PRAISE F
PACK UP THE

"Don't forget *Pack Up the Moon* whe
it's the perfect vacation or staycation read. It's filled with
honest emotion, a celebration of the power of love to heal even the most broken of hearts."

—Susan Wiggs, #1 *New York Times* bestselling author of *The Apple Orchard*

"A superlative architect of story, Rachael Herron never steers away from wrenching events, and yet even moments of deepest despair are laced with threads of hope. It's impossible to stop turning the pages, breathless to discover the fate of beautifully drawn characters who are ravaged by loss and rescued by their devotion to each other. Herron is an inexhaustible champion of the healing power of love."

—Sophie Littlefield, national bestselling author of *Garden of Stones*

"Rachael Herron has created a work of intense beauty in *Pack Up the Moon*. Here is love and fear, hope and deep longing. Here are people trying their best, and falling short, and trying again. Here is unthinkable loss, and its aftermath. Herron's beautifully rendered novel boldly shows us people at their lowest and then makes us fall in love with them."

—Cari Luna, author of *The Revolution of Every Day*

continued . . .

Written by today's freshest new talents and selected by New American Library, NAL Accent novels touch on subjects close to a woman's heart, from friendship to family to finding our place in the world. The Conversation Guides included in each book are intended to enrich the individual reading experience, as well as encourage us to explore these topics together—because books, and life, are meant for sharing.

Visit us online at www.penguin.com.

PRAISE FOR THE OTHER WORKS OF RACHAEL HERRON

"A warmhearted hug from a talented author. . . . The story will stay in your heart long after the last page is turned."

—Susan Wiggs, #1 *New York Times* bestselling author of *The Apple Orchard*

"Insightfully genius, *A Life in Stitches* makes me grateful that Rachael Herron put down her needles long enough to pick up a pen."

—Josh Kilmer-Purcell, *New York Times* bestselling author of *The Bucolic Plague*

"Rachael Herron seamlessly blends romance, friendship, and laughter."

—Barbara Bretton, *USA Today* bestselling author of *A Soft Place to Fall*

"A charming story whose characters captivate your heart."

—BookLoons

"A riveting tale."

—*Booklist*

"An emotional story of two people discovering who they really are."

—*RT Book Reviews*

"*Wishes and Stitches* will take you home to a place you'll never want to leave."

—Christie Ridgway, *USA Today* bestselling author of *Bungalow Nights*

Pack Up the Moon

Rachael Herron

NAL ACCENT

NAL Accent
Published by the Penguin Group
Penguin Group (USA) LLC, 375 Hudson Street,
New York, New York 10014

USA | Canada | UK | Ireland | Australia
New Zealand | India | South Africa | China
penguin.com
A Penguin Random House Company

First published by NAL Accent, an imprint of New American Library,
a division of Penguin Group (USA) LLC

First Printing, March 2014

LIBRARY OF CONGRESS CATALOGING-IN-PUBLICATION DATA:
Herron, Rachael.
Pack up the moon/Rachael Herron.
p. cm.
ISBN 978-0-451-46860-4 (pbk.)
1. Family secrets—Fiction. 2. Children—Death—Fiction.
3. Mothers and sons—Fiction. 4. Grief—Fiction.
5. Domestic fiction. 6. Psychological fiction.
I. Title.
PS3608.E7765P33 2014
813'.6—dc23 2013037401

Printed in the United States of America
10 9 8 7 6 5 4 3 2 1

Set in Bembo
Designed by Spring Hoteling

For my favorite teachers,
Perry Pederson and Al Landwehr.

Acknowledgments

Many people make a book, but my greatest thanks go to my agent, Susanna Einstein, for listening to the idea, holding up her hands, and saying, "Go. Write. I want to read *that*." (And then for reading it. Over. And over. And over.) Thanks to everyone at Einstein Thompson Agency, especially to Molly Reese Lerner for sending me my favorite kind of e-mails, and to Sandy Hodgman for the early and encouraging belief. Huge thanks go to my amazing editor, Danielle Perez, for knowing what to suggest and when to cheer. To Christy Herron, thanks for letting me borrow your Harry Potter books. I'm sorry Clara ate *The Philosopher's Stone*. To Bethany Herron, thanks for always making time for the emergency reads during my panic moments. I could never have written this book without the plotting genius and specialties of Sophie Littlefield (emotion), Juliet Blackwell (love), Dr. Nicole Peeler (plot), and A. J. Larrieu (character). Thanks go to Write or Die, Mac Freedom, and Scrivener, in that order—I don't know how writers got anything done before these programs existed (of course, writers who just used pen and paper weren't distracted by Twitter, were they?). Speaking of the virtual watercooler, thanks go to every single person who's ever chatted with me at Twitter and Facebook. It wouldn't be as much fun coming up for air if you weren't there bobbing cheerily at the surface. To Carolyn Tello, thank you for sharing the hijinks of the gaming industry with me, and to Amy Singer and Phillycheese for the invaluable boat info. Thanks to Moby, who will never know how much his song "Stella Maris" means to Kate. All errors, of course, are mine alone. To Cari Luna, my thanks always to you, for everything. To Lala Hulse, for believing in me and this and us. And for always thinking space aliens are the answer to everything.

Funeral Blues

W. H. Auden

Stop all the clocks, cut off the telephone.
Prevent the dog from barking with a juicy bone,
Silence the pianos and with muffled drum
Bring out the coffin, let the mourners come.
Let aeroplanes circle moaning overhead
Scribbling in the sky the message He is Dead,
Put crêpe bows round the white necks of the public doves,
Let the traffic policemen wear black cotton gloves.
He was my North, my South, my East and West,
My working week and my Sunday rest
My noon, my midnight, my talk, my song;
I thought that love would last forever, I was wrong.
The stars are not wanted now; put out every one,
Pack up the moon and dismantle the sun.
Pour away the ocean and sweep up the wood;
For nothing now can ever come to any good.

Pack Up the Moon

Chapter One

Sunday, May 11, 2014
7 p.m.

The day Kate's daughter found her was the only day in twenty-two years Kate wasn't looking.

"Good press showing." Vanessa's practiced smile worked like a boat's rudder steering Kate through the crowd, moving her easily away from the man who'd been trumpeting about Kate's obvious influences, artists she'd never heard of. "Grab one of those little shrimp things. You have to eat. So we have the *Chronicle, Bay Guardian,* and Channel 2. That's not to mention the line I have to a *New York Times* critic who's in town next week and is coming on Monday for a private showing. She can be a bitch extraordinaire, but she gave me the impression she's excited about your new paintings."

"Good," said Kate, and for once she meant it. The last time she'd had to deal with press had been under the worst sort of circumstances. This time they were hovering, but more politely. They had a different glint in their squinted eyes as they watched her closely, carefully. If she bolted, their merciless prey drive would be activated, so she breathed deeply, keeping her heart rate down. When spotted by a mountain lion, one was supposed to become as large as possible. Kate straightened her back, elongating her neck. Thank god she'd worn the black dress—if she'd worn the red silk she'd considered, the rivulets of sweat running between her breasts and trailing down her neck would have been obvious.

"Are you ready to say a few words?"

Kate blinked. This was the part she'd always dreaded most about her openings, especially now. She nodded.

Vanessa touched her elbow and stepped up to the small podium. Tapping the mike, she smiled quietly while waiting for—expecting—the crowd to quiet.

"Thank you," she said. "Thanks for coming tonight. I couldn't be more pleased to present Kate Monroe's newest installation. If you're a fan of her paintings, you've been as excited as I have about this. We've missed your work, Kate. We know you've been through a lot in the last few years."

Kate felt the press's level of alertness heighten.

Vanessa continued. "We can't imagine what it's been like for you, but, as always, collectors, patrons, and critics alike agree on this: your soul shines through this work. And we are the better for it. Ladies and gentlemen, I'm thrilled to present Kate Monroe."

Kate didn't hear the applause as much as she felt it, a wave of air that pressed against her skin. They would ask questions, always the worst part. Dread filled her, a green nausea. She glanced right, brushing her eyes over her favorite of the paintings, the one she knew critics would call "important," meaning, as usual, something they couldn't quite understand.

A deep black swath of land, a gray rotor blade jutting up into a night sky. Stronger now—she was strong enough to paint that. She'd worked her ass off. She could do this simple thing, she could stand in front of people and let them look at her, let them think they knew something, anything, about her.

In the back row, among the dozens of people she didn't know, she saw Dierdre and Elizabeth from her book club. Dierdre gave a finger waggle and Elizabeth smiled and raised a mini-quiche in her direction. Her heart eased. If they were here, she could do this.

"Thank you." Kate paused, taking a second to curl her fingers around the edges of the podium. "This show is the result of a year's worth of work." What had she been planning on saying again? She hadn't made flash cards, hadn't thought she'd need them. "Oh, crap. Just go ahead and ask me what you want."

The audience laughed, and it almost sounded kind. Kate took a question about process, and then one about her choice of material, why she'd switched back to oils only to stay mostly monochromatic. A thin trail of happiness ran up her spine. Kate knew how to do this. A critic who had panned her work seven years earlier—who had called her "stilted and thin"—seemed to be delighted, as if he could take credit for discovering her.

She took another question formed as an accolade, and then pointed, almost carelessly, at the woman from the *Chronicle*. "You, yes?"

"Your palette is astonishingly diverse in its uniformity. You've always been known, though, for your color. Did losing your son make you see the world differently?"

There it was. The question. The room gave a low hiss of disapproval toward the woman who'd asked, but Kate also heard the follow-up collectively held breath. They all wanted to hear the answer.

"No," she said, concentrating. "If anything, this work is about my father. You'll see parts of his helicopter in some of the pieces, and glimpses of him can be seen in shadow if you look carefully enough. He was a pilot and died when I was ten. The fog was low, and night came in faster than he'd expected." Kate watched the confusion register. They'd all thought they understood—that the grief on the canvas was the grief they'd read about in the papers. But they didn't. They wanted to rubberneck her maternal pain, drive by the wreckage, contorting their faces into something that resembled empathy. Instead, they were only witness to a cold loss, a loss sustained so long ago it was practically inscribed on her DNA. Relief surged through her. Her defenses still stood then.

She answered a few more questions; then Vanessa stepped between her and the microphone. "Thank you for coming, and enjoy." Applause again, different this time, lighter, less worried. Maybe the audience had *thought* they'd wanted to witness a mother's grief but found themselves as relieved as she was to be spared.

"Good job," said Vanessa. "I have champagne on ice in the back. Need a little break before the next onslaught?"

"Bless you," said Kate, holding tightly to her elbow.

In the back room, Vanessa slipped off her heels and perched on her desk as she poured them both a glass. "Just for a couple of minutes. Then I'll have to get you out there again."

"I can do it," said Kate. God, it felt *good* to know that again. It had been such a long time.

"I know you can. I'm proud of you." Vanessa appraised her, tilting her head to the side. "Can you tell me, though?"

"What?" The bubbles were sharp, prickling on Kate's tongue.

"Is the work really about your father?"

Kate should tell her no, let Vanessa believe she knew the secret below the darkness of the work. Vanessa would like that. In the long run, it would probably even translate to higher sales as she whispered to buyers what she thought each one meant. Vanessa thought they were friends, and for one second Kate wished to hell it could be true.

"Yes," she said. "It's really about my dad." Because after all, that *was* the truth. She'd never been able to paint her son, Robin. She'd be shocked if she ever could. She'd lost him as irrevocably as she'd lost the right to use color.

Vanessa shrugged. "Okay."

The door swung open a few inches.

"Private," Vanessa called. "Restroom is down the hall to the left."

A girl pushed her head in. "Can I just have a quick word with Ms. Monroe?"

Kate had seen the girl—no, young woman—during the talk. She'd stood in the back, her spine straight, the picture of an earnest art student. She wore a black oversized tunic with red pockets and torn black tights. Her hair was multicolored, stripes of blue and green cascading through her black curls. Kate had looked right at her, thinking she was a pretty girl who probably didn't know how beautiful she was going to be. An idle thought—that's all it had been.

Vanessa raised her eyebrows. "Maybe in a moment? We'll be out in a—"

Kate felt something twist in her stomach, an edge of nervousness, and she said, "No, it's fine," even while she wasn't sure if it was. She held the stem of her glass more tightly. Something was about to happen.

Vanessa gave Kate a sharp, curious look and then nodded. The door clicked behind her.

"It's me," said the girl.

Jesus fucking Christ. Kate had looked at the girl. *Right* at her. She hadn't seen it, hadn't seen the truth. Always, she'd known one thing—that she would know her when she saw her. And she hadn't. The one day she should have.

"You're . . ." Kate's bravery, so sorely tested already today, failed. There was no way in hell she could complete the sentence verbally. The girl looked so much younger than twenty-two.

The young woman's eyes filled with tears as she nodded. "Yeah." Her voice was the palest green of the first spring grass.

Kate pressed her fingers to her upper lip. Then she said the only thing she could think of, the sentence she couldn't keep back.

"Happy birthday."

Chapter Two

Sunday, May 11, 2014
8 p.m.

Okay, Pree was freaked. This wasn't the way Pree had imagined it would go at all. You'd think that a bio mom, confronted with her kid, would faint, or scream, or burst into tears. Something dramatic and loud. But no. Instead, Kate Monroe gave Pree a swift, bone-jarring hug. Then she guided Pree to the back door of the gallery.

"What are we *doing*?" said Pree, startled by Kate's sudden motion.

"Getting the hell out of here."

"What about your show?"

Kate said, "What show?"

Pree stared at the red sign hanging from the bar across the door. "I think that sets the alarm off or something if we open that."

"Oh," said Kate. "It's probably turned off." She pushed. An earsplitting siren went off, as if an air raid were imminent. "Shit! Run!"

Pree followed on Kate's heels, down an alley, turning right onto Market. They were near the Castro, and rainbow flags snapped overhead in the light spring wind as they ran. Neon signs blinked in windows—*CASH FOR GOLD! Closing 4ever. Sale Sale Sale!*—and the tang of urine was sharp and acidic. The alarm, so loud behind them, fell quiet as the noise of the city took over. A tiny Smart car laid on the horn as a bicyclist cut in front of it, and the packed F train rumbled past, making the grate in the sidewalk rattle.

And Pree could only think, *My biological mother's voice is red.*

At Church Street, Kate slowed. She breathed as heavily as Pree did, and her smile, though wide, was still startled. "Coffee?"

"Sure." Pree didn't care. It was enough to be here now. Looking at her. Kate had *recognized* her. Kind of. Maybe. Her hands were sweating.

"I guess you're old enough to drink . . ." Kate's voice trailed off.

"I'm twenty-two," said Pree. Didn't she know that?

Kate bit her lip. Pree took pity on her. "I never say no to coffee, though."

Kate's relief was obvious. "Good, good. This is a great place." She pushed open the café's door. "I mean, really good coffee. Just great." Pree was glad it was Kate doing the babbling, not her.

Kate ordered an americano. Pree would normally have ordered the same thing, but it felt strange somehow, so she asked for a mocha, ignoring the fact that she wasn't the biggest chocolate fan.

"Mocha, great. Good, good," said Kate. "Will you choose a table for us? I mean, do you mind?"

Pree dug in the front of her backpack for the twenty she'd stashed in the pocket.

"No," said Kate, too quickly. "I've got it."

"I have money."

"Please. Let me buy this."

Kate's voice sounded darker red now. Almost burgundy. She meant it. It was important to this woman who Pree was related to by half her DNA to buy her a dang coffee. Fine.

That was fine. Hell, maybe that was better than fine. A tremor ran up Pree's spine, a wonderful fear.

Pree chose a table right in front. She could run if she had to. Maybe she'd spend all night running: first to Kate, then with her, and finally away from her. Who knew? The muscles in her quads and her calves tensed. As Kate pulled out the chair opposite her, Pree felt so nervous she thought she might throw up.

"Here. Your mocha. I'll be right back. Oh, damn. Hang on." Kate darted back to the counter, where she picked up a plate the barista had just put up on the bar.

On it was one single piece of chocolate cake.

Pree closed her eyes and held her breath. Maybe if she kept them closed for a minute, she could figure out what this was supposed to be and what she was supposed to do about it.

"This is stupid, isn't it?" Back at the table, Kate set the cake down in front of Pree. "I thought for a minute it would be cute. When I ordered it." She pressed the backs of her hands to her cheeks. "But I got it wrong, didn't I?"

"It's nice," Pree managed, her voice a croak.

"It's creepy."

Pree didn't think that was the right word for it. Birthdays were for cake, after all. It was kind of . . . sweet. If a woman gives you up for adoption, and is then tracked down in the wild, wasn't it natural that she should know, just like that, that it was your birthday? Wasn't that something a woman doesn't forget? Did the date ring in her mind like a bell? Had Kate woken up this morning thinking about her? Or did she realize it later, when she looked at her cell phone, noticing the date?

And even though it was chocolate, Pree said, "It's fine. I like cake." She watched Kate fiddle with a packet of sugar. *My biological mother's hands are as small as mine.* In grade school, Pree's best friend, Mysti, had smashed their hands together almost daily, laughing at Pree's tiny fingers. "Short!" Mysti would squeal. "So stumpy! How do you hold a pencil with those teensy things?" Pree had been stupidly embarrassed by this small detail of herself, something she couldn't change no matter how many hand stretches she did, and even now she favored smocks or dresses with pockets so she could hide her hands as she walked.

Kate smiled at her and then glanced away, as if it had taken all her courage to smile directly at her. Pree got it. She totally got it.

"It's okay if we're both not sure what to do here," said Pree, picking up the fork Kate had set in front of her.

"Oh, crap. I'm the one who's supposed to say that, right?"

"Why?" Pree didn't expect Kate to start mothering now. That was fine. That wasn't what this was about.

Kate's gaze fell and she took a quick sip of her coffee. "Yeah."

In the front of the café, a short woman with a buzz cut took a seat on a low stool and started strumming a guitar that looked like it had been through a war. A hole was punched in the front of it, and the neck had been repaired badly with duct tape. The parts of it that were still whole were covered with band stickers. Pree recognized a few of the names from shows she'd been to in LA: Tar and Creosote, Chablis, Female Trouble. If she played the guitar, she'd cover hers in stickers, too. A different kind of sticker maybe—the kind she drew herself and filled her backpack with, the kind she was proud of. It was a good thing, to cover up something you loved with something else equally important.

Kate cleared her throat. "So anyway. Since I'm totally clueless about how to do this, and since I've already screwed it up, I'll just go whole hog and ask you how your birthday was."

Not how her life was. Just her birthday. Good, that was probably the best place to start. "Fine. I guess. I slept in."

Kate's eyes widened. "Here? I mean, in the Bay Area?"

"Yeah. I live here."

"Oh, my god."

Pree nodded. Now wasn't the time to admit that she'd taken the job a year before because she knew where Kate lived. That revelation, if it came, would be for later.

"Where?"

"In the Mission," said Pree. "Just off Sixteenth at Athol."

"San Francisco," said Kate softly. "You live *here*."

"And you live in Oakland." It felt bold to say it. It was an admission of something bigger.

"Yes." Kate's small fingers went white around her mug. "You googled me, I'm guessing?"

"Yep," said Pree simply. There was so much on the Internet, so much more than just Kate's city of residence.

Nodding, Kate looked at the guitarist. "She's good."

Instead of playing standard café fare folk or jazz, the woman was playing a classical piece. The guitar sounded rich, despite the way it looked, and the song was difficult and intricate.

"There are so many questions you must have," said Kate. "And I have . . . Oh, god. I don't know how to play this game."

"Rules, then," said Pree, proud that she'd thought of this.

"What?"

"Let's make up some rules for the game."

Kate smiled, the right corner of her mouth crinkling upward. "I'm not so great at games."

"Let's give it a shot."

"Okay, then. Rules."

Pree thought, pressing the fork against the top of the chocolate buttercream frosting. The little lines it left behind were straight and pleasing. "Three questions each. Nothing off-limits. If, after each of us has answered three questions, either of us is done, it's fine. No hard feelings. No big deal." She said the words lightly, but she knew if Kate left after Pree answered a question wrong, Pree would end up curled in a ball on the floor of the café, beyond devastated, making people step over her as they reached for packets of sugars and coffee stirrers.

"Like a speed date," said Kate.

Pree nodded. Yeah. The most important speed date in the whole world.

Kate said, "You first. Anything."

Now that the opportunity she'd been waiting for her whole life, literally, was in front of her, Pree's mind went completely blank. "No, you go ahead."

"Okay. What's your name?"

Pree's jaw dropped open, and she knew she must be showing off some of the cake she'd just finished chewing, but she couldn't help it. "You don't even know my *name*?"

"I let your parents choose."

"They don't tell you in the hospital?"

"They hadn't decided. Your hospital band said 'Jane' that first day because they wanted to take some time with you before making a decision. They wanted to get to know you. And they got to fill out the new birth certificate."

That sounded like her moms. "My name is Pree. I mean, that's actually short for Peresandra. But I go by Pree."

"Pree." Kate sat back, her arms slack at her sides. "I like that. What does it mean? No, wait. I don't want that to be my second question . . ."

Pree felt the words jumbled up inside her mouth and couldn't get them out fast enough. "No, no, they're our rules. Let's say that one doesn't count. My moms met in a tiny town in Peresandra, India. Marta's car hit Isi's, and then Marta gave Isi a ride, and Isi just kind of never got out of the car." Pree felt warmed, hearing her mothers' names. "That's what Marta says, anyway. So when I was born"—to the woman sitting right *across* from her—"they chose the town's name for me, even though the only thing in the town was a tire shop and some huts and a bank that had closed years before. Isi shortened it when I was little to Pretty, but I couldn't even say that—the closest I could come was Pree. It stuck."

"I love it."

Oh. That was unexpected. But it was okay that Kate loved it. What did it hurt? "All right, my turn."

"Shoot."

Think of a question. A thousand questions flashed through Pree's mind, and now the hard part was to narrow them down to one. To start.

"Why did you give me away?" It was obvious. Too easy. Way too early. And even so, she couldn't stop herself from asking it first, giving it the weight she hadn't meant to let it have.

"Oh, Pree." It sounded like Kate was testing the shape of her name. "I was so young. I was only barely sixteen. I was in high school, and my mother— I couldn't have kept a baby, but I didn't want to have an abortion. It was the only answer I had."

Pree could understand that. She honestly could. When she'd been in high school, the same Mysti that had teased her about her small fingers had gotten pregnant at seventeen. Pree had gone with her to the abortion clinic. There was no way Mysti could have kept both the baby and her scholarship to UCLA. It was either abortion or adoption, and Mysti didn't want to go through her senior year with a belly that she couldn't wrangle behind the steering wheel of her Mini Cooper. Pree had understood the reasoning completely. It hadn't made sense for Mysti to keep the baby.

It was an adequate answer. Pree knew there had to be more to it than that, but it was all right for now. "Okay. Moving on. Next question." God, there were so many. How did she pick the most important one out of the air? *Who is my father? What is he like? Did he ever know about me? What happened to my brother? Did you ever look for me?* They'd said nothing was off-limits, but suddenly Pree understood that they hadn't meant it. Neither of them.

Kate leaned forward. "Can I just add something to our rules?"

Pree curled her fingernails into her palms.

"We have time," Kate said.

"What?"

"I mean, I have time if you do. You live here. I live across the bay." Her voice trembled underneath the vowels. "We don't have to ask all the questions, all the big ones, right now. There's time. If you want there to be."

She did. Oh, she *did* want time. Pree felt her stomach flip in abject relief. "Yes. Time."

The taut skin at Kate's temples relaxed, and her smile reached her eyes. "So I'm just going to ask a small question, then. Um. What's your favorite flower?"

It was too easy. And it felt good. "The California poppy."

Kate's smile spread into a grin. "That's amazing."

"Why?"

"It's my favorite, too."

A small silence fell. They both took a bite of the cake, which wasn't that bad, for chocolate. Pree felt the space between her shoulder blades relax.

Then Kate said, "One more?"

"Okay."

"How did you find me?"

How could she not know? Wasn't it obvious? "That database. The one you put your info into. I checked when I was eighteen, and you weren't there. When I checked again, you were."

Kate said, "I thought keeping the adoption closed would give you the ability to belong to your family. Completely. Without my selfish wishes ever getting in the way. It was supposed to protect both you and me."

"Then why did you . . . ?"

"Add my info to that site?" Kate grimaced. "I have to admit, that was a bad night. I was drunk."

It was a gut punch, a fist to Pree's hopes. "Oh," said Pree. "Is that how you got knocked up in the first place?"

"Look." Kate shook her head, hard. "When I say I was drunk, I mean I was in a very bad place. The lowest I'd ever been. I'd lost everything that mattered to me, and I was never going to have those things back. They weren't mine anymore. And god, I want you to understand this." She leaned forward again.

"Yeah?" Pree kept her face as still as possible.

"I'd always said that I wouldn't put my information out there, that I wouldn't let you find me. You deserved better. But when I was at the bottom, I did it. I clicked, and suddenly I was just doing it. Typing. I signed up. The next morning, I wouldn't admit to myself that I'd done it. Kind of like a . . ."

"A one-night stand?"

Kate looked surprised. But she nodded. "Like something you do that you don't want to admit to yourself. I never consciously thought about it. If someone had asked me if I'd done it, I would have said no with a clear conscience because I believed I hadn't."

"I don't get it." Pree pulled her backpack up off the floor and held it on her lap under the table. She could run if she had to, she could get the hell out . . .

"In my mind, there was the slimmest chance that you'd want to see if you could find me. Maybe you would register with the site, just to check. And you'd probably live in New Mexico or someplace, and you'd write me an angry letter that would devastate me and I'd cry for six weeks straight, and then finally we'd meet."

Pree felt her grip on her backpack slip in spite of herself. "In an IHOP, probably."

Kate blinked. "Yes," she said. "On some lonely highway. We'd order pancakes and use every kind of syrup on the table. And you'd hate me."

"You'd think my hair was funny."

"I'd never think your hair was funny."

"But sometimes it is." Pree tugged on a messy blue lock that hung annoyingly in her eyes.

Kate leaned back in her chair and rubbed her neck. Pree realized she wanted to do the same thing, make the same exact motion, in the same way.

And there it was. Pree felt a wild rush go to her head, a dizziness as if there had been an earthquake, as if the ground had lurched beneath her. Kate was her birth mother. Kate was smiling at her, at Pree.

The birthday cake tasted like joy.

Chapter Three

Sunday, May 11, 2014
10 p.m.

Nolan had seen her today. He was sure of it. Wasn't that something? Seeing her again. Just like that. Out of nowhere.

It was only because they'd been working at that end of Highway 13 on the Thornhill off-ramp that he'd noticed her at all. He'd always hated the way that exit came to a sudden and curved stop on a downhill. Kate had never cared—she'd come swooping off the freeway, pumping the brakes at the end, hard and fast. Nolan was the opposite. He'd start braking before he even hit the exit, and he'd leave plenty of room between his car and the one in front of him. Then he'd sit with his shoulders knotted up as he watched in the rearview mirror, waiting for the car that would be there any moment, unable to slow, ready to smash into his rear bumper and shatter his world.

It didn't happen like that.

Nolan opened a beer and took it back to the couch. He sat with a long sigh, as if it had been a treacherous journey from the kitchen to the sofa. It was barely seven steps. The studio apartment was just one main room, a bathroom he could barely turn around in, and a kitchen so tiny he had to use a dorm fridge. The couch was his bed, and when he woke in the mornings, he folded his two quilts and laid them along the back of it.

At least it was easy to keep tidy. Small, like his life now. In his previous life, he'd worked at the office all day and come home to Hurricane Kate, who was always sprouting paintbrushes from her pockets, streaks of gesso on her elbows, red and orange paint caught in her hair. He'd called her the Pig-Pen of Oil Painting. Now his life was reversed: chaos, dirt, and noise all day, then home to peace and quiet. Even his dog, Fred Weasley, was normally quiet and tidy. Big and shaggy-looking, the orange-colored Fred seemed like he would shed, but he didn't. He liked to lie around snoring softly until Nolan took him for his walk, during which he frolicked like a puppy; then, at home, he went back to whuffling in his sleep. As if he knew Nolan was thinking about him, Fred Weasley opened one large eye, fixed him with a look, and rolled over, his tail thumping twice. He'd had his dinner and a walk. Fred didn't need anything else.

Nolan reached out and dug his fingers into the dog's fur, kneading the sweet spot just behind his shoulder, pleased when Fred groaned in pleasure. Then he leaned back and closed his eyes, resting the beer on his thigh. The Saab that had blown past this afternoon had been the right color green and sported the ding in the driver's-side door that she'd put in it at a gas station when she'd thrown open the door into a concrete post. The driver had Kate's brown curls. He couldn't see her face, but it was her. He'd been astonished at how he'd felt when he realized it—his whole body reacted as if he'd been using the jackhammer, and he was left juddering with a low and uncomfortable leftover buzz.

That Saab was the car that had driven Robin to most of his appointments. Robin had puked in the backseat more than once. Nolan had a vivid memory of switching on the radio, not caring what station was on, just wanting something to distract him while he mopped out the vomit and cleaned the leather seats. A Coldplay song had been on, definitely not one of his favorite things in the world, and now when that song played in his vicinity as he was grocery shopping or waited for an oil change, he'd feel his gag reflex jump as he swallowed back bile.

Nolan would have guessed she'd have sold the Saab by now. Put it out to pasture. Not that she'd ever mentioned the car in an e-mail one way or the other. That wasn't part of what they wrote about. They e-mailed about Robin. Period. Not what car she might or might not have. It wasn't like she didn't have the money for a new one—he'd made sure she did. He'd left her everything, left her every cent they had in savings. He hadn't taken a penny.

The car. Jesus. When Robin was five, seven years ago now, she'd complained so much about their station wagon that he'd bought her the convertible. It was sporty. Small. "Completely unreasonable. I'm trying to be more down-to-earth," she said, which was exactly why he'd gotten it for her. She deserved unreasonable. And it could carry a car seat, so it made sense. The whole family, all three of them, could fit inside, and when she drove it, with him in the passenger seat and Robin tucked behind them, Nolan knew his whole life was inside those metal walls.

If she'd noticed him today, she wouldn't have known it

was him. Good god, he'd been a *lawyer.* Suits. Expensive haircuts. Kate would never think to recognize her ex-lawyer ex-convict ex-husband in a group of men wearing orange doing maintenance on the roadway.

Nolan killed the beer. He stepped over Fred Weasley and limped to the kitchen, cursing the foot he'd dropped a shovel on earlier in the day, and got another beer. Two was just right lately. Another thing he'd never had to think about before: drinking alone. When you drink with someone, you can drink a little faster, a little more sloppily. You can always blame the other person, even if it's only in your mind, for finishing the bottle of wine, for making you open the next one.

When you lived alone, there was no one else making fallen soldiers. The empty bottles were all his.

Fine, it helped him keep it under control. Because, god knew, there was something so attractive about the idea of giving in. Did anyone ever set out to become an alcoholic? Plan it? When Nolan was twenty, he'd set out to become a smoker, which he'd accomplished with astonishing ease. He was a pack-a-day addict by the time he was twenty-one, at which point he couldn't afford it anymore and made himself quit. That hadn't been easy, either. Fucking brutal, actually. This was his last beer of the night, then.

Because he knew he had to, he finally dragged his laptop over and popped open the cover. It was a beater, the only one he could afford at the used-computer store on Telegraph. But it connected to the Internet, which was all he needed it for.

It dinged as it received e-mail. The notes populated into the box. An e-mail from Kate landed, the most important kind of e-mail. She'd been the one to initiate this kind of communication after he'd gotten out. Nolan had been astonished but so grateful. Not since that last moment in the courthouse had he had any kind of contact with her at all.

She'd laid down those first terse rules: only memories of Robin. He could feel the anger vibrating in the air between their computers. Only memories. Nothing more.

It was a fine rule. Her rage was justifiable in a way nothing else in the world was. He didn't deserve more. He didn't deserve the e-mails at all. So he was just grateful.

> *Remember when Robin was five? And how he loved the hydrangeas next to the outdoor tub so much he'd almost drown them by throwing water at them? There was never a dry towel left after all his baths. An hour after he got out of the indoor tub, he'd want back in, and we'd let him, thinking that when he was sixteen he'd be a normal stinky, dirty teenaged boy, thinking that we'd look back at his clean phase and laugh. We thought there would be time.*
>
> *Kate*

He read it twice, and a third time, wishing he could hear her voice reading it to him. He wrote back simply, "I remember." There really wasn't anything else he could say.

And then he found the e-mail he dreaded, lying in wait among the spam and solicitations. There was always at least one.

> *Please help. She's dying, and she's hurting. I'm too scared to do anything, and I'm too scared not to. Tell me what to do.*

It was signed "Anonymous," but the sender hadn't changed the autofill signature, so he could see that it came from Jaime Cruz. A common enough name. Thank god. If it had been uncommon, he would have googled it to see if he could find out the situation, find some press on it.

Not that Nolan would help. Jesus, he wanted to, but every time he hit reply and moved his fingers to hover over the keyboard, he started sweating and shaking and felt like he was going to throw up.

He moved it into the "Saved" file. With the others.

That was the thing about the Internet, he decided as he brushed his teeth while leaning over the tiny enamel sink, thinking again about Jaime Cruz. Things stuck now, things that in the past would have hopefully just gone away, slunk off into the night to be forgotten. He wasn't forgotten. People could find him. Maybe he should have changed his e-mail address, since it was listed on a million sites from before, but it was the only thing he'd been stubborn about keeping. And it had worked—it had been where Kate had reached him.

So he kept the e-mail address. A tiny punishment, but every one counted.

Once he was back on the couch, he did just one more thing before he closed the laptop for the night. Google Maps came up, and he typed in the address on Ronada Avenue. He switched to street view. For twenty, maybe thirty seconds he let his eyes rest on the house he still thought of as his sometimes, before he remembered he'd been removed from the deed. The front door, almost but not quite hidden by the deep garden, was antique solid-core mahogany, intricately carved. He'd found it at the overpriced salvage yard in the industrial west end of Berkeley, and Kate—only ever frugal on accident—had been shocked at the price.

"It's just a door. It has to be able to stand up to a knock. Why on earth would we pay that for a *door*? Let's take a trip or something instead."

But for once, he hadn't justified it. Kate had done the bulk of the interior design at their house, even though he was the one who maintained it, picking up behind her as she spun through the rooms as if she were the wind. He'd balked only once, when she wanted to paint the ceilings in the rooms different colors. Reds, oranges, yellows . . . It was one thing when they were on the walls—a green ceiling was where he drew the line. But everything else she could have. She could choose.

The door, though, was for him. It made the house sturdy. It stood as protection. Fortification. Not from anything, not really. Just sound. Safe. They were the only people on their street, probably in all of the East Bay, who didn't have an iron security door. Why would he get one of those? It would take a battering ram to splinter theirs.

And it was still there. At least, in the most recent satellite images, it was. And Kate's green Saab still sitting there in the driveway.

He zoomed in one more notch. Right now, Kate was in that house. Ten miles away. Somewhere in there, maybe in the living room, reading . . . A second later, he felt like a stalker, as if at any moment he'd see Kate as she put the can on the curb—it was Sunday, trash was picked up on Monday. Nolan wondered idly how many times Kate had forgotten to take the trash out since he'd been gone. Twenty times? Thirty? Once he'd stopped putting the can out on the street entirely just to see if she'd notice. "This is so damn full. How can we have made so much trash in a week?" she'd said, trying to smash the kitchen bag into the big bin. She said it for three weeks in a row until a raccoon found its way in the open top. Nolan had spent an hour on the front lawn picking up old meat wrappers and used Kleenex as his penance. It was nice, to have that fight. To fight about something that, in the end, didn't matter in the slightest.

He'd have sold the house if he were her. Apart from that

door—and her—there was nothing at that address he needed anymore.

Nolan shut the computer and closed his eyes. When they'd had Robin, after he'd realized the depth of the love he possessed for his beautiful blue-eyed boy, he'd forgotten the first rule of corporate finance, the mantra he'd repeated to his clients: Don't put all your eggs in one basket. When it smashes, it's a fucking nightmare.

Chapter Four

Sunday, May 11, 2014
11 p.m.

Kate filled the bathtub on the side of the hill below the house, using the hose that ran out the kitchen window. She used all the hot water in the tank and shut it off at the sink when the faucet went cold to the touch. Her cell beeped as Vanessa left text after text. Kate had checked a few of them, even starting the return text, but she hadn't been able to send one yet. Apparently, according to Vanessa's accounting of the sales, being the mother of a dead child and running away from your own opening were extremely good for a show. Who knew?

Pree. The sweetness within the sound of the name startled Kate every time she mouthed it.

Under the cover of darkness, the stars winking at her overhead through the oak leaves, she walked through the yard and down the hill. Even in daylight, neighbors couldn't see into their yard, surrounded as it was by hydrangea, oaks, and oleander bushes that rose high and thick around it. She winced as the oak leaves pricked the bottoms of her feet. She shucked her clothes, slipped into the water, and released a long, shaky breath.

Bathing outside felt better at night. More soothing. Her neck and left shoulder had ached so badly on the drive home from the city that she wondered briefly if she was having a heart attack. But no. She'd just been clenching her jaw too tightly as she'd sat with Pree, trying to keep herself from leaning too far forward, too close to her daughter.

Pree.

Pree had found Kate on her birthday. On the anniversary of the day Kate gave her away.

The beginning of May always snuck up on her, as if April were followed by June in her personal calendar. One day she was okay, and the next she woke up on the day of her daughter's birth. She knew without thinking, without doing the math, how old she was. *Three.* Was she learning her letters? *Seven.* Were her eyes still as blue as the day she was born, or had they darkened? *Thirteen.* Had she gotten her period yet? Was it as painful as Kate's was at that age? *Twenty.* Was she in college? Did she smoke pot? Had she fallen in love?

This morning when she'd opened her eyes, she'd known it was her daughter's twenty-second birthday before thinking about anything else. Before thinking about her opening later in the day. Before thinking about cold cereal and hot coffee. Before thinking about the commission she had to get working on soon if she didn't want to blow it. She thought of her daughter.

It was the only day she let herself think of her the way she usually thought about Robin. The only day.

Kate linked her fingers behind her neck and let herself float in the water. Her ears filled and the world went silent, covered by the whooshing of her blood. An oak leaf, its points needle sharp, fell out of the dark sky onto her breast. She ducked farther under the water, and the leaf bobbed on the surface.

This tub was where she'd run to back then. When things got too hard, when she didn't think she could take another minute of tests or results or needles or seeing the pain in Robin's eyes. Nolan had always known to look for her out here. Sometimes, when Robin was doped to the gills and sound asleep, Nolan would climb in with her, the water sloshing out onto the dry leaves beneath the cast iron. They wouldn't make love—the tub hadn't been for that, not then. It hadn't been for Robin to splash in anymore, either. It had been Kate's place to breathe. She would rest in Nolan's arms, and he'd put his cheek alongside hers, and that was enough.

P is for Pree. Kate smiled again up into the leaves overhead and then touched the corner of her lips. It felt good to smile.

This year, for the first time, Kate had felt her daughter's birthday sneaking up on her. The day before, while grocery shopping, she'd been compelled to turn around and go back to the bakery case. There, at the end, were the gorgeous cakes under cooled glass. Big white puffy confections covered in raspberries and slivers of kiwi fruit. Smaller chocolate ones gleaming like precious metal.

Then Kate saw it. The perfect birthday cake. Lemon yellow frosting, a spray of colorful pansies falling over the side. *Happy Birthday!* written in joyful grass green script. Kate had never seen such a happy exclamation mark, but there it was, just after the *y*.

And just like that, on the heels of the sudden, irrational

hope, a scalding flash of pain hit her so hard it was almost physical. She hated this part: she'd gotten so good at maintaining numbness that when she wasn't numb, she felt more than pain. She felt actually ill. For a terrifying second, Kate was sure she was about to vomit in the middle of the cake aisle, right in front of the nicely shod, well-mannered shoppers who would never fall apart the way she was about to. One woman looked at her kindly and opened her mouth, as if about to ask if she was okay, but in her fear, Kate turned away, instantly regretting the moment she broke eye contact. She could have used that hug the stranger might have given her, had she been braver.

Kate had breathed through the moment in front of the bakery case. The nausea had abated. She'd bought her frozen peas and a bottle of nice wine and had made her escape, cakeless.

She turned in the tub and water trickled over the edge, splashing over the rocks, watering the hydrangea that Robin had loved so much. While it bloomed, she'd always tried to make sure one huge purple flower stood in his room. It was one of the hardest things for her to get used to—not picking the prettiest bloom and bringing it inside anymore.

More water splashed as she folded her knees to her chest and screwed her eyes shut against the stars.

She'd met her daughter tonight, and she'd bought her a piece of *cake.* A piece of goddamned birthday cake. She'd wanted to die as soon as she set it on the table in front of Pree, when she'd seen Pree's expression transform into one of surprise mixed with amusement. She'd blown it, for sure. The fantasy that she'd know exactly what to do if she ever met her daughter was just that: an unrealistic, unrealized dream.

Pree with the nose that had come directly to her from

her grandmother, who would never get to see it. Pree with the pale green voice Kate knew as if she'd heard it every day for years.

Pree.

Kate knew her name. Her joyful, round, liquid name.

She slipped farther down until the water rose up to her chin, her nose, her eyes (she kept them open, ignoring the burn of the water). Silently, the water zipped close over her head. She held her breath as long as possible, counting in her head—*one child, two child*—and when she finally burst upward, splashing and coughing, the air she sucked into her lungs felt sweet and cold. Like a miracle she hadn't expected.

Chapter Five

Sunday, May 11, 2014
11 p.m.

Athol House was, apparently, having a party they'd forgotten to tell Pree about. When she pushed open the front door, a cloud of sweet-scented smoke drifted onto the porch.

"We're hotboxing! Shut the door!" yelled a girl Pree had never seen before. She wore a short batik skirt and a glittery-sequined blue bra. She looked like a Vegas hippie.

"You're hotboxing in a room the size of the grand canyon?" Pree muttered.

"What?" said the girl brightly as she was picked up and thrown over the shoulder of a punk Pree recognized from the co-op down the street.

"Nothing. Good luck." Pree pushed past five people she didn't know and raised her hand in semigreeting at a cluster of people sitting on the floor behind the piano. It looked like they were working on pulling together a drum circle, but only one guy tapped his bongo desultorily as they laughed at a joke Pieter had just made. The smell of nag champa was mixed with the scent of weed and curried lentils. Pree felt her stomach churn.

"Pree! Get over here, girl," said Jamón, one of the housemates whose nickname came from his huge hamlike hands and feet. He waved a joint the size of a Cuban cigar at her. He was a good guy, one of her favorites in the house. Usually he trailed two or three girlfriends behind him, somehow managing to make the women okay with it. Sometimes the women became friends in their own right, and even though Pree was California born and bred, it was still something else to see three or four people wandering off to bed together night after night. One night she'd fought with Flynn badly, and she'd ended up sleeping—nothing else—with Jamón on the couch (the women had ousted him that night in favor of each other, and he was okay with that). He'd held her tightly as they slept, and it had felt wonderful to be in his thick, heavy arms. His breathing was hot, rasping on the back of her neck, and he snored, something Flynn never did. Pree had liked the sound and feel of it, the shaking she felt in her chest as he breathed. In the early morning, as his cock hardened in his sleep—she *hoped* it was in his sleep—she'd sneaked away and into the bathroom, where she got ready for work, ignoring her disappointment.

Now Pree waved at him. "Not right now, thanks. I'm tired."

"Big day?" He rested his hand casually on the inner thigh of a woman with hot pink streaks in her short dreads.

"The biggest."

"Niiiiiice." He drew the word out, slow and long.

Pree made her way up the wide, dark staircase—the lighting in the hallway was on the fritz again. She skirted the boxes of old magazines that had been there since she and Flynn had moved into the collective. No one knew who had owned the old issues of *Life* and *National Geographic,* but not one person of the thirteen who shared the house wanted to take responsibility for getting rid of them. What if the owner came back? Most of the house agreed that would be a bummer, so the boxes sat, gathering dust along with the records in the hallway built-ins, the seven almost-empty jars of pickles in the fridge, the collections of glass bottles in the basement. Personally, Pree thought they were all just lazy. But she went along with the house majority vote, as she normally did. The only thing she'd fought hard for was the pest removal when the flea problem had become so out of control that she'd seen bugs jumping out of her backpack at work. It had turned the house into a war zone for a month with Tiffany and Bryony the most outspoken in their hatred of any pesticides, including all-natural green ones. They thought that using cucumber rind would do it. It wasn't until Bryony came down with full-body hives, a flea bite sensitivity flaring into an uncontrolled allergic reaction that sent her to the hospital with eyes puffed shut and lips double-sized, that they let Pree hire the guy to spray the hundred-year-old carpets with nontoxic bug killer. Tiffany still occasionally hissed at Pree in the hallway, but Pree ignored her the way she ignored the raccoons scrabbling outside next to the trailer.

A home. A family, they all said. They were making something real.

Sometimes it felt like they were making nothing but a mess.

At the café, Kate had asked Pree more about where she lived. "It's a group artists' collective," Pree had said. "We have communal meals three times a week and we grow a huge garden. I'm in charge of the tomatoes." Spoken out loud this way, it sounded idyllic, as it had sounded before they'd moved in. Before they'd realized that a matter as small as which pan meat was cooked in could start a full-fledged house war. Pree had enjoyed telling Kate about the collectiveness, the cooperation. Maybe she was bragging, maybe just a bit.

Then Kate had asked about *her* art. The art that had brought her to an artist's collective. Pree, her fingers inside the backpack on her lap, peeling the back of a sticker, had mumbled something about the game company where she was a junior concept artist and changed the subject as fast as she could.

Now upstairs, their bedroom door was wide open, dance music by Moby pouring out of the speakers that Flynn had found in the back room of an abandoned meth warehouse in Emeryville. Pree sighed. Moby on the stereo meant Flynn had had a bad day, creatively.

"Hey," she said, dropping her backpack onto the coffee table already piled high with their shit.

Flynn was draped across the bed, his head hanging off the end. He opened one red eye and smiled. "Babe."

"How are you?"

"You look pretty."

"You look upside down."

He flipped onto his stomach. "Still look pretty right side up." His consonants were softened, just the slightest bit slurred. Obviously, he'd hit the bottle along with the weed.

"How was your day?" Pree bent to undo the zippers on her boots.

Flynn groaned. "Awful."

"Why?"

"The Crucible denied me a place at the Fire Arts Festival."

"But you've been working at American Steel for months. You *know* all those people. I thought you were in for sure."

"Right?" Flynn took a huge swallow from the rye that sat on the floor at the edge of the bed. "And they loved my work. Said my ironwork is 'daring.' Or maybe that's what they say so you don't freak out when they say no. Bastards."

"You had enough money to pay the vendor fee?" The last time he'd mentioned it, he'd said he didn't.

Flynn smiled up at her, his eyes dreamily unfocused. "My girlfriend loves me. I thought, if they accepted me, that I might ask you for a *tiny* loan. Just for a little while, because then I would have sold and been able to pay you back. But it doesn't matter now, because they hate me."

"I'm sorry, baby," said Pree. And she was. But Jesus, it's not like she was loaded. Far from it. She just worked, which was more than you could say for the rest of the house . . . She looked around the room. "God, why is there so much shit in here?" She pushed a pile of clothing off the chair. Looking at the bottle he held, she imagined asking for a sip, thought about how the burn would feel as it went down.

"Want some?" Flynn held the rye out to her.

"Nope." Pree shook her head, feeling her stomach lurch again. She curled her fingers into her still-flat belly.

She looked around the room. With its two pocket doors on adjoining walls, it was enormous, an old parlor that had been converted into a bedroom years before. She remembered how it had echoed when they'd moved in. How had they accumulated so much *stuff?* They'd come here only a year ago, right after Pree graduated from art school. Everything they'd owned at that point fit in their teardrop trailer, which was still parked out back. Now if they moved, they'd have to hire a U-Haul. Not even one of the small ones—they'd need the medium-sized truck.

"This is ridiculous. Do you really have to keep *all* your tools in here?"

"I told you. If I leave them in the workshop, they walk away. And I spent a lot of money on them."

You didn't spend a lot of money.

Pree took a deep breath and released it through her nose. She loved Flynn. Her bright, beautiful boy. She'd fallen in love with his sweetness, the blond hair that brushed his shoulders in waves, his sleepy, smoky eyes. His hands, roughened by heat and fire, were gentle on her skin. He made her feel beautiful. Cared for. Safe. She didn't *need* him—they weren't like that together. She wanted him. He wanted her back. It worked.

"I found her," Pree said. "Kate."

Flynn sat straight up, his eyes finally focusing on her face. "You did? Where? What happened?"

Pree tugged off her tights and sat on the bed cross-legged, pushing her knees against his. This was why she loved him, right here. He listened. "She had this big art opening. I thought it would be easy to meet her there, in the open, you know."

"What's she like? Oh, my god, did she freak *out* when she saw you or what?"

"If you count running away with me from her own opening, then yeah." Pree grinned. "I guess she did."

"And then what?"

"Then we just talked."

"What color was her voice?" Flynn was fascinated by the way Pree saw colors in voices—he saw it as some kind of divination tool. To Pree, it was just the way she heard things. Flynn's voice was pink and pearlized like the inside of a shell. It was similar to Pree's mother Isi's voice, but his was a paler salmon pink, a more watered-down shade than Isi's vibrant coral.

"Red. Her voice was red."

"Huh," said Flynn. "Wish mine was red instead of stupid pink. Not too many red voices, huh?"

He was right, there weren't. "I guess it was more burgundy, if I had to narrow it down, with a deep plum base."

"Red could be happiness, or passion, or fear . . ."

"She's not happy. Well, she was for a little while, when we were talking. Maybe. But mostly she seemed . . . devastated."

Flynn leaned forward. "Yeah? Did she say anything about that? About the kid?"

Pree had read Flynn the online articles when she'd found them. The headlines came back to her now. *Nolan Monroe Kills Eight-Year-Old Son by Carbon Monoxide. Accident or Mercy Killing?* Months later: *Monroe Found Guilty of Negligent Homicide, Sentenced to One Year.*

Then, recently: *Kate Monroe's First Installation Since Death of Son.*

"Not a word. And no way in hell was I asking."

"But you wanted to."

Pree wanted to ask about her father like she wanted to breathe. The desire pulsed like an extra heartbeat inside her. She said only, "Yes."

Flynn took another lazy swallow. "But you will."

"If I see her again."

"If?"

"We just left. She got my number. I got hers. I think we both kind of ran away." Pree paused, wondering if she should go on. "She bought me a piece of birthday cake."

Flynn's eyes made a slow transition from sleepy to shocked. "Shit."

Pree shrugged.

"I forgot last year, too," he said. "*Shit.*"

Jimmy from work hadn't forgotten. He'd sent Pree a text earlier in the day. A simple *Happy birthday, you.* She hadn't responded but she'd reread it six times, willing it to be longer, to have more words every time she glanced at it, willing the *you* to mean more than the pronoun usually did. "No big deal."

"Gah!" Flynn jammed his fingers into his hair and dragged them out. "Um. I don't have . . . You wanna fuck?"

Pree couldn't help laughing. "That's your gift to me?"

He opened his arms. "Can you think of a better one?"

"You know what I want?"

"Tell me. You can have anything, babe."

She stood, stepping into her shower flip-flops. "I want to sleep in the trailer tonight." It was a wooden teardrop trailer built in 1946 that they'd bought at a farm auction and spent two months making roadworthy. They'd moved up to the Bay Area in it, living in it for weeks, parked in the backyard of a squat in Berkeley. They'd made the rear galley kitchen into a functional cooking space with a propane stove and an actual working sink. Pree had sewed—badly—a duvet cover with thrifted cowboy-covered fabric. She'd made matching curtains. She'd slapped her stickers with her signature, RARE, all over the curved ceiling, and she liked looking at them just before she went to sleep. Her outside art, inside.

Then she'd gotten the job in the city as an artist for a start-up games company, and she'd begun making real money for the first time in her life. They'd parked the trailer behind the collective in the Mission, and she'd opened a credit union account. They'd bought a real bed.

She missed the hell out of the tiny world of that trailer.

Flynn looked as if he was considering her request. Then he said, "You want to fuck in the trailer?"

How was it possible that he could pull off sweet while asking something like that? But he could. “Okay,” said Pree.

Flynn stood, rising tall above her. “I’ma show you some happy birthday, babe. You just wait.”

Things might be different, changing, scary, but some things were still good. Flynn, with all his faults, was good. Safe.

Pree held his hand as he led her down the dark stairs toward the outside. They’d leave the tiny windows cranked all the way open, she decided. She wanted to breathe the night air deep into her lungs and hold it there.

Chapter Six

Love

September 1991

In math class, first day of her high school sophomore year, Kate had realized she'd forgotten a pencil. Oil pastels, she had. She'd begged her mother to buy them for her, and Sonia grumbled the whole time about how color pencils should do the same job and cost less. Kate had two drawing pads and three erasers nestled against the five new Pee-Chee folders. But she'd forgotten to bring any kind of writing implement, and the class's first pretest was on Scantron.

"Can I borrow a pencil?" she whispered forward. The boy in front of her had brown, mostly straight hair. Right where it touched the back of his neck, though, it curled softly. Gently. Kate wanted to touch it, right at that curl, and her fingers twitched embarrassingly.

The boy didn't turn all the way around, just slid sideways in his chair. He looked like the kind of kid who wouldn't have anything but a skateboard in his backpack, so when he opened it to showcase a neat collection of pencils kept safely in a blue canvas case, she was surprised. Kate could have had her choice of nineteen different kinds of pencils. Little soldiers of diligence. He chose for her, handing her a silver mechanical pencil. "It's number two lead," he said. His voice was a dark blue, like new denim.

When their fingers touched, Kate jumped. *So this is why girls like boys.* For the first time, she got it.

"You break it, you buy it," he said too loudly, as if he had something to prove. His laugh sounded fake, but his wide smile reached his eyes as he showed her where the eraser was stored under the metal cap.

Kate's crush was in full bloom by the end of the period, but the boy, Nolan, was called out of the room by a vice principal who wore a look of rage. Nolan grinned insouciantly at Kate as he brushed past her, and she felt the inner arches of her feet tighten as she tucked her toes into balls. Her fingers wrapped around the pencil. She knew she'd keep it forever. It was the first thing she ever stole from Nolan.

Kate introduced him to her mother for the first time just before her sixteenth birthday. It was their second date, and Sonia had demanded to meet him before they went out again. Kate expected protest when they met. A wail of some sort. Gnashing of teeth and rending of garments, in a quiet and polite tooth-gritted manner. She knew her mother would look at Nolan and immediately read: *shoplifting, desk-defacing, school hallway fighter.* And worst of all: *loud.* She didn't have much hope that her unromantic mother would see anything good about Nolan. Sonia wouldn't see the way this boy kept his cherished pencils in such neat order, the way he hid his A papers with his arm so no one would see his good grades. Sonia would probably tell Kate never to see him again, and Kate would have to begin her teenage sneaking-around years.

But instead, Sonia had opened like a poppy on a sunny morning in the light of Nolan's smile. Nolan spoke to her quietly, respectfully. As if he had all the time in the world to answer her questions. Sonia smiled and waved as they left, as if she were someone else. Kate was astonished.

In the car, Nolan slanted her a sideways look and gunned the engine. "You ever seen the demolition derby?"

It was louder than anything she could have imagined. Dirtier, too. Kate felt coated in the smell of beer and gasoline by the time they left the noise and exhilaration of the race. Nolan slung his arm over her shoulder and pulled her close against him. "You're pretty damn tough, you know," he said. "Hung with the boys tonight. You didn't trip."

She *had* tripped, though. She'd been beset by a violent shyness that had been tempered only by the wild joy she felt being near Nolan. The joy had won. "Maybe."

"No, I know. You're tough."

Kate loved that he thought it.

As they drove away from the racetrack, Kate kept the window down and her hand outside the window, letting the wind lift and drop her hand. Rain started, lightly spitting against her arm, and as Nolan's windshield wipers flapped, she didn't roll up the window. Nolan laughed, sounding purely happy.

This boy. This one. Yes. The one who whooped and laid money down on her favorite beater auto, who bought her a cup of beer from a keg in the parking lot but drank bottled water because he was driving, the one who looked rugged when the older guys greeted him, the one who swore louder and better and faster than any of the rest but who held her hand even while they teased him for it. This one.

They'd been careful. Nolan had been as concerned as she about an unwanted pregnancy. Coming up from overheated kisses that threatened to burn out of their control, he'd gasped, "What—should we use?"

Kate had seen enough girls in the hall carrying a load of books on top of their bellies to know she didn't want to join their prodigal ranks. Not at all used to being thought of as the one in control—that was her mother and, before that, her father—she felt proud. Smart. She was in all honors classes. She was better at grocery shopping than her mother was. She wasn't quite yet but would very, very soon be an adult. "I went on the pill."

"How? When?" Nolan's lips were wet, and she felt her own bottom lip swelling from where he'd nipped it.

"Planned Parenthood. Last week."

"So we're good?" Sweat gleamed at his hairline. "Just like that?"

"Well . . ." The clinic had said she needed to wait to start them until she went on her period, but she'd started immediately. Better safe than sorry. "We should use a condom—I mean, are we *really* going to do this? What if it doesn't *work*?" Her biggest fear: that when they pushed into, against each other, that their bodies wouldn't fit, wouldn't work with each other's. That she would laugh at him on accident or, worse, that he would laugh at something she did.

Nolan pushed himself backward, his arms shaking with the effort, until he was resting on the headboard of his bed. It was safe here—his parents never checked on him. Nolan said they didn't care about him, that he was just a thing in their collection, and while Kate didn't totally believe him, in six months of dating she'd seen them only once, and that was in the driveway as they'd been leaving to go to some awards dinner. His mother had waved cheerily and told them that they could order pizza—she'd left the credit card on the hallway credenza. Nolan had grimaced. Then he'd taken them out to the most expensive dinner in the fanciest Italian restaurant Kate had ever been to. She'd ordered risotto, not knowing it was like savory oatmeal. Nolan said his mother had never questioned the charge.

Now he looked at her carefully, the way he did. "We don't have to. There's nothing we have to do. I love you. I'm not going anywhere. I want to be with you."

Kate knew they were balanced on a pendulum with *too young* on one side, *old enough* on the other. Her mother told her she couldn't even get her learner's permit. Sure, she was too young to vote, or to rent an apartment. But too young for sex? For love? For decisions this big?

Kate knew one thing, though: she wanted to have sex with Nolan. The lust she felt uncurling in her belly as they explored each other with fingers, lips, and tongues threatened to combust at her hairline. She worried sometimes they would leave char marks on his mother's expensive linen. They burned together. It didn't feel like hyperbole.

So she reached behind her into her backpack on the floor and pulled out—oh, god—a whole box of condoms. The woman at Planned Parenthood had insisted that she take them, even though she'd said they'd never, ever use that many.

Nolan gave a bark of laughter. "You think we're good for that?"

"Aren't you supposed to tell me that this won't be enough?"

"That's right, baby." But his voice broke endearingly, and

he slid down from the headboard to take her in his arms. "Katie, I want to make love to you, but I want it to be right."

She looked around. Low R&B spilled from his surround-sound speakers. His parents weren't going to interrupt them. "I think most of our friends get it done in the backseats of cars or in the quad behind the auto shop."

"How do we know this is it?" His voice was darker blue than normal—it was the color of sunset just before the light died.

"This is what?" asked Kate.

"Forever?"

Her mother said nothing was forever. But then again, her mother had been depressed since Kate's father died, never managing to come up above the clouds.

"I guess we can't know," she said. But this joy, this hope . . . it had to mean something. Something like always.

Nolan took her hands and held them tightly. This was the boy she loved. The one who was present with her, looking right into her eyes, not being loud in a hallway, not hooting to friends in class, but the one who was here now, relaxed inside himself. He didn't posture with her. He didn't pretend. "I know."

"You're just so you, so sure of yourself, in your own skin."

"What?" said Nolan, surprised. "I'm never me."

"Except . . ."

He nodded once, his eyes falling to the dark black silk duvet. "Except when I'm with you."

"Why is that?"

"I don't know."

Kate did, or thought she did. His parents returned anything that didn't work, that didn't perform to the correct standards. When the taillight of his mother's BMW went out, they'd refused the offered maintenance—a broken taillight! something so easy Kate could have fixed it herself with a screwdriver—and demanded that the dealer exchange the leased car with a new vehicle. They'd gotten Nolan a puppy not once but four times. Every time the new dog had done something wrong, and they'd sent each dog to the pound. The last time they presented Nolan with a three-month-old basset hound, he'd refused to pet it, not wanting to learn to love it.

Nolan said, "You know I'm not going anywhere, right?"

"Sure." A lie.

"You don't believe me."

The condoms on the bed had changed. Instead of signaling sexiness, they looked like the paper coupons that oozed out of a Skee ball machine. She sighed, the happiness and lust drained out of her. "Everyone leaves. Can't we just live in today?"

"Not when what I want is all your tomorrows."

"God, stop!" Kate pushed against his chest. "You sound like a cheesy movie. Now we'll part and meet again when we're ancient, fifty or something, and I'll die of cancer while you tell me I was always the one."

She'd meant him to laugh, but instead he looked suddenly grief-stricken. "I would tell you that and it would be true."

"Oh, Nolan," she said again, turning around on the bed so that she fit against his length, curling her hips into him. "I know you would. And I love you for it." She waited for the happiness she felt with him to curl back into her spine, as it always did. And it didn't let her down. Sometimes she thought he was the sun, that he could fix anything with his warmth. She waited for that heat to creep into her, waited as he breathed steadily next to her ear. Kate relaxed into him.

Later that night they had sex for the first time. Both of them cried. Nolan laughed in surprise when he came, and even later, when he worked out what Kate needed, he laughed again with joy. Kate grinned, looking up at the ceiling, knowing that this was new, imperfect, and exactly right.

Chapter Seven

Monday, May 12, 2014
10 p.m.

Kate had promised herself today would be the day she spring cleaned. Really. This time she'd actually do it. It wasn't just because in the middle of the night she'd imagined what it might be like to hear Pree moving around in the room down the hall. That would be crazy, so it wasn't that. It wasn't just that, anyway. The commission for the lymphoma auction was due next month—if she ever figured out what the hell she was going to do for them, she'd be busy working soon, trapped under layers of paint, and before she rolled herself back into the work she had to get some practical things done. God knew the *w*hole house could use a good clean out.

Kate looked at the stack of sneakers and heels that collected like piles of leaves in the hallway, gusting across the wooden floor. The shoe pileup matched the stack of coats and sweaters on the chair just inside the door. Mail slanted across the hutch in drifts. She usually opened the letters that looked important, and most of the time she remembered to pay the bills on time. Not always, but usually.

The clutter didn't normally bother her. She didn't notice until something was missing and then she'd look around with surprise to find that nothing was in its rightful place. The milk used to live on the door of the fridge—now she'd spend two minutes rooting through the fridge until she finally found it shoved into the vegetable crisper, a trail of sour liquid pooled underneath it. She'd find her sunglasses in the junk drawer and the screwdriver nestled among the potholders.

It just wasn't . . . important. Most of it.

She sat at the kitchen table and put her bare feet up on Nolan's chair. She still thought of it as his, even though he hadn't sat in it for three years now. Once she'd pulled it out with the intention of sitting in it, and instead had gotten a headache so intense she'd had to lie down.

She checked her cell. Stared at it. Clicked the button and scrolled right. Left. She pulled up the entry for "Mom" and pushed call. It rang once; then the recording said, as it always did, "You've reached a number that has been disconnected or changed. If you'd like to make a call, please hang up and try again." It wasn't that she'd even ever called her mother that much, anyway. Sonia hadn't liked the phone and always made an excuse to hang up quickly. But once upon a time Kate *could* call her. In the year since her mother had died, Kate called the number at least twice a week.

Kate pushed the disconnect button and stopped the recording. Someday someone would answer the phone and she'd know that the number wasn't hers to call anymore, but until then, it was. Life, she had to admit, running her finger along the edge of the wooden table, was simpler now. But not easier. Never easier.

Five days from now, on Saturday, Kate was supposed to go out on a boat and send her mother's ashes to meet her father's in the bay. One full year—it was time. Of course it was. And she should take the rest of Robin's ashes, too. She glanced through the open door into the living room at the mantelpiece. Only two things in the house were kept spotless and dust-free: those two boxes. One, the dark walnut one, held Sonia. The other, the cedar one, held half of Robin. (She hadn't been able to inter all his ashes at Mountain View—it hadn't been physically possible. She'd kept half so he'd continue to be close, not caring if it was macabre. Kate needed him more than a cold cemetery did.)

Kate dreaded the impending boat trip so much she felt sick to her stomach every time she thought of the event pulsing in red on her calendar. She didn't actually know if she'd be able to do it. The week before, she'd picked up her mother's box and had taken it into the backyard in order to pantomime the action of strewing the ash. She'd wanted to practice. But she couldn't even do *that*—she'd ended up clutching the box to her stomach, her eyes closed in fear.

No practicing today. She would clean. Tidy. Put things away. Today she would *do* it. Kate would make space for what might come, whatever form that might take, even if the very thought was one of a very possibly deluded, grief-stricken woman who should probably get more sleep.

The first time Kate had worked on clearing out Robin's room was the month after he died. While Nolan lay in his temporary jail cell, refusing the bail his parents offered, she'd been packing everything up. Compartments. Kate had wanted boxes to hold what she felt so she could put them away, forever if possible. Friends she'd made at the hospital, friends who also had sick kids, friends she *loved*, had asked to help. But she'd told them she was fine, that she didn't need them. She'd pushed her mother out of the house almost bodily. Alone—she would do it alone. By herself, she would remove every single trapping of sickness from her son's perfect room.

Kate had no clear memory of how she'd gotten the hospital bed down the stairs by herself—it had taken three men to get it up there. She'd remade Robin's old bed in the right place with his favorite Harry Potter sheets. She threw out the little bedside commode along with the low table covered with objects she had needed on a daily basis—wipes, masks for visitors, antiseptic. She threw out all the morphine, pushing the droppers and vials deep into the outside trash can, deliberately disobeying the dictate that she dispose of them at a medical waste site. Screw medical waste. Did anyone really think that her child's leftover twenty ounces of morphine were going to contaminate a landfill?

Now, this morning, Pree's face in her mind, she set her cup in the sink. She was only able to half remember those days, as if they'd been a feverish dream. Her hands were shaking. Maybe she'd had too much coffee, too fast.

Kate walked upstairs. She pushed open Robin's door. And then everything was too difficult all over again.

It still smelled like Robin's room. The door was always closed—she hated to let the scent get into the house, not wanting it diluted by normal house smells of cleaning products and sautéed garlic. It didn't smell exactly of Robin, thank god. He'd smelled of dust and bubble bath, of outside air and grass, of little boy farts and blue bubblegum. At the end, he'd smelled god-awful; Kate couldn't bear to think of the rubber and alcohol smells of hospital things: tubes, vents, machines. Those weren't Robin. They never were.

But this perma-crayon scent—this was his. A sweet waxiness, and a smell of plastic toys, things that were probably made in China and toxic as hell but who cared? They weren't what killed him. It was the scent she'd stepped into thirty, fifty times a day when he was alive, every time with a sense of joy, of excitement, that she got to see her boy again. That precious scent was escaping into the hallway, where it would mingle with the rest of the normal household smells.

Kate bit her lip. Already it smelled more normal in here, even though normal, she knew, was never coming back.

But now there was Pree. Instead of just someone, a girl out there somewhere, Pree was a very specific *one*, and so close.

Of course, it was completely possible Kate would never see Pree again even for an afternoon. Perhaps their meeting had been a one-off. Maybe it had satisfied every question Pree had. Kate had no rights, obviously.

But she had hope. Goddamn it, she shouldn't let herself dream like this—but if Pree ever *did* want to stay, what if she had a place of her own? What if she had a room that wasn't scented with a little boy's life? This new, burgeoning feeling made Kate feel like she could fly. Or at least as if she could stay upright, tearless, in Robin's room, which was as miraculous as flying itself.

The walls, of course, would have to be painted. Kate pulled the furniture out from the edges and into the middle of the room so she could get a good, clear look.

She and Nolan had spent an entire Saturday (while Robin had been at an all-nighter birthday party) painting the Harry Potter backdrop. Nolan, organized as usual, was in charge of purchasing supplies, marking colors off his list as Kate piled her arms with rollers and brushes of all sizes, stencils they'd never need. At home, Kate had been in charge of penciling in the artwork on the plain beige walls. It was exciting, to draw like that, to know she was doing something that would make her son over-the-moon happy. He'd been so thrilled when he got his "official" Gryffindor robe in the mail that he hadn't taken it off for days, begging to sleep in it at night until they got him matching pajamas.

Once she'd drawn the design of the cliffs and castle on the walls, Nolan followed up with the prosaic tasks—the black outlines, then colors, then shades. They'd done it all, the raised green and gray cliffs around Hogwarts with their jagged drop-offs, the castle's soaring battlements under blue skies complete with little puffy white clouds. A path led out of the room with a sign that pointed in one direction to the Forbidden Forest, the other, to Hogsmeade. In the distance was Hagrid's cottage, where friendly beasts lurked, their eyes peeking over the thatched roof. Robin had been set to start his first round of chemo the next week, and no one knew how he'd react to it. They wanted him to love his room.

Nolan's hand was careful, steady and sure, as it always was. Kate, on the other hand, got green paint on the old boom box she'd dragged out of the closet, and when she was dancing with the brush to Salt-n-Pepa—a cassette! an actual mixed tape Nolan had given her at the beginning of junior year—she stepped in a pan of green-blue paint that Nolan had just mixed for work on the Whomping Willow. She laughed so hard she had to sit on the floor, and then before she really knew what was happening, Nolan was laughing with her, and they were out of their clothes, naked on the drop cloth on the floor, having sex that was hot and wet and loud, like the days before they'd had Robin.

The days before.

Both of them thought about it, Kate knew, as they lay there afterward, sweat still drying, breaths heaving. They didn't talk about it, and the moment slipped away. Robin would be home the next day, after the party. He again (always) would be their first thought in the morning and their last thought at night. A long time ago, Kate had been Nolan's most important person, and Nolan hers. It was right that now they weren't. But linking hands and legs like that with Nolan had made Kate ache with a sorrow that she didn't quite understand.

Now, alone in Robin's room, Kate pulled up the blinds and undid the latch on the window. For the first time in three years, she opened the window. The small sycamore in the front yard, the one that had been a thin sapling when he'd died, was now close and wide, and the *shush* of the leaves filled the room. It blew the last little bits of her baby boy out of the room, and Kate sat, heavily, on the red braided rug she'd put in the middle of the room.

"No," she said, but she wasn't sure with whom she was disagreeing.

Releasing herself to her elbows, she uncrossed her legs and lay all the way down on her back.

If Pree never stayed (and why would she?), this exorcism would be for nothing.

What if Nolan finds out about her? It was the thing Kate was most afraid of, the thing she couldn't think all the way through.

She looked up at Robin's—no, the guest room's—ceiling.

Shit. The stars. She'd forgotten those, the faintly green glow-in-the-dark stars and the crescent moon that Nolan had put up right before Robin came home from the hospital that last time. They didn't know if he'd be strong enough to go out into the cool, foggy night air, so Nolan said he'd bring the universe indoors.

And he did. Even she, with her mother's love that

sometimes felt as if it could destroy small planets if necessary—even she knew that Nolan loved harder, stronger, more ridiculously. Kate loved Robin, but when he cried because he didn't get the French fries that he wanted or because he couldn't stay up late to watch TV with them, she didn't mind overmuch. It was just crying. He'd get over it.

But Nolan—Robin's tears had always torn him apart. Even when Robin had been a newborn, so small that his squalling still sounded like an angry kitten's cries, Nolan hadn't been able to handle the crying. In the middle of the night, when Robin wouldn't settle down after a feeding, refusing to go back to sleep no matter how much Kate jiggled and rocked him, Nolan would lift the baby from her arms and carry him, still screaming, out to the garage. He'd buckle him in the car seat (so tightly, so securely) and take Robin out for a night drive. It was the one thing that always soothed him.

As Kate slept, happy to claim a silent house in which to dream, Nolan would drive Robin up Skyline past the thick groves of redwoods and then back down again, twisting and turning, high above the lights of Oakland until they came down into the low rolling streets of Rockridge. The car's swaying put Robin to sleep, a state so deep that when Nolan pulled back into the garage, almost nothing would wake him up—not lifting him out of the seat, not placing him back in the crib. It usually gave them a good five hours. Nolan's breath would be easy as he crawled into bed next to Kate—his arms were wide and warm. Those were the happiest moments Kate could remember, those early mornings tangled in bed with her husband as her baby slept peacefully in the next room. Just when she thought she couldn't love Nolan any more than she already did, he would move his leg forward in his sleep, pressing his shin into her calf. Lying there in the dark, she'd love him as hard and as big as all the world itself, wondering at the marvel that she could hold *this* much in her heart for one man and one boy. How did it fit? How could it? But it did—it fit inside her perfectly—and she was full.

Now she stared at the glow-in-the-dark moon and stars until they blurred. A single, unwanted tear trickled down toward her ear.

Not telling Nolan about Pree . . .

She regretted nothing more.

But what the hell was she supposed to do about the regret? She didn't feel guilty, exactly, not now. She had, up until three years before, when the fury pushed it out of her. So what was this feeling, then? It crept into her throat, a tightness that didn't ease as she tried to clear it with a short, sharp cough.

As she started to stand, her cell phone gave a short beep. She pulled it out of her pocket.

> *Thanks for last night. The cake was good.*

Her heart beat erratically, and for a brief moment Kate felt light-headed. She swayed, wondering if she should sit back down before she fell.

At the kitchen nook downstairs where she kept her laptop, Kate sat, taking a deep breath. She opened her e-mail and entered Nolan's address. It autopopulated as fast as it always did. They'd only written about Robin, up until now. That was the rule. She couldn't—wouldn't—talk about Robin with anyone else.

Kate closed her eyes and for one second could almost feel Nolan's leg behind her in bed, that steady pressure that said,

Love, here, love. She missed that particular touch so much her throat ached. She had to finally try to set this right, if such a thing were even possible this late. She rubbed her eyes and then opened them again slowly.

Dear Nolan,
There is something I have to tell you.

Oh, god, she couldn't do this in an e-mail. Telling him in person would be even worse, but nothing could excuse it being done via an electronic message.

I should probably see you to say it. If that's something you could feel comfortable with, please e-mail me back to set up a meeting.

I hope all is okay with you,

Kate

It was a polite sign-off, something she wrote to acquaintances. It wasn't until after she'd hit send that she realized she actually agreed with the sentiment. She did hope he was okay. Perhaps only okay, but that in itself was an improvement upon actively wishing him harm.

She clicked on the sent-mail icon, hoping for a small moment that she'd imagined mailing it. But there it was. In her words. She'd aimed a gun and fired a bullet across the ether to the man with whom she'd made two children, the man who had killed one of them, the man she'd loved for so long before trying with all her strength to find the method of hating him.

Kate wondered what he looked like now.

Chapter Eight

Monday, May 12, 2014
12 p.m.

As Pree walked from BART toward the post office on Sutter, she let her thoughts swirl inside her head like ink mixed with water. This particular post office was a good one—always too preoccupied with trying to keep the homeless guys from peeing in the corners to ever notice a girl with blue-streaked hair and a relatively huge backpack.

She couldn't tell Jimmy her secret. She shouldn't. Why in the *hell* did she want to? Jimmy reminded her of an alley cat, long and rangy and sleek. He was a genius, sure, which was why he was the game designer, but that was even more reason not to trust him with any kind of secret. Cats were sly, untrustworthy. Everyone knew that. Not like good Flynn. Flynn, if covered in fur, would be a golden retriever.

Pree told herself that she was just helping a fellow artist.

That's all it was. The fact that she had a stupid schoolgirl crush on that artist—her married boss—was irrelevant.

She dodged a guy who was wielding not one but two iPhones while striding down the sidewalk as if he owned the whole damn thing. He was texting with one hand and talking with the other and came pretty close to clocking her in the eye. "Hey!" she yelled. He threw her a dirty look like it was her fault.

Graffiti were at the core of the games they were designing at Pree's job. The main characters left clues and hints in what they left behind. Jimmy Donegal, the game designer, had known he didn't understand street art, and since tagging was an actual part of the game, he'd hired her as a junior concept artist. She was an art major, yes, with a minor in computer programming, emphasis in gaming. But the fact that she also had street cred as an LA female street artist, limited though it was, was what had won her the job in the end.

She was just lucky. It wasn't like she was really someone in the scene. Pree had worked on a few group bombs that had picked up some press, had done some outlines while bigger, more experienced artists did the real work. But the *Los Angeles Times* had liked the RARE stickers that she slapped under the drawings of her girls. She couldn't help thinking that the fact she was white in a minority-dominated art scene got her extra attention, too, which was a fucking shame.

What would Bira and Sleet say now if they could see her? Working a day job, living with her guy, practically settled down. The girls she'd known on the street, the ones she'd run from cops with, laughing their lunatic heads off, those girls would just shake their heads and smile if they could see her now. Knocked up. Most of them had kids now, too. That was just what people did.

It wasn't what Pree had ever foreseen for herself, though. Nothing like it.

Pree had to tell the moms, of course. But the way she knew they'd react made her want to put it off. Maybe until she was eighty-three. And yeah, she had to tell Flynn. Obviously. Soon.

Pree shook her head and tugged on her left ear as if she could pull the thoughts out and throw them away, toss them out into the street with the spent cigarettes and dropped pennies. She pushed open the door of the post office and made her way past the perpetual line to the mother lode, the pile of free USPS stickers that lined the back wall along with the certified and international forms. There was a code, see. You didn't buy stickers. You just didn't. It was a thing. Most taggers stole the "Hello My Name Is" ones from stationery stores, but Pree wasn't good at that. She'd tried once when she was in high school, and she'd gotten all itchy. She'd ended up putting a pack of name tags inside a manila folder and then buying that, so she kind of snuck the stickers out of the store, but it felt like cheating. It was better, for her, just to get the legitimately free ones.

She lifted a stack of them and stuck them in her bag next to her black book. An older blond woman with honest-to-god pink curlers in her hair glared at her. Pree stared back. Who went out in curlers? Was this 1961?

"You can't take those." The woman's voice was abrasively high-pitched. Everyone turned to look at them.

Pree ignored her and walked past, but the woman reached out and grabbed Pree's arm, her bony fingers digging into her elbow painfully. "Hey!" Pree said. "Let me go!"

"Officer!" The lady used her free arm to wave at the postal worker behind the desk. "She stole a pile of papers!"

"Just stickers," Pree told the clerk. "The mailing labels."

"How many?" he asked.

"Is there a limit?"

He sighed and pushed his glasses up his sweating nose. "Let her go, lady."

"I pay taxes. She's wasting *my* tax dollars," the woman said, but she let go of Pree. Pree could smell dryer sheets on her, and something else, maybe onions.

"I pay taxes, too," Pree said as she threw the woman a peace-out. Okay, she hadn't been paying them for long, she supposed. As she went down the steps, she felt babyish, as if she'd gotten caught stealing a Blow Pop.

She trucked up to Union Square through the heavy mist. It wasn't cold. If the sun burned through, it would probably be about perfect.

Union Square was a tourist trap, of course, surrounded by shops that she never visited—Pree wasn't drawn there by its shopping potential. What she loved about the square were its little tables, some occupied by the mumbling homeless and others taken by families from Germany or backpackers from Australia. You could get a coffee and stake your spot, and no one besides the occasional panhandler would give you any grief. It was a good spot for drawing. Pree had told Jimmy she'd be by the flagpole, but he wasn't here yet, and she felt both relieved and disappointed.

She got out her favorite marker, a fat blue Pilot jumbo that she'd customized by flattening the tip out. You had to have speed when you worked—you had to have flow.

Pree drew for ten minutes, diving down into her name, moving smoothly over the edges of the stickers and back onto them. RARE was all she did today, all she'd done for a while now. In the world of graffiti, she could admit now she was a toy: someone who played at it. Her whole life wasn't graf anymore, not like when she'd graduated high school, when it had been all she could think of, when she'd snuck out of the house to throw herself into Valencia's pimped-out

Honda, headed for the canals, the rattle of cans in the truck as dizzying as the paint's fumes. That was a long time ago now, more than four years. But you didn't get over your first love, right? Even limited to stickers as she was now, Pree was still crazy about the big stuff, the colorful work, the murals that shone a million colors, reflecting the sun.

She drew another sticker, the *R* thick and triangular, then the jagged *A*, followed by the backward *R* and the sideways *E*. She did her standard swirl underneath with some fills over the address area at the top, and then added her signature heart in the right corner. Drawing the heart had started out ironically, something the girls had laughed at her for doing. But then—that whole cliché about San Francisco and where that guy left his heart? Since moving here, Pree sometimes felt as if she were leaving her heart behind when she slapped and moved on, signing her new city with something that mattered.

"I don't think the postman's gonna be able to read that one."

Pree jumped. The voice came from behind her, familiar and warm.

Jimmy. Pree was aware her crush was probably some kind of reaction to living with a laid-back artist for the last three years, because Jimmy was everything that Flynn wasn't. While Flynn was fair in looks and countenance, Jimmy's hair was short, his complexion dark. Jimmy favored ironic T-shirts and skinny jeans that Flynn wouldn't be caught dead in. Jimmy looked like he knew where he belonged (which was everywhere) while Flynn swam upriver, flopping in and out of the current as he went.

"You made it." Pree recapped her pen. "Sneak up on girls often?"

He gave her a look, the one he'd been giving her for a while now, the one she couldn't quite read. The one she knew she probably shouldn't figure out.

"Nope," he said simply. "It's good to be out of the office, huh? I like the hooky thing. What are you drawing?"

"My slap."

That look again. At that moment, the sun broke through the fog and hit her cheek with a sudden warmth as it flooded the square. People smiled. She heard laughter and then watched as a very small child lost a blue balloon and burst into tears, bolting away from his mother. She ran behind him, her arms outstretched to catch him. Pree looked away.

Jimmy pulled out a chair and sat, dropping his bag to the ground with a thump. Two banana stickers and red glitter decorated the side of it. Pree pointed at it. "Did the kids have fun with that?"

"What?" He looked confused. "Oh. Shit. I guess so."

"You didn't notice?" God, she almost *giggled*. Why did he make her feel so young?

"I try to ignore a lot of what goes on in my house." He gave a rueful smile, and Pree's heart tugged. "Okay, street girl. Show me how this is done."

"Yeah, okay." She pulled three more stickers out of her backpack. "This is a slap."

Jimmy turned one over in his fingers. "It's a mailing label."

"It's called a slap. You put them up wherever you can reach. People actually collect them—can you believe it?" Pree tapped hers with the pen. "I wouldn't ever do that, peel a slap. But people do. Sometimes I wonder if mine is in an album somewhere . . ."

"What else do you know about these?"

"This part is very important. You steal them when you want to draw. You don't buy them."

His eyebrows lifted. "So that's where the file folder stickers have been going. You're fired."

Her heart galloped. Console studios often laid off their

entire team after the project shipped. Their first game in the series ended production last month, and they were out of crunch, into future content support—the juniors were always the first to go. "No! I only took like five— Oh. You're kidding."

Nodding, he said, "I am. I don't give a shit. Show me what to do with this. And tell me why you do it."

Pree handed him a Pilot. "Don't inhale. Or if you do, enjoy the ride as your brain cells scream their way into oblivion. Okay, the first thing is to figure out your name."

"Jimmy. Have we met?" He winked, a straight-faced lazy drop of an eyelid that made Pree accidentally bite the inside of her lip.

"It can't be your own. Related, sure, but not just your name. Usually people pick an anagram. RARE is what I took from Peresandra, my real name." Rare was what her mothers had always said she was. She'd believed it when she was a kid.

"You need a fake name because technically this is illegal. Should I fire you again?"

Pree shrugged and hoped she looked as casual as she meant to. "Misdemeanor vandalism, that's all."

Jimmy turned the sticker over and then held it up to the light. "Okay, then. What about Mijy?"

"Sounds like a kind of drink. A Mijy drop."

"Yijim?"

"If you painted lines from the Torah, sure. Use your whole name." She scribbled "Jimmy Donegal" at the top of a blank page in her journal. It wasn't the first time she'd done so.

"I've got it," she said. "JOIN GYM."

He made a sound at her, a *grrr* under his breath with a smile at the back of his eyes, and a shiver raced down Pree's spine. "I like LEGMAN better."

"How about LOGJAM?" she suggested.

Jimmy shook his head. "Closer."

"DEMON?" She sketched it out for him. "That would be pretty street. Or A GOD."

"I like ADOG better. Because I am one." He tilted his head. "You know I am."

She felt that dizzy feeling again. "Fine. Draw it."

"Like yours?"

"Of course not. Draw it like it's *yours*." She tossed him a small stack of stickers. "Just doodle a while. I'll draw some, too."

A Russian family took over the table next to theirs, dumping bag after shopping bag onto the concrete. The father yelled something and the mother just laughed as the three children raced back and forth, from the table to the shallow steps. Pigeons scrabbled at their feet, hoping for a dropped crumb or two.

After long, quiet minutes, Pree ventured, "So I was thinking. If Abel and Wichita both have a signature slap, that could be good, you know? We're doing a lot with the bigger pieces, the murals, but what if they left something that others can find, hidden?"

Jimmy didn't lift his eyes from the sticker in front of him. "So you're bringing up work."

"Isn't that what you wanted? To get a little real graffiti in there?"

"Why do people hide the stickers?"

Pree blinked. "They don't, not always."

"But when they do?"

"I guess . . ." She thought about how it felt when she stuck a slap behind something, the inside of a newspaper box or on a café wall below a table's lip. "It's like telling a secret."

"So you like to tell secrets."

"Or to hide them."

He looked up then. "Tell me one, you." Again, that use of *you* that she wanted to mean . . . more.

And there was only one secret she could think of right

now. *I'm pregnant.* But if she told him, he'd immediately jump to whether or not she was going to have the baby, and if she did, how much maternity leave she'd need . . . She hadn't been working there long enough yet to do this to the company.

"Wow." Jimmy pushed his chair back an inch. "You got a good one, huh?"

"I met my birth mother." Pree offered the second-best secret she had.

"*That's* what I'm talking about. And?"

"And?" She shrugged. "It was fine."

"You never met her before?"

Pree shook her head.

"So that's a really big deal."

It was—oh, it was. "Nah. I'd been meaning to do it for a while." She paused. "She's an artist, too."

"So that's where you get it."

Pree lowered her head to finish her sticker. The fumes from the pen made her slightly nauseated. That was new.

"You must be freaking out."

Pree exhaled as she nodded. "I guess."

He capped his pen. "I didn't know you were adopted."

"It's not like you can see it on my skin or anything." Pree felt nervous under his intense gaze.

"Your parents . . ."

"Are amazing."

"Of course they are. Look at the way you turned out." He smiled so warmly that Pree's knees heated. He went on in his uncommonly colored dark gray voice, "So what was your . . . biological mom like?"

"She was nice. I guess. It feels kind of . . . weird that she was a total stranger. You know? If I'd passed her on the street, I wouldn't have known her. I'd kind of always assumed there'd be some spiritual link or something. Like I would just know." Pree felt herself blush. "That sounds stupid, I know. Oh, and I had a half brother."

"Had?"

She fiddled with the edge of the sticker she'd just finished. "The papers say he died when his father killed him in the garage with carbon monoxide."

The legs of Jimmy's chair reconnected to the concrete. "Accidentally or on purpose?"

"From what I've read, it was an accident. The dad fell asleep after driving the boy around. The kid was sick, and I guess he had trouble sleeping? I didn't ask her about it."

Jimmy squinted up at the sky as if looking for his next words. "So."

Pree waited.

"When are you going to see her again?"

"Dunno. I texted her. I guess if I see her—"

"If?" Jimmy's knee jostled the small table so that his pen rolled off the edge and hit the ground. He didn't bend to pick it up. "You met the woman who gave you life. You have to be interested in that story. It's part of who you are." Pree knew. She wondered if he focused on his wife and two kids like this, and if they loved it when he did.

Pree rolled her pen in her fingers. "It's what I always wanted, to know who she was. I knew who she was even before I moved here, part of why I came. And now that I've met her—what more am I really going to get from her? I mean, I have two moms already. Do I really need another?"

Jimmy arched a questioning eyebrow.

Pree laughed. "Lesbian moms. Double the fun, double the kale."

"Gotcha. So, do you think your dad is the same as the guy who did the carbon monoxide thing?"

"No. She was, like, sixteen when she had me. And that was just barely. No one stays with the person they're with when they're that age."

"True. How long have you been with . . . what's his name? Finn?"

"Flynn."

"Yeah. Him."

Pree peeled a sticker from its backing and then concentrated on putting it back, exactly where it had come from. "Not that long." *Three years, since junior year.*

Jimmy smiled. "How about that." His voice was darker gray than a storm cloud.

"How about that," she repeated.

"You two serious?"

This was where she should tell him, *Yes. We're serious. I love my boyfriend.* Instead she said, "Not really."

"Not exclusive."

She and Flynn were monogamous. It was something they'd expressed clearly to each other. "No."

The smile spread slowly over Jimmy's face. He was the kind of handsome that belonged on a TV show about motorcycles. "I like hearing that. You've got something in you, you know that? Something special." He paused. "It seems like still waters run deep with you. There's something you're not admitting. You can tell me anything, you know. I'm a good secret keeper."

What, did he *know* or something? The look on Jimmy's face was both kind and frightening in its intensity. All of this could be such a bad idea. *He* was a very bad idea.

Shit. She had to tell Flynn about the pregnancy. This cemented it. Flynn the Safe. Flynn the Good.

"So," she said. "Your slap looks great."

It did. He'd drawn ADOG just right, with enough boldness and thick/thin variation that it looked real.

"You sure you're okay?" Jimmy asked.

Under the table she removed her sticker's backing quickly—she was good at that—and pressed it to the underside. "I'm okay. I guess. Whatever. I will be."

If Flynn were a bad boy, she reasoned, he wouldn't be her Flynn, the one she needed to talk to. About the pregnancy, anyway.

"I know you will be. I have absolutely no doubt that you can handle whatever ends up in your path. You look good, by the way. Out here. Outside the office." Jimmy leaned back and grinned at her again. Whatever he was doing right now, he'd done before. She pictured herself for one second, her legs around his waist, pressed up against a dirty alley wall, getting fucked so hard she forgot about everything else.

Pree pushed the sticker harder into the underside of the table as she smiled back at him. You had to mark your spot, to sign it. Like you were praying, a wish that only God knew was there.

Chapter Nine

Monday, May 12, 2014
5 p.m.

"You got every cone? You sure?" Mario scowled at Nolan and jabbed his thick finger toward the stretch of road they'd been working on for the last two hours. As far as Nolan could tell, the look was permanently frozen on his face.

"Of course." Nolan nodded and sent a half-laugh disguised as a cough to Rafe.

"Every single one?"

"Yep," Rafe said. "Why you so worried? It's going to come out of your salary if we miss one?" He was good at teasing Mario. Their supervisor never got it, never understood that the guys were laughing at him. He was so ineffective that dealing with him was the only thing that made Nolan miss being in charge.

"It should come out of *your* salary. If I had my way, I'd charge you a hundred and twenty-five dollars for every damn cone you *pendejos* leave out on the road to get smashed."

Everyone laughed, which made Mario spit sideways and stalk back to his truck.

"It's not worth it, being a supe," said Rafe. "You couldn't pay me enough."

"You'd be bad at it anyway," said Nolan.

"No way." Rafe pushed his long black hair out of his eyes.

"You see everything in black and white. Supes need to see in shades of gray, or they suck. Like Mario." It was what Nolan had liked at the very beginning about Rafe—that good-versus-bad simplicity that Rafe believed in so deeply.

"Bullshit," said Rafe, but he shrugged as if in agreement.

"Call it like I see it," said Nolan as he glanced at his cell phone to get the time. Almost done for the day. He was exhausted, clear through to the bone. Just the way he liked it.

Walking back to the truck, he let the guys' talk wash over him. He settled in the passenger seat, drinking the last cold dregs of this morning's coffee from the thermos he'd left on the floorboards. No way did he or Rafe smell as fresh as they had that morning, but it was good to feel this tired. It was the beginning of the spring pothole blitz, his first, since he'd been on a little less than a year. All the guys said it was the worst part of the year, but Nolan liked the pace. Moving from street to street, filling in the worst of the holes, it was steady, almost soothing. Oakland's roads held up for thirty years, but they could afford to replace them only every eighty-five, so some roads had more filled holes and ruts than asphalt anymore. Job security, that's what they called it.

Rafe banged the door shut and said, "Oh, man." He started the truck and headed back to the yard.

"I agree," said Nolan. "Hey, I was too sleepy and didn't ask this morning. How's Rita? Did you hear anything?"

Rafe smiled widely, the deep dimple in his cheek caked with dirt and sweat. "I didn't know this morning. We were still waiting. But when I got that call at four o'clock, it was her. Best news ever. Just a fatty tumor. Benign."

The tension that had been coiled at the base of Nolan's neck started to uncurl. "Good," he said. "That's really good."

His friend's face was more relaxed than Nolan had seen it in weeks. "It's like God comes through, you know? You pray and pray and then, if you pray hard enough, you get your miracle."

"Not always." Nolan wanted to take back the automatic words as soon as he said them. Rafe was the closest thing he had to family now. He spent Wednesday nights and most of each Sunday at Rafe's. Rita cooked meals specifically for him, arroz con pollo and a heavy cinnamon cake that fixed his sugar craving for weeks on end. Often Nolan played Candy Land with Rafe's daughters until their bedtime, and then he watched sitcoms with Rafe and Rita until the wall clock chimed midnight. Letting Rafe have this—his belief that his prayers had cured his wife—was something a friend would do.

"You don't think?" Rafe shifted so that they were an inch farther apart on the bench seat. "God gives, and God takes away, right? Rita's prayers are good. And mine were desperate, so they were extra strong." Rafe was Catholic, sternly, proudly so.

"Sorry, man. I didn't mean that." God wasn't always the only one who took away.

"Huh." Rafe glanced at him. "Sounded like you did."

"My prayers didn't work out, that's all. Old scab. I'm sorry."

Nolan watched as Rafe shook it off. He was good at

that—quick to forgive, ready with a laugh. Nolan envied him the ease with which he swam through life. Rafe did the breaststroke while Nolan tried to approximate a clumsy dog paddle. But then again, Rafe had family while Nolan had two missing-in-action parents. They'd been decent folks all his life. Jim and Poppy, the banker and the gardener. They'd flown over from Hawaii for Robin's birth, and he and Kate had gone out with the baby once, putting Robin's ecstatically kicking legs into the warm blue ocean. He knew his parents had come out for the funeral, too, but he hadn't seen them then. They hadn't visited him in jail, saying it would make it too hard on him. Neither Jim nor Poppy had come to one day of the trial. His mother had sent a card that said they both believed in his innocence and that he should come stay with them after he was free. Adequate parents. They were kind when he was young, kissing him good night and reading him the occasional bedtime book. They hadn't *broken* him, after all, and he loved them. He'd never been the link that kept them together. He hadn't been enough.

Rafe palmed the wheel to turn into the yard. "You're coming with us tonight, right?"

"Yeah. Of course." Nolan didn't really want to go to Murphy's, but it was important. "I'll meet you at the bar." He jumped out and unlocked his old beater Honda—he didn't want to have to get one of the guys' wives to drive him back later. He'd stay sober; no way in hell he was drinking and driving. It was only by the skin of his teeth that he'd gotten this job in the first place. It wasn't easy for an ex-felon to get a job doing anything, let alone civil service. But during his last year of incarceration, his cellmate David had pulled some state roadwork because his brother was a mucky-muck up high in Caltrans, and he'd gotten Nolan in on it, too.

He'd loved it. Even with radio shackles strapped on in

case he decided to make a break for it, a guard with a gun watching his every move, a long pickup stick in his hand for grabbing plastic bags out from under bushes that scratched him until he bled, he'd loved it. It wasn't an office. There was no hum of fluorescent lighting overhead, no soft *shush-shush*es as copies spat out endless reams of unnecessary documents. No polite laughter when the other partners walked by, no pretentious lunches, no golden handshakes, no false promises.

In comparison, the road was true. The noise came from truck traffic, blasting their ears as they worked in underpasses. The sun burned his skin, even under the hard hat, even with the sunblock they provided. He felt half deaf when he finally took the noise-canceling earplugs out and found himself shouting politely at the grocery store after work out of habit.

And the people on the road crew were his friends. Outside, they were equal, instead of the fucked-up games that went on behind the bars. Nolan hadn't adjusted well to prison—what criminal with a white-collar past did? Inside, they hated him for so many reasons. One, he'd killed a kid. Didn't matter it was his own, didn't matter Robin was in pain, it just mattered it was a child. Two, he had no idea how to play the game.

In high school, Nolan had been tough. He knew how to fight, and he'd liked to do it—scrapping with boys who could barely throw a punch, always winning, liking the salty, acrid taste of a small amount of blood in his mouth. In the law firm, he'd occasionally bragged about his quick-tempered, fast-fisted youth.

In prison, he'd realized he didn't know a single fucking thing about fighting. The first beating he took left him with two broken ribs and a punctured lung. That was for taking the last white roll. How could he have known you left one on the tray in case someone more important came through behind you? He'd tried fighting harder the second time, but the guy who jumped him for cutting in line—he hadn't—was at least seventy pounds of muscle heavier than Nolan. The man's fists were mallets of solid steel. Nolan hadn't been able to see out of his left eye for three weeks, and for a while he wasn't sure he'd get vision back in it at all. He saw double for six months.

Humbling. It had been beyond humbling. To know you couldn't take care of anything, not even—especially—yourself.

But on the prison road crew, he'd made friends. Casual ones, but they were guys that later he could sit with in the yard. That had made things almost bearable, to be able to shoot the shit with someone you weren't scared of. Occasional laughter.

When he'd gotten out of prison the year before—released early for good behavior, they said, but he knew it was because the state was easing up on euthanasia cases—he'd called his ex-cellmate David, who told him where to go, what phrases to say. He checked the felony box on the application, wrote his explanation, ninety percent convinced he'd never be hired. When he went in for his interview for Oakland Public Works, he made the mistake of saying, "I want to be a flagman." He wanted to be the guy who looked into every car, watching families pass, fathers with fingers lifted in thanks from the steering wheel.

The man who interviewed him, a big guy with perma-red cheeks and sparse white hair, had roared. "It never gets old, man. I'm telling you, it *never* gets old. Every single guy comes in here wants to be a flagman. You know how you get to be a flagman? You work the roads. Some days you get to hold the flag. Some days you don't. Just like life. My crew is the best. I'd take a bullet for 'em, and sometimes I almost have. It's not an easy job—it's dirty and hot and humiliating. You can only work it if you really, really want it." He'd looked down at Nolan's paperwork, and Nolan knew, even from where he sat, that the felony box was the part standing out in neon, flashing, pulsing at the man. "You're an ex-lawyer ex-con. How do I know you're not just in it to spring a lawsuit on me? I got enough of those."

"I want the job. *Sir.*" The words were simple. But his heart was in them, and the man heard it.

"You'll get word next week."

He hadn't had to wait—the job was offered to him that afternoon by telephone. He took it, gulping embarrassingly and gratefully. He hadn't been as excited when he'd made partner.

And he'd been fucking terrible at it at first. Hands that he'd thought were hard from the work he'd done on the prison crew were soft in comparison to his coworker's iron palms. As the rookie, he'd had to do the shit work—all of it. And literally, a lot of the time, the work involved shit of some sort—animal shit, Porta-Potty emergencies. He'd kept his shoulders back, and when Seymour Cliff came at him for using the wrong shovel, he'd backed down, hands up, knowing that Seymour would not only beat the hell out of him, but he'd also lose his job. He was the one still on probation, not Seymour.

Maybe, come to think of it, maybe it was one of the best things he'd learned in prison. Posturing was important, sure. You strutted your stuff like a peacock even when you felt dull as dishwasher sludge. Marching through the yard, head so high you brushed the clouds even though you felt lower than dirt. But even more important, you had to learn when to fall. You had to learn when to roll over and show your belly. Once a seriously disturbed inmate had held a piece of broken razor to Nolan's neck in line at the commissary. The only reason Nolan lived was that he had tilted his head so that the guy could get a better swipe at his artery if he needed to. He'd offered quick, easy access to his own death, and in exchange, the guy had palmed the razor and walked away as if nothing had happened. All Nolan had had to do was show his belly like a dog.

It was the same on the paid road crew.

He did the grunt work. He played the rookie until a younger newbie came along. He never complained. If someone swiped his jacket, he just bought another one. What else was he supposed to spend money on? If a guy took his Coke right out of his hands, guzzling it while the others laughed, he brought two the next day, just in case.

The other men had watched, their eyes almost as careful as those in prison.

And one by one, they offered him the smallest things: a single sideways laugh. The extra cup of Gatorade. The first time someone had teasingly knocked off his hard hat, he almost cried with relief.

And now, a year in, no longer the rookie they could make go out in the rain while they sat in the truck, Nolan loved it. He'd spent nine years at the firm, and in all that time he hadn't known his coworkers' spouses' names. But one year on the road, and he knew Tim's wife's middle name, because he'd put it on the card that they'd all signed. Nolan had been the second to hear that Shante couldn't get it up anymore, and the first to hear that Viagra was a wonder drug sent from God. He knew when Rafe's first niece was due, and that it was a girl, and that that was because in his family they only made girls. Nolan and Rafe planned to build the baby a crib, even though neither of them were woodworkers. They'd bought the plans for it the week before.

The men—and they were all men on Nolan's crew—were his family now. He'd never had a second of this feeling at the firm. And if Stephen Schmidt, founding partner of Schmidt Cade and Whipple, parked his Mercedes on the right-hand shoulder and came over and offered him his job back, with full benefits and the guarantee that all was forgotten, Nolan would laugh in his face. He really would. He wasn't going anywhere. The only person he didn't get along with was Mario, and no one got along with Mario. That man had risen to the level of complete fucking incompetence, and as long as he could yell at someone during the day, he was happy. Nolan didn't mind if it was him Mario yelled at. Didn't change his paycheck. On the outside, people thought yelling made it a bad day. He knew better.

Of course, Nolan wasn't *happy*. How could he be? But for long hours of hard work, he forgot. And wasn't that, really, what happiness was? The absence of pain?

Murphy's bar wasn't far—a half mile at most from the yard. The drink-up itself was in honor of a somber occasion: the one-year anniversary of the day Louie Pacheco had been killed. It was a tradition on the first anniversary to honor a fallen coworker with drinking until they were all tequila-blind. It was what they did. Never forget. Most of the guys' wives had plans to come pick them up late that night—divvying up the driving and coordinating in the morning to get the cars back. That was nice of them, Nolan thought. Considerate, especially when you thought of what shape the guys would be in when they were poured into their backseats. For a second, as he locked the car door with his key—the remote was broken—he missed Kate so viscerally he could almost feel her next to him in the cold parking lot. In another life, she would have picked him up like the other wives were going to do. She would have pressed that impulsive kiss of hers against his lips, against his neck, before asking how it had gone. *How are the guys? How are you, my love?* He'd been her love and, god, she'd been his. She'd been everything. All.

Murphy's was dark and crowded, already full of smoke. Skull, the owner, kept a glass vase in the shape of a boot on the bar and told every person who lit up to throw a couple of bucks in the jar. Whenever he got cited for allowing smoking, the boot paid the fine. Skull knew Nolan's order, Bud draft, and had it poured by the time he'd wedged himself between Shante and Mario.

"We all did shots, brother. Next round's on you, right?" Shante already smelled like tequila as he slung an arm around Nolan's shoulder.

"Okay." Nolan was easy. He wouldn't actually do the shot, but he'd buy. The job paid better than he would have guessed it would, and the money just sat in his account. He didn't have anything to spend it on. Booze for the guys was a fine way to blow some.

"Lefty got here first." Shante gestured with his head to Lefty Venca, who was trying to balance a beer bottle on his pointy nose, and it looked like there was cash on the bar to go along with it.

"He's ahead of us, looks like," said Nolan. Shante laughed and clinked glasses in agreement.

After an hour of dirty jokes too disgusting to tell at work, Rafe stood on a wooden chair and clinked his Zippo against his beer bottle.

"To Louie!" A roar arose. Rafe slipped his lighter back into his pocket and used his free hand to gesture that everyone should quiet down. "A true man. A fine man. A man we lost too early. Being a road worker is more dangerous than being a cop, and normal people don't *care*, man. Drag racing the Dublin grade, texting constantly. What is *that* important? That's what I want to know," said Rafe. His words were on the very verge of slurring, but he was keeping it together better than most could. Louie and Rafe had been tight. They'd been partners—that's why Nolan had ended up in Rafe's truck at work. Once Louie had saved Rafe by shoving him out of the way of an AC Transit bus. Rafe believed he wouldn't be around anymore without Louie, and now Louie wasn't here.

"He was four months and two days away from retirement. He'd already bought his boat. He had maps of the ocean from here to Fiji. He wasn't gonna be on the roads anymore. He was gonna be on the water."

In the bar, no one breathed. It was quieter than Nolan's apartment at midnight. Even Skull behind the bar stopped moving, the water dripping from his rag to the floor the only sound.

Rafe took a deep breath and held his bottle higher. "To Louie Pacheco. Our brother. May all his ocean dreams be coming true. And may the motherfucker that hit him rot in hell after he's spent a lifetime getting fucked in the ass in the state pen."

As the men cheered, Nolan raised his glass and clinked left, right, and behind him. He doubted if the guy who hit Louie even got three months. It was better not to know, actually.

Next to him, Mario downed another shot of tequila, no salt, just chewed the lime afterward. His breath was strong as he turned to Nolan.

"So you know something about that, huh?"

Nolan felt suddenly cold. "What?"

"The state pen. You know something about getting fucked in the ass?"

Shit, shit, *shit.* He knew. No one had known, not up till now. HR was supposed to keep his file confidential, but he'd known it was a matter of time. Unadulterated fear froze the back of his neck. How long had Mario known? It couldn't have been long—someone like Mario wouldn't have been able to keep it to himself.

He kept his eyes steadily on the mirror behind Skull's back, and kept his face loose. Slack. Completely blank, like he was back behind the wall. Blank face, blank thoughts, chest thrust out—no victim on display for anyone to thump, maim, kill—make it through another day.

"No clue, huh? How long were you in prison, buddy? Four years?"

The riotous talk all around them died off again, and this time the quiet had an edge.

Nolan pounded the last of his beer. If he needed to make a quick getaway, he would.

"You didn't answer me," said Mario. "Whatchoo do for being in there? A lawyer like you? Some white-collar shit? Embezzled, I bet."

Nolan felt sweat break across his chest and back. Mario didn't know. "Something like that."

Mario's voice rose and the others glanced their way. "I always knew you were no good."

"Shut up, Mario!" yelled Nate, the biggest guy on their crew. "Before I have to make you!" He'd never dare speak to Mario like that on the road, but in here, off the clock, there were no rules. And by the way Nate was swaying, it was clear that he would like nothing better than to shut Mario's mouth by way of a haymaker.

It was nice, to be backed up like that. All the guys were

sending cold glares at Mario. It felt good. And it felt wrong. If they knew why he'd gone away, they wouldn't be acting the same way, he knew that. Killing a kid, no matter how innocently, made a person almost as hated as a dirty cop. "It's all right, brother," said Nolan. "I can handle it. Ain't a big deal." He'd never said *ain't* at the firm.

"Good thing you didn't go into retail," muttered Mario. "Good thing you don't get to touch the books."

"Only books I'm touching are your mama's romance novels I borrow after she climbs off." Nolan felt particularly pleased with his quick response.

"Oh-*hoh*!" the guys roared, and the moment was over. Nolan laughed and clapped his friends on the back as he went to take a leak. Then, without saying good-bye, which would have raised another ruckus, he slipped out the side door. The wind slammed it behind him, a hollow, metallic sound that echoed across the parking lot and against the wall of the mechanic shop next door.

They'd find out soon enough. He wouldn't lose his job, he knew that. The head honchos knew he'd been in prison, convicted of a felony, and he'd gotten the job anyway. But when the guys found out . . . When Rafe found out, there was no way his God would stay out of the conversation. And that wouldn't be a fair fight. Nolan never won against God.

Chapter Ten

Pregnancy

November 1991

With her first pregnancy, Kate had no symptoms. Her breasts weren't tender or swollen, and she didn't have morning sickness. At fifteen, she felt, if anything, stronger than she'd ever been. At first, she thought the new multivitamin Sonia was making her take was just kick-ass. Her fingernails grew faster. Her hair got so thick she had to tie rubber bands together to pull it all back. It was growing colder then, the winter setting in, but she didn't need to wear a jacket to walk between classes—a tank and skirt were all she needed. She ignored Sonia's lectures on catching cold and wore just flip-flops on her feet, so she could feel the blacktop below her, even as she floated above it.

She didn't understand the feeling (not at first) and

attributed it to being in love. Her friends went through boyfriends like Doritos, and they laughed at her when she talked about Nolan, but Kate knew better. *He loves me. I love him. He* loves *me.* In a year and a half—an eternity!—they'd be out of high school, off to college together. They'd planned all of it, lying on a beach blanket just past the high rows of driftwood. While watching the moon soar above them, they mapped out their living plans (a small apartment with a north-facing room for her painting and a desk for Nolan at a window that faced the sidewalk), their educational goals (a law degree for Nolan, an MFA in art for Kate, both from UC Berkeley, naturally), and their familial hopes (when they were twenty-eight, they'd have two children, a girl and a boy, each perfectly possessed of each other's best traits—wonderful, smart, obedient children who would make them laugh until they cried).

Kate was almost sixteen. She never thought the word "pregnant," because she couldn't be. They were always careful. Doubly careful, both pill and condoms. They'd never been careless, not once. Besides, fifteen-year-olds didn't get pregnant, not unless they were the potheads teetering on the edge of meth addiction who barely went to class, girls who ripped out their eyebrows and penciled them viciously back in, girls who got tattoos of boy's nicknames (Digger, Sully, Wrecker) without their parents' knowledge. *Those* fifteen-year-olds got pregnant. Not girls like Kate, girls who studied diligently for AP American History tests and ate spinach when their mothers cooked it and didn't stay up late on school nights. The only argument Kate and her mother had had in months was whether she was taking too many extracurriculars. Kate insisted she knew what she was doing and that all those extras were what colleges wanted. Sonia had given in, knitting wordlessly on the couch, the angry clicks of her needles the only evidence she was upset with her daughter.

But after missing two periods, still positive she couldn't be pregnant but filled with a heavy dread she'd never felt before, Kate went to the drugstore. Which of the dozens of boxes would be the correct one? The pink one, with the daisy on the side? The soft blue one, with the glittery embossed ribbon? (Where, she wondered, was the box for the girl who *didn't* want a baby? Where was the black box with red lettering, the one that came with a complimentary educational tract detailing how to tell your single-parent mother who still wasn't—and never would be—over the loss of her husband that she was going to be a grandmother?)

She chose a simple white and yellow box. Two of them, to be sure. And one more, just in case the first two didn't work. She used babysitting money because it didn't seem right to use the allowance money that Sonia handed her silently every week. The checkout girl met her eyes with a look that was probably meant to be understanding. She'd seen this purchase before. But the checker didn't understand anything.

At home, on the toilet, sudden terror gripped Kate. Even though she'd had a full Nalgene bottle of water in preparation, the urine wouldn't come. What if she wasn't pregnant? What if this thick dread she felt was actually a kind of silent, insane, unfounded joy? Everything rode on this moment. Her entire future, love, and life depended on a horizontal bar forming against a vertical one. From the kitchen, she heard Sonia start the washer. Her mother was washing a load of her jeans, completely clueless that her daughter had ever had sex, let alone was peeing on a stick under her roof. If it was true, if Kate turned out to be . . . she could *never* tell Sonia. She would have to move to Alaska. Or Antarctica or Australia.

Anywhere far, far away that started with *A* would do, as long as Nolan came with her, too. *A is for away . . .*

The box said to wait five minutes. Kate steeled herself to wait. The longest five minutes of her life, she predicted. But it wasn't—it took barely thirty seconds for the crossbar to start showing. Ghost pink at first, then stronger, bolder. So pink it was almost bloody when the X was formed—she was struck by its heady gorgeousness. She wanted to paint with nothing but this shade for the rest of her life and lamented that nothing in her acrylics tubes could come close. She peed on the other two sticks just to watch that particular, unique color form again, and then again.

X marks the spot, she thought. She slid her fingers over her belly, wondering what the swell might feel like. What would she look like with a belly stuck out, reaching rooms before the rest of her body did? What would Nolan think when he saw her naked?

The sticks changed everything, completely and utterly. In a sudden fit of something she couldn't understand, Kate couldn't wait until she was so big that strangers told her she looked like she was about to pop.

"Baby, you're mine," she whispered. "You're real, and you're mine."

M is for mine, N is for now, and for Nolan, always for Nolan.

He broke two dates with her, both times with good, believable reasons. His parents were forcing him to go to a diabetes benefit dinner, he said, and they had a ticket only for him, no extras. Kate believed this—his parents showed no interest in their son's relationship. The next night, he'd told her he couldn't go to the movies because he'd eaten something bad at the benefit the evening before. That was weirder—Nolan bragged he had a cast-iron stomach—but whatever. She'd see him on Sunday, right?

He said he'd call her.

Kate felt the first tiny knot of worry then.

When he hadn't called her by seven on Sunday night, she called him. "I thought we were going to hang out." She tried not to sound as hurt as she was—after all, he had no idea she had something *huge* to tell him. The biggest thing *ever.*

He said something about chores, and how his mother had been upset about the way the gardener had trimmed the hedge, and how she'd made him redo it even though he had precalculus to study for . . .

Kate let him chatter for a minute or two and then she cleared her throat.

"But how are you?" he said, taking his cue.

"I'm fine. I have a little bit of a surprise for you." She felt like giggling, and couldn't tell if it was happiness or terror that made her feel like tiny painful bubbles were racing through her blood.

Nolan said, "Hang on." Then in a rushed aside, she heard him hiss, "*Not now,* Mom. I haven't told her. Give me a second. God."

Kate laughed lightly. "What haven't you told me?"

Silence stretched like elastic, prickling and taut.

Finally he said, "Shit, Kate. We're moving."

She sucked in a breath and sank farther into the pillows on her bed. "What?"

"Hawaii."

"*What?*" He couldn't just go. Not now. "When?"

"Two weeks."

Kate felt the baby move inside her, a startled flutter. She knew it was supposedly impossible—the book she'd gotten from the library said she wouldn't feel it until she was five months along (she loved what it was called, the quickening), but she knew what she'd just felt and she knew it was real.

"So . . . we . . ." she started.

"I don't want us to break up," he said desperately, his voice cracking. "But I think it's best. I can't handle thinking of you here without me. I'd rather not . . ."

"Think of me at all?"

Another tight silence was her answer.

Kate slid her legs off the bed until she could dig her toes into the carpet. "But you love me."

"You know I do."

"So we'll make it work."

"No."

"Why?" She hated the pleading sound in her voice. This was awful. This couldn't happen. Not *now.*

"It'll be better. You can date someone else. Go to prom. Do the things you're supposed to do."

"Oh. I get it. You'll get to date, too. Some little island girl who goes to school in a sarong, right? Is that what this is about?"

His voice changed then, into his school hallway voice, the one she hated. "Why not? Would that be so awful if I wanted to do that?" It was the tone he used in the hallways when he was yelling at his guy friends, the sound he got when he was being an idiot in class with his homies. Whenever he was sent to the office to pick up a detention slip, he had the same tone as he tossed back, "Haven't been in detention all month! Can't wait!"

Nolan said, "It's not like we were going anywhere. Not together, anyway."

Kate gasped. *Fifteen and pregnant.* She should tell him. She had to tell him . . .

"My dad said everyone goes through this. What do we know about love? We're kids. Stupid kids. That's all. I can't change the facts—I'm leaving. You're staying. We're too young."

Usually, when she was on the phone with Nolan, he whispered so no one else could hear. When she was with Nolan in person, he said secret, sweet things about her pinky finger, said things about her kneecaps that made goose bumps rise on her arms. He was unrecognizable, really, as the same loud boy she saw in the halls at school.

Stupid boy. *Boy.* Not a man. What had she been thinking, to hope that this would work? That this could be something actually good, and not the tragedy school counselors always made teenage pregnancy sound like? It *was* a tragedy. A huge, fucking waste.

She remained quiet, devastated into silence.

"I'm sorry," he said in the voice she knew was his real one, the softer one. "Can we get together and talk? I need to see your face. God, I'm so sorry, Kate. I've tried and tried to get them to change their minds, but Dad has some big business deal there and they won't listen to me. It's like I'm not here, like I don't count. I need to see you—can you come over?"

"So you can watch yourself breaking my heart?" She would *not* sob, not until she hung up on him.

"Kate—it's just for the best. We're so young—"

"You keep saying that. Your dad tell you to say that?"

"No, but if I don't do this . . . he's right—"

"You're weak," she said. It was what Nolan was most scared of, that he would actually turn out to be the runt that his parents would return for a better, stronger son.

"Stop."

"You are. Weak and cowardly. You can't see what we have. You're willing to throw it all away—and you have *no* idea how much you're throwing away, *none*—and for that, Nolan, I will never forgive you." She hit the release button on the cordless and threw it across the room. When it rang again, she unplugged the phone.

Kate knew an hour later she should have told him that he was going to be a father. She should have said that while he was surfing, she'd be pregnant in homeroom. Just another promising girl gone bad.

She also knew she'd never tell him.

She knew Sonia would want her to get an abortion. She said as much whenever they saw a young girl pregnant out to there. "No idea," Sonia would say. "That girl has no idea how hard it's going to be."

Her mind raced, and she tried to grab any possible solution that floated by. Adoption? How did someone set that up? Didn't they have to be part of a Catholic charity or was that old-fashioned? And school! She couldn't go back to school. Not *that* school, anyway. One of Nolan's friends would see—would tell him. Nolan could never, ever know. Kate pictured herself at the small continuation high school that sat, literally, on the wrong side of the tracks, in broken-looking portables. Going there would practically guarantee she would have to get a tattoo on her neck.

Her mother was right. Kate sat on her bed, her fingers gripping the ragged teddy bear she'd outgrown so long before, and felt the world get huge on all sides of her. It was too enormous, too big. Too hard.

She had no idea what to do.

Chapter Eleven

Tuesday, May 13, 2014
10 a.m.

Kate made a pot of coffee and drank almost the whole pot sitting alone at the kitchen table, staring at the place on the doorjamb where they'd marked Robin's height every year.

Then she started moving. She dragged plastic bag after plastic bag down from the attic and into her Saab, fitting in as many of them as she could until she could barely close the passenger door.

Kate drove to the thrift store wondering if she was the most callous person on the face of the earth. While driving down Fruitvale she lost herself in a whirlpool of regret, thinking about how he was now erased, his things being given away—his room no longer *existed*. She was a terrible mother. She'd already known that, of course, but this made it even worse. She remembered an e-mail Nolan had sent a few months earlier, asking if she still had the rocking horse they'd bought him when he was two. It had always been in his room, even when he was too big for it. Several times Kate had tried moving it out, but Robin had always chased after her, clutching the horse's wool mane. Now it was in the back of the car on Robin's side, riding where his car seat had been. Biting back tears that threatened to rise, she parked in the thrift store lot.

Nothing to do but keep moving forward. Even if it was at a stumbling pace.

Inside, she found a small, mousy woman wearing a flowered apron sorting coffee mugs. "I have some donations in the car."

The woman shook her head. "No today."

"Yes, I'm here today."

"No donate today. Wednesday, Friday, Saturday only."

Kate balled her hands into fists. "You don't understand. I have to get rid of this stuff. Now."

"Goodwill in San Leandro has drop-off today."

Through clenched teeth, Kate said, "I'm not driving another half hour. *I can't.* Please, won't you take this stuff? They're children's clothes, and toys, and—oh, a whole bunch of books. Good books."

The woman folded her lips, looking unimpressed. "No one to receive. I don't make the rules."

"But can you bend them?" Kate tried smiling. She couldn't get back into the car with that scent. Burning the car and its contents was a more attractive idea.

"No bend. Sorry."

"My child died." There, she played the only card she had. Really, it was the only one left in many ways, Kate thought.

But instead of softening the woman, it seemed to anger her. "You should go. No donate." She turned her back on Kate and went back to pushing coffee mugs around, clinking them together, lifting one up, shaking out the dust, and replacing it so hard that the handle cracked off. "Shit." She turned fiercely back to Kate. "No donate. Tomorrow. Shit."

In the car, Kate beat the palm of her hand against the steering wheel until it throbbed deep inside. She wouldn't drive to San Leandro. She couldn't go that far. Instead, she drove from the thrift store to a shopping center close by. She'd been behind it once before. She and Robin had been searching for the perfect piñata. They'd heard that Lucky carried a Spider-Man one, which was exactly what Robin wanted. After jockeying for position to enter the lot, she'd gotten turned around and had ended up behind the center. Kate had noticed then the unlocked Dumpsters. It was a left-over tic from her apartment-dwelling days: she'd made an automatic mental note of their position. When she was in college, she'd made many a midnight dump run to unlocked Dumpsters, chucking in bags of trash that wouldn't fit in the overflowing apartment Dumpster.

When she was with Robin, excited about the closeness of a real Spidey piñata, she'd never thought she'd be back here. In fact, inside one of the bags she'd packed the day before was a collection of plastic cars that they'd also bought here to put in Spider-Man's chest cavity. Robin had kept them lined up on his window. Kate had thought that another kid might have liked them. Some little boy might have gotten a sparkle in his eye at the thrift store and would have pulled on his father's arm. *Please, please, Daddy. I want them. Please?*

One by one, she tossed the bags into the Dumpster. This, she could do this. And wasn't this similar to what it would be like on Saturday? When she would go to the bay with the ashes. Maybe she *would* be able to do it, to throw the bodies of her mother and of Robin into the wind.

Like so much trash, like what she was chucking into the Dumpster. She swallowed hard, pushing the tears back with sheer willpower.

On top of the bags, she placed the rocking horse. It looked obscene in the Dumpster. A tragedy. It was begging to be photographed in black and white by a college student, displayed pretentiously under track lighting. It would be titled "Heartbreak" and people would nod knowingly as they passed it, knowing nothing at all.

The last item she tossed over it all was a practically brand-new red sleeping bag that Robin had treated like a toy when he'd received it one Christmas morning when he was five. Once she'd found him in the garden, inside the bag, only the top of his head sticking out. "What are you doing?" she'd asked. "I'm a burrito!" he'd cried rapturously. "B is for burrito!"

She'd almost forgotten that entirely.

Three blocks away from the store, waiting at a light, Kate saw a woman huddled against a shopping cart under the 880 overpass. Her hair was stringy and so thin Kate could see her scalp in places, although she probably wasn't much older than Kate herself. She wore jean shorts, even in the cold air, and Kate could see track marks on her legs. Next to her, behind the cart, something moved, and then Kate realized someone was peeking at her. A little boy. Or perhaps it was a girl—it was impossible to tell. No more than eight, the child sent Kate a cheeky gap-toothed grin and followed it up by shooting her the bird.

Kate flipped a U-turn and screeched around each turn, hurrying back to where she'd just been. But in the three minutes it took to get there, it started pouring. "No, no, no," she said, unwilling to use her wipers, hoping it would stop. It had to stop.

Damn it. The Dumpster had already been used. Boxes of rotting fruit and vegetables sat oozing on top of Robin's sleeping bag. She pulled at the edge, but it wasn't salvageable. A piece inside Kate's heart, a tiny piece that had been miraculously still whole, broke.

"No diving!" a man's voice shouted from behind her. "Get away from there!"

"Asshole," yelled Kate in his direction as she sank back into her car that no longer smelled of Robin. "You should lock it, then."

But he didn't hear her. He didn't even look at her, just hurried through the rain to pull up the lid, banging it into place. Kate drove away, knowing that, like the woman and child under the overpass, no one noticed her, either.

Chapter Twelve

Tuesday, May 13, 2014
6 p.m.

Dear Nolan,
There is something I have to tell you.

When Nolan opened his computer, the return address pulsed from the screen as if it were bright red instead of regular black and white like the others. *KateMonroe2002.* He'd thought it was funny when she'd attached the year to her handle so long ago, as if they'd never enter another new year. When they'd started e-mailing about Robin, he'd been surprised she hadn't changed the address. Or, for that matter, her last name. But she hadn't changed, either.

It had been a long day on the road—they'd been putting in new speed limit signs on Mountain Boulevard, and people didn't know how to drive out there. Stupid winding road.

You'd think they'd get a freaking clue when they saw the flashing lights and all the guys in orange, but no. They had to speed *up*, daring each other to pass in the most dangerous ways possible. Shante had had to dive off the edge of the shoulder into the poison oak at one point to get out of the way of a red SUV. The driver was looking down at her phone, and Nolan didn't even think she noticed that she'd almost killed a man. She'd go to bed tonight thinking about bills and maybe have sex with her guy, instead of counting her blessings that a man she'd never know was still alive to go home tonight and think about *his* bills and maybe have sex with his wife.

People didn't get it.

Nolan did. He should be dead. Every day he knew that.

Wiping the back of his suddenly dry mouth with his hand, Nolan slowly and very deliberately shut the computer without reading the rest of the very short e-mail. It was different, he could tell. This one wasn't a remembrance of their son. He stood from the couch and put the beer he'd opened back in the fridge. It could wait. It *should* wait.

In the bathroom, he removed his smelly work clothes, and instead of taking his normal shower, he filled the tub with hot water. He lowered himself into it, hissing at the pain. He'd always liked a hot bath, as scalding as he could get the water to run. The tub in this apartment was subpar, and that was putting it mildly. It was plastic sealed, with cracks at the bottom where rust from underneath bloomed. Even when he scrubbed it, it never seemed clean. As it was too shallow to even cover him fully, he'd almost given up on baths altogether, even though it had been one of his favorite daydreams when he was in prison: a claw-foot tub like he and Kate had had out on the hill under the oak trees, deep enough for two, water hot enough to make his skin feel like it was about to sizzle right off.

But now, it was enough to soak as best he could. He kept the faucet running a slow drip since the overflow valve shunted water away from him. Fred Weasley sat on the bath mat and licked at the water every once in a while, seeming surprised and pleased by the taste each time. Part pit bull, part enormous unidentifiable orange mutt, Fred Weasley resembled the kind of dog that might knock over little old ladies and take their purses just for fun. Robin had always wanted a big orange dog so he could name him after the character in Harry Potter. Once Kate had asked Robin why Fred, and not Ron Weasley, since they were all red haired. "Ron's a terrible name for a dog," was the only answer Robin gave. And it wasn't an awful answer, Nolan thought.

Toward the end, they'd even talked about getting him a dog, not that Robin ever knew it. It was after he'd stepped on a bee while walking to the bathroom—a bee that must have crawled in during the heat of the day when they'd had the windows open. Robin had yelped, and when Nolan saw the crushed body of the insect, he'd called 911, almost unable to breathe himself. Robin was allergic to bees. Robin was weak. Robin would die, from a *bee sting,* and it would be all Nolan's fault.

But the damnedest thing had happened: Robin hadn't reacted at all. When the ambulance got there, they could barely tell where the stinger had gone in. They didn't even transport him—Nolan chose instead to just keep an eye on it, knowing they could rush to the hospital if they needed to. They hadn't—no swelling, no wheezing, not even a red spot. The doctor later explained that his immune system was so compromised he didn't even have his normal allergies. All his warning systems were shut down, closed for business.

On the back porch while Robin slept, he and Kate had sat in the wooden swing and talked. She'd pretended to sketch the rosebush, but her pencil barely moved. She said, "If he can't get sick from a dog, why not just get him one? I mean, besides the fact that you're allergic, too."

But Nolan's allergies didn't matter, he knew that. Something happy and bright rose in Nolan's chest, but it took only a second to flip through how it would go: Carrying Robin in his mask through the shelter, letting him point at the one he loved best. Taking it home. The dog falling in love with Robin. Robin expending precious energy, loving his new best friend.

Then, Nolan and Kate having to care for it after its master died.

It was an unbearable thought. Nolan had disguised his answer as being in Robin's best interest. They didn't know, he'd said, when Robin might start feeling better. When his immune system would compose itself and recognize what it was supposed to do. When Robin might spontaneously heal. And dogs were dirty, tracking germs in from outside. They couldn't afford that, and they wouldn't be able to get rid of a dog, not once it was in the house. So they shouldn't bring one in, period.

The lead of Kate's pencil had scratched louder as she continued to draw something she didn't care about, something that he'd find crumpled in the trash later. They hadn't looked at each other for the rest of the night.

Fuck allergies, anyway. After he got out of prison, when Nolan had found Fred Weasley in the pound, he'd figured the worst thing that could happen would be that he would have such a bad asthma attack that he'd stop breathing. While he'd mostly gotten over his death wish, there were still times when Nolan wondered how much he would mind dying. Yet an over-the-counter daily allergy pill was all he'd needed to be able to live with Fred. He still didn't touch the dog and then immediately rub his eyes, but if he washed his hands often and didn't let Fred sleep on the bed, he barely had any problems. Chalk that up to one more thing he wished he'd known earlier. He should have gone along with Kate's plan about finding Robin a dog. She'd been right, as she was about most things relating to Robin.

Even though she hadn't been right about him.

Fred Weasley *whuffed* in his ear and then burped gently.

"I suppose that's my cue." With a wet hand, he diligently scratched Fred behind the ear for a long moment. Just before he got out, he scrubbed himself with a washcloth and Dial soap harder than he normally did.

Kate deserved that, at least. She didn't need her e-mail read by a man who stank of sorrow and sweat. Kate, who'd never minded if every single scrap of food in the fridge turned green and fuzzy, had always been sensitive to the way he smelled. When he'd first gotten the job at the firm, she'd sniff-tested different combinations of antiperspirant and cologne. "Too sweet, and you'll bother the women's noses. Too assertive, you'll piss off the higher-up men," she'd said, coated in scents in the small bathroom of the apartment they'd lived in then. It was years before they'd been able to afford the house that was supposed to keep them safe. Hell, they hadn't been able to afford expensive cheese.

Wrinkling his nose, he'd said, "I don't think anyone's going to notice. Maybe I'll stop wearing deodorant altogether."

She'd been so *shocked*. "And smell like a punk rocker? You'll be out of there so fast your head will spin. Smell is almost as important as color." She dabbed a different cologne of the four cheap ones she'd bought at the drugstore in the crook of her elbow and buried her nose in it. "Speaking of which, which tie are you going to wear? The blue, I think. You look amazing in blue."

Kate had loved him. And god, he'd known it. Back then, he'd worried about everything—how to keep her happy and safe, how to earn more money faster, what the bumps were in the dark of the night—but he'd never worried that she didn't love him. He knew she did. Felt it in his bones. His parents had never noticed him. His teachers hadn't, either. Friends were a little better, but Kate, when she whirled through a room, throwing pillows off the couch and tossing the newspaper into the air looking for the brush she'd already misplaced twice that hour, when she stopped momentarily in her flight to press kisses all over his face, he knew it. He had everything he'd ever needed. And so much more.

Now, in the dismal studio half the size of that old apartment he'd shared with her, Nolan was out of the bath. Clean, he leaned back into the couch, pulling a pillow up behind him. Fred groaned and stretched at his feet.

Dear Nolan,

There is something I have to tell you.

I should probably see you to say it. If that's something you could feel comfortable with, please e-mail me back to set up a meeting.

I hope all is okay with you,

Kate

A meeting. In person. Hot damn.

The very next e-mail was from someone who wanted to know how to seal a garage properly in order to commit suicide. Jesus Christ. Who the hell did they think they were, e-mailing him? As if he knew. Like he had any fucking clue. He'd lived, goddamn it. Didn't they *get* that?

God, it was stuffy in the apartment. He got up and turned on the small fan and slid open the window that looked out over the back alley. Cumbia music pumped through the screen and the rain played a steady rhythm against the accordion. He stood in front of the fan, resting his cheek against the grimy screen until his heart stopped clattering. Kate had always loved this kind of spring rain the best. It had made her joyful, silly. Giggly. He wondered if she was looking outside, too.

Nolan didn't care what Kate wanted to talk about. She could want to discuss cutting off his balls with a rusty letter opener and he'd sit there and nod and agree before unzipping his pants.

He moved back to the couch.

"Dear Kate," he typed.

He stopped, and erased "Dear." Added "Dearest." Erased that and put it, just for fun, "My darling Kate," knowing he could never send it like that. But he looked at the words for a moment and remembered the feeling of rolling over in the middle of the night, reaching to find her in the king-sized bed. "My darling," he'd say against her hair that smelled of their bed. "My darling." She never woke, just wriggled back into him, letting him hold her tighter.

Dear Kate,

I'll meet you anywhere, at any time, for whatever you want.

You know, I thought it would be better to be on the outside. But I'm finding it's just harder out here, though, something you probably had to learn by yourself.

He couldn't figure out if this was something he should leave in or not. It was true; therefore, he could probably say it. Kate had always been good with truth, even when it was unpleasant. But maybe she'd changed. Maybe he'd changed her.

He should be dead. Yeah, he should put *that* in there.

I should be dead.

Delete, delete, delete.

I wish there were more I could say here without feeling like a complete fucking moron. Let me know what I can do, or where you want me to be, and I'll be there. I'm working for Oakland roads now. I think I saw you drive by the other day near the Thornhill off-ramp. Not something you'd have ever expected, right? Now I hold signs and fill potholes and pick up trash.

That was enough. She didn't need more than that. She probably didn't want more than that.

Love,

It was still true.
Delete, delete.

Yours,
Nolan

That was true, too.

Chapter Thirteen

Tuesday, May 13, 2014
7 p.m.

Pree had intended to talk to Flynn when they woke up. A sleepy conversation while still wrapped in the sheets might make it go better.

But when she opened her eyes, he was already gone. He couldn't sleep sometimes when he got a new idea in mind. He'd head down to the steelworks to twist molten metal while the rest of the world slept.

He deserved to know first. Of course. But she needed to go to work, which she did. Jimmy didn't end up coming in until three o'clock and left at four, giving her only a short wave on his way past her desk. He was on the phone as he passed, smiling and laughing, saying something about T-ball practice. He smiled at her vaguely. As if they hadn't even hung out in Union Square the day before. Pree kicked herself for thinking about him like that.

At home that night, Flynn still not back from the warehouse where he worked, Pree dialed her mothers' number without thinking. Normally Isi would be at the restaurant at this time of night, but Tuesdays were a day off for her. Marta and she would be on the couch, eating popcorn and watching whatever reality program Marta insisted on watching. Pree loved that she knew this. It felt like solid ground, and she dug her toes into it while the phone rang.

When Marta answered, Pree just said, "Hi."

"Isi! Pick up the other line!" Marta bellowed. Then, softer, "Hi, kid. How's our girl?"

Pree gulped, surprised by the wave of emotion that filled her. "Good. I need to tell you something."

"Are you hurt?" asked Marta.

"No, nothing like that."

Pree heard a fumbling noise and a rapid-fire string of curse words. Then Isi, on the other line, said, "Are you hurt?"

"No. Can't a girl call her mothers?"

"When we just talked to you on Sunday for your birthday? No. Something's going on. What is it?"

At least she had something big she *could* tell them about. "I found Kate Monroe."

Another thump, and Pree could hear Isi pulling out the soft green chair that was wedged near the hall closet. "Shit. Wow."

"It was fine. I went to her art opening. She wasn't anything like I'd pictured her. Younger, maybe, than I thought she'd be."

Marta said, "You gonna trade us in, then? For the newer model?" Her words were light but her voice was tense.

"Never," Pree said. "Never ever in a million, billion, trillion years. You're my moms, the best moms. But tell me something."

Pink relief colored Isi's voice. "What's that?"

"Tell me what happened. How you chose me." It was the

one thing they wouldn't talk about when she was growing up. *She wanted the adoption closed,* they'd say. *It's not good for you to have to wonder about someone you can't ever know.* Pree hadn't ever known whether that was an easy or a difficult suggestion for them. They'd told her only that they'd picked her specially, and that from her first moment of breath they'd been there. That she was *rare.* Precious. That was all she'd ever known.

"Shit," said Isi again.

"You look like her," said Marta. "It's what I always think when I see you in photos."

Pree rolled over and waited. She heard both of them take deep breaths. They wouldn't keep it from her now, would they? Now that she knew Kate?

"She was so young," Isi said. "We met her in the hospital for the first time. She was already in labor. There was a screwup, and we were already in the hospital to try to meet another baby, an emergency one."

"Holy *shit.* There was another *baby*?"

Marta said, "It was a last-minute thing—that mom was all screwed up. At the last second, her family came in and they didn't need emergency fostering. So when the agency called us, we thought they were kidding, telling us some huge cosmic joke."

"I was second choice?" Pree's brain stuck on this, whirred over something she'd never even imagined. That a child could be so easily passed over. Missed.

"Kate had been momentarily interested in us once, but we'd never been allowed to meet. We'd given up hope. But something went wrong with the couple that Kate had chosen, and the agency called us. Like I said, we were right there. In the hospital already." Marta, as if taking Pree's measure over the phone line, then said, "Kate had just changed her mind, and we ran into another couple that was coming out of her room when we were going in to meet her. Now that I do this for a living, I'm aware that's the worst thing that can happen." Marta worked for a foster-to-adopt agency in Malibu. "But I didn't know that then. For all I knew, it was normal to see your competition in the hallway. And god, they were perfect. I remember he looked like a dark-haired Tom Cruise, only taller, and she was beautiful with long golden brown hair and a beautiful face. I hated them so much, *and* I was so nervous that the second I saw them, I almost threw up right there in the hall."

Pree wanted to laugh, but she didn't. She didn't want anything to stop the story.

"So. Anyway. When we go in, Kate's in between contractions. Her face is all scrunched up like she's ready to cry, and she looks exhausted. I step forward, and I'm trying to figure out what I can say, since I'm sure she's going to pick the beautiful couple, and instead Isi passes me and wraps her arms around Kate's shoulders. 'You poor thing,' she says. 'Who's here to help you with this?' Kate tells us no one is. Her mother had driven her but then freaked out and went home. She was clinically depressed or manic or something. Kate just looked like she'd almost expected it, though. I remember that."

Isi said, "As if there's anything more important than being with your *daughter.*"

"Isi told her that we didn't care if she picked us or not, just asked that she let us stay with her for the birth. To help. I thought she was lying. I wanted that baby, you, so bad I was ready to say almost anything, but Isi said later she meant it. She would deal later with whatever happened, but in that moment she just wanted to help that girl."

Isi cleared her throat. "That girl was six years younger than you are now. And yeah, you do look alike." Pree could almost hear Isi rubbing her head with one hand. She always joked that she had Lesbian Haircut Number Eleven, gray flat-top, shaved on the sides, but it looked good on her. It was just her. Pree's Isi.

"So," Pree prompted. "You told Kate you were staying."

"Yeah," said Isi. The fierce sound of love in her voice warmed Pree. No matter what, she'd always known Isi loved her more than anything else in the world. Honestly, that was a pretty great feeling for an adopted kid to have. It's not a prerequisite for adoption, but it should be. A form letter should be signed and notarized: *Do you agree to throw yourself in front of a moving bullet to save your child? If not, please consider purchasing several new computer games or maybe a pony on which to spend your money and time.* And even knowing all this hadn't ever stopped Pree from worrying she could do something to make all that love dry up. Maybe what she was hiding from them, her own biggest fuckup, literally—maybe that's what would finally push them away. She felt sick with dread.

"Tell her what happened next," said Marta, her voice as dark green and soft as moss.

"Then Kate said we could stay. That she wanted us to. And *you*," Isi said, "came out fast after that. Not more than an hour after we got there. What little time she had between contractions, she fired off questions at us, one after the other, and not one of them about how we would raise a child."

"She asked where we'd traveled to. Wanted to know if we'd ever been to Buckingham Palace. And Venice," said Marta. "She wanted to know if we'd ever been on a gondola, remember?"

"When I told her that we'd taken a *traghetto* instead because we were cheap and that you'd fallen out because you were so excited to be crossing the Grand Canal, she laughed her way right into another contraction."

Pree could hear Marta grin. "She wanted to know what languages we spoke."

Isi said, "I changed the subject since we don't know any and told her we could ballroom dance." Funny, Pree had never noticed that Isi's voice was almost the shade of pearlized pink as Flynn's was. She could see it. Both of them loved her hard, stubbornly, as if she couldn't do a single thing to push them away.

Marta gave a burst of laughter. "I'd forgotten that. You made me fox-trot between the IV pole and the chair."

"There was three feet of space."

"We did good, though."

"Then you came out," said Isi simply. Her voice sounded funny. Isi was the tough one, the one who could manage eighteen waiters at her busy restaurant, fire two, and hire two extras while managing to serve a perfect espresso and seat the mayor, all at the same time. Her voice never got that shake in it, the one Pree heard now.

"And then what? She just gave me to you?"

Marta took up the story. "You weren't squalling, just bright red and covered with the whitish—"

"Yeah, I get that. Then what?" Pree didn't need to hear that part. She wasn't ready to think about the blood and pain and fear.

"She told the nurse to hand you to us," Marta said.

"Was she upset?"

"No."

Pree couldn't help saying, "She didn't . . . mind?"

Marta said, "I didn't trust it. I had a friend who got the baby taken back six days after she'd received her, because the mother changed her mind. I thought that was going to happen with you. Kate just didn't have enough . . . emotion, I guess. I thought we would leave that next day with you and that we wouldn't get to keep you. That whole first year, even after the grace period was over, I kept expecting that call. So I got my master's and went into adoption counseling. It was too important. All of it. Even now when the phone rings sometimes I wonder if it's someone who wants to take Pree back."

Isi humphed. "No one can take her back. She's ours."

Pree relaxed into the warmth. She couldn't tell them, not until she'd talked to Flynn. But they would love her no matter what. Right?

"You're always ours," said Marta.

There were things the moms couldn't protect her from. Things that she'd screwed up by herself. No matter how loved she was, no matter how much they wanted to protect and take care of her, Pree was still going to have to figure out for herself what the hell she was going to do and how she was going to fix it.

Pregnant. After hanging up with the moms, Pree rolled onto her back and tried to feel the life inside her. Could she commune with it? Feel it? Should she say something deep and wise? Could it help her decide what the fuck to do next?

She had to talk to Flynn.

She had to stop thinking about Jimmy.

After concentrating for a long moment, Pree only felt an ache at the back of her calves and the urge to itch her nose. Someone was making fish soup downstairs and the smell made her queasy.

Maybe Flynn would be home soon. Or maybe not. She rolled onto her stomach and pulled out some blank stickers. She started to draw. It was the only thing to do.

Chapter Fourteen

Tuesday, May 13, 2014
11 p.m.

Kate made herself go to book club, even though she hadn't read the bestselling tearjerker Elizabeth had picked for them. Just touching the cover of the book was enough to put a lump in Kate's throat. And by the conversation that swirled around her, she knew she wouldn't have made it through the book in one piece, anyway.

It was good enough to sit in Dierdre's living room, surrounded by the other seven women, listening to them chatter. She spoke exactly enough to keep them from noticing that she wasn't really saying anything. When she thought about that little person under the overpass, her teeth chattered quietly. The shame she felt about the lost sleeping bag felt like frostbite, skin burned by ice.

Dierdre knew something was going on. She cornered Kate in the hallway after she came out of the bathroom.

"Your art show was amazing on Sunday. I'm so glad we went. I felt so *cosmopolitan.* Even though every person I talked to probably assumed I drive a station wagon with more than a hundred thousand miles on it. Which I do, of course." Dierdre smiled at her warmly. "How are you?"

Kate used her most chipper voice. "Good. Busy!"

Dierdre placed her soft hand on Kate's forearm and said, "This time of year must be hard for you."

Kate forgot to breathe in her panic—how did Dierdre know about Pree and her birthday? Jesus. Who else knew? *How* did they know?

"I have a hard enough time with Mother's Day coming up this week and my kids are just far away. I've been thinking about you." Dierdre didn't let go of Kate's arm. The pressure remained, steady and warm.

"God. Fuck, yes." The weight of the day, the realization of how close it was, was almost too much. That, mixed with the loveliness of Dierdre's home—a perfect suburban haven of subtle potpourri, dried-flower arrangements in oversized vases, matching wineglasses, and coasters that were actually put to use—made Kate swallow back the terrifying urge to scream.

Dierdre, though, wasn't her house. She'd made this home perfect, but Dierdre herself wore her thick green glasses unself-consciously, left her roots undyed for months, and loudly lamented her varicose veins. When she leaned in to hug Kate, Kate folded into her softness, accepting it. She was pigment to Dierdre's linseed oil, assimilated completely, and Jesus fucking Christ, Dierdre's arms around her were the best things she'd felt in months. Maybe years.

As she pulled away, Dierdre touched the side of her head with one hand, brushing back Kate's curls. "It'll be okay."

A lie. A wonderful, perfect lie for which Kate was so grateful.

After she got home that night, Kate was ravenous. She'd forgotten to eat at Dierdre's, overwhelmed by the choices of tiny handmade crudités.

So she made a sandwich. It was her favorite—the one neither of her boys would ever eat with her. Havarti cheese, tomatoes, sprouts, and avocado on toasted sourdough bread. She padded out to the back deck and pulled a lemon off the tree that seemed to always have hundreds of small yellow fruits on it. She squeezed the juice over the top of her sandwich fillings. A twist of salt, then she mashed the sandwich together and cut it carefully in half before placing it on a plastic plate covered in small blue rabbits. Robin's plate.

Before she went to the garage, Kate picked up her cell and hit the speed dial. She listened to the dialing, to the abbreviated ring, then to the automated voice that told her she should check the listing. Her mother still didn't answer. The pain was a kick in the chest, just another bodily thump. Was it possible she was getting used to the dull thud of sorrow? Could that ever actually happen? When Sonia had died, she hadn't felt a thing for three days. Not one thing. Not sorrow, not relief, not grief. She'd found her mother's old compact in her purse and had taken it to bed. It had smelled like Sonia—chlorinated and dusty. Kate had stared at herself in the tiny mirror, willing herself to be able to find the grief, to locate it somewhere inside her own gaze. But her eyes looked the same. Just like any other day. Kate had thought she was broken, that after Robin's death she'd never be able to feel sad about losing anyone again.

Then, on the fourth day after her mother died, she woke up howling, her whole body shivering under the covers, feeling more alone than she'd ever felt before.

Now she held her cell phone tighter, as if it were flesh, as if it were warm. Then she put it back in her pocket.

A deep breath.

She needed a candle.

Kate took the three steps down into the garage and placed the sandwich on Nolan's old workbench. She lit the candle with the book of matches she'd found in the tool drawer and set it, flickering, next to the sandwich. Nolan had always been good about keeping things around, things that were handy, and he always knew where things lived, where they belonged. If Kate couldn't find something she thought Nolan might have owned, she simply took a moment to think like him. *If I were a glue gun, where would I live? Nolan would put me next to the iron, where electrically operated heat items lived, above the washer.* And there it would be.

The candle flickered once, then came back to life. She turned off the garage overhead light at the same time that she pushed the button for the door. It whirred up, smooth as always. As she walked to her car in the driveway, she turned her face to the rain. It was cold and thrilling. She loved the smell that rose from the grass, from the wet asphalt, and she remembered when that kind of thing could make her laugh with pleasure.

Then Kate drove her car into the garage and shut it off.

Kate heard the final *kerchock-clang* as the garage door settled closed, followed by a metallic whir as it came to rest. She got out of the driver's seat, picked up her sandwich, and got in the backseat, next to where Robin had last been seated. He'd always sat behind the front passenger seat so Kate would only have to turn her head a little bit to see his smile.

She ate her sandwich while staring through the front windshield at the candle. It winked at her, as if it knew a secret.

The avocado was perfect, just exactly the right texture against the bread. The lemon was almost sweet in its intensity.

Kate felt a wild rush of pleasure as she ate, and pushed down the guilty feeling she always had.

Still alive.

She and Nolan were still alive, and Robin wasn't. Robin, who had hated avocado and every single kind of cheese except American, which most of the time Kate refused to buy for him, maintaining that protein had to actually be made of something more than just colored chemicals. An ache tugged the back of her throat. She should have let him have more fucking American cheese. Cheez Whiz in a can. McDonald's cheeseburgers. All the things they'd kept from him, to keep him what? *Healthy.* What a goddamn joke.

An artist Kate knew, Judy, had eaten only organic food. She'd raised her own fruits and vegetables most of her life, and was a vegetarian. She exercised and volunteered and went hiking in Nepal. She ran marathons raising money for worthy causes. She'd never eaten a single item of processed food. She'd died of ovarian cancer the previous year.

Kate licked her fingertips clean of bits of mayo and crumbs, then ate the tiny piece of tomato that had fallen onto the plate. Every last bit, eaten.

Then she reached forward into the front area and turned on the car.

The Saab's engine was still strong—it gave a low growl as it came back to life and then purred quietly inside the closed garage with barely a throb as it idled.

Kate started to count, watching the candle on the workbench. One, one thousand. Two, one thousand. Three, one thousand.

Then, when she reached forty, as the candle guttered for the first time, as her courage guttered in the same way, she leaned forward quickly and shut off the car. As she always did, she threw open the backseat door and ran to punch the garage door button on the wall next to the light switch. It rolled up angrily, shaking the wall she leaned against.

She blew out the candle and then sank to sit on the top step.

She stared at her car. She indulged in her ritual only every once in a while. It used to be more often, but now it was down to once every three or four months. Whenever she really, really needed it.

Kate knew (now) that carbon monoxide bound itself to the hemoglobin in the blood with a much higher affinity than oxygen did. Once bound, it wouldn't let go, and less and less oxygen would be carried in the blood. It sounded like a violent takeover of the body, but actually it was peaceful, causing sleep, then death. It should be louder, she always thought. It should be something that was obvious, like the light of a candle going out, or the *shoonk* of a car door slamming shut. Not this silent, incredibly fast killer. A nurse in the ICU had told her it could take as little as five or ten minutes to cause death. A car idling in a cold garage. How many times did it happen accidentally in the United States every year? She'd read about an ambulance crew who had pulled into a cold bay at a hospital, forgetting to crack the outer door while they let it idle as the three paramedics napped, the heater keeping them warm. No one woke up. What must that have been like for the hospital workers, to come upon an ambulance full of their own? Accidentally asphyxiated.

Kate scrubbed her face with her hands. Her eyes itched suddenly and she rubbed them so hard she couldn't see through the dancing black spots for several seconds afterward. Then she got in the car, pulled it out, parked it in its usual space in the driveway, and shut the garage door from the outside, one last time.

She squinted, ignoring the rain that seeped down the

back of her sweater, and looked at her house, trying to see it with new eyes. It was sweet-looking. Quaint. The colors, dark green and brown, were old-fashioned. A stranger walking by would think that if anyone had died there, it would have been a lovely old couple who probably died within days of each other, unable to live without the partner they had spent sixty years needing.

Not an eight-year-old boy. And not, until the paramedics brought him back, a young father who would do anything, *anything* for his only child.

Still standing in the spring rain, she held the plate so tightly she worried it might break between her fingers, and felt the familiar feeling course through her. It felt like the playacting she did when she couldn't do anything else. It felt like sleeping with a man you knew was dangerous, a man who could snap your neck while you came, who might wring your very final breath from your body, and still you had to sink to your knees in front of him. A terrible, awful fuck, one that you had to have, even if it was your last.

Chapter Fifteen

Birth

May 1992

In the maternity ward's hospital bed, Kate clung to two things: the cold metal side rail that didn't bend no matter how she pulled, and the fact that she hated Grant Masterson and his wife so much that she'd probably never have the energy to dislike another person again.

"You're so beautiful, Kate," crooned Grant, his perfect dark hair falling in a wave off his forehead. "You're so strong. You're doing everything right."

From behind him, his wife, Stella, pressed her palms together as if in prayer and beamed beatifically at Kate. "If it's a girl, we'll give her your middle name. Out of respect for your great sacrifice."

"And if it's a boy . . ." Grant trailed off and looked at his wife. They both smiled.

But Kate didn't *believe* them. They didn't feel real. Something was wrong. She wished desperately (again) that Sonia had stayed after checking her in, but "something" had happened at the pool that needed her presence. A good old-fashioned drowning was the only thing Kate could think of that should cause Sonia to run away the way she had, but it was probably a chlorine shipment or something. It was strange, and upsetting—Sonia had been so present lately, toward the end of her pregnancy, as if she really, truly cared. As if it hurt her that her child was giving up a baby, as if she almost believed they were a real family again. And then, two hours earlier, she'd gotten a look in her eyes like a panicked horse and fled, leaving Kate to do this by herself. Hours from becoming a mother herself, Kate was pretty sure that was a fucked-up maternal instinct.

"Where will you take the baby?" Kate asked the couple she now hated.

Grant frowned. "What do you mean? You want to know where our house is? I'm not sure—"

"I mean in the world. Where will you go together?"

Stella stepped forward. "Oh, we don't travel much. Not safe, not in this political climate. We'll keep to the good old US of A, and that's good enough for us." Her words sped up. "Of course, the baby's safety is the most important thing to us."

Kate *had* liked them—she really had. They'd been one of two couples she'd asked to meet, and after she'd met them she'd told her adoption counselor that she didn't need to meet the lesbian couple. It would be too hard to go through that again, looking into eyes that were desperate to take what she didn't want. Grant and Stella had had to smile and appear friendly and, worst of all, *normal,* while they auditioned for the role of their lives. When they'd met, Kate had liked Grant's wide, trustworthy face, but now, from her position of pain, she hated his teeth—such small incisors. They were unnatural. And Stella looked desperate, as if she were ready to rip the child from Kate's womb—her jaw gritted in what appeared to be worried ecstasy.

Kate's eyes rolled back as the deep red pain moved through her once again. She held on to the rail as hard as she could, trying to breathe. Nothing else existed but the pain, not the baby or even herself. Just pain. Then, after what felt like hours, the pain eased like and she lay back on her pillow panting. "Marybelle," she said.

The adoption counselor stepped forward. "Yes."

"Can I . . . talk to you?"

Marybelle met her gaze. "Of course." She ushered the couple out professionally while they murmured encouraging things to her and was back in a moment. "What is it? Is something wrong?"

Kate didn't know how to say it.

"Have you changed your mind?"

"I can't, can I? It's too late."

"We talked about that. Nothing is too late. Remember?"

"I'm sorry," Kate said on the end of an exhalation. Then, "I'm so sorry. Has my mom called you or anything?" Kate mopped her sweaty forehead with the wet washcloth the nurse had given her the last time she'd checked in, when Kate was still only four centimeters dilated. *Mom. Please, Mom.*

"I'm sorry. No, she hasn't returned my messages. I've got a coworker driving by the pool now to check on her." Marybelle squeezed her shoulder, but Kate could read the disappointment in her eyes. "What are you thinking? What do you want?"

I want my mother. But she was gone.

I want Nolan. But Nolan was so far away from her, so long gone that she could barely see in her mind what color his voice had been. Dark blue like jeans? Or like the ocean the day before a storm? It wasn't clear anymore.

Three days after they'd broken up, he'd started calling. Three, six, eight times a day. The first few times, Sonia held the phone toward Kate, expecting her to take it. Kate shook her head and continued watching *The Price Is Right*. "She's not here," Sonia said roughly into the phone. Kate had made the mistake of answering the phone just once. Hearing his voice, the way he'd said, "Katie, please," had made her hands tremble so hard she'd dropped the phone. As she picked it up again, she was able to find the strength to say, "Are you still going? Still breaking up with me?"

"Yes," he'd said. "But you have to understand—"

She'd hung up.

"What an asshole," her mother had muttered, surprising Kate. Her mother had touched her on the head then, as she passed on her way to bed. Just the one light brush on her hair, so soft she barely felt it.

The calls had stopped soon after that—she didn't know what her mother had told him to make him quit calling, but she didn't care. Whatever it was, it worked. Somehow, Sonia and she had reached an odd truce, as if Sonia having to readjust her measure of Nolan had given those points to Kate. She hadn't protested when Kate told her she was switching to the continuation high school. They watched television in the dark and laughed at the same times. Kate talked her mother into getting a small pit bull mix, a gray-and-white female who wanted to cuddle constantly. Once Sonia had even put her hand on Kate's stomach. Her face, usually so terse and drawn, had softened. "Poor child," she'd said, and Kate didn't know which child she'd been referring to. She didn't ask.

Now, at the hospital alone, Kate told Marybelle, "I don't know what I want." It was as if she couldn't *help* but hurt everyone now. As if it was her job or something. "But I know I don't want that couple. It's horrible. I'm a terrible person." She started to cry again. She'd broken absolutely everything, from top to bottom, and this was just one more thing—breaking Grant's and Stella's hearts.

"Are you sure?"

Kate gulped and nodded. She had only a few minutes, five at the most, before the pain took her outside herself again. She had to be clear. "Not them."

"I'm going to have to tell them." Marybelle looked at the floor—this was hard on her, too.

"I'm so sorry." The guilt and sorrow seemed to trigger the next contraction—it tore into her, and then another one, stronger and more demanding, came pressing on its heels.

"And then what?"

Kate could read the question on her face. "No. Not me. I still don't want to keep—can't—"

Marybelle glanced at her watch and up at the face of the large clock on the white wall. "What about that lesbian couple whose profile you liked?"

Gripping the sheet between her fingers, hating how it gave so easily, Kate said, "Tell them to hurry."

The two women were there almost instantly, miraculously. And they were different from their picture. In the photo, Isi had looked über-butch, all flattop and button-down shirt, chest stuck out as if she had something to prove. Marta had looked a little too eager, her cheeks too red.

But as they entered the hospital room, Kate felt hope bloom for the first time. Isi came toward her, ignoring Marybelle's attempt to introduce them formally. "You poor thing," she said. "Who's here to help you with this?" When Kate's eyes filled with sudden, stupid tears again, Isi just took her hand and held on while another wave of pain rocked her for long minutes. Isi's hand felt so much stronger than the metal rail of the bed, and when the contraction stopped, she didn't let go.

"What's your favorite color?" Kate asked Isi. It wasn't a test, although Isi probably didn't know that.

Isi smiled, and her eyes were so soft against the severe angles of her jaw. "Would you believe pink?"

Pink was Isi's voice, a soft rose with lilac on the edges. "I believe it."

Marta, on the other side of her, brushed the hair from Kate's sweaty forehead. "Butch in the streets," she said, and Isi said, "Oh, stop," and the affection in their voices flowed over Kate like sunshine. It didn't feel like they were auditioning—it felt like they wanted to be there, like somehow they cared, and it had been so long since she'd felt it that she leaned toward it like a sun-starved daisy.

Isi said, "This isn't about what you choose to do. That's your decision, and it's none of our goddamn business. But please, let us stay? You can't be alone for this, and we don't want to be anywhere else."

Kate heard truth in her voice, and that was the moment she decided.

Marybelle excused herself quietly, and when the nurses weren't checking Kate or adjusting the IV, the three of them were alone. During the contractions, Isi propped her up, never letting go of her hand, and Marta murmured words, endearments, and encouragements that didn't mean anything by themselves but, strung together on the thread of her dark green voice, soothed Kate. During the euphoric lulls, she fired questions at them.

"Where do you live?"

"What do you eat?"

"Favorite grocery store?"

"Dogs or cats?"

"Football or baseball?"

The answers didn't matter—Kate couldn't have given a crap about whether they ate meat or not (Isi did, Marta didn't) or whether they liked cats or dogs (both). She just wanted their conversation to continue, to hear the way they spoke together, teasing gently, finishing sentences for each other. Fondness. Love. They were a family, just the two of them together.

"What languages do you speak?"

Marta's eyes widened. "Ooops. We fail."

But Isi said, "All right, you got us on that one, but we can ballroom dance—does that count?"

Pain was coming faster now, the contractions closer together, and Kate wished she hadn't passed on the epidural. Stupid. What had she been thinking? Stupid, *stupid.* "Show me," she whispered.

For the first time since they'd entered the room, Isi let go of her hand and offered it, across the narrow bed, to Marta. "Shall we?"

"I can't believe we're going to do this." But as she moved around the small room to Isi's side, Marta's face had a radiance that Kate wanted to never look away from. They did the fox-trot to silent music, and Kate watched, transfixed. They fit each other, Isi's leg moving comfortably between Marta's thighs as they turned tightly in the small space. They rested against each other.

Then things for Kate sped up, and every noise was dark blue in her ears. Breathing was painful but she didn't stop. The moments before pushing were pure hell. Pushing, though, was a deep relief, the only thing she'd ever be able to do again. The way the women held her hands hurt, too, but she begged them not to let go. And they didn't—they held on tighter. The doctor was there then, saying things that didn't make sense until Isi translated them, until Marta said them over again in her ear.

Then there was a darkness she couldn't remember, even seconds later. She knew she couldn't do it again, no one could live through this, and then she did it again, one last push as she cried for her absent mother again like a child, and then the relief wasn't relief so much as a difference, a change of air pressure, noises of the room falling back into her ears, coming back into herself, and as the nurse prepared to hand her the baby, Kate shook her head and took her hands away from them, closing them into fists.

"Them," she said, closing her eyes, wishing she never had to open them again. "She goes to them."

Chapter Sixteen

Wednesday, May 15, 2014
11 p.m.

Kate remembered seeing the road crew Nolan mentioned in his e-mail. She even remembered the man she'd stared at. He'd had shoulders like Nolan. She'd loved that Nolan had always been recognizable even from a distance in that his shoulder blades were so pointed, almost sharp. If he'd had wings, they'd have poked out right there. She had liked to touch them in the dark, liked to sleep with the flat of her palm on that bone, as if she could keep him from flying away in the night. She'd told him she would have been able to pick his shoulders out of a lineup. He'd laughed, but she wasn't kidding. She could have.

Under his orange vest, that man had had those shoulders. Kate hadn't been able to see his face under the hard hat, and she hadn't tried. It would have been too much of a disappointment, seeing someone else's expression over a body that looked so much like Nolan's.

But it *had* been him. She'd driven right past him that day. Nolan had known it was her, had watched her go by in the car he'd bought her, the car his son had died in, and had just stood there. Then he'd had to go back to work. As she drove south down Highway 13, she thought about how difficult it must have been for him to do manual labor. He'd always mocked his own soft hands, pointing out the blisters he got when they gardened in the spring. Ten minutes with a shovel and his hands were practically bleeding.

She bet they were different now.

Kate exited on Thornhill but there was no crew in evidence. Just orange cones. She almost hit one and cursed as she got immediately back on the freeway, going back west.

It had been a silly, impulsive thing to try to do, to find him. He'd answered her e-mail, after all. She could tell him when and where. She just needed to figure out how, exactly, she could tell him what she needed to. What she owed him.

If that was anything at all.

She headed toward the drugstore, swooping off the exit on Broadway as the roadway threaded itself under the highway and then back up. Kate needed earplugs and sleeping pills. She'd done well for a while, and this last year had almost seen the end of the nightmares, but last night they'd come back as bad as they'd ever been. She'd woken in a full sweat, the feel of Robin's thin arms clutched around her neck, so real her skin could remember the weight of him. She'd heard his scream in her dream, the sound he made only when he had nightmares, and the bloodiness of it had echoed in her ears for the first fifteen minutes she was awake, as if she'd just heard it, as if it had really awoken her as it had in the early days of his sickness. Those horrible days. (Living, waking nightmares, and sometimes, back then, she'd had bad dreams only to wake to find the day itself was actually worse, more unbearable.) Kate had hardly slept during the last year of Robin's life, and after he died, she'd slept even less.

So to go back to that, to feel last night the desperation for sleep, the conviction that it would never come back on its own, was horrible. Over-the-counter sleeping pills would help. So would earplugs; the *whoosh* of her own breath would lull her to sleep.

The car was on autopilot. When she stopped at the first red light and looked left toward Lake Temescal and saw the road crew occupying the turn lane, she forgot what she was doing and where she was going. Nolan.

Kate needed to be there, where they were. *Now.* Her car shot through the red light and turned left against an oncoming red Taurus, which honked and swerved around her. It didn't feel like it mattered that the light hadn't yet turned green. An arbitrary law, that's all it was.

Until the siren whooped behind her.

"Shit."

She pulled over exactly opposite the road crew. If this was Nolan's crew, he'd already seen her, that much was certain. Her mouth was dry.

The officer was older, with a reddened face. "You know what you did back there?"

Kate was horrified with herself. "I ran a light. Jesus. I didn't even think." What if that car had hit her? What if there'd been a child inside? A child with a specific name and a favorite dinosaur and a blanket his grandmother knitted for him? "I'm so sorry. So sorry."

"You could have been killed. That red car was going way too fast—I'm amazed it got around you safely."

And *that* would have been something. To have been killed in the front seat of the car in which Robin had died. In front of Robin's father. Kate felt dizzy with regret.

Kate, caught in this thought, didn't notice that the officer was saying anything until he repeated, "I mean right now, ma'am. License and registration. What part of that is too difficult for you to understand?"

She was so getting a ticket.

While the officer went back to his patrol car to write up the charges she deserved, she felt the road crew looking at her.

She checked for bicyclists in her side mirror and then stepped out of the car, shutting the car door carefully behind her. The cop looked up over at her and shook his head. At least he didn't order her back into the Saab. A taller man with a red beard wearing an orange vest started toward her also, but Nolan, already so close, said, "That's okay, Johnson. I got it."

The denim blue safety of Nolan's voice. She'd heard it so many times in her mind over the last few years that it felt bizarre to hear it out in the air, actually carried to her ears by physical sound waves and not her own imagination.

She leaned back against the door and watched as he approached. Still those broad, sharp shoulders. He was so much skinnier now. His body looked lean, the way it had when they were in high school. The hard hat cast an indigo-sepia shadow over his face but she could see he hadn't shaved that morning. He could usually get away with one day before he got his caveman look.

Kate drank him in for one wonderful second before she

remembered she wasn't allowed to. She gathered the anger—cold as always—around her like a wet sheet.

"Nolan." She hadn't even said his name out loud, not to anyone, not since the trial ended three years before. It sounded round in her mouth and tasted sweetly familiar.

"God. Kate." He took off the hard hat, then took off his sunglasses so she could see his eyes. They were still beautiful, the color of dark honey, a deep, heated ocher.

No way in hell was she taking off her sunglasses yet.

"You—" He broke off for a second. "I know I told you I was out here, but I didn't think you would actually find me."

Kate said, "I looked but I didn't see you on Thornhill. I gave up, but then . . . here you were."

It was too simple, too easy. It should have been hard to find him—she should have been looking for months, in torrential downpours and icy frost, to find him. It shouldn't have been in the sunshine, when she pulled off the goddamn freeway to go to the drugstore.

"I wonder how many times I've passed you," she said.

Nolan shook his head. His hair was longer, shaggier than it had ever been when he was a lawyer. "Just once."

"You see every car that drives by?"

"Pretty much."

And maybe he had. "It's an easy car to recognize," she said, and then realized how it must sound to him. She'd thought about selling it, of course. But then, to that person, it would have been just a car. A mode of transport. To her, it was a small rolling shrine, made more special in that everyone else thought it was just a car.

"Ah," he said. The sound was heavy and dropped between them like a stone thrown in a river.

Why, again, was Kate here? Yes, to tell him about Pree. To fix what she'd broken so many years ago. She'd thought she owed him nothing, not after he'd been responsible for losing Robin, but she owed him this truth. Finally.

"So," he said. He looked down at the hard hat in his hands, and Kate noticed that even the tops of his knuckles looked rough now, scraped and used.

"We have to talk," she said, and the look of hope that crossed his face, just for a second, made her want to sob, an ugly feeling that she bit back. "There's something I need to tell you," she went on. "It's not good. Or at least, it's not bad. It's . . . oh, god."

"Are you getting married?"

"No!"

"Are you pregnant?"

"*No.*" How could he ask her that?

"Then tell me."

Kate opened her mouth. She could . . . she would do it. He would just have to understand where she was, how she felt back then. She'd been fifteen and stupid. He'd left and broken her heart. She hadn't known anything about the world, and had thought there was no chance they'd ever get back together. People didn't do that. Kate had known that, even as young as she'd been. She'd thought she'd been making the most intelligent choice.

"Nolan, you have to—"

But he wasn't meeting her eyes. He was looking over her shoulder, at something behind her.

"This is important. I can't do it here—is there someplace—? Will you *look* at me, please?" And just like that, she was thrown back to when he wasn't listening to her, the days when she could talk until her breath ran out about blood counts and compatible marrow donation, and he'd never hear her, lost in his own grief. "Nolan?"

He was careening past her before she knew what he was

doing, shoving her out of his way, running faster than he ever could have five or even ten years earlier.

Behind her, at the open door of his patrol vehicle, the officer lay on the gravel. Nolan was almost to him by the time Kate realized the cop's face wasn't red anymore, but blue.

Chapter Seventeen

Wednesday, May 14, 2014
11:10 a.m.

It didn't happen the way it had in his Red Cross class—the cop didn't look anything like the dummy, and he certainly wasn't as lightweight. This guy had gone down hard and fast.

"Rafe!" he yelled. "Call 911!"

Think. *Think.* Head tilt—that was it—then chin thrust. Nolan put his ear next to the cop's mouth. He didn't think he could feel anything, but it was so hard to tell with the traffic still whizzing by—fuckers barely slowed down—and the wind coming up off the bay. "Shit, shit, shit."

"No service!" yelled Rafe. The damned thing about this affluent neighborhood was there were so many trees that sometimes none of their phones worked.

"Radio it in to dispatch, then." Nolan had to get this

guy jump-started, at least. Their dispatch would call the fire department and start an ambulance, but that might take a minute or two to relay.

He unclipped the cop's radio mike that sat on his shoulder and clicked it, waiting for a second to compose his thoughts. How did someone do this? "Mayday," he said. "Mayday!"

A female's irritated voice came out of the speaker at the cop's hip. "Last unit, identify."

"You got a cop down, just off Broadway at Highway 13, maybe a heart attack."

There was a startled clicking from the speaker. Then, "Which officer?"

"How should I know?"

"Car number, badge number?"

Nolan leaned forward to read the silver pin. "Collins. I'm starting CPR now."

A flurry of radio traffic that he couldn't understand started after that, but Nolan ignored it all as he pumped the cop's chest. Fucking bulletproof vest. He took a precious second to rip open the officer's shirt, but Nolan couldn't figure out how the hell the vest was attached, so he just pumped harder.

Kate stood beside him. He remembered when she'd bought those shoes—with their brown leather and red straps, he'd thought they wouldn't go with anything, but she'd been right as usual, and they ended up being one of her favorite pairs. Eight years later, she was still wearing them. Nolan felt sweat bead along his hairline and start trickling down his face.

He gasped for breath. "When do I mouth-to-mouth?" They'd taken the same CPR course when Robin first got sick. Just in case. Ironic, really.

She fell to her knees, putting her hand under the cop's chin. "I'll do it. I took a refresher class last year. I'll count for you. Keep going."

Kate counted to thirty and told him to pause while she gave two deep breaths. Nolan felt the man's ribs rise under his palms. "*Pump*," she said.

Kate kept counting as the sirens grew louder. Nolan felt, rather than heard, the sickening crunch below the heel of his palm as the cop's ribs gave way under the vest, just as his instructor had said they would if he was doing the compressions right. Holy *shit*.

They'd done eight cycles of compressions by the time the paramedics moved him to the side and took over, slicing the cop out of his vest, putting him on some kind of pumping board that did the work for them, hooking up the shock box. They said something about finding a rhythm on him, and the other four cops who were already with them on the side of the road sucked in deep, shuddery breaths. More sirens blared, all of them screaming toward them. One officer shook Kate's hand, tears visible. Another one ran at Nolan so intently, so fast, that Nolan's fists came up, as if he were back on C-block. But instead of knocking him over, he hugged Nolan, thumping the breath out of him. Nolan gave his name and a brief statement to another cop, who looked like he couldn't even legally drink yet, and then turned around to look for Kate.

Both she and her car were gone. Nolan breathed heavily, wiping the sweat from his upper lip and forehead, staring at the overpass above him.

She'd slipped away, and he still had no idea what the hell she'd been trying to tell him. She'd saved a man's life, and then she'd disappeared. Colors around him—the white scudding clouds, the wet green hills, the bright gold poppies—looked surreal, as if he were standing inside an oil painting. Maybe none of this was real. Maybe she'd painted it. Maybe he was still behind the razor wire, in his single-wide cot, surrounded by concrete walls, dreaming.

Then, just to the left of the officer's car, flapping in the wind, he saw the cop's ticket book. He'd filled out just her first and last name and half of her date of birth. Not even her license was written down. He looked up to see what the other cops were doing, satisfied to see them all busy with things, pointing, directing traffic, talking to the second paramedic unit that had pulled up for god only knew what reason.

With one smooth tear, Nolan ripped away the top part and the two copies of the ticket. He folded all three and put them in his pocket, keeping his eye on the guy who looked like he was in charge, the sergeant maybe. When the man walked back toward his patrol vehicle, Nolan approached him.

"I found this, sir. Didn't know if it was important."

The man flipped the book, looking at the copies. Was he comparing the numbers? Was he going to miss the last one? But then he looked right at Nolan and smiled while reaching out to touch Nolan's shoulder. "We owe you a huge debt, sir."

No one seemed to notice when he walked back to the guys—none of the cops, anyway. His guys, that was different. None of them were working; each and every one was staring as if he'd done something impossible, leaped a building or flown across four lanes of traffic.

"It was just CPR, guys."

Delacruz said, "You saved a man's *life*."

"Maybe," said Nolan. "You never know. He could just die again in the ambulance."

"Aren't they gonna tell you?" asked Rafe. "Keep you up to date on how he's doing? You have to find out if he makes it or not, man. You gotta *know.*" That was so Rafe, always black or white. Right or wrong. Alive or dead.

Nolan hoped like hell they wouldn't tell him one way or the other. He didn't want to know. It seemed too much to handle—the weight of it felt enormous, as if the whole sky were pressing down on him. "Whatever."

Rafe said, "Is that her? The ex?"

Nolan only nodded.

Rafe's head swiveled worriedly, looking for the now gone car. "But . . ."

Mario yelled from inside his truck. "Back to work! I'm not gonna dock your break for that, but we gotta get this segment done before four, you got it?"

The weight of the shovel felt good in Nolan's hands even though the way it cracked through the dirt and weeds on the steep side of the road sounded like the cop's ribs breaking, over and over again. *Kate had been there.* If he'd wanted to, he could have reached out and touched her. Her cheek looked just as soft. She'd always had the most beautiful, natural creamy skin. Perfect strangers on the street would stop her and tell her how pretty her complexion was. They always had.

She'd been there. And then she'd gone. He didn't know if it was a good thing she'd come. She obviously had something difficult to tell him, something she couldn't just blurt out.

Then someone had died, at least for a few minutes, while they stood together. First time they're together since court, and someone else dies. What were the fucking odds? Nolan felt bile rise in the back of his throat and he swallowed it back. He leaned on the shovel and watched another cloud chug over the hill toward Orinda.

Things were moving again. Every time in his life Nolan thought things weren't ever going to move again, they slid sideways. This time he prayed he'd be able to ride it out. For once.

Chapter Eighteen

Wednesday, May 14, 2014
4 p.m.

Pree held her cold Coke can against her neck and wished for a bucket of ice to shove her feet into. It was hot as hell in the office—the heater was stuck on, and the electrician couldn't come until tomorrow. She'd known about it the day before and she should have worked from home today, but when Flynn had rolled over to touch her hip, sliding his fingers down her waist—after getting in so late she hadn't even heard him come in—Pree had been so irritated she'd gotten up without saying a word to him, ignoring his protests.

As the morning rolled into the afternoon and the building got hotter, Pree's nerves shredded like wet tissue paper. Heat had never bothered Pree before, but now she was finding it almost unbearable. Just one more thing about the pregnancy that she hated.

Come on. How were you supposed to know what you'd feel until you did something, anyway? What if you were just a woman who didn't want a baby? What if you didn't want to be pregnant? What if you didn't want to have to make this kind of decision, period? Why should you feel *guilty*? Pree clicked to the Internet and googled, "Abortion + guilt." She accidentally clicked on the image search, and immediately wanted to erase the images that filled her vision.

"God*damn,*" she said. People posted harsh pictures. Pree was someone who didn't blink when a concept artist sent her porn as reference material when she was working on a character's clothing, and the pictures of corpses they sent her to work on decomposition were more interesting than anything else, but this stuff was turning her stomach.

"You sound upset for someone designing walkways."

"Shit!"

Jimmy stood next to her, and Pree hadn't even heard him approach. "Remember when I asked you if you sneaked up on girls a lot? Apparently you do," she snapped as she closed the window as fast as she could.

"Grumpy, huh?"

How much had he seen? Pree squinted and looked at him, but his face was guileless.

"Hot enough for you? Or are you watching sex tapes again?" He was teasing her—there really was no such thing as politically correct in the gaming industry.

"If I were going to complain about anything, I'd complain about Leif." She pointed behind Jimmy to where Leif was skipping toward the back hallway wearing a Pikachu outfit and a strap-on. "I don't even want to know what's going on back there."

He shrugged. "Some Furry poker game."

"They're not really Furries."

"Does he look like one?"

Pree had to laugh. "Yeah. He does."

He swung a folding chair around and straddled it. "Come on, it's quitting time."

"It's four."

"Like I said. The guys have beer."

"I'm not playing Furry poker."

"I'll give you a raise."

"Couldn't offer me enough." It was good, this give-and-take. Somehow intoxicating, easy, sweet, and heady. He felt it, too. She could tell, by the way he leaned forward, tipping the chair toward her, by the way he kept his eyes on hers. Pree focused on not looking away, not giving up first.

"You want a beer in my office?"

Saying yes would mean something right now, so much more than a beer.

"Drinking with the boss?" She didn't mean drinking.

He knew she didn't. "No strings."

Her stomach flipped. This was the moment she'd told herself she'd walk away from. She'd sworn it to herself, knowing herself to be smarter and better than just some girl Jimmy was interested in for the moment. She thought about his wife. The fact that he was a father. "Yeah," Pree said anyway. "Sure."

In his office, Jimmy didn't even bother with the pretense of offering her a beer. He reached behind her to lock the door. She didn't move away from him. "Speak now or forever hold your peace," he whispered against her mouth.

"I really think we should have an HR department," she said, pulling at his belt buckle so his pelvis hit hers. Fuck Flynn. Fuck everything. Nothing mattered but this man with the sad, smoky eyes who knew exactly what effect he had on her. "Who am I going to complain to tomorrow?"

"Me, of course. I'm *great* with people." Then he kissed her with calculation and talent, and Pree forgot about everything else. His mouth was harder than Flynn's, rougher, just as she knew it would be.

His words were rougher, too—darker, dirtier—making her instantly wet. "Come on, little girl. I want to know what that tight little pussy of yours feels like. Little thing like you, can you take it?" She didn't let him take off her pants, but she allowed him to slide his fingers inside her. He was good at it and she almost came, but she wouldn't let herself. *That* would be cheating. *Like this isn't,* her mind chided.

Pree bit Jimmy's shoulder so he'd know she'd been there. Later, she wanted him to take off his shirt in front of the mirror and see the little ring of teeth impressed next to his clavicle. She wanted the family man to have to hide it from his family.

Then she took him in her mouth. He came with a guttural growl that sounded fake but obviously wasn't. He tasted different than Flynn—thinner, somehow. Watered down. Pree gasped on the floor, pulling her bra back on. The dust of the carpet made her nose itch, and her knee was wedged against two surge protectors.

For just a minute, Pree wished that he'd been inside her, that she could just pretend the fetus inside her was his, that she could backdate the pregnancy somehow. Wouldn't it change things? Wouldn't it be better, carrying the child of a proven family man?

"I'm going to complain to management," she said. "Jesus Christ, it's hot in here."

"I could say the same about you." Jimmy twisted and wriggled sideways and opened his mini-fridge, pulling out a beer. "Want one now?"

Beer. God, Flynn loved beer. It was his religion, he

always said. The only three things he needed: Pree and beer and heating iron till it twisted.

Pree flopped backward so she could look under Jimmy's desk. Later in the week, when he was gone for the night, she'd come back in here and slap her RARE right there, just above where his right knee probably was most days. He'd never know.

"I have to go," she said, buttoning her jeans.

"Hey. Are you all right?" He smiled at her, and she couldn't read it. Was it a smile he would have given to his wife? Or his daughter?

"Yeah." She racked her brain, and then her cell beeped. She dug it out of her pocket and scanned the text.

> *Want to come to my place and talk? I'll grill something.*

Kate.

"My birth mother," she said, waving the phone at him, grateful for the excuse. "We're meeting again at her house for dinner."

"Hey, are you really okay?"

Jimmy started to reach for her, but Pree let herself out of his office before he could say anything else. She didn't meet Steve's surprised eyes in the hallway. She would blame it all on the heat in the building. And raging hormones. That's what this was.

Flynn's face filled her vision, his sweet blue eyes, those innocent, full lips. Those hands that knew what she needed before she did.

Grabbing her backpack, she raced out of the building toward her car. She texted as she walked. *Is now ok?* Maybe Kate was working; maybe she'd disturb her flow. For one second, she allowed herself a brief fantasy of going to the art store with Kate to look at supplies. Everyone who worked there would know her, would know she was Kate's daughter. They'd remark on the resemblance. Kate would put her arm around her in a quick hug, and they'd discuss the merits of oil sticks versus tubes.

Another text landed, a response from Kate. *Of course.* She sent the address, though Pree didn't need it—she'd had it memorized since she'd first looked her up in the adoption database.

Pree should feel guilty, and she didn't—not real guilt, anyway. Feeling remorse about *not* feeling more guilty was somehow unfair, right? Sorrow was stuck like a lump in her throat and she was sure if she tried to talk to anyone, she would cry.

You should have been smart enough to not get pregnant. The words rattled around in her head, knocking against her cheeks red-hot with shame.

She *was* smart enough. Or she thought she had been, anyway. Newly graduated, in a new town, new job, she'd thought she'd pulled it off, what she'd planned. She'd been so proud of herself. That was, really, the worst part.

Chapter Nineteen

Wednesday, May 14, 2014
6 p.m.

> *I apologize if this is the last thing you want to think about but my six-year-old is really sick. She's in a coma. The doctors say that it's up to us when we want to take her off life support. I know that's not what you went through, but I thought you might be able to help. To tell me how to feel. I don't think I can kill my baby.*

Nolan snapped his computer shut at the knock. He opened the door to find a camera and microphone pointed at him. A skinny man wearing an ill-fitting polyester jacket and under-eye concealer stood in front of him, so excited he was almost hopping.

The guy stuck his fist out to introduce himself. "Carey

Pike, Channel 7 News. I managed to track you down as one of the people who saved Officer John Collins today, and we'd love to talk to you for a minute."

The last time Nolan fought his way out from under the press's interest, they were anything but polite, shouting at him as he held his hand to his face to cover his eyes. *How do you feel knowing your child's last moments weren't with his mother? How does it feel to be found guilty of criminally negligent homicide? How does it feel to kill your only child?*

"You gotta be fucking with me." Nolan was still off the record, right? The camera didn't look like it was on. He pushed the barking Fred Weasley back. "Stop, Fred. Quit it."

Pike looked amused. "No, sir. We love a good hero story."

Didn't he know? Surely reporters did at least a cursory Internet search when they went out to do an interview? "What's your real angle?"

"Just that, sir. You're with an Oakland Public Works crew, and you saved an officer who wouldn't have made it today. Makes a nice piece, don't you think?"

Nolan looked at his feet. "It's all right. I guess. I was just doing what anyone else would do in my position."

Pike's face lit up. He was a young one, this guy. "Would you mind saying that again with the camera on?" He gestured to the man behind him. "Joe, you ready?"

Nolan stepped farther out onto his small porch, shutting the door so maybe Fred would quit barking already. The apartment where he lived was arranged like one of the old sixties motels, but there was no inner courtyard, just doors that faced their small parking lot. The manager, Sammy, had done what he could with flowers in halves of wine barrels, but he had also been MIA for the last three months while he recovered from open-heart surgery, and the plants were showing it. Some were spindly, and some were all the way dead, unhappy with the rainwater that was all the nourishment they got. Nolan had felt sad for them before, but now felt only embarrassment. This wasn't a good idea. What if Kate saw him on TV? What if she saw where he lived?

But it was too late. The bright light was in his eyes, and Pike held the microphone at the ready.

"I'm here with Nolan Monroe, who just hours ago saved the life of a man important to our community. Officer John Collins is well respected on the Oakland police force and has been with the department for twenty-two years. He's served on SWAT and Vice, and three years ago made the news when he was stabbed while stopping a rape in progress. Hailed as a hero by many, Officer Collins has a new hero tonight. Nolan, we understand that you found the officer unmoving by his car?"

So far it was okay. "Yeah." Nolan nodded.

"What did you think had happened?"

"I thought he might be having a heart attack." So much for excitement in journalism. Nolan knew he sounded lackluster, but wasn't sure what he should do about it. Jumping up and down as if he were winning an award didn't seem like it would be a great idea. He settled for pasting a semblance of a smile on his face. "So I started CPR."

"This was after you used the officer's own radio to alert emergency personnel of your position."

"I, um. Yeah."

"Did anyone help you?"

The reporter knew the answer to that, Nolan was sure. He remained silent.

"You did CPR on him for how long before the paramedics arrived?"

"I don't know. Maybe four minutes? Five?"

Pike looked at the camera. "Five minutes can mean the difference between life and death. And that's something that Nolan Monroe knows intimately, don't you, sir? Three years ago, Nolan was convicted of criminal negligent homicide, killing his son, and almost taking his own life in the process of asphyxiation by carbon monoxide in their Oakland home just a few miles from here."

Shit. Nolan took a step back, but the camera swiveled to his face and followed him. "Get out."

"How long did the paramedics perform CPR on you, Nolan? The report says twelve minutes. They shocked you twice. They were the heroes that day, saving your life even if they couldn't save your son's. Do you feel like what you did today evens the score a little bit?"

This was a nightmare. A bloodbath. "I was just there—I told you."

"You were there because you work on the roads, right? Picking up trash? You used to be a corporate lawyer, is that correct?"

Nolan managed to squeeze the door shut then, kicking out Pike's boot with his own, twisting both locks into place.

His breathing was heavy. Fred panted next to him. For a second, Nolan imagined reopening the door and repeating to the reporter what he'd heard in his head for the first two years, and still heard, every morning and night: *I should be dead. I should be dead.* It was the refrain that his blood sang in the morning when he woke, that his breathing echoed when he slept. He shouldn't be here now, and he shouldn't have been on the side of the road earlier that day when Officer Collins fell, and when Pike knocked tonight, no one should have been there to answer the door.

Nolan was living a dead man's life, and the pain of it was almost enough to kill him all over again. Almost, but not quite. It would be worse later, when the piece aired. When the guys found out. He'd known it was probably a matter of time, but he'd hoped anyway, hoped outrageously that he'd never be found out. That people he cared about would never look at him that way again.

Tears would hurt less than this perpetually sucked-in breath, he knew that—kind of like when you had the stomach flu and puking was the only thing that made you feel better. But he was saving them up for when he really needed them. He would bet that man who wrote him tonight about his little girl was storing them up, too, or at least he hoped he was. Nolan opened the computer and reread the e-mail.

It was still there. And in the time the computer had been closed, another had come in. Shorter and badly spelled, it carried the same sentiment.

> *How do u know its time? Once I put my dog down, but he told me with his eyes it was time. My boy keeps his eyes cloesed now.*

Nolan wanted to answer them.

He couldn't, though. He had no way to help. There was nothing he could say that could ease the pain of a parent losing a child, and god knew he wasn't going to assist another parent to kill their child.

But what if the kid was for all intents and purposes already gone? Where did someone else presume to step in? To give advice? Shit, what would he have given back then for an answer that was true?

Anything. He'd have given anything, and everything—all he had, and then he would have stolen more to give if he'd had to. If only someone would have answered him.

The space in his throat just under his tongue felt like it

was closing, and Nolan swallowed convulsively. Any day now, the tears would break free and the resulting flood would wash away everything he'd built up, would wash away Fred Weasley and his apartment and his beat-up Honda and the only photo of Robin he still had, dog-eared and tucked into the back of his wallet. It would all be gone in the rushing salt water, all of it, gone. And the easiest goddamn thing to lose would be himself.

Chapter Twenty

Wednesday, May 14, 2014
6:30 p.m.

The nervous energy burned in Kate's hands, flaring from her elbows, combusting at her wrists. She moved through the house, touching things as if she could imbue each item with specialness, with clear and obvious originality. This lamp, this couch, this chair—would Pree like them? Would she hate them? Would Pree expect a bohemian artist's studio, inspiration filtering in at the windows? Would she be disappointed to find instead a sturdy suburban home in which the Costco toilet paper was waiting in the hallway to be put away? Would she walk in and then immediately turn on her heel and leave after seeing that Kate's bills were piled on the end of the kitchen countertop, their paper edges splashed carelessly with coffee? There was so much to *do.* Kate had broken a glass in the sink yesterday and had left it there, unable to start the process of cleaning it up, but it would be unforgivable if Pree got cut on the glass just because Kate was careless. (Of course, when Kate *did* try to clean it up, she nicked her careless, restive hands not once but three times on the slivers.)

She brushed her teeth once more, still trying to rid herself of the taste of the police officer's mouth. God. It had been so different, so much more work, blowing into a full-grown man's lungs. The sound had been the same, though, air whistling into a desperate vacuum.

She was still staring at herself in the bathroom mirror, unseeing, when the doorbell rang, shattering the silence. *Pree.*

Pree stood on the porch, the darkness of the evening folded around her narrow shoulders. Her eyes, caught in the dim porch light, looked miserable, but then the girl brightened as if on cue. So young. How could this girl be twenty-two? If she couldn't see Nolan's ears, her own eyebrows, she'd wonder if this was the right girl on her stoop. "Hi . . . hi there."

No, even as young-looking as Pree was, this was Kate's daughter, no doubt. That voice was Robin's voice, always rusty as if it weren't used often.

"Come in," said Kate. Should she display how happy she was? How eager she was to see her? Or should she play it cool? Was that even possible? Feeling overcome by indecision, Kate stepped backward into the living room and let Pree follow her.

They sat, both carefully formal. Kate crossed her legs at the ankle; Pree crossed hers at the knee.

"So, how are you?" said Kate, but her words rang strangely, and she had no follow-up line. Her eyes fell to the carpet. She should have at least vacuumed. "Are you hungry? I have some chicken we can grill . . ."

Instead of answering, Pree bounced again to her feet and moved to the window. She frowned, and then cupped her hands to the glass, peering out into the dark. "Is that . . . ?"

"What?"

"Is that a bathtub down there? On the hill?"

Kate smiled. Of all things, she noticed that. "Yeah."

"But . . . it's out there. Outside."

"No one can see."

"*I* can see."

"But we're the only house that can see it. These are the only windows that look through the trees at it."

"So you think. There's a satellite up there with your name on it."

It was funny, Nolan had always said the same thing, only he'd laughed and said he'd commissioned the satellite's cameras.

Pree turned, shoving her hands in her jeans pockets, and she changed the subject abruptly. "So I had a brother?" Her eyes, the same pale blue as Robin's, bored into Kate.

The Internet told all. It was inevitable. Kate should have known, should have tried to beat the world to the punch and told her herself as soon as they'd met. But she hadn't. "You did."

"Did we have the same father? I read you married your high school sweetheart, so . . ."

This was the time to tell her. *Yes, Nolan is your father . . .* A spot under her ribs felt compressed, as if a fist were squeezing her heart, pushing words into her lungs and then out. If she told Pree, she'd have to admit the whole truth to Nolan, too, that she'd had his child. While she and Nolan had been apart during the college years, she'd never felt guilty about not telling him, not tracking him down. *He* was the one who'd left. He didn't deserve to know she'd given away a baby.

But when he'd come back into her life . . . As it was, she

hoped she could just tell Nolan she'd had *a* child while they were apart. Not *his* child. Just a random one (as if there was such a thing). Then she could work up to the rest of the truth. She could take her time, make it right. She had to keep the plates spinning for a little longer, that was all. Black spots danced at the edges of her peripheral vision, a darkness made of fear. "No. Different fathers." The lie burned in her chest, pulsed with heat. She only said it to give herself some more time to think, and even as she spoke, she had to keep herself from reaching forward to snatch the words back to herself. The phrase broke into shards, more dangerous than simple broken glass.

Pree blinked. "So he was my half brother."

"Yes." *Wrong, wrong, wrong . . .*

"And his father . . . killed him?"

The word was so sharp. It was appropriate, but it cut Kate. "I'm sure you read all about it. It's all out there."

"But it's not the same as hearing it from . . ." Pree trailed off on the last word.

"From your biological mother."

Pree rocked back and forth inside her thick black boots, as if the energy inside her couldn't be contained. "I hate it when people say that. Biological. As if that's all there is to it."

"But—"

"You're my *biological* mother. What that makes it sound like is that you made a baby and gave it away, and that's all there is to it."

"Some people would say that's true."

"But it's bullshit!" Pree's voice broke, just as Robin's always had when he was angry. "You gave me your DNA. Your body is encoded in mine. We share genes. I think the way you do. I act the way you do, in ways we don't even know about. We're both artists, and I didn't even know that about you. I share the same with my father, whoever he is. Yeah, it's biological, but it's so much more than that, and I would have really, *really* liked to know my brother." The clear green in Pree's voice shimmered, like heat waves over asphalt.

"I would have liked that, too. I wish you had."

Pree tilted her head and looked at Kate.

I don't get to make wishes. "I'm sorry."

"Who is my father?"

Fear would burn its way through her, leaving only a dried-out husk. Old lies. New ones. "Greg Jenkins." Greg was the boy she'd been dating at Cal when Nolan transferred in. When Nolan found her. And with a name like that—there had to be a million Greg Jenkinses in the world, if and when Pree googled him . . .

"Who's he?"

Greg had meant exactly nothing to her. They ate pizza together and saw movies a couple of times. There was a brew pub incident that remained thankfully hazy in Kate's memory, though she thought it had been the culmination of too many garlic fries followed by a clove cigarette after one too many beers. Greg had liked her very much, and Kate had planned to like him more, and when Nolan came back she completely forgot about that intention. Greg meant more to her in this moment, saying his name to Pree, than he ever had before. "He was sweet. Pretty blue eyes like a girl." This was true.

Pree touched her eyelashes. "Where is he now?"

Kate shrugged, her heart racing as she realized she would *have* to say more. Somehow, she'd thought for a second that the name would be enough. "I don't know." This was also true.

"What does he do?"

He'd friended her on Facebook two years before. Robin was dead then, and Nolan was in jail—she'd ignored the request, just as she'd shut everyone else out, and now she regretted that choice. "I have no idea."

"Do you know his birthday? I need to find him. Obviously."

Find him? She and Greg had had sex only twice (Greg eager, Kate surprised at her own ambivalence). If she found him, he wouldn't believe he had a daughter. Nor *should* he. It was untrue. And even while she knew she had to fix everything she'd broken and confess, Kate couldn't make her mouth shape the words. Instead, leaning into the fear and hoping to find the right words, the solution, she said, "You can't. I never told him."

"You never told my father you were pregnant with me?"

Also true, heartbreakingly true. Maybe truth could be snuck up on, rounded up in the back of the house under the washing machine, clubbed on the head and dragged to the living room later when she felt stronger. Kate shook her head.

"And you don't know how to get hold of him?"

Another shake of her head.

Pree bit her bottom lip, which was suddenly quivering. "That's okay. I have mad Google-fu."

It was such a lightweight statement for the despair in her eyes. "I'm sorry. Maybe we can work on it together." *Never.*

Then Pree was crying, swiping angrily at her eyes with her fingers. Eyeliner ran down her right cheek, and Kate felt relief flood her chest. Tears she understood. Tears she knew. Kate stood and gathered Pree to her. Her daughter was bony, all protuberances and sharp points.

Kate's arms rose around her, and she felt the knobs at Pree's shoulders.

Where her wings would be.

Pree's tears soaked through Kate's thin T-shirt at her neck, and still she cried. For long minutes they stood there together. Five, maybe six. Then, when the tears dried and Pree started sniffling, moving her feet in an embarrassed postcry shuffle. "I'm sorry. I don't know where all that came from."

Kate made a flapping gesture. "Are you kidding? Some days it's all I do."

Hic. "This is going to sound weird . . ."

"Tell me."

"No, it's a question," said Pree.

Kate's heart fluttered. "Okay."

"Can I take a shower here?"

Surprise felt like joy. "Yes! Of course."

"I just, I mean . . . I just want to wash off the day." Pree blinked and wiped smudged mascara off the back of her hand.

Then Kate asked what she'd longed to ask for so long, even before she'd met the person she'd ask it of. "Do you want to stay? I have ice cream for dessert and a spare room."

Wednesday, May 14, 2014
11 p.m.

Kate's bedroom was next to Robin's—no, Pree's—room. She'd spent so long untraining her listening ear that it was difficult to hear if Pree was moving around. Was she asleep? Did she like the Harry Potter walls, really? Or had that just been something she said (who wouldn't exclaim in surprise at being confronted with a towering painted Hogwarts)? Was she comfortable? Was the bed too small? Too soft?

Kate lay still, willing her breath to be silent. Over the beating *shump-shump* of her heart, she felt a splinter of unexpected pain as she thought she heard a floorboard creak, the same board that had always given Robin away as he crept out to peek in on his parents. But no noise followed that one, and Kate's heart slowly calmed.

Since Robin died, no one but Kate had ever spent the night in their home (first Nolan had been in the hospital, then in a hotel, then in prison). No, that wasn't true. Her friend Dierdre had stayed one night. She'd come over three days after Robin's death. She'd planted herself in the red armchair in the living room and said, "I'm not going anywhere."

"I can't," started Kate, exhausted by the thought of making her friend comfortable.

"I'm not here to talk to you, to feed you, or to do anything but be in this room." Dierdre picked up a magazine (*Parents*, Kate noted dully) and flipped the pages. "Nothing you say can make me leave. I love you. Now go do your thing and feel free to ignore me. I'll just be here."

Kate had ignored her as long as she could, and then late that night, she'd found herself lying on the couch with her head in Dierdre's lap. Her friend had stroked her hair and cried with her and had then put her to bed, holding her hand until she slept. Kate sent her home kindly in the morning. She was grateful to Dierdre but not willing to indulge herself again with that kind of comfort.

Kate's mother, Sonia, was almost as brokenhearted as Kate was. Robin had repaired some of the broken pieces in his grandmother (they'd shared that love of the water—their sealskin, Kate called it) but when he died, the work came undone. Sonia did her best, Kate knew that. She dropped by with food, simple, bland things that could slip down without burning Kate's tear-locked throat. She sat next to her in the trial, and never once said a cruel word about Nolan, even though Kate could see the words simmering on her lips. And

Sonia had never spent the night, had never tried to. She knew better, understood more about grief. When Sonia had died two years after Robin, Kate had been astonished at how the shades of pain were similar when she closed her eyes—Robin, her mother—deep, bruised blues marred by cadmium trails that flared angry green where they met.

Now Kate took a deep breath and rolled onto her back. She looked up at the blank ceiling, tracing the crack that ran from the wall to the ceiling fan with her eyes.

Not even the accountant Kate had dated for three months earlier in the year had ever been allowed to stay the night. She'd met him in line at the library, a safe enough place, she supposed, to meet someone. At least he read. She'd slept at his place twice, long, uncomfortable nights during which she missed the breath, the air of her own home. Esau's place had smelled like new leather shoes and roasted garlic, and he liked the windows closed at night for safety—Kate had felt, each night, as if someone were holding a towel over her mouth. She'd hated rebreathing the warm, stuffy, used-up air.

Esau had been sweet, though. He'd been exactly what Kate had thought she'd needed: a quiet distraction, some physical companionship. She liked his strong, broad arms (so different from Nolan's rather thin ones), and he always brought her gerbera daisies—her favorite flower. She loved them for their showy hardiness. Their sloppy messiness. They reminded her of herself, the way she used to be when she could still handle big things, before her bones had taken on this unbearable breakable feeling.

It had been another thing to like about Esau, that he thought of her as strong. He said she was resilient and that he knew she could handle anything. He admired her for it, and said it to her in the night, the time she needed it most. Kate used to like Nolan's dirty words whispered in her ear, but when she was dating Esau, she craved his phrasing: "You're strong as a bull, as strong as steel." When he said she was like a fortress, she actually got wet.

Once, as he moved against her and in her, Kate had wished for one horrible moment that the condom would break. She was only thirty-seven; it wasn't like her time had run all the way out. He would never know because she wouldn't tell him. She pushed away the forbidden thought and considered whispering to him to go faster, harder, but she didn't whisper things like that to him. She never said much of anything when they made love. She didn't need to. Esau was attentive, and smart. He knew what to do to make her come. Esau was reliable.

The same night of her shameful condom wish, Kate had felt something build in her chest. She'd cleared her throat, trying to get rid of it, and then, with Esau's arms firmly around her, on the solidity of his chest, the thing that was building finally broke and tears came, fast and violent. In surprise Esau said, "Hey, now," but there was a pale yellow undertone to his voice that Kate recognized—he had been as happy to have her crying on him as she was horrified. This wasn't what Esau was for, but it was what he wanted to be. "Hey, now, you. I've got you, Katie."

No one had ever called her that but Nolan, and she hated Esau for it, pushing her face farther into his neck and letting the tears soak the edge of his pillow.

"I'm sorry," she said what felt like but probably wasn't hours later.

"For what? Crying? It's good for what ails you. Talk to me."

Kate snuffled and reached behind her for a Kleenex, not caring that she sounded like an elephant, knowing that she had to find the right words to make him leave that night. She wished he were the kind of person with whom she could just have a good, massive, no-holds-barred screaming match that ended in broken china, kisses, and the absolute knowledge of the strength of flawed but true love.

The last time she'd seen Esau, he'd said earnestly (with a sheen of tears in his eyes that Kate wished she could also summon, if only to make him feel better) that he wanted her to find happiness again someday.

(Happiness had been Robin's sweaty fingers twisted into her hair while she read Harry Potter to him. Happiness had been Nolan's long legs sleep-heavy, her own feet asleep under his in their shared bed under the wide-open window.)

Now she consciously relaxed her ears, which had been pulled back as if she'd been about to smile, or grimace. She couldn't hear Pree, nothing at all. The girl was probably asleep as she herself should be.

She continued to stare at the ceiling. She'd painted all the other ceilings in the house—why not this one? Nolan had always said they should put up those silly glow-in-the-dark stars like they'd put in Robin's room. Nolan loved those damn things. They would pretend they were making love outdoors. He'd have brought her a night picnic in bed. She knew he would have.

Chapter Twenty-one

Marriage

October 1996

When Kate saw Nolan for the first time four years after their breakup, she was wearing a pale pink dress that looked like the inside of an oyster's shell. She was the pearl inside, naked and exposed. It was nothing she would have ever chosen to wear, all plunging neckline and taffeta flaring at the knee, but the host of the Halloween party, Josie, had insisted that all the women wear thrifted bridesmaids' dresses.

At twenty, Kate was in her junior year at Berkeley, finally feeling as if she might make it. She'd almost flunked out in her first year, going on academic probation twice. She'd spent way more time drinking than painting or studying, and she'd tried coke more than a few times, liking it so intensely it frightened her. She'd slept with too many men—boys, really—so many she didn't remember some of their faces.

She'd been on the edge of failing at everything that mattered, but one morning she opened her eyes at three a.m., fully awake, her roommate snoring on the other bed.

It was her daughter's third birthday. Somewhere, a child might be laughing, a child who didn't know her at all.

What if, someday, that child wanted to find her?

It would never happen, she told herself firmly, believing it.

Kate made it to class on time that morning for the first time all semester.

Now she had her own apartment, a small, damp, extremely cheap cottage in Oakland pressed against the side of a hill, and Sonia had given her an old VW Bug that ran most days. She went to most of her classes (except economics) and never missed Painting 307 (emphasis on abstract portraiture—she was in the middle of painting herself as a wooden chair). Greg Jenkins probably thought she was his girlfriend.

At Josie's party, Nolan stood across the room from Kate, better-looking than ever, finally grown into his breadth. He wore a deep purple shiny suit with a pearl-colored bow tie.

How . . . ? Shit, it didn't matter how. He was there. Ten feet away. Less. She felt as vulnerable as she'd been that day she'd hung up on him for the last time. She was as broken-hearted as when she'd kissed their baby girl good-bye. And she was about a million years older.

B is for baby.

Careful not to look directly at him, Kate kept her eyes on the back of Don's head as he primed the keg.

Then Josie turned up the music as "Breakfast at Tiffany's"

by Deep Blue Something came on. Heads bobbed, and people Kate barely knew started to dance. One guy wearing a pink ruffled tux danced as if he were fighting off a swarm of bees, and a girl rushed out onto the porch to vomit in the bushes.

The singer sang, *I think I remember the film.*

Kate tried so hard, so very, very hard not to look at Nolan. She tried until she gave up. And there, in that moment, it all came back. All of it. In his face she saw the long nights spent laughing until their stomachs hurt, late afternoons spent watching golden light slip into sunset on the beach, fingers threaded, limbs light with hope. His gaze said the words to her, the same words she didn't even know she'd been missing.

As I recall, I think we both kind of liked it.

Kate's heart flew up toward the skylight open to the moon.

Nolan didn't break eye contact. His gaze was the apology. The profession.

Kate's fingers started to shake.

Josie and Don yelled something about the tap on the keg.

Neither Kate nor Nolan even spared them a glance. Inside her chest, a million wishes thrummed and soared, frantic hummingbirds of hope.

And then in front of dozens of people who weren't paying any attention to either of them, Nolan crossed the room with long strides. He took her face in both his hands—Nolan's hands!—and kissed her. The red cup of warm beer Kate held splashed into her dyed pink pumps, and she went up on tiptoe, kissing him back. Half her heart rejoiced, soaring to the skylight above, and out to the moonlight. She kept the other half carefully swaddled away, protected by canvas and plywood. *Nothing is this easy,* she warned herself, but then the feel of his mouth, so perfect, so *missed*, pushed everything out of the way.

By the time the song—and that kiss, that perfect kiss—was over, Kate's powers of critical thinking had come back. This was the man who'd broken her heart when he was a boy.

This was the man from whom she'd kept the biggest secret in the world. She should tell him. The very first words to fall from her lips should be, *I had your child.*

But Nolan spoke first. "I found you." His voice was hoarse.

"You did."

"I love you."

And once he said those words, all her courage deserted her. He loved her? Four years and a lifetime later? How *dared* he just show up? She could be living with Greg, for all he knew. She could be *married.*

Kate could still taste him on her upper lip.

She took the beer Becky passed her and turned away from Nolan.

"Wait," he said, putting his hand on her elbow. "Aren't you going to say something?"

There was so much she *should* say. And yet, her mouth stayed shut, the words locked so far inside her she couldn't even feel their shape.

He followed her outside, past the pool of vomit, stepping over the legs of the passed-out girl who was now laughing in her sleep. There at the edge of the party, at a dark table that held two overflowing ashtrays and one abandoned bong, Kate sat and kicked off her heels. She undid her hair. As it fell around her shoulders, she watched Nolan's eyes burn. "Can I sit down?"

"Why?" Kate honestly wanted to know, even though it was the wrong word, not what she should have said.

"Because I love you."

"How can you know that?" Loneliness felt like an ache, deep inside the marrow of her leg bones.

"I can't ever start to tell you how sorry I am," he said, clutching the top of the wooden chair. He swayed, even though Kate doubted he'd had a drink. "But I want to try. I want to tell you for the rest of our lives. I transferred to Berkeley on purpose. To find you."

"So what? You've just been waiting for tonight? For four years? No e-mail? Not one fucking phone call?"

"I didn't know. Until I saw you today . . . I didn't know, Kate. I've been an idiot."

Kate sipped her beer and tried to keep her eyes on the people dancing. "We're twenty. Who knows anything at twenty?"

"My parents were eighteen when they fell in love," he said, leaning toward her. "And they're still in love so much they barely see me. How old were your parents?"

They'd been nineteen. Sonia still kissed Kate's father's picture every night before she went to sleep. She'd kissed the picture more than she'd ever kissed Kate.

"Anomalous."

"Or," he said, "young love is in our blood. Our birthright."

He was so cocky. The way he tossed the word about, "love," like it cost the same as all the other words, "chair" and "floor" and "Tuesday," maddened her.

Nolan sat, turning the chair so that he could lean in toward her. She could just make out the wings of his shoulder blades. "I did everything wrong."

"Yeah," she granted, trying to pretend she couldn't hear the ice melting and cracking inside her.

"You never answered, though. I called, again and again. I came to your house a year later, when we were visiting, and your mother wouldn't open the door to me."

It was a jolt—Sonia had never mentioned that.

Nolan rubbed his eyes, then took one of her hands in his. The chill left her fingers as soon as he touched her. "I'll spend the rest of my life making that up to you. If you let me."

Part of Kate, the part that touched his hand, longed to say, *Yes, yes, yes.* The other part, the part that still mourned for her unknown daughter late at night, the part that was lying to him by keeping quiet, made her say shakily, "No."

"Will you let me try?"

"No," she said, but the word hung, untethered, in front of them, about to fall.

"Please, Kate. Let me find you."

She leaned forward. He did the same. Their eyes closed as their foreheads touched. They breathed together. She peeked through her eyelashes at his face, and the shape of his mouth was so familiar and sexy and at the same time so dear. The planes of his cheeks were higher than she'd remembered and she felt a little shock of surprise as she noticed them again. She leaned forward, sliding her cheek against his until she could rest her head against his shoulder—but what she was really doing was reaching her arms around him, to see if his shoulder blades still felt like the wings were hiding underneath, and yes—she breathed a sigh of relief—there they were.

"I'm not letting you go this time," he said against her ear, and she trembled.

"Promise me that we'll never talk about the past," she said.

"I'll promise you anything."

Kate pulled back. "I mean it. If we . . . if we do anything with this, the past is gone. We start again. Here. Fresh. As if we had nothing before."

"But what we had was perfect . . ."

"We lost everything we had. We start over or we do nothing. At all."

"I promise. A new start, Katie."

"We'll see," she said.

Nolan leaned forward and kissed her. "I found you."

He'd found her. Even more than that, he'd been *looking.*

Under Kate's worry grew a thin green tendril of hope.

April 1999

Three years later, on a plane somewhere east of the Nevada border, Kate and Nolan made a bet.

"It's your first trip to Vegas, and it's important to make a bet early," Nolan said. "It gets us in the right frame of mind."

"You're planning on us being high rollers?"

"I always spend at *least* forty dollars gambling in Vegas."

Kate sucked in a shocked breath. "That much?"

He nodded solemnly. "Stick with me, kid. I'll show you the ropes. This is gonna be a fancy wedding."

"Probably the fanciest ever. I can't believe we're not telling your parents."

Nolan pressed the bridge of his nose. "I know. They'd fly in from Maui in a heartbeat if they knew we were doing it. But taking Dad away from his golf? They'd just be keeping an eye on the time, wanting to get back. Are you sad we didn't tell Sonia?"

Kate laughed. "No."

"She used to like me. I know she did. I'll win her back somehow."

"I hope so." Kate looked out the window, seeing nothing. Since Kate and Nolan had gotten back together, she'd barely had contact with Sonia even though they lived half an hour apart. Sonia always claimed busyness at the aquatics center, but Kate knew it was the hundred-foot wall that had grown between them. Sonia had protected her once—keeping Nolan away when he'd come back. And now Kate could feel the disapproval radiating from her mother in unhappy waves, could feel it every time she showed her mother a new painting, every time she heard Sonia *humph* when she talked about the art class she was teaching at the local charter school. Nolan was someone Sonia had dismissed, and once Sonia's approval was lost, it was almost impossible to get back. No one knew that better than Kate.

Sonia did, thankfully, approve of the fact that Nolan was almost done with law school, top of his class. That was something, at least. Everyone approved of that, even Nolan's parents. He was doing something right.

And it was fair, wasn't it? Their parents, both sets of whom had clung to each other more tightly than they'd clung to their respective children, would understand them honoring the same type of relationship, right?

Turning to face Kate, his elbow wedged between them in the cramped seats, Nolan said, "Are you sure you don't mind? The opposite of fancy. Will you regret it later? That we Vegas'd it?"

She put a hand against his cheek and felt the stubble starting along his jaw. "Even if we were married by a midget Elvis in drag, I would think it was a better wedding than any other in the whole world. And besides, I don't want momentous."

"No?"

"I don't even want romantic, really. I just want you."

Nolan colored, a deep rose lighting the top of his cheeks, something she knew only happened when he was almost overcome. He cleared his throat. "Okay, so now we *have* to bet something in honor of sighting the city."

"I bet I can get your clothes off within three minutes of stepping into the hotel room."

"Sucker bet." Nolan pointed. "There it is."

Kate looked outside at the desert, and there, off in the distance, was an enormous sprawl of buildings, the outer lines distinct against the barrenness of the desert. "All of that is Las Vegas?"

"Yep."

He'd been to Las Vegas a couple of times with friends, and she wanted to ask if he'd come here with another girl while they were apart, but that broke their unspoken rule of never talking about the past. But she'd put her heart back in his hands again, knowing the choice was *hers*, and it felt somehow richer—more true—for it. "It's big. I bet you can't throw a quarter across the main drag."

"Waste of good money. I could probably win a million dollars with that exact quarter in a slot machine."

Folding her arms across her chest, she said, "So what, big guy? What's worth betting on?"

"This," he said, serious again, and so very Nolan. "This is."

"Yes," she said. "Yes. Good god, we're getting *married.* Do we need witnesses?"

"Won't the chapel provide them? Like in the movies?"

Kate shook her head. "How many weddings have they witnessed? Half those end in divorce, and I don't want their bad juju."

"Old witnesses are used up. I can see that." Nolan fiddled with the tray table lock. "What about this? I bet I can get two people on the street to witness our wedding for us."

"Total strangers?"

"Why not? We're not telling anyone else."

It didn't feel right to Kate. Not just anyone. "Not a good bet. They could be drunks. Or murderers."

"Killers on a Vegas binge."

"Right. It can't be just anyone."

Nolan pursed his lips as if he were going to whistle. "I bet I can find two people completely in love to be our witnesses."

That was better. "They have to be as in love as we are."

"Naturally."

"What do you get?" she asked.

He thought for a moment. "You have to tell me your biggest secret."

That was the last thing she could do. "What makes you think I have any?"

"You do." He cleared his throat. "Sometimes I can almost see it."

Uneasy, Kate shifted in her seat. She fit her hand into his and leaned against his shoulder, keeping her eye on the city as it unrolled toward them. "A couple as in love as we are. That's going to be hard to find. Probably impossible."

"That's what makes it fun."

Despite the cool spring weather outside, the air conditioner was on full blast at the House of Eternal Love and Friendship. The chaplain, Roy, wore a black puffy coat over his "clerical" garb, a cheap-looking dark polyester robe and white collar crookedly affixed. Kate shivered.

"You need witnesses? My employee"—he gestured to the girl who couldn't be more than eighteen filing her nails in a side room—"and me can do that. Fifty extra dollars. No charge if she cries."

"She cries?" Alarmed, Kate looked up from the papers on the counter in front of them. "Is that normal?"

"She's good at it. A nice tip doesn't hurt, though."

Nolan signed one page and slid it to Kate. "We don't want her to cry. We'll have our own witnesses."

"Where?" The chaplain peered around them as if their witnesses were hiding somewhere.

"How much time do we have?"

Roy glanced at his oversized watch. "Thirty minutes, fast wedding, you can be back here in twenty and we'll still get it done."

Kate heard Nolan give his nervous giggle, and it infected her. "Speed wedding," she said. "Let's get married lots. Next time, we'll do it on ice skates."

As they left the chapel, Nolan said, "Over Niagara Falls in a barrel."

"Skydiving from a helicopter."

"Underwater in scuba gear," he said, ushering her to the right on the crowded sidewalk, pointing out a bench.

"Mile twenty-five of a marathon."

He raised his eyebrows at her and pulled out a red handkerchief that had come with his new suit, using it to dust off the seat for her. "I'm not so into the marathon idea."

"Okay. Triathlon."

"We can discuss it."

Kate arranged her dress—an outrageous red cocktail dress from a boutique in the hotel. It was knee-length, covered in sequins and small burgundy bugle beads. It clacked quietly as she moved, and the weight was delicious on her shoulders. She felt like a gaudy flapper and wished she had a cigarette holder even though she'd never smoked. Nolan wore a red suit made of some shiny material that gleamed in the cool sunlight. "You kind of look like a pimp," she noted.

"Fantastic! That'll make finding people that want to help us out even easier!" He sat next to her. "Hey—" He nudged her. "How about them?" He nodded toward a young couple strolling hand in hand toward them. The man wore an oversized white T-shirt that read "GUMMY" and the woman's bangs were three inches tall.

"Divorce pending," Kate said.

The couple paused to kiss.

"Cynic," said Nolan. "Why?"

"You see her bag? Coach. Easy three hundred. And look at his shirt. Thrift store central."

"You don't know that."

"He bought a new pink T-shirt that says 'GUMMY'? On purpose?" She wrinkled her nose. "Won't last two years."

"Okay." Nolan sat back.

The parade of humanity in front of them looked like a mixture of every part of America—every race, gender, social class. Prostitutes on heels higher than the Stratosphere roller coaster wobbled by, followed by women leading tiny dogs dressed in couture. Couples of all compositions strolled past, and although some looked very happy, none were exactly right.

"What about them?" said Nolan.

Both the man and the woman carried weight around their middles, and their steps were tired. They were pale, with forearms and cheeks stained bright pink by too much sun. Even in the cool air, they sweated through their matching "Vegas Baby" T-shirts. They held hands and walked with their gazes up at the tall, flashing buildings that lined the Strip.

"No," said Kate. "No one from Michigan."

"You don't know that. And why are you prejudiced against a whole state?"

"I'm not. It was just fun to say."

As the couple walked past, the woman cast a longing eye at the bench. There was a space next to Nolan, but not a very big one.

He jumped to his feet. "Would you like to sit?"

"Oh, gracious," she huffed. "Bill? Do you mind?"

Bill shook his head. "Of course I don't mind. Sit as long as you want. We'll call a cab if you get too tired."

"I'm not too tired. I'm still just so excited." She smiled cheerfully at Kate and Nolan, and a gap between her front teeth made her face look sweet and less exhausted. "Newlyweds, you know." Kate felt a flutter of surprise—they had to be in their late fifties, and they fit so well together she'd assumed they'd been together forever. "We're having the *best* time. Where are you from?"

"California. Bay Area," said Kate. "What about you?"

"Detroit." She held her purse on her lap as if it were a large sack of salt. It looked like it might actually physically hurt her to hold it, and Kate was opening her mouth to ask if she wanted to set it on the bench between them when the man, Bill, stepped forward.

"Let me hold your purse, love." He took the brightly colored bag and held it easily in front of him, rocking on his heels. "There. That's better. She's had the cancer, you know. She's getting better but I still like to baby my Diane. How long you kids been together?"

"Since high school—" started Nolan.

"Since college," corrected Kate. "Three years."

Diane confided, "Us two met in our twenties but it took till we were both divorced and I was sick for us to finally get it right. I finally got my football star."

Bill smoothed his thinning hair, grinning while he wiped the sweat from his brow. "And I finally got my beauty queen."

A look passed between them, and Kate felt its warmth wash over her. She met Nolan's eyes. He nodded.

There was no Elvis, not even on the chapel stereo. They asked for Etta James, not Pachelbel.

"Do you take this woman to be your wedded wife? To have—"

"I do," said Nolan. The chaplain fixed him with a glare.

"To have and to hold, from this—"

"I do, I do, I *do*."

Bill and Diane, standing to either side of them, laughed. "I think he does, Preach," said Bill. Diane clutched her spindly bouquet of daisies tighter to her chest. Goose bumps rose on Kate's arms.

"I do," Nolan said again for good measure.

The chaplain gave up and looked at Kate. "What about you? Same thing?"

"I do!" Without waiting, Kate put her arms around Nolan's neck and held on as if he might fly away, taking her away with him. She kissed him, hard, so he would know.

Against her mouth, he whispered, "Now tell me that secret."

"I missed you every moment we were apart." It was true, even if it wasn't a secret, and Nolan wrapped his arms around her even tighter. Kate heard the click of Diane's camera behind her.

She hadn't needed momentous. She hadn't even wanted romantic. But Kate got both, all, everything, and she felt stunned by the brightness of the future suddenly spread out beneath them. And if Nolan ever did sprout those wings she suspected were there, just underneath his skin, if he ever flew away, she knew one thing: she would hold tight to his neck and wrap her legs around his body, sticking with him no matter what.

Chapter Twenty-two

Thursday, May 15, 2014
8 a.m.

Pree should have called Flynn the night before. It had just been so easy to turn the cell phone ringer off, to fall into a deep, dreamless sleep in a strange bed under the open window, the sound of a large house breathing quietly around her. In the morning, the light that slanted through the blinds hit the walls at an angle she didn't recognize. The blue comforter smelled too plasticky, as if it were new, but she liked the smell of the room underneath it, real and like . . . a home. Something about the scent reminded her of her old room at the moms' house. Pree wanted to stay, and she wondered briefly if that was part of Kate's plan: to trick her into never leaving. She couldn't decide how much she would mind. There were worse things.

She stretched and reached for her phone, resting in

sunlight on a small blue nightstand. Two missed calls and four texts from Flynn. She was surprised, actually. He was normally mellow to a fault, not noticing if she worked till three or four in the morning during a crunch. Apparently he noticed when she stayed out all night.

She sent one text:

```
I'm all right. With Kate. Will
call later.
```

Then, on second thought, she added: *XO*. Goddamn it, she loved him. She just didn't know what to *do* with him.

Bringing up a browser window on her phone, she typed, "Greg Jenkins."

Yep, almost two hundred thousand matches. Without more specifics from Kate, she'd never be able to figure out which one it was. It looked like there were more than a hundred in Northern California alone. What if Kate had been lying? What were the other reasons for giving up a baby? With one finger Pree flicked through dozens of Greg Jenkinses on Facebook as she contemplated the worst reasons.

Incest. Pree shuddered at the thought that perhaps she was made of a commingling of an already mingled gene pool. But according to Kate's wiki, Kate's father died in a helicopter crash while she was young, so—thank god—that probably wasn't it, unless there was a barbaric uncle or cousin in the mix.

Rape. Kate had been sixteen when she'd had Pree. It was possible. It wasn't like Pree hadn't had the thought before, after all, imagining herself the product of force and anger. If so, would Kate have given Pree a fake father's name, just to throw her off the scent? Is that something a woman had to keep her child from ever learning, or was it something that would be on the adoption forms? Did the moms know? They'd kept so much from her for so long, after all . . .

The anger Pree felt was low grade, sitting on a back burner. She could turn up the gas at any moment, and it would boil over, hurting everyone. Didn't she get points for trying to play it cool? To understand? Pree wished for the equivalent of a gold star, wished that someone would notice her Herculean effort to understand Kate and the moms. Pree knew—better and better each day—why a woman could decide to give away a child. There were a million reasons, and more for a teenager. But knowing this with the front part of her mind, the logical, rational part, didn't smother that slow molten flow of anger that Kate—this smart, intelligent, interesting woman—hadn't chosen *her.* Childish. She was being so fucking childish.

Pree stood and draped herself in the long black terry cloth robe Kate had left on the bed the night before.

The image of the underside of Jimmy's desk flashed in her mind.

Ignoring the dull headache that tugged at her temples, Pree wandered out into the hallway wearing the robe over the T-shirt and shorts Kate had given her to sleep in. She craved cereal. Sweet cereal, with cold milk. It was something she never had—Flynn didn't like milk and Pree normally tried to stay away from processed grains and sugars. It was a leftover from when she'd lived at home with the moms. They'd always believed in starting the day with protein. "A day without an egg is a day wasted," Marta had said almost every single morning of her life. She and Isi had even talked about getting chickens once, but then they went to a dykefest urban homestead party where everyone got to kill a chicken, pluck it, and bring the meat home. Isi, who had worked with dead chickens in every restaurant she'd ever been in, came home pale, and Marta, normally vegetarian, went vegan for three months. Without dying from lack of eggs, too, Pree had pointed out. They didn't get the chickens.

Oh, shit, what if this need for cereal and milk was her first baby craving? Did the fetus want carbs? The thought was alarming.

There was no sound in Kate's house as Pree padded toward the staircase. It was already eight, a time when Pree's own normal routine was already buzzing—she was usually up and drinking coffee while she read the grisly parts of the paper to Flynn as he lay on top of the covers and stretched lazily. Then she'd zoom around their room looking for whatever part of her clothes she'd mislaid that day. By eight forty-five, Pree had to be on the road, headed south to the Peninsula. It was a reverse commute, which was good, but it still meant she sat in her old car for way more than she would have liked. Every once in a while, when traffic got snarled, she'd sketch while driving. She knew this was technically a bad idea, but she'd do it only when the average speed was less than ten miles an hour, and she never looked down at the pad of paper on her lap, never glanced at the tip of her pencil. She drew quickly in the blind, grabbing—stealing—the faces of people in cars around her: women singing along with their radios, mouths open, eyes wide; men scowling and punching their dashboards as if that would make traffic move, obey.

Pree should be thinking about going to work, not wandering the hall of Kate's house in clothes that weren't her own. But that would mean going home for a fresh outfit, facing Flynn, and then facing Jimmy . . .

Pree touched the smooth rail of the unfamiliar staircase. Nolan, Kate's ex, had lived here, gone down these stairs a million times. What was he like? Why had Kate loved *him* enough to keep a child with him?

The steps ended in an open area of pale wooden floor where a sideboard stood, so cluttered you couldn't see even an inch of its surface. Mail, books, a pack of red thank-you cards half open—things were spilled everywhere. A pink lamp leaned at one end of the sideboard, and what looked, improbably, like a hat covered in black feathers rested on the top shelf next to five or six votive candle holders. On the floor below, a pile of shoes spread out into the hallway. Pree counted at least fifteen pair. Kate was a clutterer. Like her. Marta said Pree had a problem with stacks—everything she touched she put in a pile somewhere until, inevitably, and sometimes with great sound, the pile tipped over. But it was a system that her brain understood. She knew exactly what pile everything was in. If she'd been forced to use an actual system, she wouldn't have had a clue where to look for things.

So she got that from Kate.

Pree looked over her shoulder as she entered the kitchen, feeling guilty. Maybe she should wait for Kate to get up? But there was something so satisfying about this, prowling around Kate's house, seeing the way she kept it, without having to keep her face politely composed. She pulled open drawers at random: cutlery, foil, potholders. She found the junk drawer, full of forks with bent tines and knotted pieces of string. Matches and rubber bands vied for space next to thumbtacks and a level. She pulled out three measuring tapes, only one of which let her measure more than four inches without snapping back. A satisfying jumble. Pree had one drawer in the dresser that she and Flynn shared full of exactly the same things.

She shut the drawer quietly and went back to her mission: cereal. Would Kate have the healthy stuff or the crap?

Hot damn, jackpot! She not only had Honey Nut Cheerios, Pree's favorite, but she went one step further: Cocoa

Puffs. Years and years ago, Pree had bought a box with babysitting money. She'd hidden it in her room and had eaten it one puff at a time, sitting on the edge of her open windowsill so the smell of chocolate would waft out, not in, so Marta, who would have died a thousand fiery deaths before she'd let something like that cross her doorstep, didn't find her out.

Pree filled a blue bowl with it immediately.

She guessed that if Kate *did* find her at that moment, she probably wouldn't mind. She might even be pleased Pree felt comfortable in her house. But as soon as Pree poured the milk into the bowl, she felt nervous and jangled, and instead of staying in the kitchen, she stepped out the kitchen door and sat outside to eat on the small side porch.

Heavy fog dripped from the trees and telephone lines, and she was glad for the thick robe. The wetness of the air weighted down a massive cobweb draped under a low bush. The cereal was sweeter than anything Pree had ever eaten before ten in the morning, and it went straight to her head. The darker thoughts she'd had upstairs dissipated, and a bright happiness as sweet as the cereal filled her brain. It wasn't until she was almost done eating that she realized she could not only see the corner of Kate's driveway, but that she could see a guy—a neighbor, probably, waiting to pick up a child—waiting in his car across the street. She felt suddenly skeevy, sitting there in Kate's clothing, eating purloined cereal.

She grabbed her bowl, and carried it in, thankful she hadn't accidentally locked herself out, something she hadn't even thought of until she felt how easily the lock flicked closed when she got inside.

Then she scurried back upstairs to wait to hear something. When she heard Kate get up, she would pretend she'd slept in. As she pulled the blanket again over her and looked out at the fog wreathing the willow, she felt a sudden joy floating inside her, as if she'd swallowed a sweet balloon. She felt safe. It was misplaced, of course—you had to admit that feeling safe just because you were near your bio mom was pretty dumb, especially when she was the one who'd abandoned you so long ago, that she was, actually, the prime mover of your whole unconventional life (lesbian moms! artistic tendencies! attachment failures!).

But the feeling was good, and she drew it closely around herself, determined to lie in the warmth of it as long as she could.

Chapter Twenty-three

Thursday, May 15, 2014
8 a.m.

Nolan rubbed his face with his hands and then rested his wrists on the steering wheel. Fred Weasley rumbled low in his throat next to him on the passenger seat. Not in the almost year he'd been out had Nolan been by the house, not until now. There were guys he worked with who treated spying on the ex like a game. They took a grim delight in coming to work and relaying what a whore their ex-wife was, how she was out banging some dickwipe while a sitter stayed with their kids. *My* kids, they'd say, shaking their heads before pulling on their work vests. *Mine.* The single guys avoided those conversations, and the married ones looked horrified, but all the divorced men leaned in and listened, Nolan had noticed. They couldn't help it.

And now here he was.

If only he could figure out how to get out of the car. Go knock on that thick strong door he'd loved so much. But so far, he couldn't.

Mr. Foster, a grumpy retired English teacher from the local high school, stepped down off his front porch to pick up his newspaper, dressed in that same old ratty green robe he'd always worn. There was no reason he'd look at Nolan other than simple nosiness, which he did. But Nolan's old beater wasn't anything Mr. Foster would recognize and Nolan kept his shades on as he pretended to look at his phone.

Nolan had to admit the outside of the house looked good. From his parking spot, he couldn't see the claw-foot bathtub in the garden. Of course he couldn't. That was the whole point. She must have kept the gardener, that much was obvious. From jail through his court-appointed lawyer, he'd hired a guy sight unseen to take care of the front and side yards in his permanent absence. Kate had always loved having pretty grass and joyful flowers, but she had absolutely no talent when it came to gardening. Watering once a week was too much to remember, and for her it was just like cleaning the house: something she never noticed needed doing. Yeah, he'd left her well taken care of, at least. He'd signed over the deed to the house and had moved all his money into her account before taking his name off it. He'd refused to pay for an attorney, saying the state-appointed one would be good enough. Nolan *was* a lawyer, after all, and he could have worked with the young guy more than he had. He hadn't, though. He'd let the kid do the best he could in court, which wasn't bad, actually. Nolan hadn't fought a thing. Not a single goddamn thing. He had no ground to stand on to fight—he was in the wrong. If he'd had to live through it, he also had to be punished, he knew that. Even a lifetime in prison wouldn't be long enough to fully punish him. He'd hoped for the death sentence—prayed for it, courted it like a lover, imagined what he'd whisper to Kate as they dripped the poison into his veins—even while knowing in California the state would never kill a man who'd mercifully killed his terminally ill, suffering child.

This was the real punishment, this right here. *This* was what he'd signed up for. Looking at their house, wondering if she was alone inside. For all he knew, Kate had a man in the house with her. Loving her.

Would another man be able to make her laugh the way Nolan had? For a selfish, dizzying moment, he allowed himself to remember the sound of her laughter. No one in the world sounded like Kate, he'd decided long ago, while still in high school. It didn't matter what she was actually laughing about as her voice trilled up and then went so satisfyingly back down again. It was solid. You could rest a cup of coffee on that laugh. He'd just wanted to hear it, to be in on the joke. And he'd always, *always* been in on it. He missed her laugh more than he missed sex.

Kate probably wasn't missing sex. Nope. A noble part of himself wanted to wish her the best in this—to hope her lover was skilled and handsome and kind. And the base part of him wanted nothing more than to storm into his old house, up the stairs, and drag out any asshole who might be in her sheets and beat the living shit out of him, to have the satisfaction of hearing him wheeze after a well-seated blow. He flexed his fingers and knew he could do it. Right now.

But Kate wasn't his to fight for, though. Not anymore.

Nolan probably didn't have too much time left here on this street before someone got interested in why a guy was hanging out in his car with no obvious reason. The neighbors all had their local beat cop on speed dial, something this part of Oakland could boast, and one of the biggest reasons he and Kate had bought here. The annexed city of Piedmont, a few blocks away, had a response time of under three minutes for all medical emergencies and felonies, and the rich citizens of this part of Oakland insisted on a similar response even while the deep east and west areas of the city were still torn by violence.

A woman getting in her parked Buick in front of him raised her perfectly plucked eyebrows and glared through his windshield. The look appeared to be directed at Fred Weasley, however, not at him. Fred tucked the top of his head under Nolan's chin and pressed the rest of his long, shaggy body as hard as he could against him, sitting sideways on the emergency brake. Nolan wrapped his arm around the dog as Fred shook in paroxysms of delight.

In front of him, the Buick pulled out, the woman casting one more glare over her shoulder. It was time to start his own car. Drive away. He told himself to turn the key, but it was harder than it sounded, especially since he was dying to know what Kate had to tell him, what was so important she'd come looking for him. But there was no way he could make himself go up that walkway. No way in hell.

At that moment, as he reached to turn the key, a girl walked out of the side door. Really, she snuck out, as if trying to avoid being noticed. Had she broken in? She was young, and had something in her hands, but she didn't look like the burgling type. She was wearing . . . was that Kate's robe she was wearing? The one he'd given her the Christmas before Robin died?

Nolan sucked in his breath and leaned farther forward. There was something familiar about the girl . . . She was young, maybe late teens or early twenties? Maybe she was one of Kate's friends' kids; Vanessa Hutchins at the gallery had a girl who would be about that age now, didn't she?

His heart started racing, thumping uncomfortably in his chest, and he had no idea why. A fine trembling started in his right hand as he touched the car key. *Turn the key. Just leave.* It was time to go. Fred was due for his day-off ramble on the beach.

But the girl. So familiar. That brown hair, curled like . . . Those shoulders—they reminded him of . . . *Shit.*

Nolan shook his head and rubbed his eyes again.

He'd been seeing Robin everywhere lately. At the grocery store the other night, he'd almost run after a little boy he'd seen rounding the end of the cracker aisle. He'd been there only a second, and Nolan had just seen the back of his head. But that split second of *knowing* it was Robin was both the best and the worst second of his life in recent memory. The very highest hope, followed almost instantly by crushing despair.

The hope had made it worth it.

The girl picked up the bowl she'd placed on the porch.

In that moment, he saw it.

She didn't just remind him of Robin. She *was* Robin, an alternate version of his son. Nolan could see it in the set of her head, the pointed slope of her shoulders, the way her left foot turned in as she stood, as if she was about to trip.

And he had no fucking idea who she was. A child she'd had with someone when they'd been apart during their early college years? That was *impossible.*

Nothing could be more impossible. Kate didn't lie to him.

Wasn't it impossible? He did math as quickly as he could—if she'd had a baby while they were apart, that child could be anywhere from eighteen to twenty-one. Shit, fuck, hellfire, the girl looked as if she'd fall into the age range.

She disappeared into the house through the side door, and Nolan closed his eyes and rested his forehead on the steering wheel. He tried to think, but his brain was spinning too fast for him to grab and tease out any single discrete thought. Robin. Kate. Robin. Robin . . .

While they were apart, Kate had given birth to a child. Shit, fuck, shit, what the *hell* was going on?

Kate had a daughter.

Chapter Twenty-four

Thursday, May 15, 2014
8:30 a.m.

Kate knocked gently on the bedroom door, and it opened quickly, as if Pree—suspiciously bright-eyed—had been waiting for her.

"Can I make you breakfast before you go to work?"

A guilty look flickered across Pree's face. "I think I might play hooky today."

"Pancakes, then?" Hope smelled like maple syrup and butter. Kate had never wanted to make pancakes so much in her whole life.

"Um. I'm not that hungry, really. Maybe some coffee?"

In the kitchen, they stood in silence while the coffee hissed into its carafe. Unsure if it was a companionable silence or not, Kate worked at carefully picking out the few shards of glass still remaining at the bottom of the sink. Pree didn't ask what she was doing.

Kate poured Pree the first cup, and then waited until there was enough to pour for herself. Pree pushed a blue-black curl out of her eye and then stared into her coffee cup as if she were having a hard time deciding whether or not to take the first sip. She was so *beautiful.* Young. Gorgeous in her casually worn luminous skin. Alive. For one second Kate allowed herself to bask in this feeling of pride in a person she'd helped create. It had been a long time. She'd almost forgotten what it felt like.

What if, on the very small chance, Pree was here because she wanted to talk? What if she wanted something from a mother she'd never had, a mother she didn't know?

Sternly, she reminded herself a child with two mothers doesn't lack for maternal advice. But oh, god, if she did . . . There weren't words in the English language to describe how she'd feel. The color didn't exist that would paint the happiness it would bring.

To be a mother. That's what Pree's mothers had had this whole time. Kate hadn't been a mother in three years, and the urge to be one was almost overwhelming. The urge to touch Pree (to smooth the hair back off her face, to touch the tip of her perfect nose) burned in her knuckles and made her fingers twitch. It was ridiculous, not to mention socially and morally unacceptable. And still it was there, inside her, a feeling that might knock her down, physically, all the way to the ground.

Carefully, she sat at the kitchen table. Pree sat in Robin's place and Kate chided herself for noticing. There wasn't a better place, after all. It was the only seat for Pree.

After a moment, Kate said, "I want to ask you something."

Pree's eyes widened.

"An easy question, I mean."

"Okay," said Pree.

"What kind of art do you do? I mean, your medium. You didn't really tell me."

Pree looked surprised. "Um. I guess right now my medium is pixels. Lots of pixels. I draw vehicles, props, environments, all for this console game we're building. They bring me ideas—like, tell me to fill this room in a certain way, or that they need a samurai sword. I go off and research whatever it is, and then I render it for the scene."

"That sounds cool." Joy thumped around Kate's chest, lodging itself somewhere near her heart.

"I like it." Pree looked at the table. "I mean, it's okay. Sometimes I wonder if I've sold out, you know?"

"You're making money by being an artist. There aren't very many people who pull off that scam."

"You do."

It was true. Kate did. Finally. "Yeah. I worked my ass off for a really long time and I support myself now. But it wasn't easy, and I'm not a normal case. Most people give up before I did. It was just a question of how long I could hold on. And honestly . . ." Kate paused. "My husband's job took care of the bills. They took care of this house. It wasn't until less than five years ago that I really started making a living wage. And if I were really honest, I'd admit I don't even love the work I've been selling."

"Seriously?"

"People like the dark stuff. They like bleak." Kate looked at her fingertips, remembering when they were always stained with color. "I used to paint with every sliver of the rainbow, every tiny piece of it. Every single shade. But that's neither here nor there, really. What?" She paused. "What's that look?"

"No, it's just that . . . You'll laugh."

Kate wouldn't. No way. "I promise not to."

Pree appeared to be deciding something. Finally, she

said, "Hang on." She pattered up the stairs and clattered back down, this time clutching her backpack.

"You have work here!" Kate felt like clapping her hands and sat on them to prevent herself.

"Kinda." Pree took out a black Moleskine that looked well used. It was battered, the corners of the cover bruised and soft-looking. "It's probably not your thing."

"Try me."

Pree opened the book, shielding the contents with her body. Then she opened to a page and pushed it across the table toward Kate. "It's not very good. I mean, it's okay, but it's . . . the kind of thing I really like to do."

It was a drawing of a girl, bold black lines done in thick ink. The girl wore ragged shorts and a short top with suspenders. Heavy combat boots. Dark square glasses sat on an oval face, and her mouth was open in a shout. She was muscular, with biceps and thick thighs. She was young, cocky, and Kate could almost hear the yell coming off the page. "Cerulean," she murmured. Cerulean was the color of determination that rose from fear.

"What?" Pree looked startled.

"Oh. Sorry. I know it's bizarre, some kind of weird synesthesia, but sometimes I see color in voices. If you could hear her, this girl's voice would be—"

"Cerulean. Yes."

They stared at each other.

"Whoa," breathed Pree.

"Do you know—?"

"Can you tell—?"

They stopped.

"You first," said Pree.

"What color is my voice?" Her whole life, Kate had longed to know.

"Red."

Kate sat back in her chair, strangely relieved. That's what it *felt* like. "Red . . ." *Red for passion.*

"More like burgundy, with plum undertones. So not true red, very purply." Pree paused. "It's pretty. What about me?"

"Green." *Green for strength.*

"Right *on.* That's what I thought."

"Pale, fresh green, like the inside of a cucumber."

Pree pulled back the book and stared into the drawing. "I can't believe you heard that."

Kate shook her head, trying to clear it. "Damn. That's so fucking cool."

Laughing, Pree closed the book. "I heard about this guy who sees numbers as colors, and each color is a different emotion. The low numbers are primary colors and emotions, and the higher colors are combinations of them. He recited the numbers in pi for five hours, twenty-two *thousand* numbers, all in order, all correct, just because he remembered the poem he'd written in his head about the emotions of the colors."

"Wow. That makes me feel almost normal."

"Right?"

"So, what do you do? Comics? Graphic novels? More?" Kate said.

"All of it. I have this fantasy of doing all of it. But time, you know, there's never enough of it. Right?"

Kate touched the cover of the book lightly, with one finger. "What else?"

Suddenly, Pree looked shy.

"What is it?"

Pree pulled something from her bag. It was something important, Kate could tell by the way her shoulders rounded protectively.

"Stickers."

Thick black lines curled over the blue-and-white sticker, which looked like it might have once been some kind of label. "RARE. Nice slap."

Pree gaped. "You know street art?"

"Graf's cool. I've never done any, but I love it. I studied it for a while, looking specifically at their shading. There's some great grayscale stuff. Have you seen the warehouse over on Mandela Parkway? A big group of women got together and bombed it a while ago."

"I read about that."

"I've been there. I'll take you sometime. If you want to."

Too much, slow down. Kate added another spoon of sugar to her cup, even though it was sweet enough already. "You sure you don't want some toast?"

"I'm okay. I, um, woke up early and stole some of your cereal."

"I had cereal?"

"Two kinds. I had the Cocoa Puffs."

Shit. Kate had left those in the cupboard, next to her own Cheerios. It had been a small concession, just a tiny one. She knew she'd throw them out at some point—she just hadn't gotten around to it just yet. The pain knifed her gut, as sudden and unexpected as always. She breathed. In. Out. Hold on.

"Must have been kind of stale," she managed.

"They were kind of chewy."

Kate stood, willing her knees to stay steady. "I'm going to have toast, then. Let me know if I can get you anything."

"So . . ."

"Mmm?" Maybe if she didn't look at her . . .

Pree cleared her throat, a soft noise. Then she said, "What did your mother say to you? When you were pregnant with me?"

"Not much, actually."

"She didn't know?"

"Oh, she knew. I think she knew before I even told her somehow. She just never had much to say to me even on a good day."

"Is she alive?"

"No, she died last year." At Pree's stricken expression, Kate realized she should have softened the blow, but she hadn't seen it coming.

"Oh. You weren't close at all?"

Was that yearning in Pree's voice? Kate said, "No. Not the way I wanted to be."

"You were alone at the hospital. My moms said that, anyway."

So alone. Kate sucked in a breath and nodded. "She tried, but she was in a dark place then. And she wanted me to keep the baby, as crazy as that was, as young as I was. She thought, if I kept you . . . Anyway. She gave me a hand-knit sweater afterward. A gorgeous, cabled Aran wool sweater. She must have been working on it when I was pregnant, hiding it in her bedroom. I guess . . . it told me she didn't wish me dead or anything. But still. We never talked about it after." About the baby. About Pree. That had been the worst part of all, actually. Worse than giving birth naturally, worse than signing the papers in the hospital. Kate had at least known Marta and Isi would love the baby. Even as young and naive as she'd been in everything else, she'd known that. But Kate had just wanted to go home, to her mother. She wanted Sonia's arms around her. She wanted to be able to cry for days if she needed to, and she wanted her own mother to take care of her. Not just a sweater.

Pree blinked. "Sad. What about your dad?"

"Died when I was young."

Pree propped her elbow on the table and her chin on her knuckles. "What do you remember?"

Kate held the bread in her hand and considered the question. "His hands smelled like motor oil, even when he wasn't working, but his jackets smelled like the cinnamon rolls he made on Sundays. He was loud, but only accidentally. He was ex–air force, and he flew helicopters, mostly commercial. On the weekends, he contracted for the parks department, flying paramedics. It was his favorite thing in the world, flying in and scooping up someone from a hillside who'd fallen or had a heart attack while hiking. He didn't hear that well from the rotor noise, and to compensate, he yelled all the time." Kate hadn't thought of him, not like this, in years. She missed him suddenly, something she'd thought she was over.

"What did he look like?"

"That's another good question." Kate couldn't really remember. She could visualize the photos she had of him, but the man himself—his image had slipped away over the years, no matter how hard she'd tried to hold on. It was why, in her last series, she'd painted only pieces of his helicopter, the sky, the ocean he loved, a jutting spit of beach. Pictures of her father. "Big. As tall as his voice was loud, and wide as a redwood."

"But you were small then." Pree kept her chin resting on her hand.

It was true, in the photos of him with Sonia, he didn't seem that much bigger than his wife. "Yeah. Maybe I just remember him that way."

Pree wriggled so that the chair creaked, a noise Kate hadn't heard in such a long time. "So he never got to see what you became."

A mother with no child. A wife with no husband. "No. He

would have thought being an artist was silly, probably. Military to the core." Kate pushed the bread down into the toaster. Damn fancy olive loaf from the farmers market, it would probably burn in there. "First-world problems," she muttered. "So. Tell me more about that Flynn you mentioned when we met. He's an artist, too, right?"

Pree shifted in her seat, her knee thumping the underside of the table. Instead of answering, she said, "I'm sorry, but I can't stop thinking about it. What was my father like?"

Kate stilled her face, making sure her lips didn't give her away. *Loving. Kind. Sexy. Sweet. My best friend.* "I told you, he was nice."

"Nice?" She smiled winningly, and Kate saw her own crescent moon crinkly eyes in Pree's face. "Can't you give me just a little more?"

"It was a long time ago."

"You must remember something. Do I look like him?"

Pree's question jolted her back to the present, and she almost answered truthfully. *So much so that it hurts me to look at you.* But she said instead, also truthfully, "You look like Robin."

Kate could almost see the war within Pree, the tension scribbled across her face. She wanted more about her father so desperately. What must she think? Had she bought the Greg Jenkins lie? What came up when you *did* google his name? Kate should have done that already, should be ready to back up the stupid, ridiculous, necessary lie.

Pree glanced down at her lap, and when she looked up, her eyes were less intense. "Well, then, what was Robin like?"

Kate softened inside. This was the only question that was safe to answer. "When he was born he weighed eight pounds, two ounces. His eyes were blue except when he cried—then they were bright green. The first movie he ever watched was *Star Wars*, because Nolan wanted to start him out right. He could read at age three, and he loved Harry Potter more than he loved ice cream. I never finished reading him the last book because there was too much death in it, and I regret that every day. He had scars on his back from the spinal taps and I worried that they would never go away, that he'd still have the reminder of his pain when he was grown. Then I'd wonder if he *would* grow up, and I'd pray for more scars, anything to buy him more time. When he went into a giggle fit, he sounded like a baby seal barking, something he knew, and on his birthday every year, he asked to go see the seals at Fisherman's Wharf so he could show them what a good barker he was. He was perfect."

"He was?" Pree's voice had a wistful tone and Kate regretted her word choice.

"Of course not. He wasn't perfect at all. He farted in front of my mother on purpose and he snuck lizards he caught outside and put them into the basket where I kept coffee filters just so I'd freak out. Once he told me my ass was fat in front of his first-grade teacher. And yes, he used the word 'ass.' But no matter what, he was perfect." Kate smiled. "You two have that in common."

Pree snorted, but Kate saw delight in her eyes, and something similar danced within her.

"What else?" asked Pree. "What was his favorite color?"

"He said red but he always reached for anything green. He loved green clothes, green crayons, green paint . . . I think he only said red because of the Gryffindor colors."

"That's why you painted his room Harry Potter."

"He was the biggest fan ever." Even now, the past tense was still so fucking difficult to use.

"Where is he now?"

Kate's brain stalled, then nosedived toward the ground, the blades whirring and cracking. "In Mountain View Cemetery, around the corner. Or half of him, anyway. I kept some ashes to bury at sea."

Pree frowned. "So part of him . . ."

"Is on the mantel with my mother." Should she tell Pree the rest? Might as well, now that she'd crashed and was lying in the wreckage. "I'm going to toss both of them off a boat on Saturday, actually. I've had it scheduled for a long time." She didn't mention she'd been considering canceling it as she had the other times. If ever it was time, it was now. Now that she had this slender hope to perch on. She would do it. That was, if she could let her boy go, the biggest *if* of all. "Robin and my mother loved to swim together."

"Shit."

"Yeah." Kate paused, taking inventory. She would live. Probably. "I want to show you his favorite place. Will you go somewhere with me? If you're really playing hooky?"

Pree nodded. "Yeah."

"Good," Kate said. It was so good.

Chapter Twenty-five

Thursday, May 15, 2014
9:30 a.m.

Kate's car remembered all the turns. It remembered the entrance onto the bridge and it exited at Octavia as if it had gone there just last week instead of years ago. Pree was quiet—not a bad quiet, but still Kate worried. Did she want out of the car? Did she regret saying she'd go someplace an hour away with a person she barely knew? Pree played with a thick pen, rolling it in her fingers, and Kate recognized the motion—she did it herself when she was thinking, only she liked holding her favorite Winsor & Newton brush and rubbing her thumb over the broken end (she'd sat on it once on the couch in her studio and refused to get rid of it).

They drove through town in heavy traffic, weaving through the park, then slicing down Lincoln through the Avenues. They were in Pree's city, but she didn't say anything about her place or her boyfriend.

"You don't need anything from home since we're so close?" Kate would have given her left eyebrow to see where Pree lived.

Pree kept her eyes out the window and tapped on the door handle. *Tap tap tap.* "Nah. Thanks for the loan of the clothes."

The jeans were two sizes too big for the girl but exactly the right length, and the red Blick sweatshirt set off the crimson streaks in her hair. A gorgeous color, actually, what she'd managed to do with those red curls that rested next to the blue. Alizarin.

Warmth spread through her. *P is for Pree.*

At Ocean Beach, Kate turned left and headed south down Highway 1.

"I love it out here," Pree said, her voice a mantis green. "Look at those surfers. They're insane. Do you *know* how cold that water is?"

Kate did, actually. "They have wetsuits," she said mildly.

"No way. You couldn't pay me enough." Pree propped one foot up in the corner of the dashboard, then seemed to catch herself. "Sorry."

"Don't be sorry," said Kate. "For anything."

"Can you tell me more about Greg Jenkins?"

A sneak attack. Kate's fingers twitched on the wheel, and she felt herself wince. "I will. Soon. I promise. I'll try to remember more. But now—look, we're here." It was mortar to the brick lie, another layer she'd have to deal with someday. Some far-off day. Next to her, Pree cleared her throat.

Kate turned right into Fort Funston at the small brown sign almost lost in the dunes. For a Thursday morning, the parking lot was packed. Mostly dog walkers, Kate knew, and her heart lifted. "Don't you love it?"

Pree leaned forward to look out the car window as Kate parked in front of a massive carpet of ice plant that rolled out to the cliff's edge. "I've never been here."

"You're kidding."

"I wanted to stop a couple of times but whenever Flynn and I drive down here we're usually on our way south to Duarte's for pie, and we don't slow down till we get there. Oh!" Pree unbuckled her seat belt and flung herself out of the car.

Kate grinned as she locked the car and moved to join her. "Aren't they awesome?"

"Dude." Pree breathed.

Dangling low overhead, three hang gliders soared. They wove, turned, and dove. Flying on the updrafts at the cliff's very edge allowed them to hover only feet above the ground, or so it seemed to those walking on the paths below. They were so close that Kate could see the color of their sunglasses. She could hear them calling to each other.

Pree dashed ahead, up the path and then out, closer to the edge. Twenty feet above her, a man flying a green hang glider whooped at her, and she looked up, mouth hanging open. He put the glider into a dive, coming straight at her. She matched his joyful shout with her own. At the last minute, he turned and flew below the cliff's edge, below Pree and down, toward the ocean's choppy surface, and then rose back up.

Kate could hear both the man and Pree laughing uproariously. Joy. That's what she'd missed by not allowing herself to come here. She'd denied herself this particular gladness.

"Come on, Kate!" Pree took off down what had been Robin's favorite walk—the one that led through an old military battery and out to a sandy expanse that looked over the whole Pacific. Pree ran the way Robin had, a rapid, exuberant lope, her long legs eating up the yards to the edge. Kate had spent so much time calling Robin back from that edge that at least now she knew one thing: the cliff didn't fall when someone stood on it. The bottom might fall out from other things, yes, but not here.

Kate reached the edge and stood next to Pree, who gazed at the water as if it might give her the answers she wanted.

"Robin used to say that on a clear enough day, you might be able to see Japan."

Pree smiled. "Nice."

"It was his favorite place in the world. We came almost every weekend with donuts and milk. He loved the hang gliders, but he loved the dogs more than anything."

As if she'd called them, a pack of dogs came through the battery, tumbling over one another as they leaped and bounced. There had to be nine or ten of them, but it was hard to tell exactly—they moved so quickly, a swirling mass of dripping tongues and feathery tails.

"Look at them," said Pree, and there it was again, that joy.

"Yep."

A black dog with white border collie blazes bounded up to Pree and poked her with his muzzle. Pree laughed in surprise, and then the dog was gone again, chasing a Great Dane that lolloped toward the dog walker, a young woman with a poofy vest and dreadlocks.

"It's wonderful. Can we keep going?"

Kate just waved her hand in assent.

The fog had been rolling out since they'd first seen the water, and now the bank was all but invisible, a low white line on the horizon. Bright sun lit the tops of the waves. Far down below, a small boat motored north. Two hang gliders, one a rainbow, the other decorated with blue lightning bolts, flew overhead, following their air current. And out on the horizon, a container ship hung still and motionless. From seeing them at the Port of Oakland, Kate knew it was enormous, almost a quarter mile long, but from here, it looked like a tiny toy she should be able to reach out and nudge with the tip of her finger.

The path turned, went downhill, and then curved back toward the edge. Kate bit her lip. It was obvious what direction the path took here—Pree would see it, and of course, she'd want . . .

Another pack of dogs came racing up the trail, a tired-looking man following them, his neck strewn with leashes.

"It goes all the way down to the beach here!" Pree kicked up sand as she ran to look. "It's really steep, but I think we can make it. Can we go down?"

Kate jerked her head in agreement and motioned her ahead with her hand. How many times had she done that? she wondered. A hundred? A thousand? As soon as Robin had learned to walk he'd hurtled down this path. No, earlier than that. Kate had a vivid memory of Nolan worrying about Robin being on Kate's chest in a snuggly as she careened down the dunes toward the water. His very first jump had been after he'd climbed up on a driftwood log and sailed into the air to land in the sand.

Pree zigzagged down toward the water, traversing the sand as if skiing, using her body to naturally slow herself down as she went. Kate preferred the hell-for-leather approach herself, always had. She liked to run hard, right downhill, until she came *this* close to tumbling head over heels. Two or three times, she'd done exactly that, coming up with sand packed in her ears and up one nostril, screaming with laughter as Robin rolled, helpless with giggles, in the sand below her. "Mama, Mama, Mama," he gasped through his laughter. The sweetest word in the world. If she could have fallen like that every time, to make him laugh like that, she would have.

Today, though, Kate didn't fall. As she almost lost control, she ran up a short dune to the ice plant, using it like a runaway-truck ramp. She did it several more times until she was at the bottom with Pree, who was out of breath, her cheeks bright red with pleasure.

Robin had always called the dogs down here the Serious Dogs. On the long, flat expanse of beach, these were the ones who were diligent in their jobs. They picked up driftwood and dragged it to more advantageous placements, bolting in and out of the waves, biting at the water as it rolled in, barking at seagulls. Down here, two hundred feet below the top of the cliff, was no place for froufrou lapdogs. This was strictly Serious Dog territory.

Both she and Pree left their shoes at the base of the trail, and then they turned right, walking north without discussing which way to go. The wind echoed Kate's thoughts and then blew them away. She felt emptied again, and realized how damn much she had missed this scoured, windswept feeling.

And today, she'd stay out of the water.

"Look! The moon is up during the day!" Pree's voice was still delighted.

Kate's eyes had been resting on the low sliver of the visible quarter moon for long seconds without realizing what she was looking at. A day moon—the one that had upset Robin so much a month before he died. She and Nolan never figured out what had made him panic when he saw it, but he'd burst into tired tears in the backyard. "Pack up the moon, Mama. Pack up the moon." They'd put him to bed, pointing out the full, glow-in-the-dark moon hanging over his head, and he'd closed his eyes, drifting into a fitful, feverish sleep.

The day moon. If Kate could have reached past Pree and

shoved it out of the sky, she would have. Instead, she turned her head and looked at the water, hard, willing the glints to burn the tears out of her eyes.

After long moments of walking, Pree said, "Did Robin have a dog?"

"No," said Kate. "Did you?"

Pree didn't follow her lead. "Why didn't he?"

"He and his father were both allergic."

"A little allergic? Or a lot?"

Robin had been so allergic he couldn't ride in a car that had ever had a dog in it. So allergic he couldn't hug his kindergarten teacher because she had three dogs at home. In fact, when he first got really sick, they'd ignored some of his first symptoms because he'd gone home a lot recently with Sammy Willits, who had a dog out in an adjoining kennel, and they'd blamed the wheezing first on that, then on the cold.

"A lot allergic."

"But he could come here?"

Kate stepped over a bulbous piece of glistening seaweed, resisting the urge to touch it with her toes. "If a dog licked him, like that dog did to you earlier, we'd wash him down. I carried a ton of wet wipes with me, and used them every time a dog breathed on him. It didn't stop him, though. Every time I turned around, I'd see him trying to touch one sandy mongrel or another. It wasn't good for him, but then again, neither were chicken nuggets, and I let him have those sometimes, too."

"You were a good mom."

Something in her voice made Kate look sideways at her. Pree's gaze was out at the horizon again.

"I tried." God, how she'd tried.

"My moms were good parents. They *are* good parents." She said it defensively, as if Kate had asserted the opposite.

"I'm sure they are. I chose them for that especially."

A pause. "Maybe I shouldn't have stayed at your house last night."

"Watch out. Jelly slime." Kate pointed it out and Pree sidestepped it. "Why do you say that?" She felt suddenly worried that she'd blown it without knowing it.

"What if you—? No. Never mind. Hey, look up there!" Pree had turned and was staring back at where they'd come from, the bluff to the left. "Kites." And with that, she was off, padding barefoot back to where they'd left their shoes, leaving Kate behind with the pale quarter moon she didn't want.

Chapter Twenty-six

Thursday, May 15, 2014
9:30 a.m.

Nolan had tailed them.

Kate and the girl had gotten into the Saab, and they'd backed out of the driveway. They'd been laughing as they passed him. Kate hadn't glanced his way, not once. And then, like someone out of a late-night cable cop show, he followed them.

He was behind them by one or two cars all the way over the bridge and through Hayes Valley, all the way across San Francisco. Out on Ocean Avenue, Nolan put three cars between them, which was safe enough. Confusion he didn't know where to place in his body moved through him, making his eyes itch.

Because now it was obvious where they were going.

Nolan's breath came faster as he made the right-hand turn past the wooden sign.

Kate had a daughter.

And she was bringing her to Robin's favorite place.

It couldn't be possible, not really. She couldn't have kept something like that from him—Kate had always been a bad liar, her cheeks reddening every time he caught her in the tiniest untruth (yes, she'd called her mother; no, she didn't mind spinach again with dinner). There had to be a better, more obvious explanation for the young woman who looked like Kate. Who looked like Robin.

Jesus, who was the girl's father? She looked too young for it to be Nolan, thank god, which would have been completely impossible, but then *who*? That meat locker of a guy she'd pointed out to him once, when they were back together? Named Zippy or something stupid. Or that Greg guy she'd gone to Josie's party with? Kate had barely looked at him again, not after Nolan was back. Fucking hell.

He parked the equivalent of a city block away from them in the huge, windswept parking lot and got out. Fred Weasley gave a small, sharp whine at his feet. "Sorry, buddy." Nolan released his tight hold of the dog's leash, letting him romp in front, and as soon as they hit the sand, he released him. How Robin had loved that this whole area of Fort Funston was off-leash. Doggy dogs just being themselves, as far as the eye could see. As always, he wished for one long, unbearable moment that it was Robin with him, not Fred Weasley.

Kate and the girl were ahead of him now, a quarter of a mile out front so that he could barely see them. It didn't matter. She'd go to the same place she always had—he would bet all $8,432 he had in his savings account.

"Hey, Nolan!" a voice yelled from behind him. "Wait up!"

Not now. He turned and waved at Boris, one of the older dog walkers. A transplant from Brooklyn, Boris had never quite gotten the hang of the Bay Area. He hated BART, saying it was everything wrong with the subway in New York and none of the parts that were right. He wasn't good at driving, but to get to Fort Funston he drove an old VW van that broke down every other week. Nolan had picked him and his five dog clients up off the side of the road three or four times already as he waited for yet another tow. The man loved his dogs, though. There was a particular reason he walked each one: "This is Monty, and his owner got in a car wreck. Paraplegic, can you imagine? No one to walk him. That's Silo, and his people own the bakery on my street. If I didn't take him out, his only walk would be on leash at three in the morning before they go in to bake. No way." Nolan liked the way Boris thought and would have normally welcomed a conversation, but not today.

"Going down to the beach," he called and Boris nodded, waving back. Boris had had his left hip replaced twice already. He walked around the dunes on the paved trails, not down them.

Nolan followed Fred, who bounced a Pomeranian and got a loud bark in payment. They wound through the ice plant to the top of a small dune. Fred, who liked a little modesty and always picked the farthest place away to do his business, turned his back on Nolan and pooped. Nolan muttered under his breath as he tromped through the plants to get the shit. "Come on, come on. Get it over with, Fred." What if he lost Kate in the dunes? Or conversely, what if he caught up with her? What the hell would he say?

Shit. He had no idea what he was doing, besides following his ex-wife and a stranger (to the exact place *he'd* been heading, he reminded himself in belated justification, to the beach where he spent every Thursday morning, always).

At the top of the rise, he kept his eyes on Kate's hair as he scoped out the nearest trash can, the warm bag swinging heavily in his fingers. There, by the fork, was a waste bin. Nolan tightened the knot on the plastic bag and started down the dune, almost tripping over a knob of dead ice plant.

Nolan lost them for a moment while at the trash can, so he broke into a slow lope, which Fred Weasley thought was a fine idea, whuffling and bouncing loudly next to him. "Come on, buddy. That's right. Find Kate," he said, even though the dog had no idea who Kate was. What a concept! The only two things he loved anymore didn't know each other.

Then he jogged around the curve and there: Kate stood at the top of the trail that led down.

Kate was really there. With the young woman, whoever she was.

They still hadn't seen him. There was time to turn around, to take another trail. Or fuck that, he'd just go home. Fred could have a leash walk today instead.

No! He shook his head, hard. This was *Nolan's* place now. His. She couldn't have it. God knew, she could have every single other thing she wanted. He'd give—had already given—her everything else. But she couldn't just take the beach back. The images of what occurred the last time they were here together unrolled in front of his eyes. He'd tried for the past year not to think about it when he came here, and now it was flooding back, as if it had just occurred. The confusion felt thicker. It was moving up his chest, to his throat now.

But then Kate laughed, her voice tossed back to him on the wind, and she started to run down the dune, her heels flying up behind her, her body tilted forward at that unnatural angle—she'd trip, he knew she would. Nolan sat heavily on the bench next to the trash can. He watched her run out of sight, just like she'd done so many times before.

Chapter Twenty-seven

Thursday, May 15, 2014
10:30 a.m.

The way back up the sand path was practically impossible, and Pree had no idea why she'd wanted to go down it in the first place. Hadn't she noticed that it went almost straight down? And she was in pretty good shape. She couldn't ever talk Flynn into working out, but she tried to get outside and run at least three times a week. She liked the high it gave her, the feeling that she'd accomplished something with just her body, distance covered by determination. This climb, though, might just kill her.

It wasn't the baby. You couldn't feel a fetus this tiny. Right?

She struggled up the hill, one step at a time, keeping her eyes on the blue T-shirt of the old man ahead of her who was somehow climbing at her pace even though he was a hundred and eleventy. She turned her head slightly, just once, to make sure with her peripheral vision that Kate was still there. She was getting closer, and Pree put more stomp in her step. She needed to get to the top first, to be able to turn around and watch her climbing.

The old man smiled as she threw herself onto the ground at the very end of the trail, where the sand blew onto the paved walkway.

"Long way up, huh?" She gasped. The borrowed jeans that had been baggy in the morning now felt tight.

He shrugged, barely winded. "Just the right distance, I always think."

Pree's phone rang in her pocket. Flynn's ring. She took another deep breath and willed her voice to be steady when she answered.

"I miss you," he said without preamble. "I love you."

The words felt good, like warm bathwater on cold skin. "Hi, Flynn."

"You know the box you keep your paints in?"

Surprised, Pree said yes. The box was too small and the lid always flew off because one of the hinges was broken. She kept the extra oils, the colors she didn't use as often, in a brown paper bag next to the box.

"I built you a new one."

"You did?"

"I've been working on it for a few months now. For your birthday."

"You forgot my birthday."

"I know. I forgot the actual day itself, but I've been thinking about it coming up, I swear to god. I'm sorry. I couldn't tell you because I wanted to finish it and give it to you in person."

"Which you're not doing now." Pree flicked a shell into the ice plant.

"I know. I just thought you should know about it. It's big. It'll hold a lot. It's built like a toolbox because you said you liked that one case at Blick, but it's metal and wood instead of plastic, and it'll last your whole life."

Pree smiled. He'd never made her anything before—not because he didn't want to, but because whenever he started to, he freaked out, thinking it wasn't good enough. He'd melted down earrings that were "almost there" and he'd thrown out a clunky brass bracelet that he didn't think was as pretty as she deserved. "That's sweet. You sure you're going to give it to me, though?"

"It's wrapped and on your side of the bed."

Pree heard him breathe. She wanted his arms around her, she wanted to sleep against his chest. "I'm sorry. I should have called you."

"As long as you're okay."

Pree watched Kate, still climbing, halfway up now.

"I'm good."

"Come home soon, okay?" Flynn said. "I mean, no hurry, but hurry anyway."

Pree hugged the phone against her chest after she hung up. Kate was almost to her now. Pree wasn't sure why the anger at Kate still roiled beneath her skin, despite all her efforts to rid herself of it. Kate had obviously done the right thing. She hadn't been ready to be a mother as a child, for whatever reason that Pree would probably never know. Kate had chosen a loving family for her. Pree was the one who had profited most—she'd gotten great parents, a loving home, and a wonderful education. A great start.

A great start that she'd already blown. Anger, quick and hot, moved from being directed at Kate to slicing through her own veins. This was her own fault.

She turned her face to the wind and closed her eyes. Pree's cheeks stung and burned; they were used to neither this sun nor the chilled breeze. She fingered the zipper on her backpack, suddenly desperate to slap a sticker someplace, but where? The cypress trees behind her wouldn't hold one. They would curl up on the gravel of the path. She saw a bench occupied by a guy and his big red dog farther down the path, and got a sticker ready inside her bag, peeling the corner back.

Was it silly, to still be so addicted to her slaps? Was it childish, something like mac 'n' cheese from the box, not good for her, but too hard to give up? Sometimes Pree suspected it might be. The stickers reminded her of late nights in high school, hiding in underpasses, cars angled out so that if CHP rolled past they could be out and gone before the cop flipped a bitch. They reminded her of the fumes of her friends' paint on the wind and the way the sun crept up over pieces that were gorgeous and monstrous at the same time and the calls that went with tagging: *Run, stop, fuck,* GO, GO, *fuck, do it,* GO!

While Pree watched Kate climb, she reminded herself again that Kate was the one who'd put her on this road. She should be grateful. She was who she was because of where and with whom she'd grown up, right? If Marta hadn't loved her so hard in junior high when she'd honestly thought there was no one uglier or more pathetic than she was, when she thought the acne would never go away and that she'd be a social pariah forever, who knows which way she might have turned? And if Isi hadn't told her, over and over again, that she had talent as an artist, that it was something she should pursue, she might have thought she had no ability when in reality she just hadn't had enough practice. She might have given up on the one thing she loved more than anything except them. She might work in retail, taking credit card payments for thin Mongolian cashmere sweaters in some store in LA instead of being a working artist. She got paid to doodle on a computer. All thanks to Kate, right?

Kate, who looked so small. She was working hard at making it all the way up. "You're almost there!" Pree finally called to her. Kate smiled at her, and from there, looking down at her, Pree could see the crooked part in Kate's hair, the way she had a thick cowlick at the crown of her head. She reached up and felt her own matching one.

Or maybe, without the moms, if she'd been raised in some Republican heartland family in Iowa, she would still have had the acne and would have brought herself out of depression on her own. She still would have been drawing, watching the shapes grow under her pen. She would have fallen in love with street art even if the roads nearby were narrower and cleaner. She would still have been Pree, because of the genes she carried.

She would still have fallen in love with Flynn. She would still have fucked up, getting herself pregnant too young, too early.

Kate dropped to the sand next to her, as out of breath as Pree had been.

"I always regret going down there right at the halfway mark coming up." She coughed, clearing her throat. "I tell myself I'll never do it again." She raised her fingers to her lips, as if she'd been going to say more.

"It's been a long time since you were here."

Kate nodded.

"Since before Robin died." Pree didn't phrase it as a question.

"Yes."

"Are you glad? Now?" Pree regretted the longing in her voice, but it was too late—it was already out there, the stupid emotion mingling with the wind.

Kate clapped her hands together, smacking the sand off them. For one terrible moment Pree wondered if she wouldn't say anything, wouldn't respond. Then she turned slightly and took Pree's salt-sticky hands in hers.

"I have never been more glad of anything in all my life."

Pree felt warmed, as if Kate had draped a blanket over her shoulders. She heard one quiet lemon-colored word in her head. *Yes.*

Chapter Twenty-eight

Thursday, May 15, 2014
10:45 a.m.

When Kate and Pree started walking again, Pree turned to the right, back the way they came instead of keeping going around the inner loop. That was fine—anything Pree wanted was fine. Their togetherness seemed thin and fragile, and while Pree probably didn't know it, Kate knew, if asked, she'd let her have anything she desired. Money—she'd write a check without hesitation. Her Saab—link to Robin be damned, she'd hand Pree the keys without hesitation. The house—Pree could move in, bring her boyfriend and all her favorite artists, every stoner she knew, and they could turn the living room into a rave space and rip out the backyard to build a clay studio, and Kate would help.

Pree could ask Kate to leave her alone (forever, even), and Kate would do it.

So turning right instead of left on the trail was easy.

A big, ugly orange dog tore past them and doubled back, knocking the back of Kate's right knee with a hefty head butt. "Hey!"

The dog took no notice, racing past Pree and then around her again. Pree laughed as he leaped onto a fallen eucalyptus trunk, climbed to the end, and brayed into the wind.

"Fred Weasley!"

Nolan's voice. It was Nolan's voice, blue as the sky, raised in a shout.

And there, impossibly, standing on the trail in front of her, his chest stuck out the way it did when he felt defensive or scared, was Nolan.

"Holy shit," said Kate.

"Fred!" Nolan yelled, making Kate jump. "Come!"

"Fred Weasley," Kate whispered.

"Following commands isn't his strong point," said Nolan. "Fred, come!" Instead, the dog tore around the cypress trees behind Kate and Pree and disappeared down a dune.

"You . . ."

Before Kate could finish her thought, before she could even figure out what the thought might become, Fred ran back into sight, raced toward them, and promptly blasted into Pree's knees, knocking her over into the sand.

"*Fuck*," said Nolan. "I'm sorry! He's harmless!"

"Jesus, Pree. Are you okay?" Kate knelt next to her.

Pree sat up, brushing sand off her elbows. She gave a laugh of delight as Fred stuck his nose under her chin and then barreled off again. "He's fun. And cute."

"That hideous beast is not cute," said Kate. Fury filled her along with relief that she recognized the emotion, knew the anger for what it was. "Fred *Weasley*?" She stood, brushing the sand from her jeans with rapid, brutal strokes. "You stole that."

"What?"

"Don't play dumb with me. Did you *follow* us here? What's your dog's name?"

"What are you doing here?" he countered.

"What are *we* doing here? Bullshit. What is your dog's name?"

"You heard me." Nolan's voice was low.

"You stole that name."

Nolan shook his head. "I didn't. It was as much mine as it was yours. You could have gotten an orange dog, too, you know."

"That was Robin's name. And you're *allergic.* I was going to get a dog someday . . . I had that name reserved." Her voice broke. "You don't deserve it. You have no right."

He ignored her glare and leaned over the girl. "You sure you're all right?" He turned his head and looked for Fred Weasley, who was still careering up and down the dunes. "My dog's an idiot. And clumsy."

"He seems nice. Just fast," said Pree.

"I'm Nolan Monroe," he said.

Kate jumped in before Pree could speak. "What are you doing here?"

"Oh, c'mon, Kate. I'm walking my dog. On *my* beach."

No, she didn't believe it. There were no coincidences. He must have followed them, and if he'd done that . . . "Were you at the house?"

Nolan opened his mouth as if to answer, then turned his head in the direction of a wild yelp. Fred flew through the trees, partway down the sandy trail toward the water and then back up. He barreled back toward them just as a small brown terrier ran through the trees. With a growl, the terrier threw itself at Fred and the two dogs snapped, clacking teeth and frothing spit.

Nolan launched himself toward them. "Fred, no!"

It escalated quickly as the terrier's owner, a woman wearing pale pink sweats, ran around the path's curve into sight. She yelled, "No, no! Rosie bites!"

The terrier was now attached to Fred's front paw. Fred spun and tried to shake the other dog loose while Nolan came in closer, Pree just behind him. A brindled boxer drawn by the noise jumped into the melee.

Kate yelled, "Pree, don't!"

"Grab them by the back legs," said Nolan. "Back legs! Then pull!"

The noise was terrifying, vicious growls marking the battle. Nolan and Pree lunged together, Nolan grabbing the boxer by the back legs, Pree taking the terrier. That left Fred still barking, confused. Fred bared his teeth and aimed at the smaller dog, but Pree whirled at the wrong time and Fred's mouth grazed Pree's ankle instead. She yelped, but kept hold of the terrier while kicking Fred away.

"Fuck! I'm sorry!" yelled Nolan. "Did he bite you?"

"Back up," said Kate. "Pree, get out of there!"

The woman in the pink sweats grabbed her dog out of Pree's hands. "I told you, she bites!"

Nolan flung the boxer away from him and lurched forward to take Fred by the collar. The fight was over as quickly as it had started. Pree looked white but stood in place. "It's okay."

"It's *not* okay," said Nolan. He shook Fred. "What the fuck, dog?" He snapped the leash on Fred's collar and tied him quickly to a low branch on the cypress.

"Are you hurt? Did he get you?"

"No," said Pree. "His mouth brushed me but he didn't bite. Just slobbered a little."

Nolan said, "I'm so sorry. I can't tell you how sorry I am.

I'll never walk him off-leash again." He looked at Kate. "He almost bit your . . . your daughter."

The word floated in front of them.

"That dog obviously loves off-leash. You can't do that," said Pree, who was staring at Fred, who was sitting patiently on his leash under the tree. "He's a nice dog."

Nolan said, "You don't know him."

"*Is* he a nice dog?" she asked.

"The nicest dog in the world."

"You're . . ." Pree started. "You're him. Robin's father."

The sentence buzzed like neon. Kate realized Pree hadn't meant to make them both jerk upright the way they did. Her voice, soft and a little unsteady, sounded merely as if she were trying out the words.

"You're Kate's daughter." Nolan, too, was practicing saying it. It was a challenge directed at Kate, but she kept her eyes on a plastic bag caught in the cypress just above his head. It snapped, shredded and brittle. "She had you in those years we were apart."

Pree nodded.

"Jesus, Kate. I had a *Chia Pet* then."

"It's what I was . . . what I was trying to tell you yesterday."

Nolan lifted an eyebrow and strode past her. He held out his hand. "I want to introduce myself again. I'm Nolan Monroe."

"I'm Pree Carleton."

Kate's daughter and her ex-husband shook hands. No, she would think of it in the right words: Kate watched her daughter, Pree, shake hands with her father. Kate shivered in the damp fog. "We should talk," she said.

Nolan looked at her. "You think?"

"Come over."

"Now?" A challenge colored his voice cobalt. "Come to the house now?"

Kate stood straighter. "Not now. Tonight. For dinner." They could talk, all of them. This would be the time. She would finally be able to put this right (if right were a thing that could actually happen, could actually come out of all of this). Nolan hadn't asked who Pree's father was. But soon, so soon, he'd ask.

And Kate would make it right. She'd correct the lies, all of them. Even if it pushed Pree and Nolan away forever—and it would, of course—she would make things right. Finally.

Chapter Twenty-nine

Thursday, May 15, 2014
10:45 a.m.

Nolan walked last, behind the two women. That determined walk—they both had it. Their feet landed fully and pushed off the sand purposefully. They were practically the same height, Kate and Pree, Pree only an inch or so taller, and if Pree's curls weren't so vividly colored and just a bit shorter, their hair would be almost identical.

The cold salt wind slapped against his cheeks.

The last time Kate and he had been here together was two weeks before Robin had come home from USF for the last time. He'd been sleeping off a new medicine in his hospital bed and the health aide assigned to him said he wouldn't wake for hours and that she'd stay with him every minute—she said they should go out, do something together. In unspoken agreement, they came to the beach. Once they were down the trail, on the sand, the waves crashing in, sending cold spray against their faces, Kate had started to run south, her feet bare, her curls tangling in the wind. Nolan chased her, never trying to stop her, just trying to keep up. A half mile, maybe a mile down the beach, she'd veered right, dashing into the waves.

No one swam here. No one surfed here. The tides were too dangerous, the current too strong. She knew it. She'd told Robin a million times it wasn't safe for him to go in.

Nolan had gone after her. She'd battled the waves, but they beat her backward, relentlessly, until he could catch her, putting his arms around her. They fell twice on their way back in, huge waves knocking them over, but Nolan hadn't broken his hold on her. Not once. She wasn't going anywhere without him, and sure as hell neither of them was going without Robin.

He'd been so furious by the time he'd dragged her out that he'd released her to the sand and moved away from her, many yards, before dropping down himself. He'd breathed hard, trying to figure out what to say to her when he could finally speak again.

Kate had gotten up, dripping water and tears, and had walked up and slapped him across the face as hard as she could. She'd never hit him before and later told him she'd never hit another human being in her life. "You shouldn't have," she said, her voice breaking.

"Shouldn't have saved you?" Nolan rubbed his cheek and tried to look around her, anywhere but at her face. "Screw you."

"Shouldn't have let me have him in the first place, just to lose—" She'd sobbed, dropping to her knees, then rolling to her side, still streaming water.

He'd gathered her to himself, cradling her sand-coated

form in his lap, and they'd sat there in the cold wind until both of them were shaking so hard they could hardly drag themselves up the path to the car. They'd never spoken of it, not a word. And they'd never come back here together as a family.

Kate had had another child. She'd kept the fact from him somehow. Why? That's what escaped him entirely. But there would be time for that later.

Now he walked behind her daughter.

Chapter Thirty

Thursday, May 15, 2014
7 p.m.

It was weird, all of it. Not bad weird. It actually felt good, Pree thought. Just odd. The three of them, in this big backyard in Oakland, grilling burgers. Just like anyone else, just as Pree had done about a million times with the moms growing up. As if it was normal.

And even stranger, they were small-talking as if there was nothing so fucking bizarre as an evening where you sat down with your biological mother and the man who caused your half brother's death. But that's how it had gone since Nolan had knocked on the front door, since he and Kate had done that weird step-shuffle dance in the foyer. Pree assumed it was the first time he'd been to the house since the trial—or maybe it was since Robin died? Was that why Kate kept looking at him like he was something breakable she was about to drop on a tiled floor?

At least out here in the backyard, if Kate dropped him, he'd fall only onto soft grass, of which there was so *much*. A swath of it rolled out from the edge of the small porch like a putting green, running to the edge of the trees that lined the yard space. The fading sunlight cut through the tops of the trees, and a songbird sang its heart out in the golden light. So many trees, thought Pree, craning her neck to look up. It was like a dang nature preserve, right here in the middle of town. There were so many trees and bushes that even now that she knew where the sky blue tub was, she couldn't see it from where she sat, hidden behind the hydrangea as it was. It was a property that money had bought.

At home, in LA, Marta and Isi had never had that much money. Their 1920s bungalow had old, warped windows and an attic full of spiders that Isi hated to spray. They'd taken Pree camping instead of to Disneyland—cheaper, she knew, but Pree'd honestly thought there was nothing better than sleeping on the beach, listening to the waves as she fell asleep. She bet Robin had gone to Disneyland plenty of times, but she didn't envy him, not at all.

Pree slipped out of her shoes under cover of the picnic table and curled her toes into the grass. It was perfect, cool and springy. Kate had to have a gardener, didn't she? The woman barely did dishes—Pree couldn't imagine her keeping the outdoors so neat.

As if he'd heard her, Nolan said, "You kept the yard guy, huh?"

Kate nodded as she took the last burger off the grill. Pree wondered if she'd always done the grilling, or if it was something she took over after Nolan left. He looked awkward, moving his hands as if he wanted something to do.

"He's good. He's online now, even the payment system. So—"

"So you never have to see him. Do you need pepper?"

Kate smiled and shook her head. "Why do in person what you can do on the computer, right?"

Pree opened her hamburger bun and added a bit more mustard, then wiped the knife on the side of her plate. So far they'd talked about the weather (a touch crisp, but with a promise of sun on the weekend), Kate's health (good, she was getting fewer headaches now, thanks), and Pree's job. *I like my coworkers,* she'd said, feeling a twist in her stomach at the thought of Jimmy, which only got more painful at the follow-up thought of Flynn. She'd been gone from the house a whole night and a day. Now, going into the second night away from home, she knew she should go back, but Pree just wanted to sit here, on a wooden bench, on a mild spring evening in Oakland, watching the colors change in the sky. Kate and Nolan and she had things to say—she could feel them underneath everything they said—but there was time. It wasn't even full dusk yet.

"Damn, forgot drinks. Wine?" asked Kate. "Nolan, white?"

Nolan looked surprised. "Oh. Yeah. White's good."

"Pree?"

"No, thanks."

"Sure?"

A nod. Of course. Pree wasn't sure of anything, though.

"Can I help you?" Nolan asked. It was a thin excuse.

Kate nodded, and Nolan followed her inside.

They kept their voices down at first, but the side window of the kitchen was open—Pree doubted Kate had noticed or they would have been whispering. If she held her breath, she could catch almost every word.

"I still can't believe you followed us." Kate's voice was lipstick red.

"I told you already, I was going there anyway."

"You were watching us?"

"We go to the beach every week on one of my days off."

"You go with your dog with the stolen name."

"You wanna talk about Fred Weasley?"

"Let's," she said. "You know he died? In *The Deathly Hallows*? Does that make it an even better name? What right do you have—"

"I have no right. I know that better than anyone." Nolan's voice was suddenly outraged. "But what about you, Kate? A daughter? You have a fucking *daughter*?"

Another silence and then Nolan said, "Whose is she?"

Kate's answer was quick. "It was when . . . in college. Before you came back."

"She's not mine?" A pause. "I'm sorry, but I have to ask. She looks too young. She's only, what, nineteen? Twenty? You're *sure* she's not mine?"

She couldn't hear what Kate said in response to him.

"Jesus . . ." Nolan said. "That guy, Greg what's his name."

Kate moved away from the window, saying something Pree couldn't make out, then said, "It always comes back to that, doesn't it?"

Nolan's voice went darker, shaded dark purple with something that sounded like regret. "When I found you again, so long ago, everything made sense. And you know what? I never kept a secret from you in my whole life."

"You know that's not true." A *pop* of a cork exiting a bottle. "You didn't tell me the story of every girl you fucked while we were apart. You didn't tell me their names, or where they lived, or what you liked best to do to them because you knew I didn't want to know. We didn't talk about that time. We promised we wouldn't."

"I would have if you'd asked me. I would have told you every single thing you wanted to know."

"Well, me, too. If you'd asked."

"No, you wouldn't have. That moratorium on speaking about the past was your idea." A barked laugh of pained anger. "Jesus, Kate. I was supposed to ask if you'd had a *baby* while we were apart? Was I supposed to be able to tell? And then, oh, god. The whole time . . . when you were pregnant with Robin, and I thought it was a miracle, and that no one had ever gone through something as beautiful before, and *you'd already had a child*? How could you?"

It sounded as if Kate took a shuddered breath. "I had a *life* without you, Nolan. I was so young then, but I had a life. Just like you did. We both have our secrets."

With shaking hands, Pree reached into her back pocket and pulled out a slap, sliding it under the top of the picnic table. She pressed it on over the bumps of wood, over the splintered cracks. She hoped it wouldn't drop off later when the fog rolled in and curled its edges, leaving it to blow away in tomorrow's wind.

"I just didn't—"

"I don't know who you are."

Kate said something Pree couldn't hear.

"Maybe you're right," said Nolan, sounding defeated. "Yeah, maybe you're right."

Pree ached for them. Floating from their voices was this . . . thing. She recognized it. When Isi and Marta fought—when they *really* fought—the very rare nights when something made one or the other so mad they couldn't see straight, and they argued in low tones in their room until dawn—this was how it felt.

But with Isi and Marta, no matter how sad they got, she knew—and maybe it was childish, but she still believed it—they belonged to each other. They weren't going anywhere. Under the fear and anger there was always that absolute bedrock of peace, and through the emotion, she'd dive down and sit on that foundation until one or the other remembered it and joined Pree down there, and they'd wait for the last one (usually Isi, of course) to come around. It seemed Kate and Nolan had that, too. As if they were in love or something. But also as if they were really, really fucked up.

Pree exhaled, pushing her palms into the table, looking at her nails with the chipped blue polish. It was bad enough that she had this decision to make, that she was carrying it every minute of the day. This, all of this, was too much. Too heavy for her hands, her shoulders to support. She couldn't take Kate's hunger another minute, couldn't take the way Kate stared at her, as if she'd been starved for years and Pree was her first meal. Kate had been nothing but awesome today, taking her to the beach, bringing her back to the house, and tucking her in for a nap, for chrissake. And Pree had taken it, had accepted it as her strange due. The prodigal child returns. Kate had gone to the store while Pree slept. The bottle of wine she'd shown Pree when she woke definitely wasn't a brand the moms bought at Trader Joe's. The meat itself had cost thirty dollars, according to the sticker on the wrapper. Who spent thirty dollars on hamburger steak?

And now a little family dinner. In the backyard. No. She wasn't ready for this. Yet.

Pree moved quickly, her hands fumbling inside her backpack. She took out another sticker and scrawled, "Sorry, I'll call you later." She attached it to the edge of her plate. Then, thinking ahead, she took a large bite of her burger. Even if she didn't want to eat with them, it was a shame to waste such good food. She shoved another huge bite into her mouth and hiked her backpack onto her shoulder.

Then she careened down the small hill, past the tub, pushing her way through a stand of oleander until she emerged on the road. It was only half a mile to BART. She could be home in an hour. Home with Flynn. She could fill her new paint box.

Chapter Thirty-one

Thursday, May 15, 2014
7:30 p.m.

Kate should have told him. Fuck, she knew she should have. But wasn't that the whole problem? That she'd *never* told him?

Nolan pointed at the half-eaten burger. "At least she ate something."

Kate supposed it shouldn't have been such a surprise that Pree took off. It had been a huge day for all of them. But it jolted her, seeing that sticker on her plate, her absence at the picnic table when they finally came back out.

Kate nodded and clutched the stem of her wineglass. In the growing dark, the kitchen light glowed through the open window. She pointed. "She must have been able to hear us."

Nolan frowned and spoke around his burger. "We didn't say anything she shouldn't have heard."

No, they hadn't. How much worse would it have been if Kate had told the truth? She'd meant to tell him. She'd had every intention of doing so. She was going to say, *Nolan, she's your daughter.* The words had been right there on the tip of her tongue. In the kitchen, she could have reached out and touched his cheek, right there where the stubble started. She could have said, *She's your daughter. I'm so sorry, love.* That's what she'd hoped she'd be strong enough to do. Tell him first, lead him back outside, and tell Pree.

Instead, she'd let Nolan believe that Pree was younger than she was. Another lie. To protect him. To keep him from pain. Jesus, how long could this go on? Now that she'd failed, would she have to maintain vigilance? Keep them separate forever? It was almost a relief that Pree had left. Nolan, in making small talk, would have probably asked something awful: whether she wanted to go to college or what Pree wanted to major in. Kate's lie wouldn't have held up for even an hour.

Kate drank her wine too quickly and she felt it go to her head.

"Eat your burger," Nolan urged in his it's-good-for-you voice. He'd used that exact tone to cajole Robin into drinking his protein shakes how many times? Hundreds?

Kate picked up her burger and then set it down again. She wasn't hungry. It was possible she'd never feel like eating again. "I'll just keep it for later."

"Then you'll never eat it."

He was interrupted by the beeping of Kate's cell phone.

"Pree," said Kate, digging frantically in her pocket. But it wasn't a text from Pree—it was from Vanessa. Probably something about the art show. She clicked to open the message.

> *Nolan's on TV, channel 7. You should watch.*

"Nolan." She stared at him. "What did you do?"

"Nolan!" The unseen man's shout came from behind them, from the driveway. "Nolan Monroe! Are you here? Can we ask you a few questions? Kate? Are you out there?"

Kate and Nolan stared at each other. Only a certain kind of person yelled like that, with that much authority. Without discussion, they bolted for the house, leaving the plates and wineglasses behind, slamming the kitchen door behind them.

"What did you *do?*" Kate said again, her voice only a breath.

Nolan bit his bottom lip. "Shit."

There were three news vans parked in front of Kate's house, and if she wasn't mistaken another crew was just down the street filming at the corner. After seeing the segment on Channel 7, it made sense. It was a short piece, but even Kate could see it was powerful, the way Nolan's face had turned to raw pain as the reporter sucker punched him with the surprise twist, the way he'd stumbled backward into his apartment (that ratty apartment, was that really where he lived?).

They were a hot story again. There had been so many reporters after Robin died, and this had the potential for being even bigger. Every media outlet loved a follow-up. "Where Are They Now?" segments sold papers. A reporter had actually told her that once, to her face. *If I could just do a follow-up piece on you, it could be huge. I might even get a promotion.* Why on earth would Kate have cared if a reporter advanced her career? For opening her private box of demons? No, she didn't think that would be good idea, she'd said, and when the woman had shoved a microphone in her face anyway, she'd let loose a string of expletives so filthy not one could have been aired on cable.

Nolan pulled the curtain back an inch to peek out again.

"Careful," said Kate. "Don't let it move too much—"

Too late. They'd seen the motion.

"Mr. Monroe! Is it true you're reconciling with your wife?" one shouted in a voice loud enough to be heard through the glass.

Another one yelled, "What do you say to the people who still think you're the children's Kevorkian? Was it really accidental?"

"Will you have another child?" shouted the one knocking at the door.

Nolan stood still, only his fists moving as they clenched in rhythm with his jaw.

"It's okay," said Kate. "We'll just wait them out. They always leave eventually." She needed to hold herself together. For just a little while longer. "Why don't you sit? For a while." Her voice shook and she hoped he didn't hear it.

Nolan sat on the couch politely, as if it were a social visit. "If you don't mind, then yeah. I'll wait the fuckers out."

Together. They were waiting out the reporters again. Together. The surprise Kate felt was deep and cold, as if she'd plunged into a river without knowing she'd jumped.

"Do you want another drink?" The words were automatic. Kate's shock over the news piece had made her almost forget the terror she carried for twenty-two years of Pree and Nolan meeting. But it had happened. And the world hadn't exploded, the sun hadn't rained molten lava.

But then again, the fear had been based on Nolan finding out who Pree actually was. And neither of them knew the truth. Yet.

Nolan nodded. "No more wine, though. Just water."

The glass she gave him was from the set he'd bought her after she'd clumsily broken most of their glassware—it was thick plastic with cheery yellow daisies on the side. He'd told her they were Kate-proof, so she'd refused to use them out of principle. It was only after he was gone that she started to enjoy them, liking the way water tasted out of them.

"Thank you." A pause. "I thought, if we met up again, that I'd do nothing but apologize. For years, maybe . . ." He trailed off. Kate heard what he didn't say. *I didn't expect I'd have something to be angry about.* It was only right he was angry. And he didn't even know the worst part of it all.

"It looks so different in here," Nolan said slowly. "But I don't know why. The furniture's all the same, and the pictures are the same, mostly. That one's new." He gestured at the painting behind her. It was a prototype for a commission she'd done last year; she'd been happy enough with it to keep and hang it. A hydrangea. It was Robin's favorite flower, but it barely looked like one: it was a gray-and-black landscape, bleak in its emptiness.

"It doesn't look like you," he said, peering more closely at it. "There's no . . ."

She waited for him to say "color."

"There's no joy."

All her biggest sales came after she went monochromatic. Maybe losing her father so long ago had made her a master of grays and browns. She'd seen the world that way, after all, after his funeral, hadn't been able to see color for months. She'd been struck color-blind by grief, even though the doctor her mother took her to had said it was impossible. People's voices lacked depth and truth without their colors. Her vision's palette had come back slowly, first the yellow family burning faintly through the grays, followed by blues and finally reds.

Kate tugged on her diamond stud. She'd bought the earrings for herself after her first really large sale. "I got a review in the *New York Times*. Did you know that?" Of course he didn't. "They called me 'commercially successful.'"

"Um . . ."

"And I quote: 'Technically talented but unequivocally soulless.'"

"Shit." Nolan tilted his head to the side and continued looking at it. "I still like it. But I have to admit it's hard for me to look at."

She understood.

He turned his head. "There are more books on the shelf, but that's not what's different. I can't put my finger on it."

Kate almost hated to tell him. "The ceiling."

"Oh, *man*. That's it."

The color blindness happened again after Robin died. The doctor was wrong; it wasn't impossible. It was a relief, actually, to not have to process beauty. It felt right to not be able to understand dull gray words. When colors finally started to bleed back into her vision, slowly, she'd painted the ceilings with each hue as it came to her, as if rewarding herself. She'd been obsessed at one point, long before, with the idea of painting the ceilings. She'd wanted to leave the walls white and have color floating above, but Nolan hadn't ever gotten on board with the idea. He believed in traditional colors on walls; he wanted white, boring, bland ceilings. After her son's death, when she looked at her easel, her mind went quietly blank. But she'd needed a paintbrush in her hand, even if it was a heavy, thick one. She hadn't used a roller—she'd just stood on the ladder and painted every ceiling downstairs a different color, working into the small hours until her arm shook. Her favorite was in the kitchen—it was the pale green of spring grass. The same color as Pree's voice, down to the exact shade, she realized now.

Kate hardly noticed the ceilings anymore, but she felt them. They warmed rooms that had desperately needed warming once she was so alone. But when she'd gone back to her real work, her painting was monochromatic, as if she'd used up her allowance of color on the house.

"I was wrong about that," Nolan said. "It looks great."

Kate inclined her head. "Thanks." If she held up her hands, she'd be able to feel the invisible, unsaid words, to push them around, move them out of her way. *Banal. Stick to banal.* "How are your parents?"

Nolan looked at her and she could almost read on his face the words he wanted to say. *You lied to me. You never told me about her. You* lied. But instead he said, "Fine. Still in Maui. Dad had gout, but it's better. They don't e-mail you?"

"I haven't even gotten a Christmas card in years."

"Oh. Well, they never were—"

"No," Kate agreed. Her feelings had been crushed when Robin's grandparents were so heartbroken they couldn't even return an e-mail, but she tried never to dwell on it. "They weren't."

"How's Sonia?"

She felt a sudden, stabbing pain behind her right eye. "She died. Last year." There had to be a better way to say it, but there it was. "I'm going to spread her ashes on Saturday. I'm not sure how I'll . . . I've hired a boat." *Tell him about taking the rest of Robin's ashes, too. Tell him. Tell him you'll be able to do it. Make yourself believe it.*

"Christ, Kate." His eyes went wide, filled with real sorrow. "I'm so sorry."

She shrugged. "It happens. She fell and got a bleed in her brain. Or maybe the bleed made her fall. They never did figure it out. She was in the ICU for two months and she didn't wake up again." Her casual words were belied by the way her voice shook.

"Kate."

She would *not* let him make her cry. "Anyway." A silence

hung in the room for a long, crystalline moment. On an exhale, she said, "I'm taking Robin, too."

Nolan's body became absolutely still. "You did the first funeral without me."

Nervous chills danced along Kate's spine. This was important. Maybe this was why he was here. "That's why I'm telling you. Meet me at the Berkeley marina at ten, and you can come. I mean, I'm inviting you."

"Mighty big of you."

Anger snapped through her, unbidden but welcome. "Oh, I was supposed to wait *years* to bury my son? For you to get out of prison?"

His voice was soft, but strong. "You can start by telling me how I never fucking knew you had a daughter." She'd never heard this particular tone of voice from Nolan, and she would have sworn that she'd heard every color his voice could possibly take over the years. This was different, the cold confusion an iridescent blue-gray like the cold winter fog when it crept over the hills.

Panic spread through her veins. He'd have to learn the truth sometime, but Kate wasn't ready yet. *Not ready, not ready.*

"Does he know? That Greg guy?" His tone was darker gray with blackened edges.

"No." A pounding started at her temples. God, she was bad at lying. But the consequences of not lying were too terrible to contemplate. Fear gripped her, the same fear she'd felt so long ago. "I never saw him again."

Nolan kept his body still and his voice low. "You got pregnant, gave the baby away, and never, ever once thought to mention it to me? Even when you were pregnant with our son? Why should I believe that you didn't lie about every other thing we had together?" Nolan blinked hard, lines gathering at the corners of his eyes and disappearing again as he fixed her with his bewildered stare.

But there it was—she saw it. He believed her. Relief filled her.

Nolan went on, "How could you do that to us? Pretend like that? Your pregnancy was the happiest time of my life until Robin was born, and then everything got even better."

Kate realized she *had* lied to Nolan, in the most fundamental way possible, for many years. She wasn't a bad liar then; she was a *good* one. A small weight lifted. "In my mind, Robin was my first. I tried to forget that whole chapter of my life. We had started a new life." How could she make this clearer to him? Their new life was the end of her old one.

"But Robin . . ."

"Had a sister. Half sister," she corrected herself quickly. "I know."

"He would have loved that. He was always asking—"

"I *know*," Kate repeated. She picked up a ballpoint pen from the coffee table and twisted it in her fingers, loosening it, then tightening it back up. A piece of metal dropped from it, skittering across the carpet noiselessly.

"How could you not tell me?"

Kate said nothing. She was at bottom. This was the lowest she could go. And maybe that was why the question she'd never quite been able to ask him, the one that had filled her mouth so many times until she could have chewed the words, finally—finally—came out as if torn from her body. "How could you take him from me?"

Nolan gasped, and then said, "*My* son, Kate. Robin was my son, too."

"That makes it better?" God, why hadn't she asked him this then? Why hadn't she railed at him, beating him with her fists back *then*? She'd wanted to. More than anything, she'd wanted to. Nolan had *lived.* She remembered wishing through her blinding fury that he hadn't. That he'd finished the terrible job he'd started. He'd tried to leave her. He'd wanted to leave her all alone in her pain. Alone. Which he'd done anyway.

Nolan said, "He was dying."

"But he wasn't dead."

Nolan was white around the eyes. "I told you a million times how sorry I was. I'll tell you a million more times how sorry I am. But I'm not sorry he isn't in pain anymore. That he got where he was going that much sooner."

Kate felt the tears well, and she hated herself for it. She was weak. Exposed, in front of the person who knew her best. *You left me,* she almost said. *How could you want to kill yourself, too? You said you'd never leave me.* "Robin didn't *get* anywhere. He was just gone."

"He comes to me, you know." Nolan's voice lost the bewildered gray and was back to its normal dark blue.

"No." It was impossible. Too unfair to contemplate. "He doesn't."

"I see him in my dreams."

"I don't believe you." Kate's only dreams about Robin had been awful corporeal ones right after he died, fleshy dreams in which she touched his clammy skin, knowing he was dead, moving his arms and legs, giving him CPR, kissing his cold blue mouth. Just a few months earlier, she'd dreamed that she was touching Robin and that, finally, he was warm. She woke in a panic to save him, to find she was wrapped around Esau so tightly he was pulling at the sheets to get away from her. It was the last time she'd slept with him.

"And it's like he's there. Like he's just been in another room." Nolan looked directly into her eyes. Now *he* was lying. She'd always been able to tell—his face became more controlled, almost perfectly still, and he tapped his fingers in that way he did when he was nervous—*tap tap tap*—on something, anything that was close. "He tells me he's always around."

For a moment there was nothing but the sound of their mingled breathing, as harsh as if they'd been running. Then her cell phone rang. The song she'd programmed it to play, "Blue" by Lucinda Williams, was too intimate, telling him a secret she didn't intend to tell.

Kate stood. She didn't recognize the number. "I have to get this." No matter who it was, she was grateful to the caller. She walked into the kitchen before hitting the button to answer.

"Is this Kate Monroe?"

"Yes." She didn't recognize the voice.

"Carey Pike, with Channel 7. I interviewed your husband last night. How are you responding to the news about him?"

"Ex-husband. Pardon?"

"Did you hear he saved a man's life yesterday?"

"I was with him when he did the CPR. I helped him." She'd helped the man who'd let her son die. And she'd do it again. Of course she would.

"So you're confirming that you've reconciled with the man responsible for the death of your child?"

Kate hung up, regretting that all it took was a click of a red button. She wanted to be able to throw it into its cradle, to hang up with fury, with a bang, rather than just a quiet beep. Lucinda's song was stuck in her head now, *I don't wanna talk. I just wanna go back to blue.*

"I'm sorry," said Nolan from behind her.

She hadn't heard him enter the kitchen. "I'd forgotten what they were like." *We don't talk about heaven, and we don't talk about hell.*

"Kate. I'm sorry."

"How could you talk to him?"

"He tricked me."

She sighed and leaned against the edge of the stove, the handle squeaking the way it always had. "Remember the time the one woman found me in the locker room at the gym and pretended to need a ride home so she could get in my car and take those photos of the inside? I really thought her car had broken down."

Nolan jammed his fingers through his hair and made it stick straight up. She'd always been a sucker for that look of his. Then he closed his eyes for a moment, and she remembered how he used to do that, to hide there, behind his eyelids, as he thought. "I still think we should have sued over that."

"Like we needed more time in court. And I would have had to do it alone. Besides, the one thing we learned was that they get tired of the same subject fast. In a day or two they'll be gone again."

Nolan picked up the pink hula girl saltshaker he'd bought her at a barn sale when they'd taken a leaf-peeping trip back east the year before Robin was born. They'd always thought it was funny that a hula dancer reminded them of Vermont.

"I get e-mails," he said.

"What?" Kate didn't follow the jump in the conversation.

He set the saltshaker down, making the dancer sway gently. "From people. Like us. Who want advice."

It took a moment to sink in. "They want your *help*?"

Nolan nodded.

"For fuck's sake."

"Yeah," he agreed.

"What do you say?" What would Kate say? *Fuck off, fuck you, shit, damn, I'm so sorry, so sorry, sorry sorry sorry no one else understands, I'm sorry . . .*

"Nothing. I just . . . put them in a file."

"You save them?" Kate rolled the hem of her shirt with her fingers.

"I want to respond—I just . . . I just can't."

He'd never been able to send the important e-mails or make the essential phone calls. When Robin was sick, she'd had to write the updates to friends and family. Nolan couldn't physically bring himself to do it. When he'd called his parents in Hawaii to tell them Robin's diagnosis, he had thrust the phone at her so he could throw up in the wastebasket.

"But that, Nolan—it's important." It had been important that she tell Nolan she'd had another child. Fuck, it was important that she tell him he had a daughter. And she didn't do it. Surely this guilt would stop her heart soon and she'd fall to the floor, breath gone forever, the last Monroe to die in this house. And she was on him about *e-mails.*

Nolan didn't say anything, just sighed heavily and sank into his old chair at the kitchen table. She hadn't heard its particular thick-boned creak for years, had forgotten it had one. He scrubbed his face with his hands and then sighed a second time.

"I know," he said. "Why the hell else am I still here? To do road work? To pick up dead raccoons and paint yellow stripes and watch my coworkers jump out of the way of cars like they're playing dodgeball? I thought my friend Rafe's wife was sick, and I wondered if that's why I stayed. To help him. But she's okay, thank god, and that's selfish, isn't it? To think I'm that fucking important? But there has to be a reason, Kate, and I just need to figure out what it is."

He rocked back in his chair, just as he'd always done.

Robin used to worry he'd fall backward, until one day Nolan had done just that, on purpose, to prove he would be okay and instead ended up breaking his wrist. Robin had refused to sign the cast, saying Nolan didn't deserve the attention. Then he'd relented and had drawn a small picture of Hedwig the Owl with crossed eyes on the plaster.

Nolan bowed his head. Then he said, "I'm so sorry, Kate." She knew he wasn't talking about the e-mail anymore. He didn't articulate the full thought, didn't speak all the words. It was all right. She didn't want to hear them again anyway.

Chapter Thirty-two

Thursday, May 15, 2014
10 p.m.

It was Flynn's idea. After he'd held Pree for the ten minutes it took her heart to still, for her to be able to speak to him, he'd listened in that accepting Flynn way as she told him where she'd been for two days. He hadn't been mad. He *should* have been angry, and Pree told him so, but he just shook his head, his soft blond hair falling around his face like a piece of sheer, shiny fabric. "Why would I be mad? You're working some stuff out."

The paint box, a true artist's toolbox, made of steel and oak, was gorgeous. It was a labor of love, everything she'd ever wanted, and nothing she ever would have asked for. It made her love Flynn more desperately, which made her want to run. Pree cursed her own fickleness as she ran her fingers over it again and again.

She thought of Jimmy and how close she'd come to fucking him. She thought of the fetus. Flynn's baby. "Yeah." She pulled the box close to her on the bed again and flicked the clasps. Then she took out a pen she'd already stored inside and reached for her pad. She didn't think—she just moved the pen around the page. Her eyes were open the whole time, but her brain was somewhere else, and suddenly she realized she had a full drawing in front of her. She could barely remember doing it. Her suspender girl was sitting on top of a brick wall staring down at the ground, where a shattered egg with legs lay. The egg's legs were wearing combat boots, just as her girl was.

Pree's hand stopped moving. Had her girl just pushed Humpty? Or was that another part of herself lying on the ground?

"Did she tell you where he was buried?"

Pree started. "What? Robin? Yeah. In a cemetery near her house. Mountain View."

"We should go there."

She reached out and touched his face. That was so Flynn. "That's a great idea. We should. We will."

Flynn slapped his thighs and unfolded himself into his full height. "Let's go."

"Now? It's dark. I'm sure they're closed."

"That makes it even better. Let's go have an adventure." He challenged her with the words that had never failed before—that particular sentence was how they'd ended up hopping a freight train one spring morning in Tulare, how they'd gotten matching penguin tattoos on their ankles, how they'd spelunked for the first time. Those words had been why Pree had applied to a job so out of her reach, and why she'd accepted it when it was offered to her. Since she'd met him, Flynn had been both her challenge and her reason for trying.

Pree directed him, and they got lost only once. Oakland was huge, and the roads around Kate's were confusing as they twisted up and around small treelined hills, but she liked the feel of it, the motion. Flynn, using impressive street smarts, parked in front of a florist shop a block away from the big iron gates at Mountain View Cemetery. "We don't want the license plate to be on camera," he said, his voice electric with excitement.

The gates were high, ornate, and very closed. Pree looked for a security camera, and found it, on the east side. "Let's pretend we're just looking for a make-out spot," she whispered in his ear, and then she realized it wasn't pretend at all, which made it even more fun. It was hard to tell exactly where the camera was aimed and where it wasn't, and she was distracted by Flynn's mouth, his hands . . . *Robin,* she thought. She was here for a bigger reason, not just to kiss this man. And she suddenly wanted to tell Flynn the truth.

"One thing," she started, and then stopped, scared.

He looked at her, and his eyes were all melty and soft and sweet and she almost didn't go through with it.

"I'm pregnant," Pree said.

He grinned, as if she'd made a joke. Then he looked at her face again and the grin melted away. "Oh, shit."

"I know."

Flynn folded like a grasshopper and sat on the curb, then looked up at her, his blond hair gleaming white under the sodium glow of the streetlamp. "What are we going to do?"

Pree loved him fiercely in that moment. He went—always—directly to *we.* "I don't know."

"Do you want . . . ?" he started.

"I don't want a baby."

"Oh." Flynn swallowed, his sharp Adam's apple bobbing in his throat. "An abortion. That's gonna be hard, right?" He reached up and took her hand, holding it tightly. "I'm with you. I'll help in whatever way I can."

Pree sucked in a breath. She hadn't imagined him saying this, hadn't imagined him going along with her so easily. What if Kate had gone to her birth father back then? What if he'd been this helpful? Would Kate have held his hand as the fetus that became Pree was vacuumed out? Who would have fought for her then? "I don't want an abortion, either."

He frowned. "Adoption?"

A pulse beat frantically at Pree's temple. "It worked out in my case, yeah, but it's not what I want for a baby. To be separated from her blood family forever." *Her.* When had the baby become a girl?

"Then . . . what's left?"

She couldn't be angry at him. He was just so earnest. He would believe anything she said, wouldn't he? Why was that so frustrating? Pree shook her head and pulled him up off the sidewalk, going up on tiptoe for a swift kiss. "Let's find Robin."

He stepped closer, taking her hands, pulling her close. She had to crane her neck to look up at his face.

"Okay," he said, his voice soft. "Okay, then." Guilt tasted like Flynn's tongue and the sweet coconut scent that drifted up the street from the tiki bar. Pree tried to lean into the kiss, but incongruously—horribly—she needed to find her brother.

A burst of laughter drifted up from the end of the street and jarred them apart. Flynn touched her chin and repeated, "Okay." Then, smacking his hands together, he said, "Let's *do* this."

He pointed out a place where the two fences joined, hopefully just out of sight of the camera. Without discussing how they'd do it, Flynn hoisted her up and tossed her over as though she weighed nothing. He came over next, landing with a thud. "Oh, yeah. That's what I'm talking about," he said.

"You're pretty good at breaking and entering, huh?"

He had the grace to look a little embarrassed. "Eh. I'm no angel." But there, under the halo of light, next to the wide shooting fountain, which was still lit as if the grounds were open, Flynn, with his blond, floppy hair and beautiful, beautiful face, looked like one.

Was it wrong to wish that he'd gotten upset with her? That he'd chastised her—and himself—for being so careless?

Flynn's gaze slid past her and up the darkened treelined pathways. "This is huge. How do you think . . . ?"

"I have no idea," she said.

They walked under thick boughs of wisteria just in bloom, the fragrance heady and sweet. To the left and right, headstones stretched as far as she could see, flanked by burial vaults of all sizes. As the road wound up the hill, the crypts got bigger, guarded by stone angels and creepy as hell, the old glass broken, open to the elements. Flynn had a small flashlight on his keychain, and they peeked inside one that was labeled *Barton-Sykes*. Pree fully expected to see bones—a whole skeleton laid out inside, leaves trapped in the chest cavity—but instead there were just two stone boxes, one on either side, faded fake flowers in a plastic vase resting on top of the left one. A Snickers wrapper caught by an eddy of air whirled in the far right corner. It was gorgeous. All of it.

Pree was ready to run, but so far they'd seen no sign of security. She wondered if trespassing was a misdemeanor or a felony. Flynn wound his fingers with hers. "There has to be some kind of organization to this," he muttered, casting his flashlight over to a crypt that looked like a mini-mansion with Ionic columns and a stained-glass door. Then he turned, sending the beam toward a low-slung white building that ran almost a block in length.

"There," said Pree. "Shine it there."

She led them to a small pedestal that kind of resembled an old phone booth if it had been miniaturized and painted white. Inside a small glass door, attached with a length of silver chain, was a laminated book. The pages had rows of tiny numbers matched to names. "Bingo."

Her fingers flipped the pages, Castorini, Foster, Giovans, Lemos . . . Monroe, Monroe, there were two and half pages' worth. Who knew there were so many dead Monroes? Then, there it was. *Robin Monroe. Plot 17.68.*

They cross-referenced it to the attached map, then took off uphill. Something snapped behind them in the building, and even though no lights came on, they ran faster.

Plot 17 was wide and sloped downward on the back of a hill. Five deco crypts stood at the top, but the rest of the plot was filled with plain marble slabs, simple and clean, old deaths lying next to new ones. *Robert Wooster, b. Missouri, 1897.* And next to that, *Agnes Wu, Oakland, 1972.*

Pree scanned the newer ones while she used the moonlight as best she could, but it wasn't enough. Without asking, she slipped Flynn's flashlight from his hands. Carmela Justice died in 1979. Pablo Flint in 1987. Ace "Buster" Neville in 1997. Closer, closer . . .

And then, just like that, the narrow beam played across the name that had been spooling across her mind on repeat. *Robin Isaiah Monroe. 2002–2011. Our Perfect Love.* The slab was tall and thin, almost up to midthigh, and a flower detail trailed downward. No plastic roses here, but Pree spotted something nestled in the grass at the base.

It was a tiny figurine, so small that at first glance it looked like one of those little GI Joe figures. But as Pree knelt to pick it up, she saw it was a teensy Harry Potter, an inch and a half tall, as if Hermione had used the Reducio spell on him. His arms were raised, robes flying behind him, his wand above his head, his features contorted as if he were about to throw down with a Dementor. Goose bumps rose along her arms and legs. A cross was generic. Flowers were silly if they were fresh, and just plain stupid if they were plastic. But this? A tiny, very special boy, casting a spell? Tears ached in the back of her throat, and she put the plastic toy back exactly where she'd found it.

"You okay?"

She nodded. She was. Really, she was. It was just . . . more than she thought it would be, being here. And Flynn was a distraction. She should be using that time to really *be* with Robin. Pree looked sideways up at his face and said simply, "Hey . . ."

Flynn got it, with that one word. "I'm going to go see if I can find the Ghirardelli crypt. A guy at the steelworks told me about it. Maybe there's chocolate inside or something. I'd do that if I were a Ghirardelli. I'd always leave candy on the steps. In a skull-shaped bowl—*yeah.*" He grinned and stuck his hands in his pockets as he ambled away, long-limbed as a giraffe. She heard him whistle low under his breath, a tune she didn't recognize, and rather than being alarmed that a security guard might hear it, she felt better. Not so alone.

She spent a minute looking at the marble as if something would reveal itself to her. More words, perhaps, scrolling across the bottom if she just waited long enough. But nothing. Just his name, the dates, and *Our Perfect Love.* It must have been nice for him to be that to someone, even while he was sick.

She turned, sitting so that her back was against the marble. Was she aligned the same way he was? Were his feet pointing downhill the way hers were? She hoped so. Five years earlier Pree and the moms had gone camping in Yosemite. Pree's tent had been on a slope so gradual she hadn't noticed it until she'd slid downhill all night toward her head. She woke up again and again, her neck twisted, the top of her head pressed against the cold tent wall.

Better to be like this, feet down, face up, looking up at the night, at the fat quarter moon that shone somehow brighter than she'd ever seen it. As an experiment, more to test herself than anything else, she scooted down, easing her butt along the grass until she could lie on her back on top of the grave. She fought a heebie-jeebie horror movie moment as she imagined Robin's skeletal arms exploding out of the ground to wrap around her, pulling her under. Then she dug her fingers into the grass. Just so long as the ground didn't give way beneath her, she was good. She didn't think she could handle falling into a grave, something she'd read once could happen in older graveyards as coffins degraded and the air pockets below collapsed.

She stilled her heart by taking a deep breath, and then one more. As she gazed upward, the fog parted for just a moment, reminding her of someone pulling a cotton ball apart—thinner, thinner, until the fibers slipped against each other and then the two pieces came free. And even with the Oakland lights, the moon gleamed bright at her. It looked down at her, and even though she knew she was perhaps being the most ridiculous girl in the Bay Area at that moment, she let herself imagine that her brother was there, a small little man in the moon, glowing toward her.

A gift.

It was almost like meeting him.

"I don't have anything for you, though," Pree said quietly. "Unless you want a piece of Juicy Fruit, which maybe you liked. I don't know. Or a pen. But what would you do with a pen?"

She lay there another moment, thinking. Then she said, still so softly she could barely hear her own voice, "Hey. I'm pregnant." She paused. "I guess you'd be too young to understand that when you died, but you'd be, what now, twelve? You'd be getting the gist of it by now. And if you were around, and if I knew you, I wouldn't tell you. Obviously. Not unless I was showing, I guess. No one else knows. No one except the guy. I just told him." She paused. It felt silly to talk out loud like this. It also felt right.

"I can't help thinking that if I had a twelve-year-old brother I'd take him to the batting cage or to the arcade or something. Just to forget about it for a minute. Because I *never* forget about it. Not even for a minute." She brushed an ant from the back of her hand. "I wish I'd gotten to meet you, brother." The word felt bittersweet in her mouth, round and heavy with something that could have been.

Then Pree thought of what she could leave behind with Robin. It was so verboten she surprised even herself. But she leaned forward and reached into her backpack anyway.

A normal predrawn slap wouldn't do. She needed to make a new one. She got out her black book to use as a lap desk. From an interior pocket, she pulled a "Hello My Name Is" sticker—she'd had to buy the pack, so it wasn't quite street but it was the most traditional slap, and she was, after all, introducing herself.

Her Pilot squeaked as she dragged it across the paper. She did the *R*s perfectly, sharp and bony. The *A* was a thing of thick, jagged beauty. She just had to nail the *E*—and she did. She almost wanted to save this one for herself. *This* was her tag. She added the swirls below, the two dots above, and the most perfect heart she could possibly draw at the end. She held it out, and in the dimness it was as if she were looking in a mirror.

Pree pulled off the backing and, without looking, reached around and stuck it on the back side of the marble slab.

From below her, she heard a distant engine sound, a tinny clatter, like a stuttering golf cart. Then there was a piercing whistle and Flynn came running. "They saw me! Hit it!"

Pree leaned forward and kissed the top of the stone. Her lips, afterward, tasted like chalk. "Good-bye," she whispered.

Then Flynn took her hand and they ran.

Chapter Thirty-three

Thursday, May 15, 2014
11:15 p.m.

They waited until the coast was clear, until the last news van had pulled reluctantly away after the last newscast. They wouldn't be back, Nolan guessed. They hadn't gotten anything from them, and new atrocities, new tragedies would be waiting for them to report on by noon tomorrow.

When Nolan was leaving Kate's house, at the last minute, at the front door—*his* old front door—Kate reached out a hand and brushed the top of his forearm for a split second before she drew it back. "Wait."

Nolan stopped immediately. He'd do anything she said.

"Can you . . . ?"

He waited. It didn't do to rush Kate, ever.

"Will I see you again?"

For a second Nolan's heart soared so high he could have

touched a satellite if it was going by. *I didn't want to leave you.* He should say it. God, he should say it. "Of course."

"I'd like that." She bit her bottom lip. "Not for . . . Just to talk and—"

It broke his heart that she thought she had to spell it out. "Katie. Of course. Anything you want."

She shut the door.

"Anything. Anytime," he said quietly to no one. *I didn't want to leave you.*

Nolan drove home and pulled up in front of his apartment complex. He caught his breath as the pain hit him, as it always did, fresh as ever as he realized again that the man his son had known was gone. That man lived in an apartment now. Alone.

When Robin turned two, it had been as if he'd gotten the memo straight from the Department of Children. He was a Terrible Two from his second birthday until the instant he turned three. There were nights when he'd scream for three hours in a row—nights when nothing would soothe him, and his voice went raw from shouting his utter outrage. Those nights, Kate had looked at Nolan, exhaustion in her eyes (but nothing like he'd see, five years later, when they were up all night for different—worse—reasons), and ask, "Is he always going to be like this?"

"No," Nolan had said, putting a hand on top of her head. "He'll be seventeen someday and he'll be out all night, and you'll call all the hospitals and the morgue and the police, and when he comes home at six in the morning smelling like beer and weed, you'll be the one screaming louder than he is now."

She'd grinned at that, and they'd known that, no matter what, they'd be together. With Robin.

And then they weren't.

He unfolded from the car and stretched. Late as it was, he'd take Fred Weasley for a lap around the block.

"Hey."

The voice behind him in the courtyard made him jump.

Rafe stepped into the light, with Johnson on his heels.

Happiness warred with confusion and was quickly snuffed out by realization. "Shit." They knew.

"Yeah." Rafe nodded, his baseball cap pulled low, casting a dark shadow over his eyes in the dimness.

"Brother, it wasn't that I was hiding it from you—"

"Brother?" Rafe asked.

Something fragile inside Nolan broke into tiny, sharp shards. "You want to come in?"

Johnson and Rafe looked at each other. Rafe pulled a work bandanna out of his pocket and moved it back and forth, threading it through his fingers. Nolan had seen him do that a million times when he was thinking about where exactly to start a job or what kind of gravel to use next.

Finally, Rafe said, "A minute."

Inside, Nolan poured them the best scotch he had. Okay, it was the only kind he had, a Glenlivet that had been on sale at Trader Joe's. He splashed a little water in each and handed them the glass tumblers he'd found at a garage sale.

"Fancy shit," said Johnson from his perch on the wooden side chair. He didn't look comfortable, and he didn't look as if he wanted to stay.

"Just whiskey." Nolan looked at the carpet.

"You killed your kid?" Rafe took a deep swallow of the alcohol, and it didn't seem to faze him—he breathed as easily after it as if he'd shot an ounce of plain water. "Your son?"

Rafe had daughters. All three of them girls. He'd admitted to Nolan once that he thought it made him less of a man that he couldn't make a boy.

"Yes."

Rafe pounded the rest of the pour and then leaned forward, running his hands through his hair, tugging hard when his fingers got stuck. "Jesus, Monroe, how could you let us think you were in for something stupid?" His words were on the edge of slurred. The scotch wasn't the first drink he'd had that night. "White-collar shit, that's what we all thought it was. It's my ex, Tanya, that calls me. I've got the kids, and she's screaming something about the TV, and I turn it on and it's you, and then she says she's gonna come get them from me because she's worried that you'll come around. And now Rita's pissed that Tanya's calling me freaking out and I don't know *what* to think." Rafe thought in black and white, good and bad. That left no middle ground for Nolan to stand on.

"I'm so sorry." This was why he'd never wanted them to know. That, and he knew they wouldn't care about him the way they had.

"You were our family, *pendejo*." Rafe's voice broke. "And I'm gonna take you to my mom's for her birthday, huh? Murder? Premeditated? What about our kids? Rita's not so freaked out 'cause she says it sounds like euthanasia. I didn't even know that word till today. That's some kind of mercy? I'm trying to wrap my head around it, how you would do something like that. What about the man I know? Huh? Where's that guy?"

During the surprisingly short trial, the entire world had broken into three camps. There were those who supported Nolan, who thought it was just a horrible accident, who said it could have happened to anyone. They tried to shake his hands in the courthouse's hallways and used his name as if they knew him.

Then there was the group of people who believed in and

fought for the idea that people could take care of their own loved ones, including escorting them to the grave. They were the ones who felt sorry for him, because he hadn't managed to off himself, too. Nolan had become—unwillingly—their poster boy for a year or two, the man who was prosecuted and imprisoned for loving his son too much. They'd never gotten the quote they'd wanted from him, though. He wouldn't talk to them. They could think what they wanted.

Then there was the third group: the ones who felt that only God should decide, that continued medical intervention was necessary for all struggles for survival, and God would decide the final outcome. Because Nolan didn't verbally embrace the voluntary euthanasia side—never said a thing either way, in fact—the God-people chose him for their example, too. He was their example of how badly assisted suicide can go. He was left without his child and for a time without his memory, never able to know exactly how long medicine could have extended his boy's life. Indubitably, the Catholic Rafe would fall into this camp.

Nolan had fit into none of the groups. For a long time, he'd had no memory of what had happened that day. None at all. It was common, he'd been told, after carbon monoxide asphyxiation.

Rafe continued, "I don't even know who you are, man."

"Who knows?" said Johnson, who'd been worrisomely silent until now. "Who knows if you won't do something like that again?"

Rafe glared. "You know that's bullshit. It's *Nolan*." But he didn't look convinced.

Nolan held up empty hands. "Won't happen. I'm fresh out of kids."

Rafe winced.

Johnson poured himself another shot.

Nolan waited.

After a long pause, Rafe finally said, "I know it was an accident and all, but *man.* You take *care* of your kids, you get me?"

"I guess that's for you to—"

"You still look like the Nolan I know. Far as I can tell. Shit, man. You don't *lie* to your family like that. Not telling us about why you were in prison? That's a lie, nothing less. Biggest lie I ever heard." Rafe took a deep breath and closed his eyes. Then he opened them again. "Okay." He scooted forward so he was sitting on the edge of the old couch. "Tell us. Go."

Nolan lost a scrap of his patience. "You saw the news. You know what happened."

"I been on the news twice in my life, and neither time they got it right," said Johnson.

"TV ain't truth," said Rafe. "*You* say the truth. Then we decide what we have to do."

These were the only friends Nolan had, and while he'd been on the road with them, he'd tried to give them the real deal, the real Nolan. With them, he'd been the kind of man he'd never been at the law firm. He was strong. Necessary. They relied on him and he relied on them. They were good men. Johnson once spent his entire lunch break on his hands and knees in the Big Longs parking lot, helping an old lady find her glasses that she'd dropped. He kept looking, even when she'd given up, and when he found them, he'd called the number she'd given him. When she said never mind, that she'd found a better pair at home, he'd tucked the glasses into his shirt pocket after wrapping them in paper towels. Just in case.

And Rafe, knowing nothing at all, had taken Nolan for a friend. They'd talked late into tequila-flavored nights about everything, the stars, the women they'd known, fights they'd had; they'd talked about larger thoughts, depression and hope and honor. They'd trusted each other. Rafe had let Nolan fly his three-year-old daughter around the backyard, her arms and legs spinning and diving while Rafe was inside cutting onions and tomatoes for the burgers. Nolan knew that was the hardest part—for Rafe the father to forgive himself for trusting his children with a man who'd killed the son God had seen fit to give him.

Leaning forward in an echo of Rafe's motion, Nolan lied, "I don't remember."

"Bullshit," said Rafe.

"I fell asleep in the garage, and when I woke up, I'd been sent to hell. Been trying to scratch my way out since then." Another lie—he hadn't tried to help himself for a long time, more than a year. He hadn't cared what happened to him. He slowly straightened to standing and said, "I got out, and got the roads job. And I met you guys, and you were . . . my new family."

Rafe had listened with big eyes and clenched fists. Now he stood. He pulled back and smashed Nolan so hard in the eye that Nolan couldn't breathe for a moment. Fred Weasley barked sharply, then scrabbled away to hide in the bedroom. Rafe immediately cradled his hand. "Fuck. That hurt like a motherfuckin' *fucker.*"

Nolan stood in place, wobbling, unsure if he should sit back down or just go for the floor, which was what his body wanted. Instead, there was another roar, and this time Rafe threw his arms around Nolan and clung to him as if they were wrestling, stuck in a grapple hold. Was it a hug or was Rafe just holding him up so Johnson could finish the job?

Nolan waited to find out which it was. His eye throbbed and the relief of the pain was astonishing. Somebody else making him hurt was the best idea ever.

Rafe released his death grip and stepped backward. "I gotta think all this through. I gotta think hard. You get me?"

Nolan nodded.

Rafe turned and left without another word, Johnson on his heels. They slammed the door so hard the thin walls shook.

Nolan found Fred huddled inside the laundry basket, head shoved into a pile of towels. "Hey."

The dog pushed farther in.

"Hey, Fred. Hey. It's gonna be okay."

But Fred Weasley wouldn't come out, and Nolan figured he knew the truth, too. The tears finally broke through then, hot and fast, his back aching with how he leaned forward digging his fingers into Fred's fur—the pain sucking at his gut as if it could bust right out. Any second all the tears and blood would pool in front of him until they filled the room, filled this shitty apartment, until everything was under the salt water and the bile.

Chapter Thirty-four

Robin

January 2002

Fear was the first symptom of Kate's second pregnancy. She woke up one morning and heard it, a rumbling inside her, a generalized, low-grade, thrumming worry. When she realized she'd missed two periods, the tremors grew louder, shaking and rolling through her: she didn't deserve this, it wouldn't work out, this time the baby wouldn't make it to full term. Because she'd given the last one away, this one wouldn't be healthy, or it would be born with an important part of its brain or heart missing.

Kate had to tell Nolan, but thinking about it terrified her. Would he read in her eyes that she'd gone through this before? Jesus, would the doctor know this was her second pregnancy even though she planned on lying about it?

While standing with Nolan as he picked out deodorant in Safeway, she picked up a box of tampons and said, "I guess I won't be needing these for a while."

Nolan glanced at her and then back at the deodorant. He tried to place it carefully back on the shelf but it fell out of his hand, clattering to the floor. The plastic base spun off.

"Are you . . . ?" The happiness in his voice was unbearable, and Kate walked away, taking refuge in the cracker aisle. From over the top of the saltines, she heard him yell, "Are you *pregnant*?"

A woman who was studying a package of rye crisps looked up, alarmed.

"Nolan!"

He yelled over again. "You tell me in the *grocery store*?" But then he was in her aisle, and he was crying, holding her tightly, kissing her over and over.

"I think so." She laughed. "I'm pretty sure."

They moved to the paper products aisle and he opened a box of Kleenex. Noses blown, Nolan led her by the hand back to the first aisle they'd been in. Then, pink box in hand, he led her through the store, back to produce.

"Bathroom?" he asked the man spraying the radishes.

Wordlessly, the man pointed through the big plastic flaps that led to the back.

"She's pregnant. Probably," said Nolan conversationally. Kate's heart flip-flopped. The radish man gave them a grimace and a thumbs-up.

In the bathroom he opened the box and put it in his pocket—"So we can pay for it on the way out"—and turned his back as she peed on the stick.

Then she watched, with a growing sense of something that felt like happiness as the plus she knew would form formed.

"Oh, Katie," said Nolan reverently.

"Is it . . . okay?" *This time, is it going to be okay?*

"Okay? There's nothing better in the whole world. You're a miracle." He kissed the side of her face and then the crown of her head. "My miracle."

"No," said Kate. "It's just nature."

"It's a miracle. I'm going to be a *father.* To your baby." Somehow he managed to turn around in the small space, raising and lowering his arms as if he were praying in a Baptist church. He spun twice more, laughing. Kate laughed with him, unable to stop herself. They laughed their way out of the restroom, through the checkout line, where the girl looked startled when Nolan pulled the used box out of his pocket and handed it to her to scan, and then through the parking lot and out to the car.

The bubbles of laughter rising in her chest felt good. They felt wonderful. And they were wrong, too. She didn't deserve this kind of happiness. She tried to push the effervescent feeling of joy back down so she didn't get used to it. She would do something wrong. She'd lose both of them.

But the baby stuck, growing inside her. The ultrasound said it was a boy, and they laced their fingers together over Kate's stomach, talking about toy trains and baseballs and firefighter hats. Together, they built a nursery, cursing over the mobile that neither of them could figure out, laughing at how small the socks they bought were. How could anything *be* that tiny? Sonia swam up out of her depression for the first time in years and came over at least once a week, her arms full of the knitted items she made at night. After the unborn baby had more than twenty tiny sweaters, Kate asked her to stop, or at least to slow down.

"I didn't get the chance to dress your daughter, did I?" was the sharp response. "Who made *her* sweaters?"

"Shhh." Kate looked over her shoulder. "Don't *talk* about her. I wish—" She couldn't complete the sentence. Their silent collusion made what small connection they'd created over the years feel even more breakable.

"Just tell him, then."

"I can't. You know I can't."

"He has to be able to trust you," said Sonia.

"He already does." Kate folded her lips. She was right about this.

Sonia harrumphed and shoved her circular knitting needles, newly free of a robin's egg blue hat, into her project bag. "So anyway. I can knit your son a motorcycle if I want to. He gets whatever he wants."

Once, during her sophomore year, Kate had been doing homework in her mother's office at the pool. She'd needed help with a thesis statement, but Sonia had just looked down at her desk calendar before shaking her head. Then the office door had crashed open and a girl with dripping hair barged in.

"Mrs. Brashear! Julie needs you—Caitlyn slipped and she cut her head wide open. There's blood everywhere!"

Her mother left the office at a dead run.

On the wet slab of concrete next to the diving board, one of the coaches held a towel to a girl's forehead. The blood spread dark in the puddled water, but Sonia took over easily, directing another coach to call 911 while she stanched the wound with a bandage and said things that Kate couldn't quite catch from where she sat on the bleacher. Her mother was smooth. In control. Soothing.

As the ambulance prepared to load their patient, Sonia signed forms and patted the coach on the back. Another little girl, white with fear, leaned against Sonia's side, and in what appeared to be an unconscious gesture, Sonia petted her, smoothing her hair off her forehead while she talked to a medic.

Now, her knitting needles pausing in their flight, Sonia looked sharply at Kate. "And he'll *swim*. Not like you. He'll swim." She held up the tiny hat and spun it on her chlorine-reddened finger. "I'm making you a matching one, by the way."

Each day that Kate got bigger with Robin was a day she

grew happier. As her body got heavier, her heart got lighter. On the day Kate gave birth to Robin (the pain was so much easier without the heartbreak attached), the joy she'd been feeling became unimaginable. And as she looked at Nolan's face glowing so brightly she hardly recognized him, the joy finally, *finally* eclipsed the fear.

August 2007

Robin was born a water baby. His favorite thing in the world was anything wet—a pond, a pool, a tub. He swam every Monday and Wednesday with Sonia, who dubbed him her little merman. They clung to each other, laughing, in the shallow end, and Sonia shouted encouragement as Robin splashed past her best swimmers into the deep end.

The outdoor tub on the hill was Robin's brainchild—he'd seen it while wandering the salvage yard with Nolan and said, "We could run a hose with hot water outside! Like inside! Then we could be like birds and I'd flap around and squawk and sing in the outdoors." That weekend, the tub came home with them. They painted it sky blue and Robin took the inaugural dip.

But the regular inside bath worked well, too. Robin, at five, no longer wanted supervision. He wanted to be able to play with his toys and make up his stories all by himself, without Kate or Nolan hovering overhead.

"Fine," said Kate. "But you have to sing."

"Huh?"

"Sing the whole time so I can hear you. If you're singing, I know you're not drowning."

Robin giggled. "So if you hear *glub-glub*?"

"Then I come running. And it's not funny, Robin. I'm serious. I'll leave you in here alone only if you sing."

He nodded gravely. "I'll sing."

So he sang, with great ceremony. If she was downstairs, on the phone with one doctor or another, Kate could always hear the sound—the tone—but couldn't always hear the words. If she was putting things away in the hall closet, she could hear the song itself: "I'm not drowning, Mom. Mom, I'm still alive! Me, me, me, *me*—I'm still alive and can breathe!"

Kate kept Robin out of the pool only when he was sick, and even then he liked a warm bath—it couldn't hurt, she thought. Not long after they got the outdoor tub, he got a bad cold. It wasn't a big deal. In fact, Kate and Nolan both had it, and there were two weeks when one or the other of them was walking around with pockets full of used Kleenex. Kate laughed as she always did and said that she'd never gotten sick before she'd birthed a germ magnet. "You get them all over you, don't you?" she'd say into Robin's sticky neck. "You roll around in germs and then come home and pour them in my soup, is that right?"

"You can't spread them like that, Mama." Robin was practical. "You can't pour germs like you pour salt."

"You're right. How did you know that?"

He shrugged. "I just know."

Of the three of them, Robin had it the worst—a wheezing in the chest and a sick thumping sound to his cough. When she and Nolan were better and Robin still had it, she took him to the doctor, who said, yep, his glands were swollen and it was going around. Nope, there was nothing they could do, but he could give him antibiotics if it would make her feel better.

Another week went by. By then Nolan was losing sleep.

"He's still sick," said Nolan at three in the morning.

It took Kate a minute to wake, to come to herself, and then she said, "It's a cold. The doctor said so."

"I don't like it."

"Who the hell likes to have their child sick? Go to sleep."

Behind her, Nolan curled into a ball, and she had to roll over in order to spoon him. As she drifted back to sleep, she felt Nolan kick. He worried too much, that was all. He always had. If she were a good wife, she'd stay awake and comfort him. Maybe have sex—that always made both of them feel better. But sleep called and she answered.

When Robin's cold was going into its fourth week, Nolan and Kate went together with him to the doctor. The doctor was out, but the nurse-practitioner told them that she wanted to run some tests.

"What kind?"

"Just some routine blood work. Make sure he's really getting over this cold that's got him down. How long has his neck been swollen like that?"

Robin, nose dribbling, didn't look up from playing his Sony PSP. He barely seemed to notice when they took the blood. The next week, when they did the needle aspiration of the lump in his neck, he just blinked as they numbed him. Kate was a wreck and Nolan still wasn't sleeping. Robin, though, sat patiently through the appointments and barely complained at the prodding.

When the results came in, they were inconclusive at first. Standing on the staircase's top landing, the portable phone in her hand, Kate gripped the rail with her other hand, amazed that her voice stayed normal. They were trying to rule out non-Hodgkin's lymphoma, but hadn't been able to yet. "Non-Hodgkin's. Is that the good kind? Or the bad?"

In the chamber of her body—somewhere between her heart and her throat—where she'd stored the fear away, something started to twinge again. A dull, low ache, and she recognized it as what she'd felt back then, when she was first pregnant with him. *Nothing is this good. Nothing can stay safe.*

Kate and Nolan said nothing to Robin while they and the doctors decided on his treatment. They knew it was a reprieve, no matter how short it might be. They wiped his nose, and gave him treats and read to him in bed, whatever book he wanted, at any time. She nodded reassuringly when he said he was bored. "Soon. Soon you'll be able to go outside and play, but look, it might rain. Let's stay in and build that paper castle we were talking about, okay? Daddy's home from work at five, and I'm going to ask him to pick us up a pizza. Would you like that?"

But he was almost six, for god's sake, not a baby. He had the language and the understanding to know that whatever was happening to him wasn't a good thing.

One morning, when she was carrying clean laundry into his room next to the bathroom, she heard a song she hadn't heard before. "I don't have cancer, Mom. Mom, you worry toooooo much! Mom, you should let me have my bath all day, all the time, all the day, and I don't have cancer, Mom!"

She pushed open the door so fast it knocked over the small stool Robin had set next to the tub to hold overflow bath toys.

"Robin!"

He looked up, wide-eyed.

"Where did you hear that?"

"What?" He pushed at his hair to remove the bubbles that had collected over his left ear.

"What you said. What you don't have."

"I don't know."

"Robin."

He shrugged and wriggled his knees so that the water splashed up the tub sides. "I just heard it."

Kate knelt and gathered his skinny wet body to her and kissed him fiercely. "Don't you worry about a single thing.

Daddy and I are taking care of it. Do you hear me?" She kissed him, her cheeks damp. "You don't worry."

He pulled away. "That's what I was *saying*. Don't *worry*. Jeesh." He held his breath and then slid under the water before popping right back out with a question. "Do I have to take medicine?"

Oh, baby. So much medicine. "Yes, sugarplum. You will."

"Will it taste bad?"

She nodded, her heart dropping. "Probably."

Robin's mouth, always the barometer of his emotions, tightened. Tears formed. "I don't wanna."

Everyone said he would be fine. All the books, all the sites on the Internet. Even though signs were pointing to bone marrow involvement, the prognosis was still good: eighty percent chance of long-term survival. But the number took poisonous root in her brain: eighty. Eighty percent meant that twenty percent of kids in stage four didn't make it. Wasn't that what it meant? Was it truly that awful? Could it possibly be?

"I don't want you to, either."

Everything will go wrong. Nothing can stay safe.

She would have given anything to stop the train that was speeding toward them, the train carrying everything she couldn't name, everything she was afraid of. *We don't deserve him. Nothing can stay safe.*

Everything will go wrong.

Chapter Thirty-five

Friday, May 16, 2014
11 a.m.

Bree felt like starting a fight. Anyone would do, really. She wasn't picky.

After their escape from the cemetery, Flynn and she had gone home, where he'd wanted to talk more about the pregnancy, but she'd cut him off by taking off her clothes. The sex, however, didn't quite work out, which was probably just what she deserved. While Flynn was going down on her, she'd felt his tongue slow as his fingers fell away. All motion ceased, and she heard a faint snore. He'd been horrified when she'd poked him in the head with her index finger, but the moment was dead for her, and she rolled over, ignoring his apologies, refusing to let him touch her belly as he wanted to.

She just kept thinking about Robin, the boy she would never meet, and the child inside her, who she didn't really *want* to meet.

A green Suburban cut Pree off on her way to work, swerving without warning into her lane so that she had to stomp her not very good brakes, and she could suddenly see the attraction road rage held for some. If she'd had a water pistol, she would have brandished it, just to see the look of fear in the man's eyes. He had a thick gray mustache, and even through the window she could see that his face was red and sweating. She didn't think she'd ever disliked anyone as much as she disliked that stranger who didn't even seem to notice he'd done anything wrong.

Jimmy rolled into the office at ten, smelling of aftershave and starch. Was it possible that his wife ironed his shirts? Were there women who still did that? For men who wanted to fuck their employees under their desks?

He smiled and said, "You good with the rendering Sean sent you?"

"Yep."

Had she really expected more from him? Had she *wanted* more? A heated glance? A look of knowing? She'd had his cock in her mouth, for god's sake.

Jimmy nodded once and moved on, laughing as Janice threw a stress ball at him that bounced off his head.

She managed to work for an hour before she lost it.

Slamming his office door behind her, Pree said, "So, what is all this?"

Jimmy looked startled.

"All what?"

Pree felt like screaming. "Are you kidding me? The flirting. Meeting me in the city, pretending to be interested in street art. The . . . what we *did*, right here."

Jimmy rubbed his hair with his hands, making his hair stick up even more wildly than it had been. "I'm sorry, I didn't mean to confuse anything."

"But you did."

He stood slowly. "I thought you were with me on this. Casual, right?"

"Excuse me?"

"I *asked* you if you and that Finn—"

"*Flynn.*"

"If you and Flynn were serious, and you told me no. You told me that you saw other people. Did I hear you wrong?"

Pree's inexplicable lie hung in front of them, and she didn't say anything.

"Did I?"

"No," she said, hating everything about him. She hated the dark piece of hair that hung in front of his ear, hated the way the collar of his black shirt was halfway folded under. She hated the fact that he was being kind to her, and she hated how she saw a flicker of pity in his eyes.

"I love Flynn," she said. Maybe if she said it out loud enough times it would keep being true . . .

"Good," Jimmy said. "That's a good thing."

"I have no idea why I did . . . what I did with you."

"That's fine. We won't do it again. I understand."

He was being so *nice.* "But we—"

Jimmy shook his head. "We just messed around." That pitying look again. "Very minor. That's all it was. I'm sorry for my part in it because I can see that you're hurting . . ."

"Just stop."

"Pree, I'm sorry—"

Pree spun and left the office without another word. *I should quit!* Yeah, that would show him. On second thought, no. She wouldn't give him that satisfaction, ever. She sat at her desk and fumed. She slammed her desk drawer so hard a screw popped out and the handle fell off.

The worst of it was that Pree *had* asked Jimmy to meet her that day in Union Square. She *had* implied she was basically single. She'd kept her pants on, as if that meant anything, but she'd undone her fly and she'd led his hand to her pussy. And then she'd skipped work the next day, as if she'd somehow earned it. And the whole time, she realized now, she'd resented him for not being Flynn. She'd been almost as mad at Jimmy as she was at herself, and it wasn't his fault, not at all.

With a sigh, Pree lowered her head to her desk. She inhaled the comforting smell of eraser rubber and charcoal.

She was supposed to be better than this. Flynn thought she was better than this. The thought should have eased her, but didn't.

It would be okay. Pree hid behind her monitor and kept her head down and clutched the thought, writing it in her mind, tracing it over and over the way she did on her stickers. It would be okay. She would make it okay. Somehow.

Chapter Thirty-six

Friday, May 16, 2014
5 p.m.

On Friday, Kate did something she hadn't done in weeks: she attempted to work. First she put on her painting sweater—the old cream Aran her mother had made for her after Pree was born. It had specks of colors inside the cabled twists from paint that had splattered, marrying the fiber over the years. Kate loved the weight of it, the way it hung from her shoulders, the clean, sheepy smell of it. She felt almost forgiven when she wore it.

She cleaned off the back porch swing and brought out her coffee and her sketchbook. Every time her mind veered toward Pree taking off, or how Nolan had looked when he left, she pushed down with her pencil harder, leaving a darker, more permanent line. By noon, she had a solid plan—the new work was going to be huge. It would take her the whole month she had before it was due to complete the pieces. In her head she saw color for the first time in years. She saw cadmium red and almost knew where she'd use it. Her fingers ached to use cerise. Electric purple breathed within her. Bright orange sat next to deep plum. She looked up at the chartreuse edge of a new acacia leaf and the color tangled with ebony in her mind. Kate wanted all of it, now. Finally it was back—the feeling of a low motor shifted into gear inside her. Motion. She didn't know if she'd be able to harness it at the canvas, though, and she was frightened.

The plan in place, the sketches outlined—only a shadow of the more detailed plan she'd come up with next—she made herself another cup of coffee and went into her studio at the back of the house.

What she *wanted* to paint was Robin's hydrangea. Not the grayscale one that hung in the living room. The real thing—the one made of glorious purples, reds, undertones of cream and yellow against the darkest greens stems, bowing under its own weight.

But instead, she'd do more helicopter scenes, the twisted metal against the hillside. They would sell, she knew, which was what the auction needed. But this time she'd use color.

Kate ran her fingers across the oils. The metal tubes, dented by her thumbs, were cool and familiar.

She had no idea what to do next.

There was a tap at the French doors of her studio. Pree's face, pale and wide-eyed, swam in the fading light.

Joy lit her heart, a color she'd never be able to name.

"I'm sorry," Pree said as Kate opened the door. "I knocked at the front door, but you didn't hear me. I saw your car . . ." Pree's voice trailed off in doubt. "I shouldn't have come around back. I'm sorry. I'm interrupting your work."

"The only thing you're interrupting is me from doing nothing. Or, worse, starting a bad painting."

Pree came closer and looked at the blank canvas. "Oh. I get doing nothing. It's a lot harder than doing something, isn't it?"

And there, in her daughter's words, was a simple, overlooked truth. It *was* harder to do nothing than to do anything else, no matter how badly. How much she'd missed by not knowing this smart young woman earlier.

Pree said, "I'm sorry. I just had such a crappy day at work—"

Kate shook her head firmly. "No apologies. I'm glad you're here. Maybe you can help me." It was a spur-of-the-moment idea, and Pree probably wouldn't want to . . .

"Me? Help?"

Kate led Pree up the stairs and into Robin's room. She'd already put the yellow paint cans on the plastic floor covering, and earlier in the day she'd taped off the light fixtures and ceiling to do the edging. She just hadn't been able to start. Maybe now, with Pree, they could get it done. Make a room for her. Together.

Pree bit her bottom lip. "You want to paint over Hogwarts?"

"All of it. It's time."

Pree reached out a tentative finger and touched the roof of Hagrid's cottage. Kate had been proud of the way she'd gotten the moss to look, almost as if it were growing out of the wall.

"You can't."

"Sure we can. Then . . ." Kate paused, gathering her courage. "You don't want to sleep in a little boy's room. Then, after it's painted, it can really be *your* room. For when you, you know, stay over. If you want to stay over, that is . . .

I just mean that you're welcome. You're always welcome. I can give you a key tonight." Oh, she was screwing it up again, wasn't she?

Pree's eyes widened again and she stuck her hands into the deep pockets of her purple smock. "I don't know."

"No pressure," Kate hurried to say. "None at all. Just know that you have a place to stay, if you ever need a break from home. A little vacation."

"I'm pregnant."

It was such a non sequitur that Kate at first almost didn't recognize the words as English. They sounded familiar, and she knew if she concentrated, she could figure out what they meant. Pregnant. Pree was pregnant.

"And before you ask, I don't know what I'm going to do."

Oh, the anguish that lay under Pree's words, a dark green miserable sound. "It's okay," Kate managed. Puny words. She could do better than that.

But before she could figure out what to say next, Pree said, "So I'm not sure I'm someone you should paint a whole room for. I'm not proving to be very good at managing my life, am I? Who knows where I'll be next week? I could up and move to Nebraska. Or go to Maine and hire on with a crab boat."

"Do you want to go to Maine?"

"Oh, you know." Pree swiped at her forehead as if angry at the dyed blue lock that hung in front of her eyes. "I'm just saying. I'm not a good bet."

Kate gestured to the bed. "You want to sit?"

"No." Pree crossed her arms in front of her and looked out the window at the sycamore. "I don't know what I want. That's the whole problem."

"How long have you known?"

"Two and a half weeks."

Kate breathed slowly. "So that's why you decided to find me."

Pree nodded once, hard.

Did she need advice? God, Kate would be the wrong person for that, wouldn't she? But she could try at least. "You want to talk about it while we paint?"

Pree said, "I really think you shouldn't do it."

Kate popped the can's lid and stuck the stirrer in. She lifted it dripping. "But look. It's a good yellow, right? Warm, with that red undertone. I thought you'd like it."

"I like the color fine. Just don't cover him up." Tears filled Pree's eyes. "You can't just cover him up like that. You can't forget him."

"Oh." Kate's knees felt wobbly, and she sat cross-legged on the carpet. "Oh. Honey. No." She rubbed her eyes briefly as if it would ease the pain. "I can't forget. I can't cover anything up. Robin was everything to me."

Wrong words.

Pree's face crumpled. "Yeah. He was everything."

"No—" Kate started.

"It's just something to adjust to, that's all. To this family, I was nothing, right? Your husband didn't know you'd had a child before Robin, and Robin never knew he had a half sister. You knew about me, but how often did you even think of me?"

As little as possible. All the time. "I always let myself have your birthday to think about you."

"Oh, good. A whole day."

There was no way to justify it, but Kate said, "It hurt so much—"

"And now I'm pregnant, too. Fertility runs in the family, right? Shit, I was on the pill. I forgot one. Just *one.* I'm supposed to be smart and make my family proud of me, but that tiny slip is all the stupidity it took on my part to end up here. With no fucking clue what I'm going to do next."

Kate reached a hand up toward her, but Pree pulled herself farther away. She leaned on the windowsill.

"There are so many options . . ." Kate said.

"Like what? I could keep the kid? No way. I'm not ready for that. I don't *want* that. I could have an abortion. I always thought that would be the way I'd go if this ever happened to me, you know? I'm pro-choice. Every woman should have the right to control her own body. But now . . ."

Kate remembered. She'd felt the same way.

Pree continued. "Now I can't think about that. I can't do it."

"That leaves . . ."

"Adoption. And that's a bullshit solution."

Kate felt as if Pree had struck her. "But you—"

"Yeah. I was one of the lucky ones. I got good parents, blah blah blah. And still, do you know how hard it was?"

Kate shook her head.

"Every day? To wonder if I'd passed you on the street? Or if you were dead? I'd make up whole stories about my family. Sometimes I'd pass a junkie on the street picking at her skin and wonder if it was you. Maybe your dad or your uncle molested you and I was the by-product. Maybe you were raped."

Kate blinked, wishing she could stop the assault of words, knowing she shouldn't.

Pree continued, "I'd wonder if I'd end up on the streets, some biological imperative pushing me toward addiction. Then I wondered if it could have been a mistake, if my birth mother wanted me desperately and regretted her decision with every breath."

"Oh, Pree."

"But you didn't. And that's fine. That's good. You had a life. I just wasn't part of it. And I don't want to do that to another child."

Kate felt a kick from somewhere deep inside her. A thought, a completely unacceptable thought grew inside her. A forbidden thought.

But she spoke anyway. "What if . . . oh. What if I . . . ?" Kate's courage failed as her arms crept around her belly. Good god, it would be her grandchild. She was thirty-seven, and as of yesterday she hadn't completely ruled out ever trying to get pregnant again herself.

But to raise Pree's baby . . .

"What if . . . ?"

Pree's glare slammed into her. "No. Are you insane?"

The dream, thin and insubstantial as it was, dissipated as quickly as it had come. Covered with embarrassment, Kate stammered, "I'm sorry. Of course. So sorry."

"I'm just confused," continued Pree. "That's all. I'm not trying to give you a *baby*. Shit." She covered her mouth with her hands for a second. Then her shoulders dropped. "I didn't mean to dump it all on you. I guess I thought you might have . . ."

"Some advice." The girl had two mothers. Kate couldn't hope to compete.

"Yeah." Pree moved her gaze out the window.

"I don't have much. Not really. But I'm here for you in every way. If that helps at all."

"What Robin died of . . . Could this baby . . . ?"

"Oh! No, lymphoma has no hereditary cause, not that they've been able to find."

Pree turned and met her eyes. "Please don't paint over Hogwarts. It means a lot to me and I've only seen it this week. I can't imagine what it means to you."

And suddenly, it did. It meant everything, this painted

world that her son had lived and believed in. His best nights were the ones he dreamed about Harry Potter, waking to tell her excitedly about the spells he'd cast and the people he'd seen—he'd flown on a broomstick over the ocean with Neville Longbottom, and Mrs. Weasley once knitted him a sweater out of licorice.

"You're right. I just wanted to paint with color, I think. I can't seem to get it on my canvas downstairs."

Pree brushed her hair back again. "Have you tried just doing it?"

"What?"

"Just throw out some color. Let it land. Who cares what happens?"

Kate picked up Robin's favorite wand, one of the few items she'd left on his bookcases, and moved it like a paintbrush. "I'm not ready," she said.

"How do you know until you try?"

Kate stared at her daughter.

Pree said, "Just try. Okay?"

"How'd you get to be so smart?"

Pree ducked her head. "I won't talk to Flynn about the pregnancy even though I told him about it. He's probably going to break up with me, and I can't even say I care that much, even though I know I should. I haven't told my moms, which feels like a *huge* lie, and I picked a fight this afternoon with my boss, who I almost slept with two days ago."

"Oh."

"I'm not that smart." Pree bit her bottom lip again, the way Nolan always did. "At least I finally told you the truth. I'm sick of lying. I'm sick of pushing people away. And anyway, the truth is usually better than the alternative, right?"

Kate's heart sped up. "Usually."

"I heard you the other night. Arguing with Nolan in the kitchen."

"That's why you left."

"You kept secrets from him, and they're coming to the surface now. So maybe it's just easier to tell the truth earlier. I guess I'm working on that."

Nolan is your father. Kate thought the words so hard she thought she heard them out loud, but Pree didn't even blink. *Say it. Say it.*

Clapping her hands together, Pree said, "I have to go."

"Oh, no—please stay . . ."

"I have to call my moms. And then I'm going to talk to Flynn. And then maybe apologize to my boss. I have a *lot* to do."

She hugged Kate quickly, and Kate wished she could freeze the moment forever, wished she could keep her daughter safe. But she couldn't protect her from life any more than she protected Robin from disease.

"Thanks," Pree said. Kate heard a rainbow's worth of emotion in that tiny, practically useless word.

Kate said, "I'm going out on that boat tomorrow. The one I told you about."

Pree nodded.

"I'm taking my mom's ashes out to the bay. She wanted to be there, with my dad's ashes, and I haven't been able to do it until now. I'm taking the rest of Robin's ashes, too." She grimaced. "He loved the ocean—I told you that already—and I kept half to . . . put out there someday. Saturday, tomorrow, is the day. If you wanted to go with me—with Nolan, too, of course—" Kate paused and then raised her hand to the back of her neck, rubbing at the sudden tightness. "It's a dumb thing to ask. Never mind."

"I want to go," Pree said.

Hope flared. "You could meet me at the Berkeley marina at ten . . . But obviously you don't have to."

"I know." Pree's voice was strong. Vibrant. "I want to. For Robin."

It was astonishing, hearing Robin's name said in Pree's pale green voice. Kate managed, "Okay. Good."

Pree moved like she had springs under her shoes. "I'll see you tomorrow, then. And now you should paint. Throw some color at the canvas. See what happens."

She made it sound so simple, and Kate wrapped her arms around her waist as she listened to the girl tromp down the staircase.

Then, without thinking, she went to the kitchen. She opened her computer and composed an e-mail.

Still without thinking, without second-guessing or talking herself out of it, she hit send.

Nolan,

Pree is your daughter. She's 22. I lied. I'm so sorry.

Love,
Kate

She went into the studio and uncapped her favorite cadmium red.

Chapter Thirty-seven

Friday, May 16, 2014
11:45 p.m.

Bree is your daughter.

The hollow inside his chest felt as if Nolan had crashed his car, as if he'd veered off the road and flipped upside down, rolling over and over. As he drove, he seriously considered doing it. If he didn't have Fred Weasley to take care of, he would, and goddamn it, he hadn't had to fight those urges in a while. Just speed up—that's all it would take. He'd hit seventy, eighty fucking miles per hour and aim for a light pole in a deserted location. The only ones affected by it would be his buddies at work who would have to clean up the blood and glass after the car and his body were carted away.

This pain—it was so bad, so fucking *bad*. It didn't have his usual guilt all wrapped up in it, either, the regret that slowed pain into a thick liquid fire. This was sharp and intense, the flames of it whipped up by fury.

Pree was his daughter. He'd never known he had a daughter, and the worst part was that he could never call her that. Kate had stripped that right from him. If he'd known—oh, god. He let himself imagine for one terrible moment a world in which Robin was fine, a world in which Nolan had always known his daughter. A world in which, even without Robin, he would have still been a father . . . Such a different world.

He drove on autopilot. The only thing he was conscious of was steering the car carefully between the yellow and white lines. He felt Fred's hot breath on his wrist every once in a while. Nothing else. He didn't even know where he was going until he got off the freeway at Keller. He took the winding road down Fontaine like he was riding a skateboard, leaning back, barely braking on the long hill lined by oaks as old as Oakland itself. At the bottom he went into the treeless flats south of MacArthur. It wasn't safe here, not this late at night, and he knew it, but he didn't lock his doors. After all, he wasn't the target here—he wasn't young or black, although the groups of kids huddled on the corner at MacArthur and Eighty-second gave him a look like he didn't need to slow down. According to Rafe, there were two reasons why white men cruised the streets down here, and Nolan was interested in buying neither drugs nor girls. At Dowling he hung a left, dodging two people that stood talking in the middle of the street. They, too, stared. He nodded, and they nodded back, dismissing him.

Rafe's house was an older bungalow built with Craftsman touches that had all been ripped out by an earlier occupant. It was pale yellow, the grass a little too long, the driveway gate stuck permanently open. The porch light was off. Nolan glanced at his watch: 11:54 p.m. He left Fred in the car.

Nolan rapped on the iron door, sending a hollow, clanging noise inside. There was a pause, and then a twitch of the curtains in the room on the other side of the glassed-in porch.

Rafe, wearing a brown terry robe he was still belting around his waist, opened the door. "What the fuck, man?"

Without hesitation, Nolan punched Rafe across the jaw.

He hit him so hard he thought he'd broken his hand—pain sliced up his arm and he gasped. But it was a good, clean, cold pain. Concentrated.

Seemingly unsurprised by the sudden blow, Rafe held his jaw, stretching it out, his eyes narrow. "What. The fuck."

"She had a baby."

"Huh? While you were in?"

Nolan shook his head and his hand at the same time. "Twenty-two years ago. *My* kid." In his head echoed the road crew's divorced guys' lament: *That's my kid. Mine.* He went on, "A girl. A daughter. I never knew. And she's a good kid. Nice." Covering his face with his hands, he said, "I met her yesterday."

From behind Rafe, Rita said, "Nolan? Rafe? Should I call 911? What's going on?"

"No, baby. It's okay. Go back to bed." Rafe rubbed his jaw some more. "Come in, brother."

Rafe poured him a shot of tequila—neat, no lime, no salt, just a straight-up shot. He got two bags of peas out of the fridge and wrapped them in red dishcloths. They sat together, frozen peas held to their cheeks. "Throw it back."

But Nolan still felt frantic, out of control, and the tequila fueled the fire instead of cooling it. "I had a family. Rafe, I had a *family*. I wrecked it. But she wrecked it first, and I never even knew."

Rafe leaned back slowly in his chair until the front two legs lifted. A shuffling noise behind him in the hall said someone small was watching them, but Nolan didn't turn his head. They'd go back to bed. That's what families did. Slept at the same time, under the same roof . . . together.

"So this daughter. You met her."

"Not *as* my daughter. Kate said she was someone else's. And I believed her. Fuck, now that I think about it, she has my nose. My shoulders. She looked so much like Robin I could hardly bear to look at her, and when Kate said she wasn't mine, not the same combination of genes, I just believed her." He leaned forward so that Rafe met his eyes, held them. "I was a father. It was the most important thing to me, and I was so fucking good at it. And then I couldn't be one anymore. But . . ."

"If you'd known, you would have still been one."

Nolan gave a short nod. "We were just kids, but we could have raised her together. I'd have been the father of a full-grown daughter now, not just some dead boy's dad."

Rafe shook his head and after a long, considerate pause said, "She should have told you." He poured another shot for both of them, and when he passed it to Nolan he thumped him on the shoulder before picking up his frozen peas again.

Silence fell and, with relief, Nolan fitted himself into it. He belonged in this kitchen, next to the laundry on the dining table and the pile of clean dishes. Rafe sat with him. Together. Rita, awake and waiting for Rafe, would forgive him for hitting her husband eventually. At least if he had nothing else in the world but his dog, who was probably howling right now out in the closed-up car, he had this. A tiny, refracted shard of a family, but one that saved him a chair.

Chapter Thirty-eight

Death

November 2011

Kate didn't believe it until the very last minute. Until what felt like the last second, actually, although they still had a week. Had she known that then, she wouldn't have been able to move a single muscle.

As it was, she was still able to smile at Miss Evelyn when she entered Robin's room at the hospital. She was his favorite nurse, and the only thing that made leaving her okay was the fact that he was going home.

Going home. It had been presented as an option, and Kate had grasped at it with both hands, as if it were the life preserver that would pull them all up out of the river of pain that was carrying away her whole family.

"Yes, we want him at home."

The hospital's social worker, who went by the perky and very young name of Brittani, said, "Hospice at home for a child is a huge undertaking. We can talk about what that would mean for you, but let's talk about your other options now, too. There's a group house for end-of-life children in Hayward that does amazing things, for example. Your insurance would cover it."

Kate clutched Nolan's thigh through his jeans. Her fingers were claws, but she couldn't help it. "A whole house?"

"It's lovely, with a big garden, and the people who work there are—"

"A *house* full of children who are . . ." She couldn't say it. She hadn't said it once yet. If she didn't utter the words, it made them stay not true. For a little while longer, at least.

Brittani nodded. "Or he could stay here at the hospital. That's an option."

The hospital where he was woken every three hours to do something, take something, get something drawn. It was one of the best children's hospitals in the western United States, but Kate was furious about the fact that nothing could be done to get rid of the smell. Sick children shouldn't have to inhale that soul-crushing, antiseptic, singed-plastic scent.

"Home. *Our* home." She impressed herself with the firmness of her voice. Its solidity.

Brittani looked at Nolan, who nodded once. She brought out a pamphlet, flipped it open, and began to talk about hospital beds and ventilation needs.

Kate split herself again. One half—no, perhaps an eighth—of her was listening intently. At the time the bed was delivered, she would remember what Brittani had said about it. She would have already bought the supplies from the hospital store Brittani had recommended. She had the name of the bedside potty chair memorized, and she understood the catheterization process for when the hospice nurse wasn't available to help.

But the rest, seven-eighths of her, wasn't in the room. This part wasn't surprising to her. What unnerved her was that the rest of her wasn't with Robin, either. She didn't imagine that she was tucked up next to him, although that's what a good mother would do, probably. That part of her wasn't even painting, something she'd been completely unable to do since he got sick. She imagined painting now—yes, she imagined her darkest, her most frightening work. She knew that if she could get to the canvas, it would be the best work she'd ever done. But she couldn't. Every time she picked up a brush, she felt as if she were drowning, her head pushed and held under a mile of dark water. She knew that for every tiny piece of emotion she might be able to capture, she'd be holding a thousand—no, a million—times more in her heart, in her blood. How could she even dream of painting when her son was dying? And all the emotion that wasn't going anywhere while she *thought* about the paintings was just circulating in her body like the cancerous cells that circulated inside Robin. As he got sicker, she knew she was failing as a mother. Why would she try to succeed at something that so obviously didn't matter to anyone? It was just paint piled on a static canvas. Who the fuck cared? For the first time in her life, she wasn't an artist.

Instead, now, in the office with chipper talkative Brittani, desperate to be anywhere else—*anywhere* in the world—she thought about trips she'd taken to Europe, before he was born. Once she'd gone with Nolan, and twice she'd gone alone. These were the trips she lived in now. Walking in a soft, surprisingly warm spring rain late at night in Barcelona when sleep wouldn't come, the streets full of young people like her who apparently had no place better to go than the cafés and bars that lined the old streets. They stood inside looking out at her, probably wondering why she had no umbrella and yet wasn't walking quickly. But she didn't mind getting wet. The smell of the paving stones mixed with the scent of tobacco and wine. The sight of damp coats cheered her. In a high window, she saw an old woman in an orange kerchief gazing down, as if looking for someone. Kate waved, and the woman waved back nervously before drawing back out of sight.

And there was the time she spent in Venice. A whole week, by herself, in a tiny rented apartment. She remembered the cold, echoing marble stairs that led up to the fourth-floor rooms, and the way the stone felt harder than any tile under her bare feet in the bathroom. A terrace not even five feet wide gave her a view of all the roofs in Cannaregio, and when she slept in the flat, flat bed, she counted how many different sets of bells she could hear. Seven. Maybe it was nine. During the day, she sat at the canal's edge at a café and listened to the water slapping the walls as the boats passed by. Once, she saw a UPS boat, as brown and blocky as their American four-wheeled counterparts, and she laughed so hard the waiter raised an eyebrow.

A pub in London. A bridge in Prague. A train in France. Anywhere but here. The pain was too bad, the fear was too much. Anywhere else, maybe it would be bearable. It wouldn't, but she let herself have the fantasy.

When Brittani said, "Do you have any other questions?" Kate didn't. She'd already asked them and she'd been given the answers. But most of her hadn't heard them. Most of her wasn't even a mother. She wasn't a painter. She wasn't even here, because if she wasn't here, if she'd never been here at all, her son, the person most important in the whole world, wouldn't be dying.

On the worst day of her life, Kate had been headed to San Francisco to meet a friend at the De Young. Everyone had been nagging her, Nolan included, to get out of the house, if only for a couple of hours, and she'd finally agreed, exhausted from arguing about it. Then the friend had canceled, citing a family emergency that later turned out to be a sick cat. On learning that, Kate had almost laughed.

So Kate went home. She looked for the boys. Robin rarely got out of bed then—it hurt too much—but sometimes Nolan would talk him into being carried downstairs and placed in his wheelchair, then rolled around the house and the garden. Lately, though, he'd been saying he didn't want to go outside. When he looked out the window into the backyard, at the tetherball pole, out at the pond where he liked to lie on his stomach and watch the koi swim up at him, their mouths begging for food, instead of pulling toward the out of doors, he turned his face to the wall. Kate wondered with sick despair if it was because he knew he didn't have many more days left, but when she'd tried asking him, he'd closed his eyes and asked her to read more of *The Deathly Hallows* instead.

"Oh, honey. What about the part in *The Philosopher's Stone* when they're playing Wizard's Chess?"

"Do too many people die at the end, Mom? Is that the reason you won't finish reading it to me?"

She'd shaken her head at him, momentarily unable to speak.

"I figured. Who dies?"

"I can't—" Kate choked.

"Remember when Cedric dies in *The Goblet of Fire*? And Harry sees him and talks to him before he carries him back to Hogwarts?"

"Yeah, baby."

"I like that part. I like that Harry can see his parents in the Mirror of Erised. I just wanna know one thing."

"Yeah?"

"Is it real?"

"That Harry can see his parents?"

Robin said, "You see your greatest desire in the mirror, right? So a desire isn't really real. So maybe they're not there?" He paused to cough. Then he said, "I know what I'd see in the mirror."

It took all her courage to ask, "What?"

I'd see myself healthy. I'd see myself as a teenager. As an adult. With my own children.

"I'd see myself playing Quidditch. And *winning*." Another pause. "Does Ron die?"

"No," she could answer truthfully. She'd never tell him about Fred Weasley. Tonks and Lupin. She couldn't read aloud Dumbledore's line, "Never pity the dead, Harry. Pity the living, and above all, those who live without love." Nor could she tell him about Harry dying. And then his returning, alive, which was the most terrible part of all.

The day she came home early, Kate hadn't found them upstairs. The wheelchair was in the hall, but she looked in the backyard anyway. Maybe Nolan had taken him out for a drive? It was one of the few things that still made Robin feel good. It was as if they'd traveled backward in time, and Robin was a baby again, and the only way they could get him to sleep was to drive him around and around the hills of Oakland. Nolan would strap him in, careful not to bruise him, and then he'd drive like a little old man: slow to the stop signs, even slower to start. If he saw a pothole, he went around it, and speed bumps he negotiated like land mines. It worked, though—on nights when Robin couldn't sleep and the medicine wasn't helping, nights when the drugs backfired and left him anxious and in pain, the drives were the only thing that helped.

Kate normally didn't go along. Not that she wasn't

invited—it was her car and her child; obviously she could have gone, too—but the care with which Nolan drove Robin, as if he were about to break, made her insane. She wanted speed for her little boy. Ninety miles an hour on a hot summer night with the top down, an arm stuck out to dance in the wind. But Robin couldn't ride like that anymore.

That afternoon, she'd thought they were driving. Out somewhere. She'd taken Nolan's car when she'd left, knowing Robin liked hers best.

So when Kate had gone into the garage and smelled the exhaust, when she'd heard her Saab *putt-putt*ing along, when she'd seen the garage door all the way down, she hadn't panicked. They were getting ready to go. Or maybe they were just getting back; Robin was asleep in the backseat, she could see through the window.

When she saw Nolan slumped at the wheel, though, she couldn't quite make her brain work fast enough. *Something. Do something.*

Thwack! She hit the garage door button. She ran through the house and grabbed the portable phone and dialed 911 so quickly that it felt like she'd always had the phone in her hand. The dispatcher asked questions Kate couldn't answer, and she hung up, hurling the phone into the bushes. While she waited for the sirens, at first so far away, to get closer, she dragged Robin out. She pulled him more roughly than she ever had before, knowing somehow that the tilt of his head was just wrong, and if she could get him out on the lawn, she could get it right. Get him normal again. As normal as he'd been that morning, maybe. Or even better, the week before. Or the month before, before they'd lost what was left of their hope.

Robin wouldn't go like this. It wasn't supposed to be like this. It *couldn't* end this way.

Nolan was still in the garage, still slumped at the wheel.

Kate pulled open the driver's-side door and undid his seat belt. He was heavy, slouched forward as if his spine had softened. She didn't know how to get him out, only that she had to, so she leaned in and put one arm under each of his and then pulled as if her own life depended on it. He moved more easily than Robin, perhaps because if she looked into her heart to examine it, she cared less, if only by the smallest—almost immeasurable—fraction. She moved faster, with a tiny bit less caution. She was stronger, too. The fear had by then become a raging beast inside her, and she probably could have picked up the car and shaken it over her head if she'd needed to.

She had to move fast with Nolan, because the sooner she dragged the man she loved outside to the good air, the sooner she got to go back to Robin, the boy she loved most.

Nolan on the grass. Faceup. Not breathing. She knew he wasn't, and there wasn't anything else she could do, just pray the ambulance got there in time to help him.

She chose Robin.

His mouth was still warm, and the feel of his lips on hers gave her hope. She could taste the banana he'd had for lunch, the food that sat best with him now. And there was the acrid yellow smell of his medicine, the smell that made both of them gag when she gave it to him.

His chest, under Kate's hands, moved perfectly. She was strong. Nolan always told her how strong she was—it wasn't even hard to do this, to keep his lungs moving for him, to give him her breath. She willed herself not to use any of the oxygen before she gave it to him. She didn't need it, and her boy did—she knew that—even though his lips were still pink, his cheeks ruddy, as if he were in the best of health. When Robin was a baby, still healthy, Kate would sneak into his room, convinced he'd stopped breathing. It was only by sheer force of her own will that his chest had risen and fallen—staring at him was what started him breathing again. She knew it was a ridiculous idea, but it was one she believed. She had given birth to him. Her body had made her son breathe. She should be allowed to do it just one last time. For fuck's sake, she was finally getting good at it.

In between breaths, she screamed for help. From anyone, from God, from Mr. Foster next door. The screams ripped from her lungs, shredded terror that she sent out with nothing returned. While she pressed Robin's chest again and again, she thought bitterly of the two-income houses they were surrounded by. All their neighbors had fabulous jobs, fantastic lives. Their perfect, healthy children were either in day care or in expensive charter schools. Where the hell, then, was the help? Kate saw maids go in and out of people's houses, saw their gardeners with their leaf blowers and poison sprays—where were they now? Where was someone, anyone else that she could direct to do CPR on Nolan?

No one came. No one saw. No one helped.

She felt incredibly small, as if the grass were falling away beneath her and Robin. The only thing left was her, pumping his chest, putting air in his lungs—above them, a vast sky of blue that reached so far into the heavens that not even God could see them.

When the engine pulled up, a firefighter who looked barely old enough to drink had to hold her in his arms, had to lock her there while two full crews attended to each of her men. Two police officers helped him hold her—she was a wildcat, a banshee, a hurricane—while more, so many of them, stood along the lawn's edge watching. She fought the firefighter so hard she knew his face and arms were bleeding by the time the ambulance left the scene, sirens blaring, but she didn't apologize.

Nolan was put in the hyperbaric chamber. The carbon

monoxide was forced from his hemoglobin so that regular carbon dioxide could reattach as it was supposed to. The chamber was used for divers who had the bends, they told her. Kate wondered if they would let her borrow it someday, since she was at the bottom. She'd float up eventually, right? Wasn't that what she would have to do? Bodies underwater bloated and, at some point, surfaced. But while they saved Nolan's life, no one could bring Robin back. The doctor said his lungs were too weak. It had been too much for his body to handle. Robin hadn't felt a thing, he said. Not a thing. He'd just drifted off into his last nap.

Kate felt a jealousy that she'd never felt in her whole life, an envy so thick and viscous she could almost see it, a film in front of her eyes. Robin drifted off.

R is always, always R is always for Robin.

Chapter Thirty-nine

Saturday, May 17, 2014
7:45 a.m.

Fred Weasley looked at Nolan with rheumy, wary eyes as Nolan dressed to leave Saturday morning. "Never seen me like this, have you?" He meant the way he was dressed, although he was never this deeply furious, either. Nolan put on his one pair of slacks, a thrift store find, dun-colored with a slight stain at the right hem, and a nice blue shirt he'd bought in the city on a whim one day when he'd passed Brooks Brothers in Union Square, remembering all the money he'd dropped there over the years. He'd thought maybe he'd someday need an outfit for a date, though it had felt like an impossibility even then. Now it just felt ridiculous. The knot forming of the dark blue tie came back to him as if he'd done it yesterday instead of more than three years before. He tugged it harder than he needed to, rage coursing through his upper arms and into his fingers. He watched his face turn red in the mirror. Only then did he loosen it. His eye was deeply purpled, and he felt satisfaction that one part of him, at least, looked the way he felt.

Other than the black eye, he looked okay. For a funeral.

It was still early, before eight, when Nolan pulled up in front of the house. Only one cameraperson had come out, was still waiting on the sidewalk.

"Mr. Monroe! Do you have any statement about whether or not you're reconciling with Kate?"

He gave what he hoped was a crazed smile and waved with only his middle finger. Tomorrow there would be none of them left.

When Kate opened the door, she looked almost happy. It was just for a second, and then she brought the lines of her face back under control. It made him even more furious.

"Come in," she said.

Inside, through to the kitchen—it was tidy, the dishes put away. As if she'd sent that e-mail and then gone about her business cleaning up. All of it was so unlike her.

"Coffee?" she asked, holding out a cup—his blue mug—the way she had a million times before.

"Were you ever going to tell me?"

She said nothing. Just stood there, her eyes swimming with tears he didn't want to see.

"You kept my *daughter* from me?"

"She wasn't ours. She couldn't be."

"You sure seem to have her now."

Kate shook her head. "Up until the day she turned eighteen, it was a closed adoption. Still is, technically. I *couldn't* tell you."

"She found you somehow." Nolan's feet remained planted rigidly apart.

"Internet. You know, like the kids do." She smiled again, thinly. "I put my info in. Late one night. I was drunk—I barely remember doing it. I wanted to tell you a thousand times."

His hands balled into fists at his sides, then starfished out. "You told me everything else."

"I did."

"Everything. You were the most honest person I'd ever met. Too honest."

Kate nodded. She looked as miserable as she had in the courtroom, her skin white, her eyes wide.

"But you didn't tell me I was a *father.* Even after I'd lost that part of myself."

She shook her head and sucked in her lips.

"Jesus, Kate! You took my *daughter.* The only chance I had at a daughter. You stole it from me."

"Wait—"

"You robbed me of the chance to keep doing the only thing I was good at." His shoulders shook.

"We couldn't have found her. We weren't allowed to. If I'd told you, it would have been worse. I thought I was protecting you. And I was scared."

"Of *what*?"

"Of losing you. I was used to losing things by then. Dad. I lost Mom even though she was still around. Then you. The biggest mistake of my life was not telling you when we found each other again—it should have been the very first thing out of my mouth. When it wasn't, it was too late. That sealed the lid of it shut. I didn't know what else to do. You were gone. You'd left for Hawaii with your parents. As far as I knew you were never coming back."

"We should have had her, Kate. She should have been *ours.* This whole time, she could have been our little girl. We'd be the ones sending her to college. We'd know her favorite color. She'd come to me when she was scared. There'd be no cause for her to be frightened of me."

"She's not scared of you . . ."

"Her brother's dead. Of course she's terrified of me. She has to be. Everyone else is."

Kate jumped as he kicked the bottom of the cabinet next to the stove. It flew off its broken hinge, the one he'd always told Kate he'd fix but never got around to. It clattered across the tile with a crash.

He'd have been good with a daughter. He knew it. Crouching, he tried to put the cabinet door back on.

"This hinge is blown."

"It has been."

"I'm gone for three years and you don't fix a single goddamn thing." It wasn't a question. "The bathroom sink still not draining?"

"Oh, love . . ."

That word was what did it. He stood and was forward, inside her space before he knew how he'd gotten there. Kate pressed herself against the edge of the counter, her back bending as she moved backward. She couldn't go any farther. He pushed against her.

"She's *mine.*"

"But I—"

"I could kill you for this." The pain in his fists, in his chest, told him it wasn't an idle threat. Her breath was warm on his cheek, and every single fucking thing he wanted to do to her was physical. He wanted to put his hand to her neck and tighten until she went as red as he had that morning with the tie, holding until she went blue. He wanted to pin her arms back and fuck her hard, standing up. He wanted to kiss her so that she couldn't breathe. He'd never felt such a need to hurt someone. Ever. "*Fuck.*" He pushed back, the lower half of his body pressing against hers before he moved away from her. He focused on Robin's chair. He knew she'd felt his cock and he didn't give a shit.

She was even paler now, so white Nolan wondered if she would faint. What would he do if she did?

Kate said, "It was what you loved the best. What you were the best at. Being a father."

"Is that supposed to make me feel *better*?"

"I'd managed to give that to you. With Robin. You never needed to know how much I'd screwed up back then. It was so long ago, and I'd had to let her go completely. I pushed her away. I almost never consciously thought about her. Only on her birthday. I'd compartmentalized my brain so much by that point that it didn't even feel like lying. I can't explain it. It was like it had happened to another person, someone who wasn't me." She paused. "It's not something I'm going to apologize for, Nolan. Not after what you did."

Nolan clenched his hands and then released them to hit the tabletop, which shook as if it might collapse. He roared, a noise he'd never made before, not even when he'd woken in the hospital to be told he'd lost his son. The sound went on and on, filling the kitchen, filling the house where Robin and he both used to live.

Then Nolan sank to his knees and her arms were around him. He struggled against her. He kicked, flailing against her, and his shoe hit her shin, but she didn't cry out. She was stronger, in this moment, than he was. She held on as if she were riding him, as if there were a cash prize for staying on top of him as he thrashed and wailed. He kicked the wall and the chair; his arms beat the floor. He heard her gasp and then she twisted again, wrestling him so that he was holding her on his lap. Then she launched herself at him, this time in a kiss—not so much a kiss as a battle. The winner would be the most ferocious. Blood bloomed inside his mouth and he wasn't sure whose it was. Kate gasped for air. In that fraction of a second, as her body relaxed for a short moment, he pulled at the top of her jeans. She retaliated by yanking his belt so hard it slapped against her forearm.

When their clothes were disposed of, strewn around them, under them, he paused, holding himself above her, right at the very edge, his arms shaking with the strain of holding himself up. He looked down. Kate's eyes were full of tears and rage. He wouldn't . . . he couldn't just—

She did it for him, shoving her hips upward as hard as she could, taking him in his moment of indecision. He was in her then, and collapsing on top of her; he pinned her as they bucked against each other, their sobs disguised as gasps. When he came, there was nothing left but the feeling—he'd chased everything else out, away, and the blank silence felt like forgiveness. She clenched against him, her eyes screwed shut, her fingers digging into his upper arms, pulling him harder against her as she reached her own release on a strangled curse.

Kate shifted then, rotating on the floor so that she was tucked in against his side, her face pressed into his neck. She cried, softly, the way she'd never let herself cry in the old days. Then she'd been stiff, holding her tears back until they burst from her violently all at once. Now the tears were slow and steady.

When eventually she stilled, he sat up, taking her hand. They walked upstairs without discussion and he led her into their old bedroom. It smelled different now, but Nolan found he didn't care. They pulled the covers back and slid in, he on the right, she on the left, as they always had. She laid her head on his shoulder and his arm still fit around her. The morning light streamed through the glass and lit up the side of her face the way it used to. Through the bed and up through the floorboards, he could feel the strength of the front door he'd chosen and hung by himself.

Kate cleared her throat. "Do you want to know how Mom died?"

His answer was a kiss to her temple.

"I was going to pull the plug."

"Kate."

"She wasn't breathing on her own. Her heart was barely putting up a fight. They said she was most likely brain-dead and wouldn't be coming back. I'd been waiting for her to wake up. I wanted her to say she wished she'd met my daughter. Or to just *look* at me and really see me. I knew she'd wake up and we'd say everything. Finally. But then she didn't. The doctors said she never would. The thing I'd wanted from her for so long was never, ever going to happen. So I made the decision to have them shut off the machines. It's funny, I guess I'd always kind of seen an actual plug in my mind. Like someone bends down to the wall and yanks out the cord. I was sitting here at home, sitting on this bed, choosing the time my mother would die. But then . . . I went to the hospital that morning, and she'd just died. Five minutes before I got there."

Nolan started to say something, but his voice choked. Finally he simply said, "I'm so sorry." It was enough. Long minutes passed as they stared up at the ceiling. Their ceiling.

"Pree doesn't know who you are," said Kate. "I told you but not her."

"You should have told both of us." But the rage had left him, the heat of it burned out by the shape of her in his arms.

"I know. And you shouldn't have left me alone."

"I didn't want to." She didn't know it for the truth it was, and he knew he couldn't explain it to her, not in a way she'd believe.

They kissed again, and this time it was different. It was the way it had been the first time. And on their wedding day. And over Robin's head, the first time they met him. How they should have kissed when they let him go.

Chapter Forty

Saturday, May 17, 2014
10 a.m.

Pree steered her car into a small parking lot along the water. Dozens of boats bobbed at their moorings. Tiny white birds battled the larger seagulls over the fish guts a guy was tossing off the pier. She had no freaking idea how to find Kate. She'd never thought there would be this many boats here and they hadn't set up a real meeting point. She drove slowly through the lot, easing into the next one, craning her neck to look at the various people.

But then there she was. Kate was walking down a short dock. A man, his face turned toward the water, was behind her. Nolan. Pree felt her throat muscles tighten and pulled into a parking spot.

Kate waved when she saw her. Nolan smiled. He had a black eye that went from his temple down to the middle of his cheek. Pree wanted to ask about it, but she felt tongue-tied. She hid her hands inside her dress pockets. Kate held a brown Trader Joe's bag with one hand and pushed her wind-blown curls out of her face with the other. Pree could have told her it was no use—her own curls were already halfway to dreads. Once they'd all said hello, she pulled an elastic band out of her backpack and snapped it around her hair.

"Do you happen to have another of those?" Kate asked.

She dug in her pocket and handed one over. It was silly and minor, but it felt intimate somehow, giving Kate the hair band.

"We're waiting for that one." Kate pointed at a blue sail-boat slowly scudding under motor power through the gray water. Pree nudged the rubber bumper on the dock with the edge of her sneaker. Then she noticed Nolan was doing the same thing on the other side of Kate, so she stopped.

"What's that?" she said, pointing, trying to fill the spaces in the awkwardness.

"Oh," said Kate. She looked down. Her face twisted.

"Shit," Pree said, getting it. Really? A Trader Joe's bag?

Kate's words were rushed. "They're in nice boxes, I promise. Mom's is walnut, and Robin's is cedar. I just needed some way to carry them . . ."

"Shit," Pree said again. Nothing else really seemed appropriate.

And then Nolan laughed, the reverberation deep in his chest. The air turned brighter and Pree didn't want to hurl herself in the water anymore.

As the sailboat moored, bumping the rubber guards with a hollow sound, the fog thinned and a skinny beam of sun-light touched the edge of the dock. Brian, the guy driving the boat, looked like he was born to do nothing more than tool a boat around the bay, pulling up fish as he went. He was a little scruffy and maybe thirty-five. Pree shoved her hands into her pockets and listened to him tell them where to stand and, more important, where not to stand. Brian showed them the ropes—literally—and told them he might ask them for help. At any minute Pree was going to screw it up by getting knocked overboard by something sail related. She told herself to duck whenever anything at all happened.

This whole stupid thing was too romantic an idea. When she'd woken up that morning, she'd thought it might be cool, going to sea to bury the brother she never knew. And hey, she might turn out to be a born sailor. Maybe she'd find out she was meant to live someday on a boat in a ramshackle marina somewhere. Alone, except for one of those boat cats that prowled around the bow.

But Pree quickly learned that the motion of the boat didn't agree with either her or her condition. From the dock, the water had looked flat, but in reality it was pocked and marred by tiny waves that instantly made her want to hurl. She took a deep breath through her mouth and told herself to hang the fuck on. Mind over matter.

Brian aimed the boat toward Alcatraz. "We'll take the scenic route. Maybe see some harbor porpoises. They were hanging out near Angel Island earlier this morning." He said it as if they were tourists at Pier 39 or something, as if they'd come for the view. But Kate and Nolan nodded along and looked as if there were nothing more interesting than perhaps getting to see some marine wildlife. Then Kate disappeared into the underneath part of the boat. Belowdecks, Brian had called it. Pree followed her. Maybe it was smoother down there.

Kate stood behind a tiny counter, the two wooden boxes in front of her. She looked up when Pree clattered down the stairs, and half smiled.

"You all right?" Kate said.

"Sure." Pree wasn't. She scoped out where the bathroom was—she could make it if she needed to. Knowing that calmed her stomach for a minute. "Are *you* all right?"

Kate pressed her fingers one by one against the countertop. "I guess when I booked the boat I didn't expect it to be so . . . real."

The boat lurched and both Pree and Kate toppled to the left. One box slid to the edge of the counter—Pree caught it the second before it went airborne. It was surprisingly heavy. Kate took it, propping her hip against the counter for stability.

"I'm sorry," Pree said.

"For what? You haven't done anything wrong."

"I guess, for all of this. That you have to go through." A tiny part of her felt an odd guilt for not being there for Kate when Robin died. Not that she'd had a choice in it. But the guilt remained, small and uncomfortable.

"Oh." Kate shrugged. "I've done a lot of the going-through already. This is just . . . punctuation."

Pree stared at the lighter-colored box.

"That's Robin," Kate said. "I mean . . . you know."

She wanted to see inside, and at the same time she didn't. "Do you throw the whole box?"

Kate shook her head. "Not encouraged. You just shake out the ashes. You're not even supposed to do that—bad for the bay and all—but we're not asking permission. See?" She took the lid off and inside was a clear plastic bag, like the kind you put vegetables in at the grocery store. It was even sealed closed with a twist tie. Inside was gray dust that looked, from the outside, like the clay Pree had used in college during her pottery phase.

"I just have to . . ." Kate undid the tie and peered in. She took a small ziplock bag from her pocket. Turning it inside out, she put her hand inside, as if to pick up dog poop. Then she reached into the bigger bag and took a handful. She flipped the plastic bag as if it were something she did every day and sealed it. Tucking it back into her front pocket, she gave Pree a quick look. The boat swayed again, and Pree wasn't sure what made her feel more sick, the rolling of the boat that made her knees feel like they were made of Silly Putty or the idea that Kate had just stuck her hand into Robin's ashes and put them in her pocket.

Pree barely made it to the bathroom in time. It was harder than she would have thought, wearing a life jacket and puking in a tiny little toilet while pitching back and forth. When she came back out, Kate was leaning forward, whispering urgently to Nolan. The noise of the boat slapping through the water masked whatever it was she was saying, but Nolan looked up, and his face was transparently guilty. His hand had been resting on top of Kate's, and he pulled it back as if he'd touched an iron.

It reminded Pree acutely of a picture at home that Marta kept in the living room, framed, on the wall next to all her school portraits. The wall of shame, Pree called it, and she hated almost every single photo. But even she could see the humor in this one: in it Pree was sitting in her cow pajamas not next to but *under* the Christmas tree. She was lit harshly by the flashbulb and she was completely caught: the partially unwrapped box still in her lap, one hand on the toe of her new Rollerblades. She looked guiltier than anything.

Nolan had that exact look on his face.

Like, *the exact look.* Pree couldn't quite figure it out. She could almost get it, but then she shied away. "I should go back up . . ."

"Pree," said Kate. "I have to tell you something." Looking terrified, she gripped a brass railing affixed to the wall.

"No, that's okay. Thanks anyway," Pree said, as if Kate had asked her if she wanted a snack. *No, no chips for me. I'll pass on the chocolate milk.*

"He's your father."

It all came together in one bright flash, as if Isi's camera had flashed again the way it had that Christmas morning.

"Nolan's your biological father. I should have told you that right off. I know that, and I'm sorry."

He stepped forward, and Pree ducked back into a tiny alcove next to the head. "No, no. Don't."

"He just found out, too. Yesterday," said Kate.

"I don't understand," Pree said. She felt so stupid. And she couldn't get away. She was on a fucking *boat* with no way off. "What about Greg Jenkins?"

"It was Nolan."

"You lied."

"Yes," said Kate miserably.

"I don't— Why?"

"I was scared. I'd been so scared—"

"Did you just want to keep me for yourself or something?" She walked past both of them to the bottom of the stairs, where she held on to the railing with all her strength. "Because you didn't want to share?"

She saw the truth of it reflected in Kate's eyes. And there was a tiny, shameful part of herself that liked it—that liked that Kate wanted her so much she didn't want to share her with anyone.

But Kate had shared Pree right out of her life twenty-two years ago, hadn't she?

"Pree, that's not it," started Nolan. He was holding the rail next to the sink as if the boat were going over twenty-foot waves.

"Did Kate tell you I'm pregnant?"

It was Nolan's turn to look shocked. He shook his head dumbly.

Pree started up the stairs. "Like mother, like daughter, I guess." She wanted one of them to stop her. But neither of them did.

Chapter Forty-one

Saturday, May 17, 2014
11 a.m.

If anything, Kate should have been scared of flying. On planes, she should have gripped her armrests and prayed to a God she didn't understand while soaring through the clouds. But she didn't. She loved flying. It was always water she'd been scared of without a good reason. And now there were so many reasons to hate being on this boat, to hate being this terrified.

"This was your idea, you know," said Nolan. He still had that ability to read her.

She ignored him and went up the steps.

The closer they got to the Golden Gate Bridge, the windier it became. Brian had told her on the phone that the best place to dump ashes was in the ocean, outside the bay, but she was worried that it would be even rougher. If Pree had been sick on the little wavelets, what would happen out there?

Brian stood with his hand resting lightly on the wheel. His legs were planted far apart and he gazed straight ahead. He didn't acknowledge her. He was obviously accustomed to these trips of grief, used to pretending he wasn't there. Kate was grateful.

Pree sat at the bow, her legs slung over the edge, her arms wrapped around the rail in front of her, watching Alcatraz glide past to her right.

Kate stopped, unable to move forward or back. She held the rail but only lightly. Ironically, her legs seemed to take to this—she swayed from her kneecaps as if she'd been on boats all her life.

Brian looked at her over his sunglasses and blinked. The skin of his eyelids was pale in contrast to the rest of his face. Then he looked past her to Pree. "Hey, you wanna steer the boat?"

Pree turned her head. "Me? No."

"Come on."

"No way. I'd put us on those rocks."

"I won't let that happen."

"No." Pree was firm. "Never."

"You don't want to be able to say that you steered a sailboat under the Golden Gate? You won't regret that someday?"

Kate saw Pree bite her lip.

Come on, Pree.

"Show me," Pree said, standing.

Brian put her hands on the wheel and stayed next to her. "That's right," he said. "You're a natural."

Pree looked jittery. "But how do I avoid the legs of the bridge? They're huge."

"Same as you avoid things in a car. Just think your way

there. Watch with your eyes—your hands already know how to do it."

Pree narrowed her eyes the same way Nolan did when he was concentrating. The boat's sail guttered as the wind shifted.

"What do I do?"

"To the left a little," said Brian calmly. The sail filled again and they darted forward. "Yeah, good."

Kate felt, rather than saw, Nolan come up the stairs behind her. He put his hand, as he always had, on the small of her back to tell her he was there, and she tucked her body into his, the top of her shoulder fitting exactly under his arm. She stayed in the lee of his arms for the space of two breaths, long enough to fill her lungs with courage. Then she stepped out. She wanted to feel the wind. Still moving easily even though the boat bucked, she took Pree's abandoned place at the bow.

She threaded her legs under the rail, letting them hang in the air. The salt spray dampened her jeans and Brian warned her that her feet might get wet. One part of her cared—her feet should *not* be getting that close to the water, period. The other part of her exulted in the salt and wind hitting her face, the slap and clank of the sails above her.

The Golden Gate drew closer, and Kate risked a backward glance. Pree's face was as bright as the sun glinting on the waves. As the sailboat glided under the steel girders, the cars thumping far overheard, Pree barely glanced up. She appeared transfixed by the water in front of her. Behind her, Nolan looked just as transfixed by Pree.

As well he should be. Pree was remarkable. A sense of pride surged through her, as misplaced and strong an emotion as she'd ever had.

The boat sailed into open waters. They could sail due

west for days, weeks, and not run into anything until they hit Japan, just as Robin had always said. It was dizzying, and Kate held the rail tighter. The swells were different here, wider somehow, more spaced apart. While earlier the boat had jogged like a trotting horse, now it swayed like an enormous rocking chair.

"I'm done," said Pree. "That's all I need. Can you do it now?"

Brian took the wheel. "I'll take her out a ways and then we can heave to. Rest for a while. Do our thing."

Kate considered what "our thing" meant and thought about the small boxes belowdecks. A boat with bright green sails came into view around the curve of the Marin headland, and she wondered what the people on board were doing. Drinking champagne and toasting a celebration? Or dumping loved ones over the rails also?

She expected Pree to go sit in the back, away from her, but instead she swung forward, gripping the rope and dropping onto the edge next to her. Nolan sat next to Kate on the other side. If she reached out, she could touch them both at the same time.

"I fucked up," Kate said, her voice loud enough to reach both Pree and Nolan. It probably reached farther, over the slapping waves back to Brian. She didn't care. "What I did, I just fucked it all up. I should have told Nolan about you when I got back together with him so long ago. I should have told you about him, Pree, the first time you asked. I've had secrets locked so long inside that I'd forgotten how to open that part."

Kate would lose them both because of this. She knew it. This morning with Nolan had been a mirage. Whatever she might have had with Pree was evaporating into salt mist in front of her, and it was her fault. She held the cold metal so tightly her thumbs went numb. She had to keep being brave until she was alone again.

Pree faced away from her, toward the open ocean. "How was I supposed to figure anything out if I didn't know my past? Where I came from?"

"Easy," said Kate lightly, motioning with her head toward the land behind them. "You came from them. Isi and Marta."

A pause. Then Pree said, "Robin's dead."

The words sounded worse coming from Pree. Kate closed her eyes and leaned her forehead against the railing. It was cold and smelled of steel.

Pree continued, "I'm the only real link you have left to him. You're not related to each other by blood, but both of you are related to me. That's your connection. To him and to each other. You need me. But I still don't get why . . ."

Kate looked at Pree. She wanted to touch her, rest her hand on her arm, but she didn't want to risk chasing her away. "I missed you every day that I didn't see you. There wasn't a moment that you weren't part of my life."

"Bullshit." But Pree's word was weak and got lost in the spray.

The sailboat turned slowly, heading west and then south. The Golden Gate was farther away than Kate had realized. The only noise was the splashing of the water against the hull and the creaking of the sails overhead. Kate knew she had to speak, but she didn't have a clue what to say.

Pree was the one to finally break the silence. "And you kept him from me. What were you thinking, Kate? Yesterday, I was just hanging out with you guys, and he's my father? And you knew?"

"I'm sorry." Weak, tiny words, so impotent in the face of Pree's sorrow.

"Were you worried I couldn't be trusted or something? Oh, maybe you're right. Maybe I *would* have asked why he killed my brother, the one I never got to meet."

Nolan blinked once slowly and the color drained from his face.

"Pree."

"What? I just found out half my genes are his. You think I'm not a little worried? That I have the genetic marker of a suicidal killer? Maybe it's hereditary, the whole not being able to take care of anything. Good thing I don't want this kid." Her nose was pink and her eyes were wet. Kate couldn't tell if she was crying or windblown.

Nolan stuffed his hands in his pockets. His lips pressed thinly together.

"Robin was sick," Kate said. "Really sick. Don't be mad at him. Be mad at me."

"I'm not mad at either of you. Or maybe I am. Maybe I'm going to be. I'm just confused—don't you get that?" Pree covered her belly with her hands.

No one spoke then. Kate wished she knew the right thing to say, but she suspected it didn't exist. Everything was wrong. Everything. Again.

They sailed another ten minutes until Brian judged they were at a good spot to stop. He turned the boat just off the wind and luffed the mainsail. He turned the tiller in the opposite direction, and the boat went still in the water. Behind them, the ocean was clear, calmer this far out.

It was time.

Kate retrieved the boxes from below. She felt a solid clunk inside, as if she were grinding gears, going from forward to reverse too suddenly. But she kept moving, up the stairs back onto the deck, her legs still working easily with the sway of the boat. It was quiet now without the flapping of the sail. Small waves splashed at the side of the boat, and two pieces of metal clanked overhead.

She didn't know how to do this. She'd gone through Robin's funeral without the man she loved beside her, and now he was here, and she wanted more than anything to hand him his son's box.

But before she handed it to him, she needed to know one thing. Kate said, "Have you ever visited his grave?"

Nolan blinked.

Pree opened and then shut her mouth.

The ocean grew even more still, as if it were also waiting for his answer.

Chapter Forty-two

Saturday, May 17, 2014
11:15 a.m.

"Me?" Nolan said. "You're asking *me* that?"

The anger was back, sudden and pure, burning like gasoline through his veins. He'd never seen Kate at the grave, not once. He thought he might see her when he started taking all those walks with Fred, always stopping to talk to Robin, to touch the little Harry Potter figurine he'd found at the comics store down the street. But not one time had he seen her. "I'm there almost every day. Where are *you*?"

"Excuse me?"

"You live around the corner. It's a five-minute walk through a nice neighborhood to get to the front gate."

"That's not what I asked," she said. "I just didn't know if you'd been there. If you knew where he was."

"*Do* you go see him? That's all I want to know."

With her free hand, Kate shoved the mass of her windblown hair back. "None of your business."

He was right—she didn't go. And it was his business. He knew why she'd asked. In her typical Kate way, she'd assumed that, like her, he couldn't go. She'd probably been planning to get mad at him about it, never dreaming that Nolan had never been able to stay away from the cemetery where his child was buried. Nolan knew that if Robin actually still existed anywhere, he'd be glad his father came. But the most important person to Robin had always been, without question or doubt, his mother.

And she didn't visit him.

"That's crazy," he muttered. "Around the fucking corner."

"Nolan—"

"Did you always argue like this?" asked Pree, shoving her hair back in the same way Kate just had.

"No, Pree—" started Kate. "We weren't—"

"We didn't argue. Almost never." Nolan felt stricken.

"Whatever," Pree said. "Mostly people are just who they are no matter what's going on around them. That's what I think anyway." She lightly tapped the top of the rail as if to make sure it was strong enough. She was so like Kate when Kate had been that age—all ragged emotion and long limbs—that it twisted Nolan's heart.

He closed his eyes for a moment and felt the sun heat the backs of his eyelids. When he opened them again, he looked through the bridge to Berkeley and Oakland, so far away now. The cities looked sturdy. Friendly. A myriad of red and brown roofs, tilting upward toward them. So many lives filled those spaces, all of them loving as hard as they had, and all of them would end up in the same place with hands full of ash. It was an awful thought, terrible enough for him to want to sail away forever and beautiful enough that he didn't want to let go.

"We argued about everything except what mattered," Nolan said. "Who needed to do laundry. Who left the cheese on the counter so it dried out. Whose turn it was to give him his medicine. Jesus. I thought it was my job. She thought it was hers. We fought about who got to sleep with him. And about what we would do when he was gone."

"No."

His bait had worked—the lie of his last sentence got to Kate, broke through that look on her face, the one that scared him.

"We never fought about what we would do when he was gone." Kate lowered her voice. "We never talked about that. You know it."

"We should have. Why didn't we?"

Kate laced her fingers in front of her. Sun reflected off the water and dappled her curls. "Who tells you to do that? Who explains that to someone in the spot where we were?"

"Hospice did."

"But I hated them."

"You loved them."

Kate gave a brittle half smile. "They were angels," she said. "And I hated them more than I've ever hated anyone in my whole life."

"They couldn't have been any nicer. Any stronger. Any more loving. They told us what to do, Kate. They told us to start planning. We should have listened. We owed him that—we owed him more of us. We should have planned for this, for what happened to us afterward."

"It's like you're blaming me." The tendons in Kate's neck were strained. "You can't do that."

"We gave up on him. I should have done more. You should have, too. So damn straight I'm blaming you." Nolan felt dizzy and reached a hand to steady himself on the seat behind him.

And it was, finally, time for him to tell her the truth, fuck whether or not she believed him. "It was on purpose. I killed him on purpose." Something she'd known, of course, but something he had never admitted out loud, not once, to her or anyone. "I never planned it, though. We were just going for a fucking drive. He was hurting and couldn't sleep. But the drive didn't help. I had to turn around before we even got up to Skyline. We pulled into the garage, and I put down the door, and then I looked in the rearview mirror, and I wished to hell my baby could just go to fucking sleep. So I didn't turn the engine off."

Kate made a strangled noise behind her hand.

"And for just a moment, I planned to kill myself, too. I thought I couldn't live without him. But Jesus, just like thirty seconds later, I looked in the rearview mirror and saw that he was asleep, and I realized I couldn't leave you like that. I could never have left you like that, Katie. The last thing I remember was panicking, fighting to undo my seat belt, but I couldn't get my thumb to work right. It just happened so fast. I never knew it would happen so fast." He gulped painful, salty air. "I would never have left you. Don't you *know* that?" That had been the worst part—that she *hadn't* believed in him. "You're the one who left *me*."

Chapter Forty-three

Saturday, May 17, 2014
11:20 a.m.

Kate felt as if the boat dipped out from below her feet, leaving her standing on nothing but wind. She was dropping, falling. Everything around them disappeared. Pree wasn't watching with her careful eyes; Brian wasn't there. There was just him—just Nolan. And the box she held, the box her boy was in.

Nolan looked as if he were going to pass out. *Fuck*, she wished she couldn't read him so well. She wished she could go back to where she'd been just minutes, seconds before.

"Nolan. You don't remember what happened. You never remembered."

He shook his head. "I remembered in prison."

She could only stare at him. The doctors had said then that his short-term memory of that day might come back spontaneously, or it might never return. Then did he know . . . ?

"I remembered every minute until I passed out."

"Jesus," she said.

Finally, he spoke, and the sound was dusty, as if the words had been so long unused they creaked. "Tell me."

Pree moved silently toward the back of the boat, as if she knew this was just for them. Brian made himself busy with a manual of some kind.

"I left the search window open." Kate took what felt like the last breath of her life. "The cops used the back button and found where I'd been."

Without a sound, Nolan mouthed, *No.*

But he knew. She had to go on. She'd done this to him, brought him to this. She had to finish it. "'CO poisoning.' 'Garage death.' 'How long does death take?' 'Murder-suicide.' It was all there. They could see every search I'd done, all the way back to the original one: 'mercy killing.'"

"They didn't care I tried to commit suicide—that was only a crime against myself. But those searches were why I got convicted. When I didn't have my memory, I thought *I'd* looked them up. But it was you."

"You planned to fall asleep. With my boy." They were weak words.

"I never planned it. That's the point, Kate. I would never have planned it."

No. No more of this conversation. It was too much, too awful . . . She was crying then, and she didn't want to be. The grief felt new again, and that kind of sorrow should never, *ever* feel new. It wasn't fair.

Nolan's arms went around her. She felt him shake so hard she thought he might break apart. Against her ear, he said, "I never would have left you."

The fingers of her left hand dug into the flesh above his shoulder blades, her right hand still clutching Robin's box. "You wanted to die," she said. "With him."

"I never would have left you," he said.

Why did he keep repeating that? Grief and guilt felt like a dizzying leap, a twist in her stomach, a lurch she couldn't recover from. "Did you think you were the only one who lay awake at night wishing that you could take the pain from him? I did the math while you were sleeping. If someone had told me that I could trade another little boy's life for Robin, you know what? I would have done it. If I'd had to pull the plug myself, if it would have saved Robin, I'd have done it while I watched the boy's mother throw herself onto his bed. If someone had said, 'Here. Flip this switch, and a van full of six children will die in a fiery crash but Robin will live to see his twenty-first birthday'"—Kate's voice failed but she kept speaking—"I'd have done it. In the middle of the night, I decided I couldn't consign a whole village full of starving children to death as a trade. That's where my line was. A whole fucking village. But six kids? I could have killed six of them for Robin. I would have."

Nolan pulled away and rubbed his temples. There was a streak of gray in his hair she hadn't noticed, and it hurt her heart to look at it. "I feel like I'm at the bottom of a well. I know there's a top up there, and I know where I fell in, but I can't ever see daylight. There's no light at all. I'm trapped, and I can't get out. I can't help him. I can't help you."

She leaned her forehead against his chest. He smelled like Nolan, like soap. Like duct tape and pencils and, now, cold salt wind.

Nolan spoke against her hair again. "You should have told me the truth."

Her fingers tensed against his back. "I know."

His hands came up and pushed gently at Kate's upper

arms. He put her away from him, and there was an agony of space between them. "That's why you didn't fight for me."

"What?"

"You chose Robin."

"I—"

"Of course you chose him that day, when you brought us out. I knew you gave him CPR, not me, and that was exactly what you should have done. That's what I would have done, too. But then, later. You never chose me, and I never knew why."

"I stood by you every minute of the trial—"

"As I went down. I had no memory of what had happened—I assumed the search terms were mine. You didn't testify for me. You said you couldn't."

She'd always been a bad liar. He knew that. "I was so confused. I didn't know what to do."

"I needed you to fight for me, like you'd fought for Robin, and I didn't understand why you didn't. You were so strong, and I needed you to do battle for me."

"But you didn't fight for yourself—"

"I couldn't. That's when I knew you were gone. It broke what little I had left of my heart."

"But you're the one—" Kate broke off, scrabbling in her mind for anything she'd done right, but she couldn't think of a single fucking thing. She'd thought lying to him was her only choice. She glanced at Pree at the back of the boat. Always a lie, always. "But you're the one who filed for divorce from prison. You sent me the papers."

"Which you signed. You never protested. *You never fought for me.*" His voice broke. "And now I know why."

Too much. He was totally right and at the same time completely wrong. Turning, Kate called to Brian, "Can we go back, please?"

Brian looked up, confusion on his face. "But you haven't—"

"I'm not going to. This was a terrible idea."

Brian said, "What if you just—?"

"Fine," she said. "*Fine.*" She picked up Sonia's box and opened it. Ripped into the plastic. Dumped it carelessly, in one heavy *whoosh.* The bag slipped from her fingers, and she regretted that part of it immediately, that she'd just thrown a toxic oil by-product into the ocean. She also *did* feel lighter, having tossed the ashes, but there was no way she was letting Robin leave her that way. She put his box safely under a seat. "I can't put him here. That's the thing. Robin loved the ocean, but I hate it. It's cold. It's rough. It's not safe for a boy his age."

Nolan looked past her, over her shoulder, as if she weren't even there. Standing this close to him, standing as close to her heart as she had in years and years, Kate had never felt so alone.

She'd lost him. Again.

Chapter Forty-four

Saturday, May 17, 2014
11:50 a.m.

On their way in toward the bridge, the rocking motion made Pree feel ill again. Something huge had happened in the front of the boat, something devastating. Kate and Nolan looked as if they'd just lost their son only minutes ago, not three years before. And Pree couldn't do a damn thing except wait for the invisible storm to pass.

Thank god she hadn't been able to hear everything, not above the slaps of the waves against the hull. But Pree shouldn't even have to see this. Didn't they know they should keep this private?

But she'd signed up for it, she supposed. She'd chosen this by getting on the boat. Her *father.* That had come as a surprise. It wasn't as bad as she would have thought, though. Nolan . . . he seemed kind. A man who'd loved a child as much as it seemed he had . . . maybe it would be okay to get to know him. A little.

Maybe. Maybe not.

The marina drew closer, and Kate came back and sat next to her quietly. Her hand slipped into Pree's, cold and small. Pree almost pulled away, but Kate's grip seemed to help the queasiness. Nolan, looking wrecked, sat silently on the other side of Pree.

Pree kept her eyes on the Berkeley hills.

The night before, she and Flynn had broken up. She'd told him about Jimmy. Flynn had flipped out, way more than she would have predicted. He'd shouted, his voice going more coral-colored than she'd ever heard it. Practically Isi-colored. He threw one of his shoes through a closed window. He said he would fight for her, that he'd go to the ends of the earth for her. Then Pree had said she cared for him; she just wasn't sure she loved him.

"Did you ever?" he'd asked, tears wobbling, unshed.

"Yes."

"Fuck, Pree. That makes it so much worse."

He'd wanted things she couldn't promise anyone. Not anymore. His voice went pale again, back to its normal simple pink, and she felt it, just like that: he'd given up on her. Really, it was what she'd wanted him to do. She didn't love him, not like that.

Why did it hurt so badly, then, when he left?

Flynn didn't say where he was going or when he'd be back. Her heart had broken then, walloping her with a thudding pain she could feel now in the backs of her eyes. Pree didn't *want* Flynn—she really didn't. But she wasn't sure how to live in a world without him.

She'd called Isi and Marta, crying frantically, and she'd told them everything—all of it, from the pregnancy to

Jimmy to forcing Flynn away. They were driving up now. They had said they would try to meet her at the dock, if traffic allowed.

They were coming.

She checked her phone. A text from Isi:

We're here.

And at the pier, Pree saw them. Miraculously, the moms were there. Waiting.

Her Marta. She looked windblown and ragged. She had a white look under her eyes, a pulled tightness Pree had never seen before. Pree had put that look on her face, and she regretted nothing more. Isi, her crew cut bristling in the wind, looked as if she were about to throw herself into the water and swim to her. She kept her gaze squarely on Pree, as if pulling the boat toward her with the power of her mind.

Pree came down the ramp first, flying at them. They were there.

They were there for *her.*

Isi caught her in a hug so tight Pree could barely grab her breath. Then the moms were apologizing, and Pree couldn't figure out why. "I'm the one who let you down, and you're saying *you're* sorry?" That made Marta hiccup, and Pree got squeezed until she knew she'd have bruises later. Good bruises.

And in that moment, Pree knew. She finally got it. She already had her family. Right here. She'd had it the whole time, and while she'd known that superficially, she hadn't really known it in her bones. She hadn't known it in her blood. Not until now. She already had her people. Marta. Isi. *Hers.*

She looked over her shoulder and saw Kate coming down the ramp, followed by Nolan. Her birth parents. She knew about them now, just as she knew about her double-jointed left pinky and the fact that she was mildly allergic to strawberries. She was glad to know. But the knowledge mattered so much less when held up against the two women who stood in front of her, the ones who had driven to her as fast as they could. The ones who held her heart.

"We can get my car later. Can you take me home now?" she asked.

"Yes," Isi said, and her voice was the most gorgeous shade of rosy joy.

Chapter Forty-five

Aftermath

November 2011

Six days after Robin died, Kate was still in bed, using every ounce of self-control she possessed not to go into Robin's room, not to take up keening on his floor, the wailing that, once started, would never end. *My boy my perfect boy my love my boy my boy my child my boy.*

Nolan was in the hospital, still unable to communicate. Sonia said his eyes didn't function right—she'd checked on him every day. Sonia was as brusque as she'd always been. More so, perhaps, as if she had something stuck in her throat and couldn't clear it.

But with Robin's death, Sonia's shell had cracked, and Kate could see something inside her mother, something she'd never known was there. Sonia knew the very bones of grief, and in sharing that with her daughter, there was a softness at the curve at her cheek, a kindness in the hand that efficiently drew the covers over Kate and patted her head. There were no kisses, no words of love, but there was a rough tenderness, and Kate could tell her mother was trying. It was all she had to give. Once, Kate had woken to find Sonia staring out the window of the bedroom, with the curtain pulled back. "What is it?" she'd asked.

"I was just thinking about your father."

"What about him?"

"I should have tried harder, after he died," said Sonia. "To give you more. I should have at least tried." There was a pause. "I tried with Robin. My merman."

Kate couldn't answer around her swollen throat.

"But I'm still sorry . . ."

For one moment, Kate thought her mother was going to bring it up—would talk about the granddaughter she'd never met. She closed her eyes, as if that would keep her from hearing, but instead Sonia left the room, closing the door quietly behind her.

On Kate's sixth day in bed, the day before Robin's funeral—which Sonia had planned, dry-eyed and matter-of-factly—Sonia said, "Nolan doesn't understand it when I tell him. His eyes don't change when I explain it again. What happened. Where he is now."

Kate turned to the wall and closed her eyes. It wasn't fair that she had to live in a world like this, feeling what she did, and he didn't. After what he'd done.

"You have to go to him," Sonia said.

"No." It was the only word she was sure of.

"He needs you."

Kate needed Robin. "No."

"He loves you."

"No." He couldn't.

"You love him. You love him more than you've ever loved anyone except your son." Sonia left herself out of the equation of love.

"He took Robin from me."

"Then go," said Sonia, her face fierce. Furious. "Tell him."

At the hospital, the ICU nurses knew the story. That much was obvious in the way they lifted their eyebrows at each other when they thought she was looking somewhere else. A nurse in green scrubs took her to Nolan's room, and her glance was kind. The room was all glass and metal, and very cold, as if he were about to go into surgery. This wasn't a normal recovery room. This was serious. "He just said his first few words this afternoon. It's good you're here." And before Kate passed through the glass door to the nurses' station just outside, the nurse said, "Don't upset him. He probably won't remember anything you tell him, so don't expect much. His short-term memory is gone for now. It might get better later, but there's no telling just yet."

Kate pressed her lips together and nodded.

He was noticeably thinner. How could that happen in mere days? The fact that he'd grown a beard was an unexpected jolt.

"Nolan," she said. God, what if he opened his eyes? She had no follow-up line.

But he did. He opened his eyes, those wonderful maple-colored eyes, and there he was. "Love," he whispered.

And instead of screaming, instead of raining blows down upon him, instead of anything she'd originally planned on the way to the hospital, she did something else. She examined the side rail of his bed and pushed the right combination to drop the metal. Then, lifting the tubes that were connected to various parts of his body, she slowly and oh so carefully slipped under them. She shimmied under the thin blanket. Pressing herself against him, she felt him shudder.

"You're right. It's cold in here," Kate said, as if they'd already been discussing it. Continuing their conversation. "Let me help. Come closer."

Nolan didn't move. She could feel he couldn't, so she got closer to him instead. Her knee to his, body to body, her warmth heating his chill. "That's right," she said.

He lay on his back, tears running from his eyes, catching in her hair.

"Do you know what happened?"

"No," he whispered. "But . . . something. Did."

Kate waited. She tried to find the place inside her chest that would allow her to punish him. *You killed your son, my boy, our son. You took him. You killed my son. My boy my boy my little boy.* Each word a weapon. Each word another death that he had so unforgivably escaped.

She leaned her head close to his and softly said the words that were tangled in her mouth.

His body relaxed.

She said them again, and she kept saying them, over and over, until the words unwound and reknitted themselves together and made a blanket of words, draping a warmth over them both that allowed him to relax and fall back to sleep, pressed against her.

Robin loves you. I love you. Robin loves you. I love you. Come home to us. I love you. I found you, I found you, I found you. Come home. We love you. Come home.

Chapter Forty-six

Sunday, May 18, 2014
11 a.m.

On Sunday morning, it took every ounce of Kate's courage, every last drop she had left, to park the car in front of the address Nolan had jotted down on a Post-it when he'd left the other night. "Just in case," he'd said. A low-slung apartment building, gray and tired-looking under the overcast skies—it looked like an old motel, and maybe it was. The plants in the planters were as exhausted as the paint.

Her hands shook as she went down the walk toward number 4. She stretched them out, wishing she'd thought to tuck a paintbrush in her back pocket so she'd have something to cling to.

She raised her fist to knock, but stopped when she heard the voices inside. She couldn't make out the words, but that was his real voice, the one not everyone got to hear.

Leaning to the left, she peeked in the side window. A man wearing a red plaid overshirt leaned forward to say something to someone who was on the other side of the wall, out of her range of vision.

Nolan had friends who really talked with him? *Good.*

It was even harder, then, to actually knock, knowing she was interrupting something important. She heard Fred Weasley barking, and a sharp "Hush!"

The door swung open. Nolan was midsmile, but it slid from his face when he saw her.

"Damn," he said.

Kate stuck her fists in the pockets of her sweatshirt. "Can I talk to you? Just for a minute." She looked over her shoulder at the man standing behind Nolan. The man's face was drawn, cautious. He had a black eye to match Nolan's.

"Yeah," said Nolan. His voice was flat. Fred barked at his side. They let her in, but Nolan didn't quiet the dog, letting him bark until he wound down.

It smelled like Nolan inside, warm and soapy, and Kate's heart thumped in her chest so hard she wondered if his friend could hear it from where he stood coolly observing her.

Fred gave one last protesting woof and then jumped onto the couch to observe.

"This is my—my ex-wife, Kate," said Nolan. "This is Rafe." He offered no explanation of who Rafe was as he would have in the past. As if they were so tight she should know who he was.

"It's nice to meet you." Kate leaned forward with her hand outstretched.

Rafe didn't take it. "Yeah. Okay, brother, I'm gonna bail."

"You have to? I got Negra Modelo. Three of them have your name on 'em."

"Nah, bro. I was just checking on you." A pointed look

directed at Kate. "You call me if you need anything. Or just come over. Rita got the ingredients to cook you that mole you like—she just needs a couple hours' notice."

"Good enough. Send my love," said Nolan. They locked hands and pulled each other close, bumping right shoulders easily. "See ya."

Rafe slipped past, giving Kate the barest nod as he did. He closed the door behind him, and they were alone.

"So now you've seen the place. Kind of pathetic, huh?" His denim voice held a challenge.

It wasn't. It was cozy, warm, the furniture broken in and loved-looking. The cushions on the couch—which was possibly also his bed—looked just right to sink into.

"I wondered if you'd show me those e-mails." There was no point in taking her time getting to the point. This wasn't a social visit.

"Are you serious?"

She nodded and looked at her feet.

"Why would I?"

"Please, Nolan?"

He muttered something under his breath and then took his laptop from the side table and propped it open on the small kitchen table. A few keystrokes, and a file called "To Do" opened in his Gmail. At least forty e-mails dropped, scrolling down the page.

"There. You satisfied now?"

"Holy shit."

He nodded. "It's bad."

Kate sat in front of the keyboard, expecting him to stop her.

But he didn't. He stood next to her and watched. From the couch, Fred Weasley groaned, far back in his throat.

She opened the most recent one, dated two days before.

She's in pain all the time. Her veins have collapsed. The port actually exploded in her chest. We can hardly get the pain medicine in her. It's not fair. *How long do we have to keep this game of protracting her life going? It's the worst, most vicious game we've ever played, and we're losing more every day.*

The back of Kate's throat felt thick. She breathed around the salt that filled her mouth.

She placed her hands on the keyboard.

Then she looked up at Nolan.

"May I?"

He swallowed. Then he nodded.

She typed slowly, because everything, after all, for this family, and for her own, depended on this moment.

We, Robin's parents, can't tell you what to do. It isn't *fair. None of this is fair. And none of it is your fault, not her sickness, not her pain. And we know this: You won't know what to do until you do. And when you know, you'll know with all your heart that you're doing the right thing, no matter what that is.*

She took a deep breath and then continued typing.

Nolan still carries the burden, and Kate carries the same one. Your story will be different from ours. But know that we understand what you are up against, and we stand with you. We pray for peace for you, with you.

Love, Kate and Nolan Monroe

She pushed the chair back and turned the computer so Nolan could read it. He dropped into the chair next to her, and as he read, his eyes filled with tears. That muscle at the side of his jaw jumped, the one that twitched when he was angry. He scowled and rubbed his face.

Then he hit the send button.

He turned the computer so it was in front of her again. "Do the next one."

Now our baby only cries when he thinks we can't hear him.

Kate typed:

Robin used to do that. Kate used to do that, too, when she thought Nolan was far enough away. But it's important to cry. As a family. Hold on to each other. Forgive each other. It will be harder to hold on to each other later—practice now.

When she was done, Nolan read it, hit send, and said, "The next one."

They stopped using tissues after an hour, letting the tears fall onto the tabletop, wiping their eyes with the backs of their arms. Kate developed a headache that almost blinded her. Nolan gave her ibuprofen before swallowing four himself.

The last one, the one that Nolan had received first, so many months before, was the hardest.

He's gone. I couldn't do a thing. I couldn't help. He went, and he was alone because I took a motherfucking walk to see if they had fresh coffee in the cafeteria, and he died by himself. My child. By himself. He's gone, and I did nothing.

Kate put her hand over her mouth. She felt Nolan kiss the side of her head.

Then she typed:

You did everything you could.

She wrote their story. Robin had been alone, too, essentially. And now all they had was each other, and it would have to do. They were everything that mattered to each other.

We understand your pain.

"We do," Nolan said. "We do." He hit send.

Kate leaned against Nolan. He was solid. Sure. He put his arms around her. "It's Mother's Day today," she said. "Did you know that?"

A long, shuddered breath. She wasn't sure whose it was. Another one. It was their breath, then. An apology made of air.

"I found you," he whispered.

"Thank god," she said. And then she dug her fingers into his shirt, just over where his wings were. She hung on. "Thank god you did."

Nolan grabbed her then, wrapping his arms around her. He was strong. He was still strong. "I'm here," he said. "Still here."

She held him tighter, so tightly her arms ached. Then she put her mouth as close as she could to his ear and told him the truth she'd never said out loud. The truth he already knew.

"If you hadn't done it, I was going to."

It was the first time in years that tears felt like a relief. Like forgiveness.

Chapter Forty-seven

Sunday, June 1, 2014

Two weeks later, on Sunday morning, Kate wasn't paying attention to anything in the world but her painting. When Nolan shambled down from the house carrying two coffee cups, wearing yesterday's rumpled clothing, she had to blink hard to bring herself back.

"Hey," he said. "Am I bugging you? I can go . . ."

"It's fine," she said. "It's good."

Nolan smiled. "Great."

Fred Weasley leaped through the oleander and then ran off to investigate the ivy.

"Only for tonight," she'd said last week. "One more night." One night had turned into seven, then fourteen, and Kate knew, if it worked, it would be for longer. It was a terrifying, precarious feeling. They were both standing on the same cliff, looking at each other, each daring the other one to jump. Kate thought of the hang gliders at Fort Funston, and how they ran toward the edge until they ran out of earth. Then, when the ground fell away, they simply picked up their legs and dangled in the air.

"I can't believe you never did this before," Nolan said, gesturing at the bathtub.

Kate picked up the brush again and went back to it. She was covering the bright blue, little by little, with jewellike spots of color. She was painting a mosaic in paint, bright shards of blue and red and vibrant yellow. The porcelain tub was all together, still of a piece, but in paint she broke it and put it back together. An image was forming, and she wasn't—for once—planning ahead. It was coming slowly, and so far, she had just a leg at the top right side of the tub, a small dangling leg that reminded her of Icarus's fall. Trees, like the ginkgoes overhead, were forming on the porcelain. The hillside was the one she stood on. Small strokes of blue and green became the hydrangea next to her. She was painting her hill on the tub, and Robin was running out of the picture, just there, at the top.

Nolan nodded to the small wooden box at her feet, but before he could say anything more, a voice called down from above.

"Hello?"

Kate dropped the brush in the dirt at her feet. Never mind. A little dirt crumbled into the paint would give it texture.

Pree came down the narrow path. "Hey."

"I'm happy you came." The words seemed small to convey so much.

"Me, too," Pree said.

Nolan looked confused, as Kate thought he might. He'd catch on soon enough.

Pree, meanwhile, was looking at Nolan curiously but without antagonism. "Hi," she offered.

Nolan ducked his head. Then he gave that sweet shy smile and Kate saw the same one spread across Pree's face.

"I wanted to take a walk," Kate said. "Together. To where Robin's . . ." She took a deep breath. She hadn't been there since the day they put half his ashes in the ground, since they pulled the grass back and then rerolled it, like a living rug made more verdant by the bodies below. "To Robin's grave."

Both Nolan and Pree swayed toward each other. Kate was sure neither had noticed, but on another day in a different time Nolan would have taken Pree's hand. Kate knew it, and her heart wept. And then leaped, for having them both here.

"This was his favorite body of water," said Kate. "A bath. Any bath." She looked at Nolan. "May I leave some of his ashes here?"

Nolan nodded.

Kate opened the box and withdrew the plastic bag. She moved to the hydrangea, Robin's flower, and reached underneath it. She spilled some of the ash, feeling it float back up and brush her wrist. Looking at Nolan, she raised her eyebrows. A question.

He took the bag from her and spilled more. So small, really, what his body had been reduced to. From their sturdy little boy to this fine grit. "Leave a little," she whispered. He did, passing the bag back to her.

She put the bag back in the box and held it tightly as they walked together through the streets. It was such a short walk—a lovely one, past cottages and old homes set back, like theirs, behind gardens that had been growing for dozens of years. Tangles of jasmine bursting into bloom waved in the breeze as they passed.

Pree took the lead, striding ahead confidently. She knew the way, Kate noticed. Even once inside the great park of the cemetery, she knew which way to turn, which crypts to pass, where to head across the grass. So when they got to Robin's headstone, Kate wasn't surprised to hear Nolan say, "Motherfucker."

Pree bit her bottom lip.

"Some motherfucker *tagged* it." He pointed to the back of the stone. "A fucking sticker. Can you believe this?" Dropping to his knees, he started trying to scratch it off until Kate said, "Wait."

He looked up. "No, this isn't okay. This is so many kinds of screwed up."

"It's mine," said Pree, her voice high and as deep green as the grass they stood on. "I'm sorry." She scrabbled in her bag and pulled out a blank one. "See? It's what I do. I'm sorry. I don't know why . . ."

Nolan brushed his hands on his thighs and then rocked back to sit on his heels. "I don't . . . Well. Wow."

Kate put out her hand. "Can I have one?"

Without saying a word, Pree handed her the blank sticker.

"And a pen."

Pree gave her the thick Pilot.

"Give one to him, too?"

Nolan took the sticker and the extra pen she'd produced.

"Sign it," said Kate.

"No," said Pree. "You don't have to—I'll take mine off. It's not right. I'm sorry."

"Just . . . hang on a minute." Nolan closed his eyes again. Thinking. Kate loved watching him work it through. It felt like driving a familiar road, one she hadn't been on in years, but she knew she was close to home.

"Do I have to use my real name?" he finally said.

Pree, looking surprised, said, "Better if you don't. Lots of people respell their names or use a nickname."

"Who should I be?" He uncapped the pen. Looked at the blunt tip. "Wait." Another beat. "I got it."

Slowly, carefully, glancing at Pree's RARE sticker for reference, Nolan drew the letters NKRP. He drew a small curled flourish at the bottom and Kate smiled. He'd always been good at many things, but drawing wasn't one of them.

"That's good," said Pree. "That's nice." She scuffed the grass with the toe of her combat boot. "But I gotta say this, okay?"

"Shoot," said Nolan, and he looked as suddenly nervous as Kate felt.

"I don't know what this is." She spread her arms out wide. "All of this. I don't know what I want, and I don't know what *you* want. Neither of you could ever replace my moms."

Nolan nodded. Kate said, "You're right."

"And you can't have this baby to replace the one you lost."

Kate felt it like a blow. "*No.* Of course not."

Pree looked chagrined. "Marta just wanted to make sure that wasn't on the table."

"It's your baby, Pree."

"And I don't know what I'm going to do. But I'm probably going to give it up. Maybe with an open adoption. I'm thinking to two gay guys. Give the kid two fathers. Maybe . . ." She paused and bit her bottom lip. "Maybe, if we're all still friends then, I could ask if you could meet the baby occasionally. You know. With me. Like at Christmas or something. Marta says that happens a lot with open adoptions. But that's just a maybe. No promises."

"No promises," said Kate. "That's fine. I just want to know you."

"We can play it by ear." Pree looked at Nolan.

Nolan nodded. "Yeah. By ear."

Kate felt joy fill her lungs, easy and sweet.

"Yes," she said.

Pree said, "Good. Okay. What are you gonna write, then?"

They both looked expectantly at Kate's sticker, still blank in her hand.

There was only one thing she *could* write.

She and Nolan peeled the backs off and stuck them on the back of the stone, overlapping Pree's original. Pree put the pens back in her bag with careful ceremony.

Then together they climbed to the top of the cemetery, up to where it opened into wild green grass and live oaks. No monuments, no slabs. Just open space. Below stretched all of Oakland. Kate's house. Nolan's apartment. Lake Merritt glimmered next to the tall buildings that stretched to the bay. A cargo ship pulled lazily toward Treasure Island. In the far distance San Francisco sparkled.

A is for ash.

A is for air.

A is for all.

Without speaking, all three of them touched the bag and tipped out the last of the ash. It caught the wind and before Kate could properly even see it in the air, it was gone.

Robin would like Kate's sticker, she knew. It was a word he'd written often, on almost all of the drawings he'd ever made.

Mom.

They walked back, slowly. Together. Nolan and Pree talked about something that Kate didn't follow, about a first-person shooter game at a company where Pree was applying to work. From the pocket of her hoodie, Kate withdrew the other, smaller plastic bag. *This* was the last. Her final secret. With her thumbnail, she pierced a hole in the corner. And as they walked home, a thin stream of ash, lighter than air, trailed from the cemetery to Kate's front door.

Her son stayed outside with the tub and the hydrangeas and the stickers on the marble they'd left for him.

Kate opened the door and let in her husband, then her daughter.

Photo by Khalil Robinson

Rachael Herron received her MFA in English and creative writing from Mills College, and has a popular Web site at RachaelHerron.com. She is the author of the Cypress Hollow romance series, as well as the memoir *A Life in Stitches*. She is an accomplished knitter, and lives in Oakland with her wife, Lala, and their menagerie of cats and dogs.

CONNECT ONLINE

www.RachaelHerron.com
twitter.com/RachaelHerron
facebook.com/Rachael.Herron.Author

CONVERSATION GUIDE

Pack Up the Moon

Rachael Herron

This Conversation Guide is intended to enrich the individual reading experience, as well as encourage us to explore these topics together—because books, and life, are meant for sharing.

A CONVERSATION WITH RACHAEL HERRON

Q. How did you come up with the idea for Pack Up the Moon*?*

A. Once upon a time, I wanted to be a teacher. I got my master's in English and spent approximately eleven seconds teaching writing in an arts college. I hated every second of it. I couldn't sleep for worrying about the next day's class, I was a stuttering wreck in front of the students, and I hated the bureaucratic red tape. So one afternoon while waiting for my milk shake at a burger joint in the Oakland hills, I picked up a trade magazine and started looking for trucking jobs. I thought it would be romantic to be a truck driver, my long hair (I'd grow it) flying out the open window, my dog in the passenger seat, both of us wearing matching red bandannas. I'd write fiction at truck-stop counters. I'd drink very bad coffee. It would be amazing.

Instead, though, I noticed an ad to be a 911 dispatcher. Oh! Wouldn't that be a window on the human condition?

I've never been more right.

Every time I answer the phone at my 911 job, it's a new story. Or rather, it's a new spin on very, very old stories. I don't take notes—I don't steal people's lives that way. First, it would be unethical. And second, I don't have to. Some calls have stuck with me over the years, word for word, and nothing I do can shake loose the curses and promises and screams I've heard.

The focus of life itself has shifted for me over the fourteen years I've been dispatching. When I got out of grad school, I had stars in my eyes. Everything was going to be perfect, for everyone. I just knew it.

I know now that life is hard, more difficult than I could have imagined, and that this is true for everyone. But I also know that people love harder than I ever imagined was possible. Everywhere.

I hear it.

I've talked desperate great-grandsons through giving their 103-year-old grandmother CPR, thinking the whole time, *Let her go; isn't this her time?*, only to hang up and realize I've just heard a whole family rallying around an incredibly old woman, all of them cheering, "Come on, Gran! You can make it! You can do it!" What a brilliant, stubborn love that is. What a gorgeous brute optimism people possess.

And I've heard so many times—way too many times—parents fail in doing CPR. Blowing too hard in an infant's small, fragile lungs, breaking their baby rather than fixing him. I've heard them pump their six-year-old's chest while knowing the damage from the fall their child just took is too great, too much to heal.

There is no sound worse in the whole world, I think, than listening to a mother realize for the first time that she is losing her child forever. And there is no greater honor than bearing witness to that moment—being strong enough to know how to direct her—even as she feels her child's life seep through her hands.

I finish the call, clicking my release button when the ambulance arrives and takes over. I don't have any more instructions to give. I'm done with my part of it. It's time for lunch, and I make my salad. I laugh with my coworkers about something funny that's just happened down the hall.

As dispatchers, we're conditioned to let it go. To move on. But periodically, I think about the families. How is the sibling doing? Will today be the funeral? How is the mother now, a year later? What about this Christmas? This Mother's Day?

They aren't questions I can ever get answered. My minuscule part in their story ends when the line disconnects. I'm witness to the beginning of the worst part of their lives, and they will (rightfully) never remember my voice. I have no idea how their lives go after that. And it's none of my business. Literally.

But I wanted an ending, a real one, one I could control. So I wrote *Pack Up the Moon*. The hardest part, Robin's death, is already over when the book begins. That fateful call to my imaginary coworker about the fictional situation has already been made. Kate has felt her son's chest rise and fall under her hands, and she's seen her attempt fail.

Then we get her story. We see her today, as she lives in the aftermath of that nightmare. I wanted to give her the hope I can't promise anyone else. I wanted to give her peace.

Q. You're not a mother. Was writing a book about motherhood daunting?

A. Very much so! But there are two things I know how to write about. The first is the mother-child relationship. It seems as if everything I write, whether it's a romance or a personal essay, has a theme of motherhood. This is because my own mother, who I counted as my best friend, was perfect. By that, I don't mean she got everything right or that we even understood each other well. Over the course of years of writing about her after she died, I ended up realizing we were both flawed. But no matter what, she was perfect at loving, even when I was very hard to love.

The second thing I know how to write is grief. Because of all that time I spent grieving on the page, both personally and publicly, I know how to achieve catharsis through the written word—and isn't that release what we're all looking for in books or movies that make us cry? So I figured if I put those two things together, I could have a shot at making this book work.

That said, it was something I never took lightly. I ran the book past the best mothers I know to make sure I got those feelings somewhat close to reality. I interviewed adoptees and adopters to make sure I wasn't missing anything there, either.

But research is one thing. Real life, another. I know how a mother loves—because I had a mother who loved me hard. I would have fought an army of men armed with nuclear weapons with only my hands and my teeth if I could have saved her, and I wouldn't have cared for a second if I'd died. In my mind, if you multiply that urge by a million, you get a mother. I hope I'm somewhat close to getting that right.

Q. What's your writing process?

A. Hoo boy. I write all the time. I work long shifts (forty-eight hours at the firehouse, with nap breaks). I write on some of my breaks when I'm not too tired. Our strange schedule means that I work for two days straight and then I have four days off, which is great for a writer with no kids.

I usually go to the café so I don't end up doing the dishes or scrubbing grout to get out of doing my writing. We have three cats and three dogs, and keeping those off my lap and out from under my feet is almost a third full-time job. At the café, I turn off the Internet in forty-five-minute bursts. Sitting there, alone with my Internet-free laptop, I finally get bored enough to work. Then I take a fifteen-minute e-mail/Twitter break, and then I do it all over again. And again. And again.

I'm pretty obsessive about many things (ask me about my knitting sometime) and writing is one of those things. I write a lot. I wrote this book you're holding twice. Literally. I'm not talking about the umpteen drafts I produced along the way. I mean there are more words in the trash file than there are, total, in the remaining book. They are unused words, words that didn't make the cut. I learn what I know, what my characters need to know, by dancing around subjects, getting closer and closer to them until I know not only what I believe about the topics, but, more important, what my characters think of them. That takes a while. I'd love it if I were more of a planner. I'm working at getting better at that.

But I also love the not knowing. That's the adventure of being a writer. Never being able to predict what's going to come flying out of your fingers next. Mostly, it's stuff that makes your eyes roll, stuff you know you'll have to cut later. But sometimes, you look at the words and say, "Yes. That's what I meant. Hell, that's *better* than what I meant."

I try not to forget what Stephen King said about writing being telepathy. I'm writing these words, and you are reading them. We're not in the same room, but you're hearing my actual thoughts. We are connected, right now. If that isn't magic, I don't know what is.

That's what keeps me writing. That magic. The fact that Kate is at once a made-up, fictional character and, at the same time, a stand-in for anyone who has ever grieved. Which is, of course, every one of us. We are the same.

We are connected.

QUESTIONS FOR DISCUSSION

1. Pree's first real question to Kate is "Why did you give me away?" Kate says she didn't have any other options. Is this true? What different roads could Kate have taken? How would her life be different now?

2. The neurological condition of synesthesia can present itself in many forms: some people see colors in numbers, see time three-dimensionally, or hear music when they look at letters. The author of this book sees gender and color in letters and numbers, which inspired her to give Kate and Pree their own form of this condition. What does Kate and Pree's shared synesthesia mean about them as characters? Do you have any form of it yourself, or know anyone who does?

3. Kate feels guilt about not telling Nolan about Pree the first time she sees him again as an adult. How much guilt do you think she *should* feel, given that she and Nolan weren't together when she gave up the baby for adoption? How does the fact that they had another child together change this?

4. What effect does Kate's mother, Sonia, have on her? How has it shaped her own experience of motherhood?

5. Nolan has formed a new road crew family in the time since he got out of prison. How does this shape his character throughout the book?

6. How would Kate's life have been different if both Nolan and Robin had died that day?

7. What is Pree really looking for during the course of the book?

8. Can you forgive Kate for using the search window she confesses to opening?

9. Related to the last question, can you forgive Nolan for his decision in the garage?

10. Do you think Kate will be able to move forward now? Do you see the ending as happy or sad? Or something else?

11. Should Kate and Nolan have answered the e-mails Nolan received? What should they do next?